Praise for Matt Dunn:

'Funny and witty, a great read that gives us a look into the workings of the male mind' *Sun*

'A well-crafted tale of when love goes wrong and love goes right – witty, astute but tender too' Freya North

'Full of great one-liners, this book is a terrifying eye-opener into what men really think' *Company*

'Frighteningly funny and sometimes just plain frightening . . . the most realistic perspective on the average man's world view most women will get without hanging around in a locker room' Chris Manby

'Delightfully shallow and self-obsessed – that's the male psyche for you' *Elle*

'A warm, open and damn funny book' *Lads Mag*

'Both hilarious and touching' *Best*

'Most amusing' *Closer*

From Here to Paternity

Matt Dunn

POCKET
BOOKS

LONDON · NEW YORK · TORONTO · SYDNEY

First published in Great Britain by Pocket Books, 2007
An imprint of Simon & Schuster UK
A CBS COMPANY

1 3 5 7 9 10 8 6 4 2

Simon & Schuster UK Ltd
Africa House
64-78 Kingsway
London WC2B 6AH

www.simonsays.co.uk

Simon & Schuster Australia
Sydney

A CIP catalogue record for this book is available from the British Library

ISBN 978-1-84739-067-7

Typeset by Rowland Phototypesetting Ltd, Bury St Edmunds, Suffolk
Printed and bound in Great Britain by Cox & Wyman Ltd, Reading, Berks

For Clare and Ewan.
From your kid brother.

This is a true story, although some of the names have been changed.

And most of the facts . . .

Chapter 1

As I understand it, there are ways to celebrate the news of the arrival of your first child. Handing out cigars, for example, or the traditional glass of something alcoholic. Seeing as neither Tom nor I smoke, I've decided on the second option, which is why I've just opened a rather nice – as in on the plus side of a fiver – bottle of Cabernet Sauvignon. But while I don't pretend to be an expert in all things birth-related *yet*, I'm pretty sure it's the baby's head you're supposed to be wetting, and not the father's.

'Sorry, Will,' says Tom, handing me a tea towel so I can mop up the mouthful of wine he's just spat over me in surprise. 'But ... *you're* going to be a father?'

I dab at the red stain on my now not-so-white shirt, and grin back at him, at the same time trying to ignore the crashing of plates I've just heard from the kitchen where Barbara, Tom's wife, is preparing the Sunday roast. And although I'm not sure I like the emphasis Tom's put on the word 'you're', I react like one of those nodding dogs you used to see in the back of brown Austin Allegros.

'Yup.'

Tom shakes his head, making one of those long-suffering faces that I've come to know from my best friend over the years. Barbara, on the other hand, slams shut the oven door and comes rushing in from the kitchen. For once, she doesn't say anything, but instead gives me a look that leaves no doubt she can't quite believe what she's just heard.

You? her look continues. *Will Jackson, the most irresponsible man I know? A father?*

I keep nodding, much to Barbara's obvious bewilderment. She and Tom have been married for nearly ten years, and by now she's usually quite accepting of my various escapades. But apparently not this one, because when she finally manages to form a sentence, it's not quite the one I was hoping for.

'You're joking, surely?'

'I'm deadly serious,' I say, my idiotic grin suggesting otherwise.

'Tom?' implores Barbara, sitting down next to me at the table and putting her head in her hands. She's wearing a pair of crocodile-puppet oven gloves, which make her look like she's being attacked at a Punch and Judy show. 'Say something, will you?'

'Er, congratulations?' He holds a hand out towards me, which I shake enthusiastically. 'But I thought you and . . . What was the name of your last one?'

I have to think for a second. 'Cecilia.'

'Ah, yes. The lovely Cecilia. I thought you and she had split up?'

'We did.' I take a sip of my wine. 'Last week.'

'Oh.' His expression changes to one of confusion. 'But—'

'Typical!' interrupts Barbara. 'And I bet you binned her because you got her pregnant, didn't you? Poor girl. Well, I don't know what you're looking so happy about. There are far too many single-parent families nowadays without you adding to that number.'

I inch imperceptibly away from Barbara, all too aware of her potential to show her disapproval in more physical ways. 'No – you don't understand. I "binned" her, to use your sympathetic description, because she's not the one I'm having the baby with.'

'This gets worse,' says Barbara. 'You've been cheating on her and you've got someone else pregnant.'

'No. Nothing like that.' I make a hurt face. 'What do you think I am?'

Fortunately, Tom holds up his hand before Barbara can begin to tell me. 'Hang on,' he says. 'Let's start from the beginning. Are you, or are you not, having a baby?'

'I will be, yes.'

'So,' sighs Barbara, removing the oven gloves and placing them on the table, 'who's the – and I use the word advisedly – "lucky" girl? Anyone we know?'

I shrug. 'It's not even anyone I know.'

She frowns. 'So you haven't actually got anyone pregnant?'

'Not yet, no.'

'But you are going to be a dad?' says Tom.

'Yup.'

Tom and Barbara exchange puzzled glances. 'So what are we celebrating, exactly?' asks Tom. 'The fact that you've become a sperm donor?'

'No. The fact that I've made a decision to do something life-changing. I, Will Jackson, am going to be a father.'

As I sit back smugly in my chair, enjoying the sound those particular words have made, and Tom and Barbara look at each other in disbelief, there's a long, awkward silence. So long and awkward, in fact, that I feel I have to start speaking again. 'And I'll tell you something – the day I decided was the happiest day of my life. Finally, I realized I had a purpose. A direction.'

'Other than going nowhere fast, you mean?' Tom says. 'And what do you mean, *you* decided? On your own?'

Barbara looks even more mystified than before. 'Isn't it normally the kind of decision that takes two people?'

'It is. I mean, it will be. Eventually. Yes. And there's the thing.'

She reaches over and takes a swig from Tom's glass. 'What thing?'

'I just need to find the right woman. Which is what I wanted to ask you. Well, ask Barbara, really. . .'

'Steady on,' says Tom. 'I know we're friends, but there are some limits.'

It's my turn to be confused. 'I don't get it.'

'And you're not going to, either,' says Barbara, folding her arms.

'No – you don't understand. To ask whether you know anyone who might be suitable. For me.'

Barbara stares at me for a second while she attempts to process this particular piece of information. 'For you to have a baby with, you mean?'

'Yup.'

'Let me just think . . .' She gazes off into the distance theatrically before suddenly cuffing me round the top of my head. 'No! Of course not. What a ridiculous idea.'

'It's not ridiculous, Barbara,' I say, smoothing my hairstyle back down. 'I'm not getting any younger.'

'You're thirty,' says Tom. 'That's hardly old.'

'Yes it is,' I say. 'I found a grey hair the other day.'

'So what?' says Tom, running his fingers through his hair, in the manner of the man in the Grecian 2000 advert. 'Even I've got a few.'

'It wasn't on my head, Tom. And besides, my biological clock is ticking.'

As Barbara and Tom stare at me in disbelief, the kitchen timer rings, much to Barbara's amusement. 'Oh my word. It's Desperate Dad,' she laughs, before heading back into the kitchen.

'Will, you're a man,' says Tom, refilling his wine

glass. 'You don't have a biological clock, and even if you did, your clock can keep on ticking long past . . . Well, as long as there's still juice in the battery, so to speak.'

'Precisely,' agrees Barbara, as she places a tray of strangely shaped Yorkshire puddings on the table. She's normally an excellent cook, but hasn't quite perfected the Sunday roast yet. 'So, why the big rush? You've not got some incurable disease you haven't told us about?'

'No – nothing like that.'

'Shame,' jokes Tom, topping up my glass.

'It's just that I love kids. Well, the twins especially.' I nod over towards the conservatory, where Jack and Ellie, Tom and Barbara's five-year-olds, are sat in front of the TV, spellbound by some Disney DVD that they've already seen approximately four thousand times. 'And I see the enjoyment you get from the two of them, and I want to be a part of that.'

'You are a part of that,' says Tom reassuringly.

'When you remember their birthdays,' adds Barbara. 'Which you'd think would be easy, seeing as they're both on the same day.'

'No, I mean that I want some of that. For myself. My own family.'

'There's some merit in that,' agrees Barbara, slapping my hand away from the tray. 'At least then you won't be turning up here for lunch every Sunday.'

Tom smiles. 'What's brought this on? I never had you down as the two-point-four type.'

'I'm not. I mean, neither did I. But I'm going to be thirty-one soon. That's not thirty any more. It's "thirties". And recently, I—'

Barbara taps the side of her nose. 'Aha. Will, I'm sensing the phrase "mid-life crisis" here.'

'It's not a mid-life crisis. Heaven knows I see enough of them in my clients to know what one looks like.' I work as a life coach. Which isn't really a proper job, and certainly isn't a valid basis for taking money off people, according to Barbara. 'But there's a reason why those holidays are called "18–30". Because at thirty-one, you need to take life a bit more seriously. Have some responsibilities.'

'But you've never been on an 18–30 holiday,' laughs Tom.

'And I won't be able to, soon. So I've got to get on with the next phase of my life.'

Barbara pats my hand sympathetically. 'You're feeling broody, aren't you?'

'No – I just want to do something with my life.'

She shakes her head. 'This isn't just another of your five-minute obsessions, is it? Like the time you got the tropical fish? And we all know how that turned out.'

I redden slightly. 'Yes, well, how was I to know they'd be so labour-intensive?'

'Will, remembering to feed them every week and cleaning their tank out occasionally is hardly labour-intensive. And by the way, any fool knows you don't do it with bleach.'

'Especially while the fish are still in there,' adds Tom.

Barbara sighs. 'And if you think the fish were hard work, you obviously haven't got the first idea about looking after a child.'

Tom nods. 'It's quite a lifestyle change, you know. A fair distance from your current man-about-town existence.'

'And that's precisely why I want all this.' I gesture around the room with the hand holding my wine glass, causing Barbara to check anxiously for signs of spillage on the carpet. 'I'm tired of single life.'

'You wouldn't be single if you didn't keep breaking up with all these women,' points out Tom.

'Have you thought about getting a dog instead?' suggests Barbara, heading into the kitchen and returning with a bowl of roast potatoes. 'As a pet, rather than as a girlfriend, I mean?'

'Very funny.'

Barbara shakes her head. 'I wasn't joking.'

'Will, do you really know what it's like?' says Tom. 'Being woken up throughout the night? The constant crying? The mess everywhere?'

'And that's just when you're trying to get pregnant,' says Barbara.

Tom grins. 'Tell you what,' he says, walking into the conservatory and ruffling the twins' hair. 'We'll lend you our two for a few days, if you like. See what you think after that.'

From in front of the television, Jack and Ellie glance nervously in my direction.

'Really?' I glance even more nervously back. 'I'll, er, just take them away with me after lunch, then.'

'Fine,' says Tom.

'Great,' I say, trying to ignore the fact that Jack's bottom lip has started to tremble.

'Over my dead body,' says Barbara, fetching a plate of roast beef from the kitchen and putting it down on the table.

'Go on,' says Tom. 'It'll be good for him. Might make him think a bit differently.'

'Tom – you seem determined to put me off. Don't you think I'd be a good dad?'

'That's got nothing to do with it,' says Tom, neatly side-stepping the issue. 'I just . . . I mean, *Barbara* and I just want you to know what you'd be letting yourself in for.'

I put my wine glass down. 'Tom, you didn't ever meet my dad, did you?'

'No.'

'Well, nor did I. Not really, anyway. He left when I was still a baby. And that's why I'll be a good father. Because I'd never do that to a child of mine.'

'Maybe so,' says Tom. 'But I just want you to know what it really means to be responsible for someone else. You can't even keep your houseplants alive. Having kids . . . Well, it affects your every waking hour.'

'And a lot of your sleeping ones as well,' adds Barbara.

'It's true,' insists Tom. 'You're on call twenty-four-seven. And what's more, you look at these little things, and realize there isn't anything you wouldn't do for them.'

As he smiles down at the twins, Ellie swivels round and tugs on his trouser leg. 'Daddy, can I have a drink?'

'Not now, Ellie,' says Tom, picking her up and plonking her back in front of the television. 'Daddy's talking to Uncle Will.'

'I thought you said there wasn't anything you wouldn't do for them?'

'Yes, well.' Tom sits back down at the table. 'It's a figure of speech, isn't it?'

'It is for you,' says Barbara, fetching a couple of juice cartons from the kitchen and handing them to the twins.

Tom ignores her. 'And then there's the career stuff,' he continues. 'If you're at all ambitious then, sometimes, having a child means you have to put that ambition on hold.'

'Well, one of us did,' says Barbara archly. Until the twins came along, she used to do something high-flying in the City that neither Tom nor I ever quite understood.

'But that's the beauty of it,' I say. 'That *is* my ambition. To have a child.'

'Why now?' asks Barbara. 'What's wrong with your life the way it is?'

'Nothing. But I suppose that I just pictured it a little differently. That I'd have a family by now.'

'Well, maybe you should have thought about settling down earlier,' she says.

'Yes, well, it's called "settling down" because most people end up settling for someone they don't really want to be with, and the down part is because that makes them depressed . . .'

Tom puts an arm around my shoulders and gives me a squeeze. 'Or is it because you like playing the field too much?' he says, adding, 'Lucky sod!' before ducking to avoid the oven glove Barbara throws at him.

'Tom, "playing the field", to use your quaint expression, isn't quite the fun you make it out to be. There's an awful lot of rejection and disappointment involved. Can you imagine what that's like?'

'Will, I'm an actor,' says Tom. 'I get rejected and disappointed every day.'

'And anyway, it's you two who are the lucky ones. You've managed to find someone who you want to spend the rest of your life with and, together, you're building a family unit. This house isn't just a house.' I gesture again towards the conservatory, which resembles the aftermath of an explosion in Hamleys. 'It's a home.'

'But, Will,' says Barbara. 'I can't really see you doing domesticity.'

'Maybe not. But I still want the "family" part. And before it's too late.'

Tom makes a face. 'Too late? Too late for what?'

'Listen,' says Barbara. 'Don't rush this. You've got a while yet.'

'Maybe so. But think about it. I've got to find someone. Get her pregnant. Hope the pregnancy goes okay, and then it's a further nine months. So I can't procrastinate.' I make a lunge towards the tray of Yorkshire puddings, and manage to grab one before Barbara can stab me with a fork. 'Goal setting. It's what I tell all my clients. And so by the time I'm thirty-one . . .'

'Which is' – Tom does a quick calculation – 'less than a month away.'

'. . . I'm going to find someone to start a family with.'

As I sit back in my chair and examine the soggy piece of batter in my hand, Barbara frowns. 'What's the matter?' she asks.

'Your Yorkshire puddings are just a bit . . . mushy.'

Tom lowers his voice. 'That's what breastfeeding two kids does to you,' he says, followed by 'Ouch!' as Barbara's second oven glove catches him on the ear.

Barbara sits down next to me. 'I think you've forgotten something, Will.'

'Which is?'

'What about falling in love? It's not a business decision, having kids.'

I take a bite and chew thoughtfully. Fortunately, it tastes better than it looks.

'Well, there's another thing.'

'Uh-oh,' says Barbara. 'What do you mean?'

'How long did it take you two to fall in love?'

'Years,' says Tom, checking Barbara's got nothing left to throw. 'I mean, we'd known each other for ages before we started going out, and I think we fell for each other pretty quickly, but of course while you might be "in love", there's a difference between being "in love" and being "in love enough . . ."'

'. . . to have a baby,' says Barbara, finishing the sentence for him.

'Precisely,' agrees Tom, before realizing he's actually agreeing with himself.

Barbara looks at me sympathetically. 'What about you, Will? Have you ever been in love?'

I pretend to consider this for a moment. 'I don't think so . . .'

'What about whatsername?' interrupts Tom.

I don't have to guess who he means. 'Anita?'

Tom nods. 'You were pretty keen on her at the time.'

I shrug. 'Maybe. But I'm not sure it was *love*,' I say, pronouncing it 'lurve'.

'There's always Sadie?' he suggests.

'Sadie?' says Barbara. 'Was that someone at college?'

I blush. 'He means Sade. The singer. And it's pronounced shar-day, Tom, for the millionth time. I was head over heels in love with her. When I was thirteen.'

Barbara sighs. 'Will, I'm talking about a real person.'

'Sade was real. Is real.'

'Yes, but your love for her wasn't.'

'Yes it was. I had all her albums. And a massive poster of her on my wall. Above my bed, in fact. So I could see it as I . . .'

'Oh please. Will, be serious.'

'. . . went to sleep, I was going to say. And I am serious. Or at least I was about Sade, at the time.'

Barbara looks at me as if I'm completely missing the point. 'I'm talking about real, romantic love. Not an unhealthy obsession with some pop star.'

'It wasn't unhealthy,' I mumble. 'And anyway, what's love got to do with it?'

Barbara folds her arms. 'What do you mean, what's love got to do with it?'

'Hang on,' says Tom. 'That was Tina Turner. Not Sade.'

'What are you getting at?' Barbara asks me, a little more interested now that we're on her territory.

'Or was it Bonnie Tyler?' Tom continues, to no one in particular.

'I mean, what if I dispense with the "love" part?'

Barbara frowns. 'Huh?'

'I'm serious. What if I concentrate instead on finding someone who's going to be a great mother? Someone who really wants kids and – here's the clever part – has all the skills and characteristics that you'd look for in a mum. Surely that's the best way to ensure that the child has the best possible upbringing?' I look at them both hopefully, pleased with my fantastic solution. 'What do you think?'

Barbara grimaces. 'Well . . . It's hardly the traditional route, is it?'

'So? What is the traditional route nowadays? Get married, have a family, get divorced? It's only going to end up in tears anyway, so why not do without all that emotional bollocks and cut to the chase. Focus on what's really important. The child.'

Barbara retrieves her oven gloves from where she's thrown them at Tom and stands over me, pulling them back on in the same manner that a boxer might. 'You want to have a baby in the full knowledge that you'll probably divorce the mother at some point?'

I nod nervously. 'That's the idea. Surely if I approach it that way, at least we'll avoid all the bitterness?'

'So tell me – you'd plan to chuck her out onto the street when, exactly? As soon as Will junior goes off to college? Or turns twenty-one? I can picture it now – "Happy birthday, son. Here's your present: the key to the door. And by the way, your mother and I only got together so we could have you, and now that you're leaving home, well, so is she."'

I shrug. 'That's if I even get married to her in the first place.'

Barbara rolls her eyes. 'Welcome to Planet Will. Why you've remained single over the years just amazes me.'

'I'm serious, Barbara. Times have changed. Getting

divorced was really tough for my mum back when my dad left. Nowadays it's more of a stage everyone goes through. Like puberty.'

'Or temporary insanity, in your case,' says Tom.

'Besides, divorce isn't necessarily such a bad thing for the kids.'

Barbara sits back down. 'I can't wait to hear this.'

'Think about it.' I lower my voice, even though it's unlikely that the twins are paying attention to anything except for the cartoon on the screen in front of them. 'Say you and Tom split up, and then each marry someone else. The kids have now got two sets of parents. Twice the love. And from their point of view, two homes. Two sets of toys. Two lots of holidays. And maybe even some more brothers or sisters. Surely if the parents can remain civil because they've both moved on, then that kind of arrangement's better than when people stay trapped in an unhappy marriage just for the "sake" of the kids – who I'm sure will pick up on the bad vibes anyway?'

Barbara stands up again. 'Well, that's one point of view,' she says, making it clear with her tone that it's not *her* point of view.

Tom twists the top off another bottle of wine. 'So, assuming we *might* just know someone, have you thought about the kind of woman you want to be the future ex-Mrs Jackson?'

Barbara looks from Tom to me, and then back at Tom again. 'Hold on. Let's not discuss this as if we're actually thinking of doing it,' she says, before stomping back into the kitchen.

I lower my voice again, but this time so Barbara can't hear. 'Okay – she needs to be at least thirty. That way, I've got a good chance of ensuring that her biological clock is ticking even louder than mine.'

'What about going for a younger one? As in much younger. That way, by the time the kid's out of the picture, if you do decide to stay together you've still got yourself a nice young—' Tom stops talking abruptly, aware that Barbara's reappeared, and is standing behind him holding a hot pan of gravy.

'Nope. The way I see it, she needs to be in the same boat as me. Probably hasn't had a child yet . . .'

'What's wrong with someone who's already had a baby?' says Barbara indignantly. 'She'll be better at motherhood. She'll already have had the practice.'

'Fair point. But equally, having another child could distract her from giving mine the attention it needs, and I want her to be completely dedicated to nurturing the baby.'

'Will, don't forget you're talking about a woman here,' says Barbara. 'A human being. Not a growbag.'

'She's got to be smart, well dressed . . .' I say, counting off on my fingers.

Barbara rolls her eyes. 'What's that got to do with it?'

'. . . come from a decent home, have a good job. And obviously she can't have any physical deformities. Or mental ones. Or be fat.'

Barbara sighs loudly, then heads back into the kitchen to fetch the gravy boat.

'You really want to go through with this, don't you?' says Tom.

I nod. 'I've been thinking about it for a while.'

'Since when?' asks Barbara, walking back into the room.

'Er . . . Since last Monday, actually. But I have given it a lot of thought.'

'So I see,' says Barbara scornfully. 'Nearly a week . . .'

Tom takes the gravy boat from Barbara and puts it on the table, careful to place it on the coaster. 'Are you sure you're doing this for the right reasons?'

'Tell me what the right reasons are, exactly. I know one thing – a lot of people do it for the wrong ones, or at the wrong time, or can't afford it. I have the time. I'm going to provide a stable financial household. I even have the spare room. I'm fit, I'm healthy—'

'If a bit mad,' interrupts Barbara.

'I'm serious. My life couldn't be going better. I've got everything I need, except for . . .'

Barbara smiles. 'A brain?'

'A family,' I reply, helping myself to a couple of roast potatoes. 'Fundamentally, I just really, really, *really* want to be a dad. And there're a lot of men out there – present company excepted – who've already got kids and who can't truthfully say that.'

'But . . .' Barbara seems to be struggling to find new

arguments. 'Why do you feel this need so strongly?'

'I just ... do. It's hard to describe it. Just like Tom's always known he wanted to be an actor, I've always wanted to do this.'

'Well, why haven't you yet?' she says, passing me a plate with about half a ton of meat on it. 'It's not as if you haven't had the opportunity.'

'Because the kind of girls I've been attracted to so far, well ...'

Barbara folds her arms again. 'Well what?'

'They've been good-looking, great fun to go out with, sexy, fantastic in bed, but ...'

'But?' Tom looks at me strangely. 'How can there possibly be a "but" after that description?'

'But I couldn't imagine any of them looking after my children. Making them would have been fun, but, well, sometimes these things are mutually exclusive, aren't they?'

'Not at all,' says Tom, although a little too slowly for Barbara's liking.

Barbara smiles. 'So you're just after someone who can be a good mother, pure and simple?'

I finish my mouthful of roast beef. 'Well, maybe not so pure ... And that's my dilemma. Because there's a difference between the kind of girl I'd normally go for, and a, er, mother-type, isn't there?'

She raises her eyebrows. 'Is there?'

I look nervously across at Barbara, who's brandishing her knife menacingly in my direction, and swallow hard. 'Well, look at Cecilia, for example. A great girl, really good fun and all that. But could you really see her caring for a child for eighteen years?'

'Not for even one evening,' says Barbara.

'Don't worry about that,' says Tom, trying to strain the lumpy gravy through his fork. 'It's genetic. They may not seem like it at the time, but the second a woman gets up the duff—'

'That's the accepted medical term, is it?'

'Yup. Anyway – the moment most women catch even the slightest glimpse of a child, the old hormones kick in and they magically seem to know all this stuff about rearing and breastfeeding and the like. It's as though it's already programmed into them.'

'So you're saying that if Cecilia had become pregnant, then all the partying would have suddenly stopped?'

Tom puts his fork down. 'Well, the coke habit might have been a bit of a tricky one to kick. But essentially, yes.'

'So why didn't you ever let the two of us babysit for Jack and Ellie, then?'

Barbara rolls her eyes. 'I refer you to Tom's previous observation.'

'Ah. But in any case, I'm going to have to play it safe. I can't take the gamble that suddenly they're going to turn into supermum. They've got to know what they're doing from day one.'

'Tell me something. Honestly,' says Tom. 'You

haven't just gone and knocked someone up, and this is your way of covering it up?'

'Chance would be a fine thing,' I say. 'And thanks for your faith in my motives.'

He grins sheepishly. 'And you're sure it's really what you want?'

'Well, let me ask you a question. What's the most rewarding thing you've ever done?'

Tom considers this for a moment. 'You mean financially? Well, certainly not having the twins. Quite the opposite, in fact.'

'No,' I say, as Barbara kicks him under the table. 'Emotionally. Life affirming.'

'Oh,' she says. 'You mean the sort of rubbish you tell your clients about.'

'Er, yes. That sort of rubbish.'

'Easy,' says Barbara. 'Having Jack and Ellie. Obviously.'

I turn back to Tom. 'You?'

Tom puts his arm around his wife's shoulders and gives her a squeeze. 'Same answer,' he replies, possibly because he knows which side his bread is buttered, but more likely to avoid another bout of domestic violence.

'So can you blame me for wanting a part of that? Ask me the same question and I'd struggle to give you an answer.'

'Or at least one that didn't involve some combination of women, drugs and sex,' suggests Tom.

'Which, ironically, is what you're going to need if

you're going to get anyone to agree to join you in this hare-brained scheme,' adds Barbara. 'Where on earth are you planning to find this poor girl?'

'Well, I've got a date tomorrow night, actually.'

Tom raises one eyebrow. 'Oh yes? And where did you meet this one? As the two of you were gazing hopefully through Mothercare's window?'

'Er . . . In Tesco's, actually.'

'Tesco's?' says Barbara. '*Every Little Helps?*'

'And with a thing as little as yours,' snorts Tom, 'you're going to need all the help you can get.'

And this is pretty much how the rest of lunch goes, with Tom and especially Barbara trying to convince me of the stupidity of my plan. Eventually, I look at my watch, more for effect than because I've actually got to be anywhere, before getting up from my chair.

'Thanks,' I say, carrying my plate through to the kitchen and sticking it into the dishwasher. 'For lunch, I mean. Not the lecture.'

Barbara follows me into the kitchen. 'Someone's got to keep you on the straight and narrow. I don't know why you get offended by it.'

I sigh exasperatedly. 'No offence, Barbara, but it's because this is what you always do – look down your nose at me from your perfect lifestyle in your perfect home.'

'What are you talking about?' She pulls open the door of the huge free-standing fridge in the corner, which is packed full of brightly coloured pots of food for the kids, and bottles of wine for the adults.

'You and Tom. Sometimes you can be such ...' I nod towards the fridge, 'Smeg marrieds. Just because I've been living my life differently to you up until now, the moment that I want to change it you start lecturing me because I don't want to do things your way. It's like ... like you're in life's sixth form, and you're talking to me like I'm still doing my GCSEs.'

'I'm sorry, Will,' says Barbara, as she escorts me to the door, closely followed by Tom and the twins, who've been reluctantly prised away from the television. 'I don't mean to have a go at you. It's just that where you are now – it's quite a long way from here to paternity.'

'Barbara's right,' says Tom, nodding towards my gorgeous but highly impractical TVR parked next to his Volvo. 'And it's certainly a little different to the way we saw your life ending up.'

'Which was?'

'Well, the way you've been going' – Tom scoops Jack and Ellie up off the floor in turn, holding each one out to me so they can plant sloppy goodbye kisses on my cheek – 'a lonely, drooling wreck in a retirement home somewhere.'

And as I get into my car and start the engine, it occurs to me that unless I start doing something about it right now, that stands a very good chance of being the title of my autobiography.

Chapter 2

It's the following morning and, as is usual every Monday, I'm woken up early by Magda, my cleaner, banging around in the kitchen. I don't really need a cleaner, especially at twenty pounds an hour – I'm hardly a messy person and, besides, it is only me in the flat – but Magda also does my laundry, and quite frankly I'd pay twice what I do at the moment to get my shirts ironed.

I reach across and hit the 'snooze' button on my alarm clock before it goes off, then get up and pull on a pair of trousers over my boxer shorts, retrieving last night's T-shirt from the back of the chair, and head bleary-eyed into the kitchen. When I get there, I find Magda down on the floor on her hands and knees, and with her head in the oven.

'Morning, Magda,' I say, trying unsuccessfully to stifle a yawn. 'Things can't be that bad, surely?'

Magda sits back on her heels and frowns up at me. 'What?'

She's dressed in her usual uniform of jeans, trainers,

and a T-shirt with one of those phrases printed on the front that doesn't quite mean anything – today's says 'Rifle Sporting Limited'. With her dark, spiky hair, pale skin, and despite almost the entire contents of the Argos jewellery catalogue adorning her ears, she's pretty in a moody, slightly tomboyish way. I'd guess she's around twenty-five – if her eyes didn't seem to be about a decade older than the rest of her. 'I have seen many things,' she said once, when I told her she looked older than her years. Although, on reflection, she may have meant in this flat.

'It's an electric oven, anyway,' I say. 'You won't be able to—' I stop myself quickly, realizing that making a joke about gassing yourself probably isn't in the best taste, particularly if, like Magda, you always walk around as though the world's about to come to an end. Besides, Magda never gets my jokes, and although I like to tell myself that it's because of the language barrier, while her English has improved considerably over the past couple of years, her appreciation of my sense of humour hasn't. I suppose we didn't get off to the best of starts – especially when she first appeared at my door and announced 'I Polish', so I fetched her a cloth and a tin of Mister Sheen and pointed her towards the table.

'I don't know why I clean oven every week,' she says. 'You never use.'

'I don't know why either, Magda,' I say, although it's possibly because otherwise she'd struggle to occupy herself over the three hours I pay her for. 'Maybe one of my neighbours sneaks in when I'm not here and makes themselves something to eat.'

'It is bad not to cook,' she says, standing up and placing a can of Mister Muscle on the worktop. 'In Poland, everybody cook. Even boys.'

I grunt, not wanting to get into another one of Magda's 'in Poland' stories, and help myself to a variety box of Frosties from the cupboard, which I eat straight from the packet, much to Magda's evident disgust. Magda sometimes feels she's my surrogate mother, which at times is nice, although not when she marches into my bedroom and starts hoovering round me at seven a.m. – especially when I'm still entertaining from the night before, if you know what I mean.

I flick on the television and finish my Frosties in front of the breakfast news, then jump into the shower, being careful to lock the door in case Magda decides now is a good time to clean the bathroom, and half an hour later I'm heading out of my front door. I hurry down Richmond Hill and along the high street, past Richmond's numerous cafés, mobile phone stores and charity shops, aiming for the building overlooking the Green where my office is. It's a chilly morning, and I'm dreaming of my first cup of coffee of the day, but just as I'm passing the Ann Summers shop on the corner, a girl with dreadlocks and a pierced nostril blocks the pavement in front of me.

'Hi, there. Can I have a minute of your time?'

Too late, I spot the familiar clipboard and brightly

coloured fleece top. I avert my eyes and try to walk on past, but she darts in front of me and starts to walk backwards, talking all the while.

'Can't you spare just a moment or two? To help old people?'

This has happened to me often enough recently to know that it's not a moment or two she wants, actually, but my bank details on a direct debit form. And if I signed up with everyone who accosted me here on the high street, it'd be me who'd be the one in need of charity. Besides, I've got things to do today, particularly if I'm going to put my plan into action.

'I'm sorry. I can't. I'm' – I glance theatrically at my watch – 'late for a meeting. And it's freezing,' I add, side-stepping her at the same time, and realizing as soon as I say it that that must be the lamest excuse ever for not donating to charity.

'So are thousands of pensioners,' she calls after me, making me feel instantly mean. 'To death. Every day.'

Unfortunately, I've forgotten that the café opposite my office building is closed for refurbishment, and so I have to turn round and furtively walk back past where Miss Dreadlocks is trying to accost someone who looks old enough to benefit from the charity she's collecting for, and head round the corner into Costa Coffee instead. I buy myself a large cappuccino, dropping my change guiltily into the charity box on the counter, before checking the coast is clear and making the short walk back to my office, where I jump into the lift and ride up to the second floor. As the lift doors open, Jen, the receptionist, puts down her copy of *Heat* and smiles at me.

'Morning, Will. Good weekend?'

I shrug. 'Not bad. Up until I got accosted on the way in this morning.'

Jen rolls her eyes. 'Same thing happened to me on Friday. Bloody chuggers.'

'Who?'

'Chuggers. Charity muggers. There's a rash of them in Richmond at the moment. What was it for today?'

'I dunno.' I take a sip of my coffee through the little hole in the lid, nearly scalding my tongue in the process. 'Help the Aged, or something.'

'That's ironic.'

'How do you mean?'

'Asking you for that,' she says, smiling cheekily at me. 'You might as well just keep the money.'

'Don't be so disrespectful,' I say, trying to glare at her, but unable to stop myself from grinning. Jen's probably about twenty and, thinking about it, that makes me half as old again. 'I can have you sacked, you know.'

She picks up her magazine and pretends to be fascinated by an article about what Posh Spice doesn't eat for breakfast. 'I know,' she says.

I glare at her some more, then head off down the corridor and into my office. I run a life-coaching consultancy, which sounds very grand but basically means that people whose wives or husbands have become fed up of them moaning come and moan to me instead about how bad their 'lot' is. I spend the best part of an hour listening to this, give them a bit of perspective by reminding them that there are starving children in Africa, and then spend the final five minutes trying to get them to focus on the positives – which here in Richmond are usually related to how much money they actually have – before relieving them of some of it.

I say consultancy, but I employ only one consultant – me. And I'd like to think I'm a fair boss – I give myself the day off whenever I feel like it, and don't make myself work too late. It's not the most difficult of jobs, and aside from the fact that it can be a bit soul-destroying to listen to someone who earns slightly less than the GDP of Belgium tell me that his Porsche, five-bedroom house next to Richmond Park, and ski lodge in Val d'Isere don't quite make him happy, it pays well. In fact, at the risk of mixing my metaphors, it's the Orient Express of gravy trains. And I shouldn't really be hypocritical, because it's rewarding in other ways too. And while I'm different from my clients in that the flat on Richmond Hill and the TVR that they've enabled me to buy over the years *do* actually make me happy – to a point – so does the fact that I'm genuinely able to help some of them with their problems.

All of which is funny because I'm not really 'qualified' to do this. Sure, I've got a certificate on the wall with my name on it saying that I'm a Fellow, Life Instruction Programme Practitioners And Natural Therapists (which Tom takes great pleasure in pointing out spells 'flippant'). But while most people study for years for that certificate, I bought mine from eBay.

I've been life coaching for about four years now. And although this line of work was quite unusual when I started the company – which used to be called 'Get A Life' – now it seems everyone is doing the same thing, so there's a lot of competition. Here in west London it seems you can't move nowadays without bumping into a something-or-other coach, so I've gone one step ahead and called my method the 'Life Train'. And why take the life train? Because it gets you there faster than the coach, of course. And how did I get into this? Well, a little by accident, really. I've always been someone who other people find it easy to talk to. Or maybe it's talk *at*. But either way, people seem to like unburdening themselves to me. And to be honest, I don't mind, whether it's over a coffee, a beer, or over the course of sixty minutes.

Ironically, it's been these hours and hours of therapy that have made me decide on my own route to happiness. Because no matter who I talk to – the banker with the Ferrari, the bored housewife rattling around the huge London apartment, the ex-premiership footballer coming to terms with the fact that his career is over by the time most of us are just starting to shave, there's one thing they all take pleasure in. One subject I know

I can just get them started on to raise the mood of a particularly depressing session. Their kids.

For example, Stephen, who's a trader, complained for an hour and a half to me last week, saying how, after eleven years on the job, he was starting to wonder what it was all about. 'Well, what did you earn last year?' I asked him.

'It wasn't a very good one. Just short of four million, including bonuses,' he replied, straight-faced, from his position on the couch.

Well, that's what it's all about, I wanted to say, as he looked up at me expectantly. I stared at the notepad in my hand – I always have a pen and paper, though usually just use it to jot down stuff I need to get at the shops on my way home – and made a note that I needed to put up his session fees. But stuck for an answer, I turned the question round, which always works fantastically well. That's why this therapy lark is so easy: simply repeat the question they've just asked you, and you often find they knew the answer all along.

'Well, let me ask you something,' I said. 'What do *you* think it's all about? What did you do last year that gave you the most satisfaction?' Again, if you've got an hour to kill, asking the same question in several different ways usually goes a long way towards filling it.

Stephen thought about this for a while, obviously working out which of his deals had been the best, I imagined. But, as it turned out, obviously not.

'I taught my son Ben to ride his bike,' he replied, a

tear rolling down his cheek. This captain of industry. This mover and shaker. This big soppy git, I thought. At the time.

Because it's a common sentiment. From housewife to high-flyer, I noticed that more and more of my clients were citing their children as their reason for being. The big thing in their lives. In some cases, the only thing in their lives. Whenever I needed to help them get some perspective, all I had to do was start them talking about their kids.

I tried it out on Tom too, when he was feeling down one day, and it worked. So I suddenly had a foolproof strategy to help my clients deal with their depression – simply telling them to go home and give their kids a squeeze. But after a while it started to feel a bit hollow, because I didn't know what it felt like myself.

And it's not that I'm unhappy with my lot. I just realize that I could be happier, and becoming a dad is going to help me achieve that. So I'm going to take my own advice, and instead of spending all my time trying to make other people's lives better, focus on my own for a while.

I finish my coffee, and stare out of the window, waiting for my nine-thirty to arrive. I say that my office overlooks Richmond Green – perhaps it's fairer to say that the building my office is in overlooks the Green. My actual office, on the other hand, is on the other side of the building – the side that looks out on to the back of the Ann Summers shop on the high street, which isn't as exciting as you might think. I could have had a view – a better view than old naked shop dummies and empty Rampant Rabbit crates, that is – but first, it would have been almost twice as expensive and . . . Well, to be honest, I had thought that I might by some miracle get something slightly racier to look at than just the occasional sullen shop assistant sneaking a crafty cigarette.

There're a few other businesses in here too; some graphic designers have the whole of the ground floor, there's an accountancy firm above them, then my floor is all individual offices rented out to the likes of me – next door to my office is a guy who writes slogans for greetings cards, and along the corridor is a very attractive girl called Kate who's some sort of management consultant. Upstairs is an import/export business, although none of us are actually sure what it is they import/export, and by the looks of the guys who constantly go in and out, it's probably best not to ask.

I hear my phone buzz, and look at my watch. It's nine-twenty. And when I walk down to reception I see Joanne, one of my oldest clients, waiting for me. As usual, she's early, and again, as usual, she looks like she's been crying.

She's married to some banker in the city, and a credit to the plastic surgeon's art: stick thin, Botox-ed up to her eyeballs, and wearing a watch that probably costs more than even *my* car. And yet she's still not happy, possibly because the husband who buys her all the aforementioned alterations and adornments spends all his time at the office and not with her – probably because it's the only way he can afford it all.

'Morning, Joanne,' I say, steeling myself for fifty-five minutes of Joanne's usual tirade about just how terrible it is to live in a big house and be the wife of a multi-millionaire. 'And how are you today?' Unlike most people who ask that question, I really want an honest answer.

As Jen rolls her eyes at me from behind the reception desk, Joanne gets up from where she's been flicking through a copy of *House and Garden*, which quite possibly contains a feature about *her* house and garden, and follows me down the corridor. 'Not too good, actually,' she sniffs.

I look back towards reception to see Jen miming fitting a noose round her neck. Unlike me, she has little sympathy for some of my clients, particularly those like Joanne who she thinks have more money than sense – and Joanne's certainly not stupid. She's been coming to see me since just after I started, and while I'd like to think we're making progress, in reality every time I try and 'fix' an issue with her, she finds something else to feel bad about. In actual fact, I've come to the conclusion that she just wants to talk to someone, and I'm quite happy to be that someone, especially for a hundred pounds an hour. Oh yes, and Joanne and her husband don't have kids.

For the last few weeks, we've been working on

Joanne's relationship with her friends – a similarly turned-out bunch of ladies who lunch, although by the looks of them, 'lunch' doesn't involve the consumption of any actual food. 'They're all more beautiful than me,' she sobs, from her usual position on the couch. 'And cleverer. And with better-looking husbands. And perfect homes . . .'

I reach over and hand her a tissue from the bumper-sized box in my drawer, which Jen has christened 'Joanne's Box'. It's getting worryingly empty, and I don't have a spare.

'And so would you say that you feel a failure next to them?'

Joanne nods vigorously, causing her five-hundred-pound haircut to wobble alarmingly. 'If there was one thing, just one thing where I felt I could compete, even be better at than they are, I'd be able to look them in the eye.'

I shake my head sympathetically. 'And do you think they're happy? With their pampered lives and rich husbands who they never see?'

Joanne nods again. 'It certainly seems like it. But then, who wouldn't be, with a lifestyle like that?' she says, unaware of the irony in her last comment.

I put on my best, soothing voice. 'So, if we can identify one thing, any thing, that you can beat them at, that'd make you feel better?'

Joanne gazes miserably out of the window. 'I suppose so.'

'And do you suppose that any of them, these perfect women, have self-esteem issues like you do?'

'Of course not. How could they?'

'Hmm,' I say, sucking on the end of my Biro. 'Interesting.'

Joanne looks up hopefully. 'What is?'

'Just that, well, and this is a bit of a long shot . . .'

'Yes?'

'Would you say that you've got a lower self-esteem than any of them?'

'Absolutely.'

'Which means there is one thing that you beat them at.'

Joanne frowns at me. Or at least I think she does, as her eyebrows move closer together, although her forehead doesn't wrinkle. 'I don't follow you.'

'You've got the worst self-esteem out of them all,' I say triumphantly.

Joanne looks puzzled for a few seconds. 'And that's good?'

'Of course it is. You look at all these women and think that you can't possibly compete. That they outdo you in every respect. Well, here's one where they don't. You're the winner.'

'I don't really see that as winning,' she says suspiciously.

'But that's what I've been trying to do for the past few sessions. To teach you to look at yourself differently. You don't live a normal life, so you can't look at life normally. You have this ... *existence* that's so different to the rest of us. You tell me how false it is, and how unfair it is, and how miserable it is' – I'm in full flow now – 'and the fact that you're unable to deal with it. That it doesn't sit well with you. That these false friends of yours – and I mean that in both senses of the word – love their lives, whereas you're completely at odds with yours. Well, surely that's a good thing? Surely that means you're a better, more decent human being. That you're unhappy, and looking for a way to have a better life rather than this constant circle of parties and holidays.'

Joanne looks at me like I'm a genius. 'Well, when you put it like that ... Although I do quite like the holidays.'

It's difficult to tell, given the lack of movement in her facial features, but I'd swear I can see the merest trace of a smile on Joanne's surgically enhanced lips. And while I know that it's probably just a temporary mood swing, the sad thing is that the one thing I want to advise her to do, I can't. Because she can't. Have kids, that is. And even though there's very little else to feel sorry for her about, it breaks your heart.

Five minutes later, when I'm writing up my notes, there's a knock on my door. It's Jen.

'What on earth did you say to old Mrs Trout-pout? She positively bounded out of here.'

I shrug. 'It's a gift. Besides, I'm afraid I can't let on, Jen. Client confidentiality, and all that.'

'I'd watch her, Will, if I were you. You know all about this clients-and-their-therapists lark. I think she's got a rather soft spot for you.' Jen shudders. 'Although having said that, it'd be the only soft spot anywhere on her body.'

'Now now, Jen. And remember, I'm not a therapist. I'm a life coach.'

Jen makes a face. 'Whatever.'

Chapter 3

I finish the rest of the day's appointments by four o'clock, then hurry back home, as I've got the first phase of my plan to put into practice before my date this evening. So, following a quick trip to the Toyota garage in Twickenham, I sit down at my kitchen table and switch on my laptop. First task is to log on to Friends Reunited, to find out what most of the girls I knew at school are doing now. I can't resist checking the male section first, where they all seem to be gaining a family and losing their hair, and it idly occurs to me that maybe the two are linked. I flick through a few of the profiles – including Tom's, which makes him out to be west London's answer to Robert De Niro – before turning my attention to the girls. But despite an hour or so of pleasant reminiscence, no potential candidates leap to mind; from what I can remember, the ones that are still single, deserve to be single. The rest of them all seem to be happily married – I suppose my year are too young to be going through divorces just yet – and already have children, or are lesbians, or even (which seems a little unfair to me, given my current lack of a family) lesbians with children. After a fruitless further hour of searching the years above and below me, I'm just about to give up when I spot Debbie Smith's details.

I don't remember Debbie all that well, however I seem to recall that she was quite pretty, always wore the shortest skirt and, more importantly, stuck her tongue down my throat one night at the school disco. And although I also seem to remember that she had a bit of a reputation for sticking her tongue down the throat of any boy who so much as looked in her direction, let alone those who'd gone to the trouble of buying her a Coke and a Curly Wurly like I had, she has written something interesting on her profile: 'I'd love to get together with anyone who remembers me, particularly any guys out there who are tired of being on their own, and feel that three is better than two.' This is great – she must be feeling broody. Without any hesitation I pay my subscription, write her a quick email saying 'hi', and hit 'send'.

And while a quick snog and a slow dance to Whitney Houston's 'I Will Always Love You' was about as far as it went between Debbie and me, it suddenly occurs to me that there must have been other girls who I actually went out with back then, and not necessarily at my school. But when I Google 'Girlfriends Reunited', instead of finding a site where I can track down my exes, there's just a bunch of pornographic lesbian photographs, which I delete. Eventually.

Next, I grab a blank sheet of paper, and make a list of all the women I know. I stare at it for a moment or two, then cross off all those I've been out with, which leaves about ten. I then put a line through those people like Barbara or Jen whose situation makes them inappropriate, and then do the same with those people who are unsuitable for other reasons – either they're too ugly, they've already got a boyfriend, or they're, er, too ugly.

It's at this stage I realize that I've crossed everyone off the list, which kind of confirms a suspicion that I've had since yesterday. It's going to have to be someone new. But Debbie Smith aside, where am I going to find her? And what is it that makes a good mother, exactly? I can hardly phone mine and ask her.

Still, if my date tonight works out, I might not need to track down Debbie, or indeed anyone else, which is why by seven o'clock I'm sitting in Pizza Express in Chiswick, having dinner with Alice – a rather attractive and somewhat top-heavy girl who caught me checking her out at the checkout in Tesco's on Saturday. But as is my new resolution, I'm trying to look at her as someone who's a potential mother of my child, rather than just someone who could work as a body-double for Pamela Anderson. Not that her figure isn't practical, of course; at least the baby would eat well.

It's not my usual choice of venue for a first date, but

this was Alice's suggestion – her favourite restaurant, in fact – although I'm not quite sure what this says about her. I'm actually not sure what she says about herself either, mainly because she's only just moved down to London from Sunderland, and I'm having trouble understanding her heavy north-east accent. But I like pizza, even the ungenerously frisbee-sized ones they serve here, and as I sip my sparkling water I try hard to decipher her small talk. I've ordered my favourite, Quattro Formaggi, and after I've waved away the bored-looking waiter, who's been leering down Alice's top while simultaneously brandishing his large, rather phallic pepper grinder at her, I pick up my knife and fork hungrily. But just as I'm about to tuck in, Alice nods towards her plate.

'For Jesus.'

'Oh. Yes. Sorry. Of course,' I say, putting my knife and fork down guiltily.

I can't remember the last time I heard anyone say grace, and in fact I've never been religious, so I don't know exactly what to do or say in response. I bow my head and stare at my pizza intently for a few seconds, watching as the mozzarella melts temptingly over the crust, wondering how long I should spend in the 'grace' position, before remembering that I should perhaps shut my eyes. Thinking about it, I wonder whether Alice's evident spirituality is a good thing. Because although it occurs to me that it might sub- stantially reduce my chances of sex this evening, it also has its positive side. A child of mine being brought up religiously, and therefore with sound principles? Why ever not?

I'm already picturing myself as the proud dad at Will junior's first communion, when Alice coughs loudly next to me. I open my eyes and turn to face her.

'Amen,' I mumble.

But instead of joining me in what I believe is the customary response, Alice just stares at me strangely. 'I didn't know you was religious, like,' she says.

Is this a trick? Or was my head-bowed reverence so convincing she thinks that when I'm not hanging round supermarkets I'm actually the Bishop of Brentford?

'Well, I'm not, really. I mean . . . It's not that I don't believe, or anything, or that I do, but . . .' I begin to realize that I might be tying myself up in knots, and decide to change the subject. 'How's your pizza? What did you order, again?'

Alice still has the same confused look on her face. 'Like I said. Four cheeses. Same as you.'

'Ah. Right.' I take a large gulp of water and hurriedly try and change the subject. 'So, how do you like it here in London? You must have been relieved to get away from the north-east? With a name like yours?'

Alice frowns. 'How d'you mean?'

'Alice in Sunderland?' I say, then wonder why she's looking at me blankly. 'Like the book? By Lewis, er, Carroll?'

As my voice tails off, and I make a note to myself not to take the mickey out of any prospective partner's name in the future, Alice shrugs, and cuts a huge slice out of her pizza.

'It's okay. Chiswick's nice,' she says, emphasizing the 'w'.

'It's, er, Chis-ick.'

Alice pauses mid-bite. 'What?'

'The "w" is silent.'

'Silent?' says Alice, not sure if I'm being serious. 'That's a southern thing, is it?'

Forty-five minutes later, I'm starting to wish that Alice would take after the 'w' in Chiswick, as she doesn't stop talking, even when her mouth is full of pizza. I can't get a word in edgeways, and even my party trick of shoving a couple of dough balls into my cheeks and doing my best Marlon Brando in the *Godfather* impression doesn't shut her up. What makes it worse is that the more red wine she drinks, the thicker her accent becomes, and by the time I eventually drop her off at her flat – as well as off my ever-so-short shortlist – I can't even tell if her 'You for coffee?' is actually her way of wanting to prolong the evening or telling me to get lost.

I head back into Richmond and realize that it's still early, but past Jack and Ellie's bedtime, so it should be safe to give Tom a call. When I suggest a beer, he sounds a little puzzled.

'On a school night? Besides, I thought you were

supposed to be on a date with that girl from New-castle?' says Tom, putting on his best Tyneside accent so the last word comes out like 'nuke-hassle'.

'Sunderland. And I was. We went out for pizza. And I've ditched her to come and have a beer with you, which should give you some idea of just how well it went.'

'Pizza? She didn't fancy trying your meat feast, like?'

'Very funny, Tom. And by the way, you sound more like someone with learning difficulties than someone from the north-east.'

'Booger off, mun,' says Tom, as if he's suddenly moved to Pakistan. Despite his drama-school back-ground, accents aren't exactly his strong point. In fact, I'm not sure what his strong point actually is, apart from playing the slightly porky thirty-something dad.

He's still chuckling when I ring on his doorbell a few minutes later, but when he follows me outside, his face changes abruptly.

'What the hell's that?'

'My new car. Potentially.'

Tom stares in disbelief at the hulking silhouette of the Toyota. 'That's not a car. It's something straight out of Desert Storm. Does the US Military know you've pinched one of their vehicles?'

'It's a Rav 4.'

'"Rav" as in "raving mad", I suppose? What's wrong with your sporty little babe-magnet? Don't tell me it's broken down again?'

'No. But it's a baby-magnet I need now. So I'm test-driving this.'

'What on earth for?'

'The TVR's hardly a practical car, is it? Besides, all parents have to drive a four-by-four. It's practically the law in west London.'

This is true, although while the centre of Richmond is usually forced to a standstill at school-run times by these huge vehicles, the most off-road they ever get is when they pull onto the pavement to drop little Rupert and Rupetta off at the gates.

Tom sighs. 'May I just remind you that you don't even have a baby yet. Or a woman to make one with. So why the sudden need to change your trans-portation?'

'Because I want everything to be right. The fewer changes I have to make at the time the better. I want the potential mother of my child to look at me and see that everything's in place. That I'm prepared for all eventualities. So the trappings of my so-called bachelor lifestyle have got to go. And that starts with the car.'

Tom grabs me by the shoulders. 'Will, listen to me. The rest of us fathers only do those things because we *have* to. Not voluntarily. Most of us would kill for a car like yours. Believe me, you want to hold on to that stuff until the last possible minute, because it'll be a long, long time before you'll see anything like it again. Except driven by other people, that is.'

'No, Tom, you're wrong. When I finally meet the woman who's going to be the perfect mother, I don't want anything about me to scare her off. Anything. I want her to look at me and say, "There's someone who knows what he wants, who's thought about what he needs to do to run this parenthood lark successfully, and who's prepared to make all sorts of sacrifices to make sure that happens."'

'And a trip down to Toyotas R Us is going to achieve that for you, is it?' Tom opens the door and peers into the back. 'Besides, how many kids are you thinking of having?'

'Mate, if there's one thing I've learned from you, the big car isn't for the kids. It's for all the kids' stuff. Pushchairs. Toys. Changes of clothes. By the time you and Barbara get the Volvo loaded up for anything more than a drive around the block, there's hardly room for Jack and Ellie in there, let alone the two of you.'

'Maybe so, but this . . .' Tom just shakes his head. 'Half the reason I hang around with you is so I get to go in your flash car once in a while.'

'Thanks very much.'

'And you never even let me drive it once,' says Tom sulkily.

I suppose I am, or rather was, a little bit anal about my car. 'Tom, there are some things in life that are sacred, and the TVR was mine. Besides, I've seen the number of dents you've got on the Volvo.'

Tom sighs and climbs into the passenger side of

the Toyota, shutting the door with an echoing thud. 'To the pub,' he orders. 'To the pub.'

'Why did you say it twice?'

He grins. 'I didn't.'

Ten minutes later, after I've made the pleasant discovery that speed bumps are no longer an exhaust-scraping hazard, while at the same time making Tom bump his head painfully against the roof, we're sitting in our favourite pub, the City Barge, at a table over-looking the Thames. Even though he's already had his dinner this evening, Tom's ordered a plate of nachos, on the strict understanding that I don't tell Barbara.

As I sip my beer, Tom dips a nacho into the pot of sour cream on the table, pops it into his mouth, and grimaces, before picking up the cream and sniffing it.

'Do you think this has gone off?' he says, offering me some to try.

I wave the pot away. 'Tom, it's sour cream. How could you tell?'

'So – your Tyneside lass not quite right for the task in hand?' he asks, picking up another nacho.

'Nah. She was nice-looking, but ... It's just re-inforced that I can't base this search on looks alone. They might be nice eye-candy—'

'Or in her case, why-aye candy,' interrupts Tom, scooping up some guacamole.

'Exactly. But I can't let that be the most important factor. I've got to look for someone a little more ...'

'Mumsy?'

I shudder a little. 'But not too mumsy. I've got to think about how the child's going to look. After all, there's no guarantee it's going to take after me.'

'I know,' says Tom. 'It's funny how Jack and Ellie both look like Barbara.'

'Fortunately,' I add, thinking that they're twins, so it's highly unlikely that they're going to look different to each other. 'But I can't go too far down that road, as I'll obviously want to keep sleeping with her after the baby's born.'

Tom laughs bitterly. 'Oh I wouldn't worry about that.'

'What do you mean?'

He puts his pint glass down. 'Have you any idea what having a baby does to your sex life?'

'I've got a dreadful feeling you're not going to say "improves it beyond belief"?'

'Stops it. Dead. And I mean dead. I tell you, mate, when you're trying to get pregnant, it's morning, noon and night. Which initially is great. But then you start to feel like you do at one of those all-you-can-eat restaurants, so much so that you might even start feigning headaches occasionally. And then when she's pregnant?' He rolls his eyes. 'You might think that all the hard work's been done. Well, you're wrong, because that's when the hormones really kick in, and you can't get her off you. And the irony is, while she's feeling extra-horny, you fancy her less because she's getting, you know, fat, plus you're worried about having sex with her because there's someone else to think about – and you don't want to poke their little eye out with your—'

I sit back in my chair. 'Whoa! That's a little too much information, mate.'

Tom stops speaking momentarily, possibly because of the look of horror on my face, and then breaks into a grin. 'You need to hear this, Will. Because if you think that's bad, consider what happens once the baby's born. What you've got then is the prospect of no sex for the first few months because either she's too sore, or too self-conscious, or you're too worried because you can't quite get out of your head the sight of the last thing you saw emerging from her' – he points to his crotch – 'girly bits down there. I'll tell you, I've not taken so many cold showers in my life. Even on the odd occasion when you find that she's actually in the mood, it's been so long for you that you reach the old "they think it's all over . . . it is now" stage a lot sooner than you'd like.'

'Tom, please.'

'And then after the first six months you'd think things would be better, but oh no, because by that time, even if you're lucky, the two of you are still getting only a few hours' shut-eye each night, and so the only thing you actually want to do in bed is sleep. And then after a year or so, when you finally get the kids into some sort of regular sleep pattern, you're so worried about disturbing them that you don't dare do anything that might make the slightest bit of noise, for fear of waking them up and having them marching into the bedroom and seeing Daddy and Mummy in a position that's going to give them a complex for the rest of their lives.'

'Thank you for the mental image I'm trying hard to ignore.'

'You're welcome.'

'So you're basically saying that I needn't waste my time looking for anyone sexy?'

Tom carefully peels the melted cheese off a clump of nachos to reveal a jalapeño, which he drops into the ashtray. 'Not at all. By all means focus on the motherhood angle – it's much more appropriate for what you're trying to achieve. But bear in mind that although they might suddenly turn fat and middle-aged when they're "with child", they don't all stay that way.'

'Huh?'

Tom grins. 'Haven't you heard the phrase "yummy mummy"? You know – the allure of the mature?'

I peer at Tom over the top of my glass. 'What on earth are you talking about?'

'Tell you what,' he says. 'Come with me one day when I'm picking the twins up from school. You'll see what I mean.'

'Fine,' I say. 'Although I'm sure I can still bring myself to do the business afterwards, whatever she looks like. After all, I've got to fancy her enough to get her pregnant in the first place, don't forget.'

'And have you thought about how you're going to do that?'

'Sleep with her? That, I believe, is the usual tried and trusted procedure? Though, thinking about it, I suppose I'd only have to do it the once, wouldn't I?'

Tom looks at me condescendingly. 'Will, that's like expecting to win the lottery the first time you buy a ticket.'

'What do you mean?'

He folds his arms and leans on the table. 'Well, for one thing, timing is critical.'

'Oh. Right. Well, that shouldn't be a problem. I always, ahem, aim for simultaneous, you know . . .'

Tom makes a face. 'Thanks for the imagery yourself, Casanova. I forgot that you skipped most of biology class. I don't mean that sort of timing. You have to plan it around her time of the month.'

'What, if she's got PMT she won't want me anywhere near her, you mean?'

'No – her fertility cycle. There're only a few days when she's actually capable of getting pregnant, and you have to make sure that you strike while the iron's hot, so to speak. Especially because you've only got a small—'

'Window of opportunity?' I interrupt. 'And please keep your voice down.'

'That's right.' Tom gestures towards me with his pint glass, spilling some lager onto his plate of nachos. He picks up one of the beer-soaked chips, puts it into his mouth and chews it appreciatively. 'And don't forget, you have to be sure that you're both actually fertile in the first place. In fact, that's a very important factor to consider. If I were you, I'd start wearing boxer shorts, watching your diet . . .'

I nod towards Tom's half-eaten pile of nachos. 'That's rich, coming from a man whose idea of health food is a bar of Cadbury's Fruit and Nut.'

'I'm serious. In fact, before you head off on this wild goose chase, I'd get yourself checked out.'

I frown at Tom. 'Why on earth would I need to do that?'

He stands up and leans across the table towards me. 'Because apart from anything else, if you're firing blanks and you don't know it, you might end up sleeping with an ugly woman for nothing.'

As Tom heads off to the bar to get us both another beer, I sit and stare out of the window thinking about what he's just said. It's all very well me trying to anticipate problems with my potential partner, but it's never even occurred to me that there might be a spanner in *my* works.

I'm still preoccupied with it when he sits back down at the table. 'I'm pretty sure I'm okay.'

'How do you know?' says Tom, dipping a nacho straight into his beer glass then into the sour cream, chewing on it as if he's conducting some sort of taste-test.

'Well, I don't, um, have any problems.'

'I'm not sure I want to hear this.'

'You know, on the' – I clear my throat – 'volume front. Every time I, you know . . .'

Tom pushes the sour cream away from him. 'Thanks for sharing that, Will, but it's not about quantity.'

'Of course it is. Like everything, it's a numbers game. Only one of the little blighters has got to get through, surely, so by statistical analysis, the more I produce, the higher the chance that one of them is going to make it.'

Tom shakes his head. 'I think you need to do a little more research, Will. It's about quality. All that, er, stuff, isn't just the little folk, you know. It's just like their transport medium.'

'Pardon?'

'Well, think of it like the London Underground. Look at it at rush hour, and then again at eleven o'clock at night. The tubes are still the same size, but there are fewer passengers.'

'Huh? So it's about the size of the tubes? Well, in that case . . .'

'Okay. Bad example.' Tom taps his pint glass. 'Think of lager.'

'Lager?'

'Yup. If someone handed you a glass of beer and you drank it, do you think you'd be able to tell straight away if it was normal lager or low-alcohol lager? You'd still be drinking the same amount, it would still, if you excuse the thought, taste the same, but, and here's the important part, it wouldn't be as potent.'

'Which means?'

'If it was low-alcohol lager, you'd need to drink an awful lot more to increase your chances of getting drunk.'

'Or pregnant.'

'And it's possible that no matter how much lager you drank, if it turned out to be alcohol-free . . .'

'Then I'd be wasting my time.'

'Exactly. And even then, it's not just about the alcohol content of the lager.'

'What? Now you're going to tell me it's down to the quality of the glass.'

'More like the way you get her to drink out of it. It's actually quite a complicated biological process, this pregnancy stuff. Not just like making a bowl of porridge, where all you have to do is add the hot milk.' Tom grimaces. 'Yuk. Sorry.'

'So it's nothing to do with technique, then?'

'Nope. You can be the most skilful footballer in the world, but you're never going to score unless you've actually got the ball at your feet.'

Football. Finally, Tom is talking a language that I understand. 'But how do you know all this? You obviously have no problem in front of goal, judging by Jack and Ellie.'

Tom smiles, and lowers his voice. 'I'll let you into a little secret. It was taking us ages to get pregnant, and Barbara is, as you know, a little older than me, so we decided to go and do something about it.'

'Don't tell me the twins are adopted? I saw Barbara get very fat. Or was that just a pillow up her jumper for those nine months?'

'Nope. IVF.'

'You've what?'

'IVF. In vitro fertilization. We got ourselves checked out, and while we both seemed to be okay, it just wasn't happening. So . . .'

I stare at him for a few seconds, before realization dawns. 'So you gave yourselves a helping hand. As it were.'

'Quite.'

'Hence the twins.'

'Yup. Which was a blessing, in a way. Barbara didn't have to go through the trauma of childbirth twice and, from their point of view, they've always got someone to play with.' He clinks his beer glass against mine. 'Result.'

'And it didn't seem . . . weird?'

Tom shakes his head. 'No, not at all. Still Barbara's eggs, and my, you know, sperm. We just needed a little help getting them to meet.'

'What, like a dating agency?'

Tom nods. 'Precisely,' he says, draining the last of his beer. 'A dating agency.'

And that gives me an idea.

Chapter 4

But first, I've decided that I ought at least to follow Tom's advice and get myself 'checked out', as he's so succinctly described it. So, after I've dropped the Toyota back at the garage, and following a somewhat nervous phone call, I find myself driving along Chiswick High Road, trying to find the family planning clinic.

Tom's recommended this place, although that's probably because it's the only one he knows, rather than because it's particularly good – it's not the sort of establishment you'd normally find yourself recommending, I suppose, like a restaurant, or a good dentist. The building itself is quite innocuous, in between a kebab shop and a branch of Barclays. 'There's a bank next door,' Tom said, 'just in case you need to make any other kind of deposit,' before collapsing with laughter.

I'm a little early, and there's a parking space right outside, so I sit in the TVR for a few minutes while I try and work out how long I need to put money in the meter for. Eventually, when I've looked at my watch for approximately the seventeenth time, I get out and stand on the pavement, and after a couple of minutes of pretending to be fascinated by a poster in the bank window advertising Unit Trusts while actually checking no one I know is actually walking by, I do a final scan up and down the street, then duck into the nondescript doorway and climb the stairs. As I walk towards the reception desk, I can't help noticing a couple of doors on either side of the lobby. They've both got the word 'occupied' on a sliding sign above the handle, and when I listen carefully, strange music seems to be coming out from behind one of them.

The receptionist looks up from her copy of *Hello!* and gives me a bored smile.

'Can I help you?'

'Yes, I . . .' I clear my throat. 'I've got an appointment to, well, you know . . .' Bloody hell. Why does it have to be a female receptionist? 'To have my . . .'

After I've finally stopped spluttering, she consults her appointments diary.

'Mr Jackson, is it?'

'That's right.'

'Take a seat in the waiting room, will you?' She nods over to one side of the reception area, where there are a couple of plastic chairs next to a water cooler. 'And if you could just fill out this form?'

I take the clipboard and pen she's handed me, sit down and start to fill in my details as requested. It seems straightforward enough, until I get to the section marked 'partner's name', where for a second I consider writing 'don't know yet', but end up leaving it blank. After a couple of minutes I walk over and hand it back to the receptionist, who stares at it for a few seconds, then gives me a strange look before picking up the phone.

'Dr Scott, Mr Jackson's here,' she says, followed by, 'No, on his own.'

She tells me to sit down again, and so I head back and sit on my chair and flick through a leaflet on family planning – which is, after all, what I'm trying to do – that I find on the coffee table. My mouth is dry, and I'm hoping the rest of me won't be, but as I'm helping myself to a drink from the water cooler, the music I'd heard earlier suddenly stops, and a red-faced man comes out through the door. Rather worryingly, he's carrying a toolbox, and as the door swings shut behind him, I catch a glimpse of a bed with what appear to be a pile of pornographic magazines on the pillow.

'Success?' asks the receptionist.

The man nods. 'Yes. Just needed a few tweaks and out it came.'

'It's always the way,' says the receptionist. She reaches for the petty-cash tin and hands a wad of notes over. 'Thanks for coming.'

'Any time,' replies the man, before winking at me and heading out through the door. As I watch him go, the receptionist notices my bewildered expression.

'Something wrong, Mr Jackson?'

'No, it's just, I, I mean ... Was he a, you know, sperm donor?' For some reason, when I say those words, I can't help thinking of the kebab shop next door.

The receptionist looks puzzled for a second, before bursting out laughing. 'No,' she says, between gasps. 'Repair man. The video player in one of the cubicles had a cassette stuck.'

'Ah. Oh. Right.'

I'm just processing this piece of information and trying hard not to blush when Dr Scott comes out to meet me. She — and she would be, wouldn't she? — is a rather attractive and stereotypically sexy forty-something doctor — the kind you used to see in those cheesy old BBC comedies; her hair up, a pair of glasses perched on the end of her nose, and dressed in a long white coat.

'Mr Jackson? Come this way, please.'

I look at her face to see whether that's meant as a joke, but then realize that she's probably heard them all, so just do as instructed, and follow her into her office. There's a bed at one end with a screen behind it, and a desk with a chair where, fortunately, she tells me to sit. She scans through my form and makes a couple of notes, before putting the clipboard down on the desk.

'So, what seems to be the problem?'

This time, I can't stop the reddening of my cheeks. 'It's, er, a little embarrassing, really.'

Dr Scott takes off her glasses and rubs the bridge of her nose wearily. 'Mr Jackson, I can assure you that after ten years of treating fertility problems, nothing embarrasses me any more.'

'Well, I don't have a problem. Not really. As far as I'm aware, that is. I just wanted to check that I was, you know . . .'

Dr Scott smiles at me. 'I don't know, actually. I'm not a mind-reader. In fact, my particular area of specialism is quite a bit further down than that.'

I smile back at her, pretty sure that her last comment was meant to put me at my ease. 'Sorry. It's just . . .' She really is very attractive, and I just can't seem to bring myself to start talking about my sperm in front of her.

'Are you having erectile problems? Because if so, I can give you a leaflet, and—'

'No. Nothing like that,' I say, perhaps a little too quickly.

'It's nothing to be ashamed of. It happens to most men at some point in their lives.'

'Well, it's never happened to me,' I say, *and not to any men who have ever been in bed with you, I'll bet*, I think, trying not to fixate on the way Dr Scott is absent-mindedly sucking on the arm of her glasses. 'It's just that, well, I'm trying to have a baby, and I just wanted to check that I wasn't, you know, firing blanks, so to speak.'

Dr Scott leans back in her chair, puts on her glasses,

picks up the clipboard again and uncaps her pen. 'How about your wife? Many fertility problems can be down to the woman and not the man.'

'Well, that's a relief,' I say, before realizing that probably sounds a bit harsh. 'I mean, a shame. But I'm not married.'

'Well, your partner, then,' says Dr Scott, a little testily.

'I don't have one. Currently, that is. I mean, I'm looking for someone. I just want to check I can, you know, procreate, before I go to the trouble of—' I stop talking, because Dr Scott is looking at me in a rather strange way.

'So, let me get this straight,' she says, all traces of a bedside manner evaporating rapidly. 'You don't actually have anyone to have a baby with, but you basically want to find out if you're fertile?'

I nod. 'That's about the size of it. If that's something you do?'

Dr Scott re-caps her pen and puts the clipboard back down. 'It's your money.'

'Great,' I say, before shifting awkwardly in my seat. 'So, what happens now?'

By now, Dr Scott seems to be enjoying my discomfort. 'Well, we'll require a sample, of course,' she says, reaching into one of her desk drawers and handing me a plastic pot. 'As soon as you can.'

'Oh,' I say. 'Right.'

'So.' She smiles at me. 'Off you go, then.'

I'm not sure if I've heard her right, but when she makes no move to get up, I can't help but ask.

'Er . . .'

'Is there some problem?'

'Aren't you going to leave me to it?'

'Pardon?'

I nod towards the bed in the corner. 'I just thought it'd be a bit more private, you know? That I'd get my own room.'

'Mr Jackson, I don't mean right here. You can use one of the cubicles out by reception. Or take the container home with you and bring it back later, if you'd prefer.'

'Oh. Of course.' I stand up, and take a closer look at the pot. It seems rather, well, large. 'How, er, much do you need? I mean . . .'

Dr Scott shakes her head. 'It's not a competition, Mr Jackson. Don't feel you need to do any training. But I'm assuming you've gone without any emission for a day or two, so we can expect a decent volume?'

I look suspiciously at the plastic pot, suddenly anxious. 'A decent volume? Which is what, exactly? I mean, do you expect me to' – I swallow hard – 'fill it?'

She half-smiles at me. 'If you could fill it, Mr Jackson, you probably wouldn't be here in the first place.'

I laugh, though more from nerves. 'No. Sure. And when do I get my results?'

'We can do it for you in forty-eight hours,' she says, standing up and leading me towards the door.

'Depending on how quickly we get the sample back, of course.'

As I walk back out through reception, I glance at the cubicle door, but decide immediately that this isn't the route I want to take, despite the variety of artificial stimulation on offer. Besides, I'm worried that these places might have hidden cameras, and I don't fancy the tape appearing on some strange Japanese television programme some day. I don't want to produce my sample under pressure, either – it might affect the results, plus, I can't quite face walking back out again after however long and the receptionist judging me on the time I've taken. I realize that if I'm going to do this properly, then a, ahem, homecoming is the only way.

Half an hour later, I'm back, clutching my precious cargo. Miraculously, the same parking space is available outside the clinic, although I don't know whether to be happy or depressed with the realization that I've been able to perform so quickly that there's still some time left on the meter. I've driven extra carefully on the way here so as not to risk spilling, and when I head back up the stairs and into the waiting room, where there's now a young couple sitting, the receptionist does a double take.

'My, that was fast,' she says, a little too loudly for my liking.

'Yes, well, that's because I don't live that far away, and the traffic was light, and I've got a powerful car, and not . . .' I stop talking because, frankly, I just want to drop it off and get going. 'Where do you want it?'

I hold the pot out towards her, beginning to wish they'd given me a bag to put it in rather than just expecting me to hand it over as is.

'Just leave it on the counter. Have you put your name on it?'

'How do you mean?'

She hands me a biro and a sticky label. 'On the side of the pot.'

It seems strange, but as I sign the side of the beaker, I'm suddenly nervous. I've gone through the last fifteen or so years convinced that I was producing a potent cocktail of baby formula, so much so that it had to be restrained behind a protective layer of industrial rubber, but within the space of forty-eight hours I'm going to find out if I've been wasting my time. If in fact I needn't have bothered going through with what is the always-embarrassing ritual of breaking away from whatever, or rather whoever, I've been doing to reach into my bedside drawer, locate the little foil packet, fumbling to open it in the dark, and then feeling that momentary swell of pride when I've not been able to get the condom on, before realizing that it's just because I'm holding it the wrong way up.

And as exciting as the prospect of no-jacket-required sex for the rest of my life might be, more importantly I'm nervous because my dreams of starting a family might end right here. This little pot is suddenly taking on a rather large significance – and so I hand it over carefully, as if it's some explosive substance. Which in a way, I suppose, it is.

'So, do I call in? For the results, I mean?'

The receptionist nods. 'Just give us a ring on Friday morning. They'll be back from the lab by then. But we'll post you a copy anyway.'

As I walk back out and get into my car, I can't help but look at my watch. Even though I know it's only Tuesday, I suspect it's going to feel like a very long few days.

I've got no appointments until the afternoon, so on the way back from the clinic, I decide to go round to see my mother – after all, I'm not the only one who's going to be affected by my plan of impending father-hood. For a while now she's been on at me to settle down and start a family, but I reckon if she's going to suddenly become a grandmother without watching me go through the settling-down part, she might appreciate as much notice as possible.

My mother still lives in the same house that she and my father bought when they got married, on a side street halfway up Richmond Hill, and just round the corner from where my flat is now. When they first moved in, they had a fantastic view of the Thames snaking down towards Eel Pie Island, she tells me. Nowadays it's not quite so fantastic, obscured as it is by Park Avenue nightclub and a Gourmet Burger Kitchen.

But the location's still pretty good – particularly if you're partial to the odd burger after you've been clubbing. Which maybe, at sixty-one, my mother isn't, really.

I still speak to her every other day, and call round for dinner at least once a week, and I've been doing this ever since I left home. It's one of the reasons I bought my place so close by, in fact. My dad's leaving may have been hard on me, but it must have been even harder on my mother, leaving her to bring me up on her own. At least it was just me, I suppose, but I don't think she ever recovered from his departure. Not enough to want to meet anyone else, anyway.

I'm like my dad, she tells me, although that's usually when she's having a dig at me in a you're-just-like-your-father kind of way. I have to take her word for it, of course, as I can't remember him at all. Well, not really. Even the few grainy photos I recall seeing before my mother got rid of them all don't quite capture the spirit, the essence, the smell of him, or how it felt when he picked me up and carried me around on his shoulders. Which I'm assuming he must have done, but because I was still a baby when he left, I can't be sure it happened at all.

I always ring the bell, even though I have a key for emergencies. Despite a couple of angina attacks last year, my mother is still the kind of person that emergencies don't ever happen to, but when I have to press the doorbell three times for some reason today,

I start to feel a little anxious. I'm just about to try and phone her when I see the familiar silhouette approaching the stained-glass panel in the door, and when she finally lets me in she's wearing one of those face masks favoured by London cycle couriers and Michael Jackson.

'William!' she exclaims, a look of delight spreading across what I can see of her face. My mother is the only person in the world who calls me William, and I've given up trying to correct her. 'I chose that name for you,' she always says, 'so it's up to me to decide how I say it.'

As she moves to kiss me hello, she has to stop herself and take the mask off, and although she doesn't refer to it, I can't help but quiz her.

'What on earth is that for?'

My mother pulls the mask away from her mouth and nose and places it on the top of her head with the elastic still round her ears, so it looks like a cheap party hat.

'I've just been doing some potting,' she says. 'In the greenhouse.'

When she motions me to follow her inside, but doesn't elaborate, I have to ask again. 'And?'

'Well, I've heard all the stories about those green-house gases. And you can't be too careful . . .'

'Mum, that's not . . .' I think about trying to explain, but decide against it, as I've got to be back at the office in an hour or so. My mother is always getting the wrong end of the stick, especially when it comes to going 'green'. For example, she won't use recycled toilet paper – because she thinks it's recycled *toilet paper*.

I help her take the mask off, then follow her through into the kitchen, where she puts the kettle on and gets a couple of mugs out of the cupboard without even asking if I want a cup of tea.

'What have you been up to this morning?'

'Oh, not very much,' I say, a little embarrassed to tell her about my visit to the clinic earlier. 'I just had to head down to Twickenham, and then across to, er, drop something off in Chiswick.'

'I thought I heard the car a few times,' says my mother, shaking her head. 'I can't keep up with your comings and goings.'

I wait until we're sitting down with our tea before I tell her my plan, and I'm expecting her to be pleased at my news. But, for some reason, she doesn't seem quite as delighted as I'd hoped.

'So you're going to have a grandchild? Just like that?'

'Well, technically, Mum, I can't have a grandchild. I can have a child, and it'll be your grandchild, but I can't actually—'

My mother shushes me. 'You know what I mean. What a silly idea.'

'What's wrong with it? Don't you think being a father would suit me?'

'Everything, William. And what do you mean,

would it suit you? A baby isn't a fashion accessory, like your Dolcis and Banana.'

I blow on the top of my tea and take a sip. 'You've been reading the *Daily Mail* again, haven't you? Besides, it's Dolce & Gabbana.'

'Well, whatever you call it.' She puts her mug down and folds her arms sternly. 'A child isn't something you "get", like a new car, or a flashy watch. It's something that's born out of love between two people. The extension of their relationship. A natural next stage to go to. Not something that you just head out to the shops and buy.'

'It's hardly like that.'

'Of course it is. From what you've said, you're going to go out and find the first suitable girl you can and' – my mother wrings her hands, as she searches for the appropriate word – 'impregnate her. That's not how to start a family.'

'Well, again, technically, it is . . .'

'No it *isn't*. A child needs to come from an inner desire. Not necessity. I loved your father. And having you was a representation of that. Not like this emotionless scheme that you seem to have devised. And what about the poor girl?'

I'm wincing a little from the onslaught. I can't remember the last time my mother told me off – and it's certainly not since I became an adult. 'She's not just any poor girl. She'll need to want this baby as much as me. And we'll be raising it together.'

'Yes, but you won't actually *be* together, will you? And that's the important part. It's bad for a baby if there's no love in the house.'

'But you and Dad weren't together for most of my childhood. And you didn't do too badly with me.'

My mother shakes her head. 'I'm beginning to doubt that. And don't forget that wasn't through choice. You ... you're starting off on the wrong foot here, William. And that's not going to be good for the baby. Or anyone, come to think of it.'

I decide to play the emotional card. 'But I thought you wanted a grandchild, Mum?'

'I do,' she says. 'But not that way. I want you to meet someone, fall in love, settle down ...'

'So do I,' I reply glumly. 'But it's not quite worked out like that, has it? And I don't want to leave it too late, in case ...' I leave the sentence hanging, but we both know what I could have said.

'I'm going to be around for a while yet, William. Don't worry.' My mother takes my hand in hers. 'So promise me something. Promise me you'll at least try to go about this for the right reasons, and in the right way. Not like some ... production line.'

I give my mum's hand a squeeze. 'I promise, Mum.'

And later, as I say a guilty goodbye to her at the door, I hope she didn't realize that I had my fingers crossed.

★

I head back to the office, grabbing an egg and cress sandwich from Pret A Manger on the way, and walk into reception just in time for my two o'clock session with Harry – a skinny, balding, fifty-something multi-millionaire software company owner whose biggest dilemma is how he can meet women who aren't just after his money. I decide against passing on Jen's advice that he should contemplate plastic surgery, but instead convince him that most of the women he's attracted to – twenty-year-old pneumatic blondes – might not have his best interests at heart, and therefore if he wants to meet a more wholesome type of girl then he should avoid his regular visits to lap dancing bars, before ushering him out on the stroke of three. I check my appointment book is clear for the rest of the after-noon, tell Jen to put my calls on hold, and sit down at my computer.

For starters, I type the phrase 'man looking for mother' into Google, but instead of the result I'm looking for, all I get are a number of links to dodgy websites crammed with pictures of fully grown men wearing oversized nappies. And so, with a quick check that the door is indeed shut, I type in the words 'inter-net' and 'dating', and hit 'enter'.

I've never been internet dating before. In fact, I've always tended to think of it as something used only by guys who can't meet women the 'normal' way. But it's become pretty obvious to me that I've become one of those guys, in terms of meeting the *right* kind of woman. Besides, if you're looking for something specific, you can't beat the internet nowadays. I found my flat on the web. Bought a lot of the furniture online. And even tracked down the TVR. And look how happy I am with that.

At first, I can't believe my eyes. There are fifty-one million, seven hundred thousand results. For a moment, it's almost off-putting, but then I suddenly realize that this is actually a good thing. If there are this many internet dating sites, then there must be an awful lot of single women out there. Hoping that the reverse isn't true, and that there aren't just a lot of awful single women instead, I shut my eyes, run the cursor up and down the list, and click on one at random: NewFlames Dot Com.

As the page loads in front of me, I read through the joining blurb. It's thirty pounds a month, and with less than that to go until my birthday, thirty quid to find the mother of my baby seems like a bargain. I quickly type in my credit card details, and with a surge of excitement, click the button that says 'Join now'.

'Please choose a username' instructs the prompt at the top of the screen. Hmm. I waste ten minutes trying to think of something clever, before just trying 'Will', then 'Will Jackson', and then even 'WillJackson', but they've all been taken, and although the computer tells me that I can have 'WillJackson69', I reject it on the grounds that it might be misinterpreted as rude. I can't believe there are sixty-eight other Will Jacksons on the site, but eventually I settle on 'WillJackson76' – a combination of my name and date of birth.

I flick through the 'Reasons for Joining', where I'm supposed to choose from headings like 'relation-ship', 'marriage', or 'fun' – there's even one that says 'sex'. And although I see that as being a key part of the process, I can't really put just that. The page won't click through unless I choose one, however, and although I can't see an option to tick 'a mother for my as-yet-unborn child', I decide that I can best put that in the 'About Me' box. I settle for 'relationship', and turn my attention to the rest of the sign-up process.

It's the 'Personal Details' section first, which seems straightforward enough. 'What do I want from a relationship?' Good question. Fortunately, there's a drop-down box, but the options – from 'pen pals', which strikes me as a rather outdated term given that any interaction will be conducted through a keyboard, 'romance', and 'fun', all the way through to the honest 'sex' again – don't quite work for me, as there's no option to select 'a family'. Maybe that'll come later, but, in the meantime, do I just click on 'not specified', and run the risk that people won't read any further? I mean, I will be wanting sex, obviously, but it's not the first reason I'm on here, is it? Also, any woman who responds to that is hardly going to want to have a baby, is she? After all, that's going to stop her having sex, according to Tom, although, thinking about it, maybe in their particular case Barbara just wanted to stop having sex with Tom, rather than stop having sex altogether. And 'fun'? Well, having a baby's going to be fun. Although not actually during delivery, I suppose. After a few minutes' deliberation, I decide to stick with the enigmatic 'not specified'. I can always go into my reasons later.

Next box – my current status. That's easy: 'single'.

Third box. 'Do you have any children?' Aha. And there's even a section that says 'I can't wait to have children'. Perfect. That'll do me. I click it and try to highlight it in bold, but, sadly, there doesn't seem to be that option.

I whizz through the rest of the front page, filling in the height and weight parts, along with a physical description that includes the colour of my eyes and hair, although this seems to be a little superfluous given that most people seem to have photographs on here. Maybe it's to catch them out if they're using someone else's photo? But who'd be that stupid?

I'm stumped a little at 'Build?', not knowing whether to click 'athletic' or 'medium'. To tell the truth, I'm quite slim really, but fit with it, thanks to my nightly running habit. But 'slim' always seems a bit of a negative word, somewhere next to 'weedy' in the overall scheme of things. 'Built like a racing snake' is Tom's usual description of me but I can't seem to find that in the drop-down list either. And as 'medium' is a pretty bland description too, I eventually settle for 'athletic', although if they're expecting someone with more of a Tarzan-like physique, they're going to be disappointed.

Great. Page one completed. I click on 'next', which takes me, not surprisingly, to page two, and 'Who Do You Want to Meet?'. I fill in the requisite 'female', and thankfully there's a box for 'can't wait to have children' again, which I select. As I scan through the rest of the physical characteristics, I have to stop and think. I don't necessarily want to seem too picky, even though, of course, I am. I stop short of clicking the 'considerably overweight' box, and I'd rather she was below six feet tall, but otherwise I decide to come back to this one.

Page two completed — sort of — and onto page three: 'Refine Your Profile'. I spend a few minutes scrolling down the page, answering more in-depth questions such as whether I have any facial hair or tattoos; all pretty straightforward. But by the time I've got onto page four, I'm beginning to find it a little more challenging than I first thought. The questions about cooking, gardening and housework I can just about deal with, but I'm stumped as to whether I'm 'feminine or macho', and how much of either I might be. I mean, obviously I'm not feminine, and I have to shave every day, so I guess I'm a little macho, but I thought macho was one of those terms from the seventies, like 'cool' and 'tank top'.

I eventually settle for 'a little macho', on account of my slightly hairy chest, but by the time I've reached the bottom of the page, I'm starting to wonder if

I know myself at all. Am I gentle? How careful, exactly? Would I describe myself as sexy? I look down at my work uniform of sensible grey trousers and white button-down shirt. Not very sexy at the moment. And I almost leave the question 'How spontaneous are you?' as I didn't know you could have degrees of spontaneity – surely you either are or you aren't?

Right. My interests. Well, at least this should be fairly simple. I speed through the eating-out section, then paint an honest picture of myself in terms of my television, newspaper and magazine habits, plus how much I like the arts; then I misread the 'Reading – like/dislike' section and put 'I've never been there', until I realize they mean books, and not the town.

Finally, just when I'm starting to flag, it's the 'About Me' section. Here there are no pop-down lists to click on. Here I can be honest, and just write a few well-chosen words about who I am, and what I'm looking for. Easy.

Or maybe not. Half an hour later, I'm still staring at the blank screen in front of me. What on earth do I put? I've typed and deleted several attempts in the 'What do you want others to know about you?' box, because what *do* I want them to know about me? That I'm desperate to be a dad? That I love kids? But assuming anyone ever gets to read this, how on earth will I differentiate myself from the thousands of other guys here?

But then it hits me. That is my differentiator. Surely

the kind of women I'm after must be bored of all the guys on here just crowing about how great they are. Let's face it, most women must use these sites because they're fed up of the normal dating channels, and of wasting time on men who don't want to commit, or don't want to settle down yet, or don't even want to think about having kids. And that's my USP. I'm not scared of commitment. I don't want to waste anyone's time – especially my own. And more than all that, I'm as desperate to have children as they hopefully are.

And it's at this point I decide that I'm not going to try and be smart with any of my answers. I'm just going to tell it like it is. Be honest with myself, and them. I delete my 'Ideal date? Heaven and back' answer, and to 'Where will you be three years from now?' I simply reply, 'Living happily with my wife and child.' And after a few moments' deliberation, I have it: 'Fit, solvent, not bad-looking, no convictions – spiritual or criminal. Looking to settle down and start a family. If you're the same (but female, obviously) why not get in touch?'

There. Finished. I take a deep breath, stand up, press 'submit', and walk over to the window to stretch my legs. But when I get back to my desk, instead of a list of potential partners, there's a screen asking me whether I want to upload a photo. After the briefest of hesitations, I click on 'yes'. It's only fair, I suppose, that they can see what they're getting.

But for this, of course, I need a decent photograph

of myself. At first, I try to take one with my camera phone, but evidently my arm isn't long enough, because despite lining up my face in the little convex mirror next to the lens on the back, I can't seem to get a photo that doesn't make my nose look twice the size it actually is. I try the same thing with the digital camera I keep in my desk for reference photos of my clients – well, the pretty ones – but just end up with a better-quality version of the same picture, and my distended-looking arm clearly visible.

After ten or so shots, each as bad as the other, I think about calling Jen in to ask for her help, but I don't really want her to know what I'm up to. Instead, I root through the drawer, find the instruction booklet, and flick through it for the first time – despite having owned the camera for the best part of a year. And on page fifty-one, I learn that there's a 'timer' function.

I assemble a pile of books roughly equivalent to head height on my desk, then balance the camera precariously on the top, and aim it at the space on the wall where my Picasso print is, then set the timer, go and stand in front of the print, and smile. And smile. And just when I'm wondering how long I can keep smiling for, the camera clicks. I head towards it, blinking from the flash, but when I check the photo on the screen on the back, I realize I've forgotten to turn on the anti-red-eye, so I look like the devil. I reset the camera and try again, but this time I've obviously forgotten to turn on the anti-gormless, and the Picasso print behind me makes me look like I've got some sort of nineteen-seventies-style perm.

I delete both photos, and remove the print from the wall before pressing the timer button again and getting back into position. I'm ready for it, and manage to put on my best mean and moody look by the time the camera flashes. But this time when I look at the picture, mean and moody turns out to actually resemble constipated.

I sit down to try several other shots, looking up at the camera from my chair, in turn happy, moody, and even surprised, but instead of the sexy, enigmatic look I was hoping for, they just make me look like a retarded version of the seven dwarfs. Eventually, after I've taken about twenty shots, I start to think that maybe the photos are actually okay, but that I can't really tell what they're like from the small screen on the back of the camera itself. After a further ten minutes reading through the instruction manual, I manage to download them to my PC; but even viewed on the monitor, there's not one that wouldn't look out of place on *Crimewatch*. In desperation, I click on Photoshop, but there doesn't seem to be a 'miracle makeover' among the edit options. With a sigh, I set up the camera again.

An hour later, I've finally got three semi-decent options. But which one do I upload? When I check a few of the other male profiles, half of them seem to have just the one photo, some of the others have two — or sometimes even three — of the same shot, and a few have the person in different settings – at work, as the life and soul of a party, or being particularly sporty. There's even the odd one of them on their latest holiday, enjoying one half of a romantic candle-lit dinner – but with their ex obviously scrubbed out. And although mine all seem to show an embarrassed thirty-year-old skulking in his office with the blinds drawn, I upload them anyway, and get a message in return telling me they're now waiting for approval, which I imagine is in case I've submitted anything rude, rather than just plain ugly.

As I sit there, I decide to have a quick browse through some of the female profiles. There's a 'match' button on the toolbar, and when I click on it and select the option for profiles with photos, a list of my top-twenty matches appears in front of me. Even at first glance, there seem to be a couple of potentials including, interestingly, someone who's the spitting image of Britney Spears. But I decide to hold off from sending any messages until my photos are up. There's nothing worse than starting a dialogue and then being rejected because of your looks – although I've just rejected the majority of my 'match' list on that exact same basis.

I'm just about to log off when there's a pinging sound, and a flashing envelope appears at the top of the screen. When I roll the cursor over the bright-yellow icon, the words 'you've got mail' appear. Mail? Already? This is going to be easier than I thought. But when I click on it, my excitement soon evaporates because it's just a mail from NewFlames, welcoming me to the site. 'Your account is now active,' it tells me. 'You can send and receive messages, and even use our instant chat.' There's also a handy hints section, telling me the dos and don'ts of internet dating, including some basic ground rules; and with that in mind, I decide to draw up some ground rules of my own.

I get a pad and pen from the desk, and start to make a list of what exactly it is I'm after, otherwise, I'm going to be looking for something when I don't really know what I'm looking for. Normally, I don't have a 'type' – if I meet someone and find her attractive, I ask her out. It doesn't matter if she's blonde, brunette, black, white; anything goes, really. Anything apart from fat ankles, that is. But this is a different thing entirely. I'm looking for someone who's perfect. Or rather, a perfect mother. Only thing is, I'm not exactly sure what that entails.

There're the physical characteristics, of course. She's got to be good-looking. And I'm not being selfish here. I want the child – my child – to have the best life possible, and that includes not being aesthetically challenged, or growing up being teased for having the FA Cup sticky-out ears that he's inherited from his mum. And when I say the child's a 'he', it could be a 'she'. I'm not that bothered, to tell the truth. It'd be like having to choose between Jack and Ellie, and they're both great kids. And he – sorry, *it* – has got to be smart. And sporty. And after yesterday evening's misunderstandings, not grow up with a strange accent.

As I note these down, I start to think about other aspects. What about the convenience factor? Do I restrict my search to a geographical area? Just Richmond? West London? Or the whole of London? On reflection, it's probably better if she's local, and doesn't have to relocate, and *I* certainly don't want to. Though having said that, if Halle Berry decides she's suddenly feeling broody but wants to stay in America, I reserve the right to change my mind.

And do I tell her exactly what I'm after from day one? Or just start a normal relationship with her, see how it goes, then, if we get on, get her pregnant as soon as she agrees? By the time I'm on my third page, my head is beginning to hurt, and I realize one very important thing. I need a second opinion.

When I hand the list over to Tom later that evening, I watch anxiously as he reads it. He grins at a couple of items before eventually passing it back to me.

'Seems pretty . . . comprehensive.'

'You don't think I've left anything out? Anything important?'

Tom takes it back and flicks through it again. 'Have you got "fat ankles"?'

I nod. 'Number three.'

He puts it down on the dining table. 'Then it seems like you've got all your bases covered.'

Barbara walks in from the kitchen, where she's

been giving the twins their dinner, and picks up the clipboard.

'What's this? Your shopping list?'

'In a way . . .'

I try to grab it, but she's too quick for me, and takes it over to the sofa to read. She scans through it a couple of times, frowning as she does so. 'What's all this about?' she asks, staring accusingly at Tom.

'It's Will's,' he splutters defensively.

As I give him a look like he's just told on me at school, Barbara turns her attention to me. 'You've made a list? What on earth for?'

'It's his ideal woman,' says Tom. 'Or rather, non-ideal.'

'This should be good,' she says, to no one in particular. 'Make me a cup of tea, will you?' But as Tom and I head for the kitchen, her 'Not you, Will' stops me in my tracks. Like a scolded child, I head back into the room, and slump down in the armchair.

As Barbara reads carefully down the page, I can't seem to detect whether she's amused or annoyed, although I do spot her sneaking a glance at her own ankles.

'And how many of these did you help him out with?' she asks, as Tom heads back into the lounge carrying three mugs of tea. When he doesn't answer immediately, Barbara just sits there, refusing to take the one he's offered her, enjoying his growing discomfort from the hot mugs he's holding.

'All my own work,' I say, after I've watched him suffer for a few more seconds. 'Honest.'

Barbara looks at Tom sceptically, before finally taking the mug with 'World's Greatest Mum' printed on the side. With a sigh of relief, he puts the other two mugs down on the coffee table and blows on his fingers.

I pick up my tea and take a sip, before making a face. 'What's this? Girl's Grey?'

'Sorry, Will,' says Tom, swapping my mug for his. 'Wrong one.'

Tom heads back into the kitchen, reappearing a few moments later with a plate of biscuits, while I sit nervously sipping my tea, waiting for Barbara to explode. But, to my surprise, she just hands the list back to me in silence, then picks up a custard cream and shoves the whole thing into her mouth.

'Aren't you going to say anything?' I ask, watching her chew.

Barbara swallows the biscuit, and takes a mouthful of tea before reaching for another. 'Like what?'

'Er . . .' I put the list down on the coffee table and help myself to a chocolate finger before Tom can eat them all. 'Like how shallow I am for writing a list?'

Barbara shakes her head. 'Doesn't hurt to put things down on paper. Helps you get them clear in your own head.'

I look across at Tom, then back to her. 'But what about some of the more, er, sexist stuff? Like—'

'Fat ankles?' interrupts Barbara. 'Even I don't think you'd reject a chance of future happiness purely based on the diameter of some poor girl's lower leg. It's just . . .'

'Just what?'

Barbara puts her mug down on a coaster on the coffee table. 'These lists are all very well, but when it comes down to it . . .'

'What?'

'Well, it's not a factual thing, attraction, is it?'

'Isn't it?'

'Hell, no. If I'd written a list about everything I was looking for in my ideal man, I'd have been single for a long, long time.' She looks over to where Tom is poking around in his mug, trying to fish out the remains of the digestive that he's dropped into his tea. 'And I certainly wouldn't have ended up with Tom.'

Tom looks up, a miffed expression on his face. 'Thanks very much.'

'I don't mean that in a bad way. All I meant was that, at the time, I would have written down stuff that I thought was important then. Whereas Tom had other qualities.'

'Better qualities,' suggests Tom, putting his mug down next to Barbara's.

'Like I said,' continues Barbara, picking Tom's mug up from where he's placed it directly on the table and sliding a coaster underneath it, 'other qualities.

And besides – he's a different man now from the one I first met.'

'Fatter, for one thing,' I observe. 'And with less hair.'

She laughs. 'All I'm saying, Will, is don't exclude anyone. Because when it comes to love, you can find it in the most unlikely places.'

'But what about compatibility? Surely that's important?'

Barbara shrugs. 'What is compatibility, exactly? Look.' She picks up my list again. 'You've written "must like old films". But what if she doesn't? That might simply be because she's never seen any. Or any of the "right" ones. It's all very well saying that you want to meet someone with the same interests as you, but the only problem with that is how are you then ever going to do anything different? So you liking old films and her liking new ones, for example, is an opportunity for you both to experience something new. Together. To introduce each other to something different. And trust me, when you've been with her for a few years, that'll be a godsend.'

Tom nods. 'It's true. You want someone who can teach you a few new things. And I don't mean in the bedroom department. Although, thinking about it . . .'

Barbara looks at him in a chance-would-be-a-fine-thing kind of way. 'Why don't you take a different approach?'

'What sort of different approach?'

'Well,' says Barbara, in the tone of a patient school-teacher trying to explain a particularly difficult maths problem, 'instead of focusing on what you think you want or don't want, why not try and learn from the women you've dated so far?'

'How do you mean?'

'Well, what was wrong with your last few girlfriends, for example? There were obviously reasons why you broke up with them, so all you have to do is avoid anyone with those same faults and attributes.'

'That's not a bad idea,' agrees Tom.

Barbara stands up and walks towards the kitchen. 'I'll just find a pen.'

I look at her, horrified. 'What – you mean, now?'

She nods. 'No time like the present.'

'In front of you?'

'Why ever not?'

'I'd be embarrassed.'

She rolls her eyes. 'Don't be ridiculous, Will. There's very little I don't know about your love life, don't forget.'

I look accusingly across at Tom, who's pretending to be fascinated by the pattern on the carpet.

'But I—'

'Come on, Will,' says Barbara, sitting back down and uncapping a Biro. 'What's the one thing that's stopped you being able to commit to any of your girlfriends in the past?'

I sit and think about this for a minute, just like I've

sat and thought about it every single time I've broken up with any of them. And as Tom and Barbara watch me expectantly, I try and put my answer into words.

'Well, it's like . . .' I put my tea down on the table, careful to place it on a coaster. 'You know that feeling when someone's trying to help you on with your coat, but you don't realize one of the sleeves is inside out, and so you start to panic a little bit because you can't work out what's wrong, and, no matter what you do, you can't seem to find the hole . . .'

'So that's your problem – you've never been able to find the hole?' smirks Tom, before Barbara shushes him by pinching him on the arm.

'Well, that's how I've felt with all of them. That awkwardness. The feeling that something's just not right.'

Barbara sits there, nodding in an understanding way, while Tom rubs his bicep.

'And so you're really just looking for someone who *feels* right? Despite,' she points to the list again, 'all this stuff?'

'That's about the size of it,' I say, picking up the last chocolate finger and popping it sideways into my mouth, much to Tom's evident disgust.

Barbara sits back in her chair and puffs out her cheeks. 'Well, you'd better get a move on, then.'

And later, as I head back home to my empty flat, I find myself agreeing wholeheartedly with her.

Chapter 5

I'm too busy with clients for the next couple of days to give it much more thought, and besides, for some reason which I'm hoping isn't aesthetic, my photos haven't been 'approved' yet on NewFlames. But this is fine, because until I get my results back from the clinic, I'm reluctant to go any further anyway.

I don't sleep very well on Thursday night, and by Friday morning I'm positively terrified. I decide that it's a call best not made from the office, and it takes me two attempts to dial the clinic's number, but when I do get through, I put the phone down the moment the receptionist answers. What if the news is bad, and my little swimmers turn out to be more Robert Maxwell than Duncan Goodhew? I feel like I'm waiting for my GCSE results all over again, except the consequences if I fail are much, much worse.

After a very strong cup of coffee, I take a deep breath, pick the phone up, and dial again.

'Chiswick Clinic,' says the receptionist brightly. 'Good morning.'

I sincerely hope it will be. 'Oh, yes, hello. It's Will Jackson. I'm just calling to get my results?'

'Hello, Mr Jackson. I'll put you straight through to Dr Scott.'

Put me straight through to the doctor? *Straight* through? Is something wrong? Why do I need to speak to her? Surely it's just a case of getting the scores on the doors. Marks out of ten. Or does she want me to come in so she can break the bad news to me in person?

After what seems like an eternity listening to a very bad electronic version of Stevie Wonder's 'Happy Birthday', which I assume they've chosen on purpose, Dr Scott comes on the line.

'Hello, Mr Jackson. And how are we this morning?'

I swallow hard, and hope she doesn't notice the trembling in my voice. 'Well, that's kind of what I'm hoping you'll tell me.'

'Hold on one second,' she says. 'I've got your results right in front of me.'

There's a shuffling of papers, and I almost expect her to announce 'and the winner is . . .'

'Well, your sperm count is in excess of twenty million per millilitre . . .' she says matter-of-factly.

Twenty million! I suddenly feel like I've won the lottery. Twenty million – and only one has to get through.

'. . . with a motility of twenty-nine per cent.'

That suddenly stops me in my tracks. Twenty-nine per cent. That's less than a third. Little more than a quarter, in fact. But surely even a quarter of twenty million is still good? I'm beginning to wish that I'd asked Tom what I should be expecting.

'Ah. So is that good or bad?'

'Well, it's in the ninetieth percentile for a man of your age.'

'Oh. Right.' I clear my throat. 'So is that good or bad?'

'It's good, Mr Jackson. It means you've got no problems. Everything else – morphology, speed, concentration – seems fine . . .'

As Dr Scott reels off a myriad of medical terms, I zone out for a moment or two. I've heard the words 'no problems', which is all I really wanted to know.

'So, as I said,' continues Dr Scott, 'you should have no difficulty becoming a father. Assuming . . .'

'Assuming?'

'Well, assuming that your partner doesn't have any problems.'

'Yes, well, I've got to find her first,' I blurt out, aware that that might prove to be the biggest problem of all.

'We posted a copy of these results to you last night,' says Dr Scott. 'I'm surprised they haven't arrived yet.'

I'm surprised too. The postman's already been this morning, and there was certainly nothing . . . Bollocks.

'What address did I give you?'

'Hold on one second, and I'll just check.'

There's the sound of someone typing on a keyboard, and then Dr Scott comes back on the line. And the address she reads out isn't my home address, but my office address. Where Jen opens the post . . .

Five minutes later, I burst breathlessly into reception to find Jen sitting there, flicking through a magazine. I try and turn my headlong rush into a casual stroll before she notices, but it's too late.

'Why are you so out of breath?' she asks.

'Lift . . .' I pant. 'Broken.'

As if on cue, the lift doors ping open, and Kate from the end office emerges into reception, causing Jen to peer at me strangely. I ignore her questioning gaze and hastily scan the desk in front of her. Miraculously, she doesn't seem to have started on today's post yet – her issue of *Cosmo* and the large chocolate muffin she's half concealed underneath it seemingly more urgent. I reach over and scoop up the letters, which I'm relieved to see include what's obviously the one from the clinic, before heading down the corridor and into my office.

I have quite a busy day again, so don't really have time to reflect on my good news. By three o'clock, I've just about finished with my last client when my phone goes. It's Tom.

'What're you up to?' he asks.

'Just finished, actually.'

'Bloody part-timer,' says Tom.

'That's rich, coming from someone who's un-employed for most of the year.'

'I'm not unemployed,' counters Tom. 'Actors are never unemployed. I'm "resting".'

'Is that what you call it?'

'Yes. Anyway, I thought you might want to come with me when I pick the twins up this afternoon.'

'Fine,' I say, pleased at any opportunity to see Jack and Ellie.

'Great,' says Tom. 'Meet me round the corner from the school in ten minutes. And try not to look shifty.'

'Shifty? What are you talking about? And why can't I meet you there?'

'Just in case I'm late. A strange man hanging around on his own by the gates might attract the wrong sort of attention.'

'I'm not strange.'

'That's a matter of opinion,' says Tom. 'Oh, and by the way – did you get your results today?'

'Yup,' I say. 'Pass. A-star, actually. So it's all systems go.'

'Good for you.'

'Yeah,' I say. 'Best two hundred quid I've spent in a long time. Now I can—'

'Two hundred quid?' interrupts Tom. 'Bloody hell – they must have seen you coming!'

At that, Tom starts laughing, and he's still laughing right up until I put the phone down.

Ten minutes later, I meet him as directed, and as we stroll round the corner and towards Jack and Ellie's school, I see exactly what he was talking about the other day. Because there seem to be an awful lot of women waiting outside the gates. Well-dressed, good-looking women too, their hair expensively cut or scraped back off their tanned faces, and with tight jeans revealing pert backsides. I point out one particularly attractive brunette to Tom.

'Oh – that's Eva. She's an au pair.'

'And the rest of them? Au pairs too, I guess, by the looks of them.'

'Nope.' Tom lowers his voice and leans in close to me, as if he's letting me in on a big secret. 'Like I was telling you. They're the mummies.'

'But they look . . .'

'Yummy?' Tom grins. 'I know.'

'But how come they . . .' I'm still a little speechless at the array of talent on offer.

'Think about it. These are West London Wives. What else do you think they do with themselves while the kids are at school? They certainly don't spend all day on their hands and knees scrubbing the floors of those mansions they live in. While little Tarquin does his ABCs, and hubby's working at the investment bank, their lives are one long cycle of going to the gym, playing tennis, having their hair and nails done, and then meeting their similarly well-manicured friends for lunch or coffee. If you spent that amount of time working on yourself, I guarantee you'd look that good too.'

'I do. Look that good. In a male sort of way, I mean. But anyway – what's your point?'

Tom smiles hello to a couple of the women. 'My point, young William, is this. Even though there's going to be a period of time when this mother-figure you're looking for might not be quite as slim and sweet-smelling as you might like, there'll eventually be a period when all the hard work's done – at least when the kid is packed off to school – and she can start turning herself back into the sort of woman you might want to sleep with again – out of longing, rather than duty, I mean. So bear that in mind when you're choosing function rather than form.'

As the school gates swing open, a tidal wave of five-to-seven-year-olds comes rushing out, to be swept up and loaded into a succession of expensive-looking four-by-fours. And although one or two of them look more relieved than happy, as if they've just been released from prison, it's lovely to see the expressions on the majority of the little faces as they run happily through the gates, proudly clutching whatever it is they've painted or made in class that day, before handing it over to their even prouder parents.

'Why have you never asked me to come and pick the twins up before?'

Tom looks shiftily at a couple of the mothers. 'What – and spoil my little treat? Besides, if you're so interested, why don't you help yourself to one of them?'

'Kids? Surely that's illegal. Not to mention kidnapping.'

'No' – Tom motions towards a group of the women

– 'one of the yummies. Ready-made family, you see.'

'Don't be ridiculous. I'd never want to break up a family unit. Besides, I probably wouldn't stand a chance.'

'How do you mean?'

'Look at them. If they all look that good, I bet the husbands take some beating too.'

Tom laughs. 'Not at all. You should see them – on the odd occasion they ever actually manage to tear themselves away from their offices in time to make it to parents' evening. Trust me – for every yummy mummy, there's a chubby hubby back at home.'

'A chubby hubby?'

'Yup,' says Tom, without a trace of irony despite his own less-than-six-pack physique. 'Who gets that way because he spends all day sat on his backside at work trying to earn the money that he thinks will be enough to keep her indoors happy, when in actual fact she spends most of her day outdoors, turning herself into the kind of woman you see here.'

As we peer towards the gates, Jack and Ellie suddenly appear, giggling with delight when they see me. With a near-simultaneous cry of 'Uncle Will', they bound towards me, and I scoop them both up off the ground – something that's getting somewhat harder the older they get – and take each of them under one arm, like I'm carrying two sacks of potatoes.

We're just about to begin the stroll home, when Tom is stopped by a rather fierce-looking blonde. She's wearing the tightest pair of designer jeans I've ever seen, and a pair of jewel-encrusted sunglasses so large they make her look like a child who's pinched her mother's. Holding onto her hand is a little blonde girl who I recognize as Hermione – one of Ellie's playmates.

'Hello, Tim,' she says, smiling at Tom, although it's only her mouth that moves. Whether that's as a result of insincerity or Botox is anyone's guess.

'It's Tom,' says Tom, blushing slightly. 'Hello, Alison.'

'Really? Tom? Are you sure?' She turns her attention to me and extends a carefully manicured hand. 'And you must be?'

I'm still carrying the twins, but I manage to twist around awkwardly to shake her hand, unfortunately swinging Jack's feet into Tom's groin at the same time.

'Hello, I'm Will.'

'Will. Of course. Alison Walters,' says Alison, looking me up and down from over the top of her sunglasses – no mean feat given the size of the lenses. 'Listen – I just want to say I think it's great what you're doing. I mean, who'd have thought it a few years ago, but nowadays . . .'

I suddenly wonder whether Tom's been gossiping at the gates. How on earth does she know? 'Well, er, thanks very much.'

'Tell me something,' says Alison. 'How do you decide which one is the mother?'

'Well, that's, er, kind of what we're trying to work out,' I say, glaring at Tom, who, to his credit, looks mystified.

'It must be hard, you know,' she continues. 'From the twins' point of view, I mean. But I suppose it would be Tim, by the look of you.'

I hoist the twins up manfully. 'What are you talking about?'

Alison lowers her voice to a whisper. 'How do you tell them? I mean, what do they think? When they see everyone else with a mummy and daddy, and you two are, well, two *daddies*.'

As I glance across at Tom, a look of realization spreads across his face. 'Alison, you've got it wrong,' he splutters, turning even redder than before. 'You're thinking of Tim and Bill. Henry's, er, dads.' He nods over towards where Eva is walking away with a little blond boy. 'It's not us. I mean, my wife's called Barbara. Will's not . . . I mean, Will is . . . We're not gay.' These last three words come out of Tom's mouth a little too loudly, prompting a few mothers to turn their heads in our direction.

Now would also be a good time for Alison to blush but, if she does, it's well concealed behind the layers of foundation.

'Oh,' she says, open-mouthed, before quickly regaining her composure. 'Sorry. Easy mistake to make.'

'No it isn't!' says Tom.

We stand there awkwardly, not quite knowing what

to say, until Jack breaks the silence. 'What's "gay", Uncle Will?'

I look down at his snot-encrusted face while I try and think of an appropriate answer, and I'm just about to open my mouth when Tom interrupts.

'Ask your mother,' he says, pulling a tissue out of his pocket and wiping Jack's nose, causing him to wriggle in annoyance.

The twins are starting to get heavy at this point, and as I look down at little Hermione, I'm already feeling sorry for her, having to go through life with a name like that, let alone a mother. Suddenly, Ellie squirms out from under my arm and tugs Alison's sleeve.

'Mrs Walters?'

'Yes, Eleanor?'

'Where's your other face?'

Alison smiles back down at Ellie, but it's a smile that instantly reminds me of Jack Nicholson in *Batman*. 'What do you mean?'

'Your other face? My mummy says that you're two-faced.'

As Alison looks at Tom angrily, I try unsuccessfully to stifle a laugh. Tom, on the other hand, looks mortified as Alison stomps away, dragging Hermione with her.

I put Jack down on the pavement next to his sister, and nudge Tom. 'Out of the mouths of babes, eh? Remind me to buy Ellie some sweets as a reward.'

He sighs. 'Thanks. There goes one less children's party invitation.'

As we stroll back, with the kids now walking either side of me and holding onto my hands, Tom clears his throat.

'So, what did we learn from that, then?'

'What – apart from the fact that Hermione's mother is a complete B-I-T-C-H?' I reply, spelling the word so the twins don't understand. 'Oh, and that you're trying to turn me into a home-wrecker.'

'I'm serious. You could do worse than hook up with a few of them,' suggests Tom. 'Well, not a few, exactly, but there are at least two who are divorced and—'

'Let me stop you there. They already have kids. And I don't want any complications.'

'But they'll have a house. And an income. And possibly even an au pair.'

'And an ex-husband. And I certainly don't want to be giving my child to someone else every other weekend.'

Tom shrugs. 'Suit yourself. But at least you now know what you're missing out on.'

I stop walking and turn to face him. 'So, hang on. You taking me there was more so I could bag myself a rich divorcee, rather than just to see that all women don't suddenly get hit with the ugly stick the minute they give birth.'

'Bit of both, really.'

'But I know that second bit already.'

Tom frowns. 'How so?'

I shake my head in disbelief. '*Barbara*?'

'Oh. Right. Of course.' Just then, Tom's mobile goes, and coincidentally, by the sound of his 'yes, dears', it's Barbara. Eventually, he snaps it shut. 'Bollocks!'

As Jack and Ellie look at each other and make Os with their mouths, I frown at Tom. 'Language, please.'

'Sorry. Sorry, kids.'

'What's up?'

'Barbara's going to be late. Optician's appointment.'

'I've been telling her she needs to get her eyes tested for years,' I say, patting Tom on the cheeks.

'Which means that I've got to cook dinner. Which also means that I have to buy the ingredients for dinner.'

'Can't you just get a takeaway?'

'Sure. Barbara comes home from a hard day at the office and I present her with a party bucket of Kentucky Fried Chicken. That'll be me packed off to the job centre first thing Monday morning.'

This is one of Barbara's conditions – that Tom is allowed to pursue his acting 'career' on the under-standing that, for the three days a week she works, he does all the household duties.

'So go shopping, then.'

Tom looks down at the twins, who are currently trying to chase each other around and in between my legs, and I have to raise myself on tiptoe to avoid being head-butted in what would undoubtedly be a painful area. 'You've obviously never tried the supermarket at school-chucking-out time with two hyperactive kids in tow.'

I shrug. 'I'll come with you, if you want. Or, if you'd prefer . . .'

Tom eyes me suspiciously. 'What?'

'I'll look after them while you're there.'

'Really?'

'Absolutely.'

A look of relief washes over Tom's face. 'Great. Take them to the park or something. They like the park. You can wear them out on the swings and stuff. And get them something to drink while you're there,' he says, rummaging in his pocket and handing me a crumpled five-pound note. 'But don't give them anything to eat.'

'Got you.' I look down at the twins, who have stopped running around like mad dwarves, and are now fascinated by a dead bird in the gutter, which Jack is poking with a stick, much to Ellie's disgust.

'You're sure you'll be okay?'

I nod. 'How many men get a chance to take twins out for a drink?'

'You're a lifesaver,' says Tom. 'So, I'll see you back at home? I shouldn't be more than half an hour. Three-quarters, tops.'

'No problem.'

As Tom hurries off towards the supermarket, I grab the twins' hands again, but as we walk back through Richmond it occurs to me that I don't know where the park is – at least not one with, to use Tom's description, swings and stuff. We head by Richmond Green, just in case they've miraculously built some in the hour since I left my office, but no such luck. As we're walking past my office, however, the twins' faces suddenly light up.

'Starbucks!' shouts Ellie.

'Starbucks! Starbucks! Starbucks!' Jack joins in.

'Starbucks?' I say, somewhat less enthusiastically, staring at the now refurbished café next to my office, which has evidently sold out and taken the corporate dollar, judging by the gleaming new sign above the door. 'You want to go in here?'

As the twins jump up and down excitedly, I peer in through the window. Sure enough, there seem to be a few families inside, fraught parents trying unsuccessfully to read the papers while the kids climb over the chairs or stuff muffins into their mouths, sometimes at the same time.

I wonder for a second whether Tom's 'something to drink' included coffee, but the kids seem to know where they're going, so I push the door open, take the twins inside, and walk up to the counter.

'What would you like, kids? Cappuccino?'

Jack wipes his nose on his sleeve. 'Cappuccino,' he repeats, although it sounds more like 'cuppa China'.

'Ellie?'

Ellie nods, although I'm not too sure either of them knows what a cappuccino actually is.

'Three cappuccinos,' I say to the barista behind the counter, adding as an afterthought, 'and you'd better make two of those decaff.'

I feel a tug on my trouser leg, and look down to see Jack eyeing the cakes through the glass display cabinet. I shake my head, but when his lip starts to quiver, I make a quick decision. What's worse – an angry Barbara, or me on my own in public with a crying child? It's a no-brainer, and I hurriedly pick three giant chocolate-chip cookies up and put them on my tray. As I reach into my pocket for my wallet, Tom's fiver not quite covering the bill, the barista asks if I want chocolate on the top of the cappuccinos. I don't have to look at the twins to know what the answer will be.

I carry the drinks over to a table by the window, Jack and Ellie following obediently behind me, and the three of us sit down. And for the next ten minutes there's an uncanny peace as the twins attack their cookies, or stick their fingers in the chocolate-dusted foam on the top of their coffees, or draw pictures on the table top in the piles of sugar they've emptied out of the small brown sachets that Jack's collected from the counter. You see, I think to myself, it's easy, this child-rearing lark. Nothing to it. In fact, I've obviously got a gift for it. Think how good I'll be when I've got one of my own. And just as I'm congratulating myself, and sipping smugly on my cappuccino, Ellie decides to stand up on her chair and make an announcement.

'Uncle Will?' she says, tugging at my sleeve, and nearly spilling my coffee in the process.

I look down at her fondly, trying to ignore the chocolate fingerprints on my shirt. 'Yes, sweetheart?'

'I need a wee.'

'Pardon?'

'I need a wee!' shouts Ellie, perhaps not realizing that in the adult world 'pardon' means 'please repeat that', rather than 'shout it at the top of your voice'.

'Oh. Right. Okay. . .' I look around, trying to ignore the other customers whose heads have just swivelled towards us, and thankfully spot a sign saying 'Toilets' in the corner next to the counter. 'Don't be too long now.'

Ellie puts her cookie down on the table, her face crinkling in confusion. 'But . . .'

'What's the matter?'

'Ellie can't go on her own,' says Jack through a mouthful of chocolate chips.

'Ah. Okay. Well, off you go too, then, Jack. And make sure you hold her hand.'

'No,' says Ellie, tugging on my sleeve even harder and, rather worryingly, hopping up and down. '*You* have to take me.'

Ah. I stand up, and wonder what to do next. Jack's sitting there, happily trying to remove a few chunks of chocolate that are stuck to the wrapper, but I can't just leave him there while I take Ellie to the toilet. Or can I? Thinking about it, I can see the toilet door clearly from where Jack's sitting, which means that from the toilet door, I'll still be able to see him, which in turn means I should be able to keep an eye on both of them at the same time. Sorted.

'Okay. Jack, you stay here. I'm just going to be over there with Ellie.' As I point towards the toilet door, Jack just nods without even looking at me, as if I'm an annoyance keeping him from spreading more chocolate round his face. I hoist Ellie off the chair, and carry her past the counter and into the toilets, careful to keep the door propped open with my foot so I can still see Jack. Once inside, there's a separate door for the Gents, and just opposite, another door that, not surprisingly, says 'Ladies', which thankfully is within reach of my outstretched arm. But when I nudge it open and try to usher Ellie inside, she stops in front of the doorway and peers in apprehensively.

'What's wrong?' I say.

'Who's going to do dabby-dabs?'

'Dabby-dabs?' I don't know what dabby-dabs is. I can guess, but I don't really want my answer to be correct. 'Can't you do your own, er, dabby-dabs?'

As Ellie shakes her head slowly, I look back over to where Jack is sitting. 'I can't come in there with you, Ellie.'

Ellie's eyes start to mist up. 'Daddy always takes me in.'

'Does he?' As Ellie nods, I realize that 'well, I'm not your daddy, am I?' probably won't get me off the hook here, and that I've really got no choice but to take her in. And maybe it's okay. Perhaps places like this are child-friendly, and expect this sort of thing. 'Okay, then. Just wait here for a second.'

I walk quickly back across to the table where, despite it being the size of his head, Jack has miraculously managed to finish his cookie, although there still seems to be a good third of it plastered around his mouth.

'Now you be a good boy and promise me you won't go anywhere while I take Ellie into the toilet, Jack.'

Jack looks up at me mischievously, and then eyes the rest of my cookie, which, after a moment's consideration, I slide across to him, reasoning that by the time Barbara starts worrying about his lack of appetite later this evening, I'll be long gone.

I hurry back to where Ellie is waiting patiently outside the toilet door, push it open and make my way gingerly inside. I've never been in a Ladies before, and I'm momentarily jealous that they get their own cubicles plus what even seems to be proper hand wash and paper towels. It's a far cry from the Gents, which by this time of day usually looks like the Somme.

'This is different to the one Daddy takes me into,' says Ellie, looking around as I steer her into one of the cubicles.

'Different? How?'

'There's no thingies on the walls.'

'What sort of thingies?'

'White thingies,' giggles Ellie. 'With yellow cakes in them.'

'What do you mean, yellow cakes?'

It takes me a moment or two to realize what Ellie's talking about, and, too late, it occurs to me that while Daddy does in fact take her into the toilets, it's usually the Gents. Too late, because as I'm nervously holding Ellie's cubicle door open, there's a flushing sound, and a pretty blonde woman emerges from the one next door. She's about my age, and by the way she's slipping a green apron over her head and tying it around her waist, she obviously works here, but when I raise my eyebrows at her in a what-can-you-do kind of way, she looks like she's about to scream.

'What are you doing in here? It's the Ladies.'

'I know. I'm just watching this one.'

I try and give what's intended to be a long-suffering parental smile, but the woman doesn't return it. Instead, she peers past me and into the cubicle, where Ellie is climbing precariously up onto the toilet, even though she's forgotten to pull her trousers down first.

'Yours, is she?'

'Oh, no,' I say, before suddenly realizing that that gives me absolutely no excuse whatsoever for being in the Ladies. 'I mean, yes.'

The woman looks at me suspiciously, and then pushes past me and kneels down in front of Ellie. 'Is that your daddy?'

Ellie looks up at me and laughs. 'No.'

The woman's face darkens as she wheels round to face me.

'Well, she's not mine, exactly, but I am looking after her. For a friend.'

She stands up and places her hands on her hips. 'Really?'

'Yes, really. In fact, I'm looking after two of them. See?'

I take a step back to the main toilet door, push it open, and nod back towards my table. But just as I'm about to justify my last statement, my heart skips a beat. I can't see Jack.

I shout, 'Back in a sec,' to the woman, and then sprint off through the café, concerned slightly that she'll think I'm making a run for it, but more worried that something might have happened to Jack. I hurry towards the table, dodging through the obstacles of buggies and pushchairs, but when I get there, there's no sign of him. I can't have lost him — Tom's going to kill me. And then, more worryingly, so is Barbara. Frantically, I peer over to the door, then through the window into the street outside. He can't have gone that far in such a short space of time, surely, particularly weighed down by so much chocolate?

As I look around, desperately trying to spot him, the woman from the toilets appears next to me, carrying Ellie in her arms. But instead of helping me search for him, she just puts Ellie down and nods towards the table.

'What?' I say, half shouting. 'Where?'

'Underneath,' she says calmly.

I drop to my knees to find Jack sitting contentedly under the table, munching on the rest of the cookie that he's evidently dropped and gone down there to retrieve. A wave of relief washes through me, and I grab him gratefully and stand up, banging my head painfully on the edge of the table as I do so.

As I rub the lump that's starting to appear above my left ear, and Jack starts to giggle, Ellie tugs my sleeve again. 'I need a *wee*,' she says, and by the look on her little face, she needs it rather quickly. I stare at her as she crosses her legs, then look at Jack, and back at Ellie, and just stand there helplessly.

'Don't worry,' says the woman. 'I'll take her in, if you like.'

Funnily enough, there's nothing I'd like more in the whole world at this moment. 'Would you mind?'

'Not at all.' The woman shrugs. 'Bit of a handful, two of them, I'd guess.'

As she takes Ellie's hand and leads her back into the toilets, I collapse onto the chair next to Jack and down the rest of my coffee, then nearly spit it out again when I discover that Jack's emptied at least five of the sugar sachets into it when I wasn't looking. I'm contemplating telling him off when he spots Ellie's half-eaten cookie, and looks at me out of the corner of his eye.

'Go on, then,' I say, past caring now.

After a minute or so, and by the time Jack's munched

most of the way through his third cookie, the toilet door swings open and Ellie runs back towards the table. I start packing up to go, but just then Jack hops down from the seat next to me and starts to march away from the table.

'Jack?' I call after him. 'Where are you off to?'

He looks back towards me. 'Toilet.'

'Jack can go on his own,' announces Ellie proudly.

'Shame his sister's not the same,' I say, tweaking her nose affectionately.

As he walks away, I notice that he's still holding what's left of the cookie, so I get up and follow him to the toilet door.

'Don't take food in there, Jack.'

Jack frowns. 'Why not?'

'It's, er, not clean.'

Jack stares at the cookie, and then at the toilet door, as if he's trying to work out which of his needs is greater, before finally putting it down on the floor outside and pushing the heavy door open.

'Well done, Jack. That's much more hygienic,' I call after him, picking the cookie up and depositing it in a nearby bin before going back and sitting down next to Ellie, where I can keep an eye on the toilet door.

Five minutes later, when there's still no sign of him, I'm beginning to get a bit worried. I tell Ellie to stay where I can see her, walk over towards the toilet and push the door open, only to find Jack on the other side, crying softly.

'Jack?' I say, picking him up. 'What's the matter?'

'Couldn't . . .' he sobs. 'Door . . .'

As Jack blubs on my shoulder, I see what the problem was. While pushing the outside door open to get in is relatively straightforward, even for a five-year-old, pulling open the actual door to the Gents is another matter entirely – particularly when you're too short to reach the handle.

I put Jack back down on the floor. 'Haven't you been yet?'

Jack shakes his head miserably. 'No.'

Checking that Ellie's still sitting safely at the table, I pull open the men's toilet door for him, and he disappears gratefully inside. Thirty seconds later, he reappears, pulling his trousers up by their elasticated waistband.

'Did you wash your hands, Jack?' I ask him.

Jack stares at his palms, which are still encrusted with chocolate and God knows what else, and then looks up at me with his big blue eyes. 'Yes.'

I peer in through the toilet door. If he couldn't reach the door handle, he's even more unlikely to have been able to reach the sinks. Or the hand dryer, come to think of it.

'Come on,' I tell him. 'I'll help you.'

I pick him up again and carry him back into the toilet, holding him over the sink and helping him wash his hands, then suspending him under the automatic hand dryer, which he thinks is the greatest game in the world. After a minute of this, my back is beginning to hurt, but when I put him down to wash my own hands, he decides to walk over to one of the urinals and pick up the bright-yellow toilet disinfectant block. I'm just fast enough to stop him before he puts it in his mouth.

'No, Jack. That's not nice.'

Jack looks at the collection of toilet blocks in the urinals, as if staring at the pick 'n' mix at Woolworth's. 'But they look like sweeties.'

'No, Jack. They're not sweeties.'

A look of disappointment crosses his face. 'What are they, then?'

'Well, they're cakes of disinfect— No, not cakes, exactly,' I correct myself hastily, as at the mention of the word 'cake', Jack's eyes have lit up again. 'Come on. Let's go and find your sister.'

After I've made him wash his hands again, we head back out and over to the table, where, thankfully, Ellie's still sitting, good as gold, but with the woman from before.

'I thought I'd better keep her company,' says the woman. 'Seeing as she was here all alone.'

'Oh. Right. Jack and I were just ... I mean, he had to ...' I stop talking, realizing that I'm about to blame my irresponsibility on a five-year-old, which would be childish, in both senses of the word. 'I didn't get a chance to thank you before,' I say instead, noticing again how pretty she is. 'I'm Will. Will Jackson.'

She holds out a hand, and I shake it. 'Nice to meet you, Will Will Jackson. I'm Emma. Ness.'

'Emma Ness?' I say. 'Like the—'

'Shop?' She rolls her eyes. 'I get that all the time.'

'The shop? I was going to say monster. You know – from the Scottish, er, loch ...' I stop speaking again, suddenly aware that that's probably not the most flattering comparison to make.

Fortunately, Emma smiles. 'I get that all the time too.'

'You work here?'

Emma looks down at her green apron and shrugs. 'No, I just happened to put this combination on this morning. Terrible coincidence,' she says. 'Still, while I'm here ...'

And as she picks up my empty coffee cup and heads back towards the counter, it takes me a second or two to realize that she's joking.

When I eventually drop the kids off, Barbara's waiting anxiously by the door. She picks Jack up first, and then Ellie, inspecting them for any signs of damage or loss of limbs before ushering me into the kitchen, where Tom, evidently in the dog house for entrusting me with the twins in the first place, is midway through cooking the dinner.

'Listen, Will,' she says, once she's plonked Jack and Ellie down in front of the television and joined us in the kitchen. 'I feel a bit bad about Sunday. I didn't

mean to, you know, suggest that you weren't ...'
Apologizing has never been Barbara's strong point. But
then, according to Tom, that's because she's always
right. 'And the twins seem to be in one piece, so ...'

'What?' I say, nudging Tom, who's obviously
enjoying her discomfort.

'So, if you're absolutely set on going through with
this, then perhaps I can help.'

'Really?' I say, suddenly all ears. 'How do you mean?'

'Well, there's this woman. Julie. At work. She's
single. Loves kids. And desperate – to settle down, that
is. So I thought you and she might want to, you know,
meet up?'

I can hardly believe what I'm hearing. 'You want to
set me up? On a blind date? What's she like?'

'She's very nice. In fact, we're all mystified why she's
been single for so long.'

'Oh.' I slump against the fridge. 'Right.'

'You don't sound very enthusiastic.'

'Sorry, Barbara. It's just that, if she's been single
for "so long", however long that is, then it's probably
for a reason, which means either a) she's ugly, b) she's
fat, c) she's got no personality, or d) all of the above.'

'None of the above, actually,' snorts Barbara. 'She's
really very nice. About my height, short dark hair,
pretty, nice figure.'

'It's true,' says Tom, stirring a pot of something
unidentifiable that's simmering away on the hob. 'She's
just your type.'

'You've met her, have you?'

'Well, no, but . . .'

'And she's desperate to have kids?'

'Absolutely,' says Barbara.

I look at the two of them, standing there as if they've done me the biggest favour in the world, and let out a resigned sigh. 'So when do I meet this Julie?'

'Tomorrow,' says Barbara triumphantly. 'It's all set up. Three o'clock. That new Starbucks next to your office.'

Oh great. 'And how on earth will I recognize her?'

Barbara smiles. 'She'll be pushing a pram. An empty one.'

Chapter 6

It's Saturday. And another Single Saturday, to be specific. With a sigh, I reach across to switch off the alarm clock before climbing across the empty side of my double bed and making my way wearily into the bathroom. Single Saturdays suck.

And I hate Single Saturdays because Single Saturdays are always the same. Wake up sometime around eight, which is the same time as during the week – not counting the days that Magda disturbs me at some unholy hour – and seeing as there's no one to spend the morning in bed with, get up straight away, chuck some clothes on, and stroll out to Tesco Metro to buy the paper and a *pain au chocolat* before heading straight back home for breakfast and my usual pathetic attempt at the crossword.

At around ten-thirty, I'll change into my workout gear and head over to the gym, in the vain hope that my Single Saturday might magically turn into a Couple Saturday. Because single guys don't go to the gym on Saturdays for a workout. We go because we hope that we'll bump into this gorgeous single girl who's stuck in the same lonely routine as us, and we'll get chatting, and maybe one of us will suggest a coffee, or a drink, or even dinner.

But, of course, there are never any gorgeous single girls at the gym on a Saturday morning. They've all been snapped up, or they've snapped up someone themselves. So, instead, I'll spend an hour mixing it up between the free weights and the machines while watching some obscure sport on the TV screens dotted around the room, but always keeping one eye on who's coming in through the door, just in case ...

Then it's back home again for lunch, because no one likes going out to eat on their own, particularly on a weekend. And because I can't face traipsing round the shops on a Saturday either, mainly because I'd have to keep pushing past all the loved-up couples who jam the town centre at the weekend, lunch is invariably followed by an afternoon in front of the football with a beer or two. Why do women think that we men are obsessed with watching sport on TV? Because for a long period of our lives, when we're not engaged in – or having much luck with – the pursuit of them, it's the only thing we've got to do.

What freedom, I used to think. I can do whatever I want. I've got no commitments. No need to be somewhere at some specific time, or to do anything I don't want to do simply because my girlfriend might fancy it. But, nowadays, I've grown tired of it. Tired of constantly being on the lookout for someone who might be girlfriend material. Tired of not being able to meet a woman without summing her up, giving her marks out of ten, wondering whether she's single, flirting with her if she is – and even sometimes if she isn't. And tired of going through the same motions, time and time again, only to watch the relationship fail because we probably weren't right for each other in the first place, and only got together because we hated the idea of Single Saturdays more.

And the reason it's tiring is because there's a real pressure on us single guys. Every time we meet a woman, the stress starts. If we think she's attractive, then we can't possibly relate to her as a normal human being. There's always this hidden – in some cases, not so hidden – agenda of wondering if we should ask her out, and more importantly, wondering what our chances of success would be if we did. We can't help thinking of every single woman we meet as a sex object, because quite frankly, that's exactly what they are to us. Even if we don't think they're attractive, we still feel duty bound to flirt just a little because if we're half decent then we won't want to hurt their feelings. And because women hardly ever, in fact never, ask us men out, we know we're safe to do that.

All of it – the sexy car, the nice flat, the gym membership, making sure I'm dressed well, even the long runs in the evening – they're not really to make *me* feel better. They're all to do with attracting the opposite sex. And they're tiring too.

Couple Saturdays are better. Couple Saturdays might involve breakfast in bed, or a lazy stroll along the river followed by a pub lunch. Couple Saturdays can mean plans for the evening, rather than a night with just the remote control for company. Maybe even dinner for two, followed by breakfast in bed, with one of you still wearing last night's clothes, if you're lucky. But Couple Saturdays aren't perfect. Couple Saturdays can contain awkward silences. 'What shall we do?' conservations. 'Where shall we go?' discussions. And 'Where are we *going*?' arguments.

Which is why what I want are Family Saturdays. Because compared to Single Saturdays, Family Saturdays are a walk in the park. Family Saturdays are fun. Family Saturdays are all play and no work. Because on Family Saturdays, you've always got someone to play with. Tom might moan at being woken up at six a.m. by the twins jumping on his bed, but, I tell you, he's got it easy, compared to what I've got to look forward to: a blind date in a coffee shop with a desperate woman, arranged by my best friend's wife because she feels sorry for me. As I stare at my reflection in the bathroom mirror, I realize that this is probably the lowest I've felt in a long, long time.

I used to love weekends when I was a kid. I'd done my penance, spending an uncomfortable week at school, and now I had two whole days to relax; forty-eight hours to enjoy myself, and not be bullied by the other kids about how I didn't have a dad. I'd get up early on Saturday morning, wanting to stretch out the whole weekend, making the most of every second before that feeling of dread would start to creep up on me late on Sunday afternoon. And every Sunday night, I'd lie awake, fearing that the coming Monday morning was going to be just as bad as every previous Monday morning. Sure, there were a few other kids at school whose parents were divorced. But at least they saw their dads occasionally. At least they knew where their dads lived. And what they looked like.

Fortunately, this Saturday, there's less time to feel sorry for myself. After a quick breakfast and an even quicker trip to B&Q, I spend the morning redecorating the spare room. And although this really just entails filling a couple of black bin bags with half a ton of old clothes for the charity shop, dismantling my pool table, and removing the 'arty' Athena prints from the walls, it still takes me the best part of two hours, particularly when I unearth my collection of Claudia Schiffer calendars at the back of the wardrobe. I flick through several months in pleasant reminiscence before binning Claudia, then give the room a quick coat of magnolia emulsion – not knowing whether to paint it pink or blue at this stage, of course – and push the sofa bed against one wall, so there'll be enough space for the baby's cot.

I finish off by fitting child locks onto the cupboards in the kitchen, and before taking a quick break for lunch, log on to NewFlames to see whether I've got any interest. I'm a little depressed when I see that my inbox is empty, but as I'm flicking through the gallery of new members – who seem to be mostly out-of-focus camera phone junkies or twice my age – a flashing icon in the shape of an eye suddenly appears at the top of the screen.

I look at the menu on the left, and feel a sudden surge of excitement: NewFlames has an Instant Messenger option where members can 'talk', and someone wants to talk to me! I have to stop myself from punching the air in celebration, but, as the chat screen loads, I'm hit by a sudden feeling of anxiety in the pit of my stomach, which immediately strikes me as ridiculous. It's not as if I'm going up to some stranger in a bar to try and talk to them – quite the opposite, in fact. They're coming over to talk to me.

I roll my cursor over the icon, and the eye winks at me – a nice touch, I decide – and as I click on it, a message appears at the top of the screen. 'Sandra wants to talk to you,' it says, 'do you want to talk to her? Y/N'. Underneath the message is a small thumbnail, which opens a photograph in a new window.

For a moment, I can't believe my luck – Sandra's gorgeous! Long dark hair, a cute nose, perfect teeth – in fact, she looks like she's had this picture taken professionally, and I don't mean by one of those scary makeover-type photographers. My first thought is that maybe she's a model, but just as this occurs to me, I dismiss it as ridiculous. What on earth would someone who looks like her be doing on a site like this? But then I remember the calendars I found earlier, and an interview I read with the lovely Ms Schiffer in GQ, where she'd been complaining that men never asked her out because they felt too intimidated by her looks. Well, maybe that's why Sandra's on NewFlames – because she's not meeting men the normal way. And let's face it – looking at the kind of losers other supermodels go out with, who can blame her?

I quickly scroll down through Sandra's profile. She's twenty-five, and lives in London, apparently, and although she doesn't say a lot more about herself, she is quite stunning. Stunning enough for me to ignore the lack of other information on her profile, anyway. And as I stare at her picture, I suddenly feel embarrassed about the quality of my photo. Still, I think, looking at Sandra's perfect features, it seems to have done the trick. I hurriedly hit Y, nearly pressing the 7 key by mistake in my urgency, and a dialogue box appears. There's one word in it – 'Hi.'

Trying to overcome my stage fright, I think fast. How to respond to Sandra's opening gambit? What to say that conveys my cool, man-about-town attitude, yet also implies that I'm the sensitive, caring type who, coincidentally, is desperate to settle down and have a baby? After an anxious thirty seconds, 'Hi yourself' is the best I can come up with.

'I'm Sandra,' replies Sandra, which I guess is a bit unnecessary, since I already know that. Still, maybe she's a little nervous too. And what's wrong with introducing yourself the traditional way?

'Will,' I type, staring at her photo again, still not quite believing my luck.

There's a pause and then 'Will what?' appears on the screen.

I type 'Will you have my baby?' and then hurriedly delete it. 'Will Jackson.'

'Nice to meet you, Will Jackson,' comes the reply.

'And you,' I type.

'Thank you,' she replies.

Er . . . 'Don't mention it.'

'Don't mention what?'

Ah. It's not quite as easy as I thought, this instant 'chat'. If we were in a bar, I could easily offer to buy her a drink at this point, thus giving us both a little time apart to digest our initial impressions of each other, and consider what our next topic of conversation is going to be. And as I think about how to steer the exchange round to finding out a little more about her, I'm starting to get worried that I haven't replied for a while. I don't want her to get bored and go off me. But what on earth do I say?

'You're very pretty' I type, then delete it. She's probably heard that a hundred times before. I need to be original. But how? 'Do you come here often?' even seems corny when it's typed, let alone spoken. I settle for 'How are you finding NewFlames?' and hit 'return', but when she doesn't reply, I start to worry that my brilliant conversational dexterity has flummoxed her.

I look back at the message I've just sent. Was it rude in some way? Might it have annoyed her, that I should be prying into her activities on the site? Does she think that I'm insinuating something? Or has she just found someone else to chat to? I click back onto her profile, which tells me she's still online. But what do I do now? I can't send her another message before she's even replied to my last one, as I don't want to appear needy, or impatient.

Just as I'm about to give up, her reply finally arrives. 'Will Jackson, I am sorry, I must go now. Can we speak later?'

Later when? Later today? Later this week? I type each of these phrases, and then delete each of them in turn. 'Okay,' I type quickly. 'Nice "talking" to you.'

I hit 'return', pleased with the inverted commas I've put around the word 'talking'. But if Sandra's impressed with my grammatical stab at humour, she doesn't say.

'Perhaps we can meet up some time?' comes the reply.

What? Meet up? Result! I look at her photograph one more time, and type 'Yes,' perhaps even a little faster than Instant Messenger can cope with. 'When?'

There's no answer from Sandra, and I stare at the

screen, willing her to respond, until about thirty seconds later the doorbell rings, and I almost fall out of my chair in shock.

I walk nervously into the hallway and press the intercom buzzer, and Tom's voice leaps out of the speaker. With an equal mixture of disappointment and relief, I buzz him in.

'Hello, mate,' I say, a little surprised at seeing him on what is, after all, a Family Saturday. 'Barbara given you the day off?'

Tom walks in through the doorway and deposits what appears to be an old copy of the *Guardian* and an industrial-size bar of Dairy Milk on the coffee table. 'The twins are at a birthday party. Again. One of about thirty every year we have to take them to. And that means thirty presents, times two, of course, because they can't just give one between them.' He sighs. 'I'll tell you, Will, open a toy shop. You'll make a fortune.'

'Why don't you just say you can't make it?'

'And risk Jack and Ellie becoming the class outcasts? No way. Besides, it's some new kid – Archie some-body-or-other – who Ellie's taken a shine to, so Barbara felt it was important.' Tom shakes his head. 'Playground politics. It makes corporate life seem like a piece of piss.'

'And you'd know that how, exactly?'

Tom ignores me, and plonks himself down on the sofa. 'I've left Barbara there with them. There're only so many screaming kids I can handle in a room at one time.'

'And how many is that?'

'None.' He looks at his watch. 'So, anyway, I thought I'd come round and watch the football and drink some of your beer. If that's okay?'

'Sure,' I say, nodding towards the fridge. 'Help yourself.'

Tom gets up and heads over towards the refrigerator, grabbing a bottle of beer from inside the door. 'Bottle opener?'

'Top drawer on the left.'

He grabs the handle and tugs. And tugs. Then tries the cupboard underneath with the same result. 'Mate, I think your kitchen's broken,' he says.

'Child locks.' I reach in, release the mechanism, and open the drawer. 'Fitted them this morning.'

Tom opens his mouth as if to say something, then just takes the bottle opener from me and shakes his head, popping the cap off his bottle and taking a long swig.

'What's all this?' he says, catching sight of the laptop on the kitchen table, where I'm still logged on to NewFlames.

'I've, er, joined a dating site.'

I wait for the ridicule, but, much to my surprise, none comes. 'Good on you,' says Tom. 'Anyone interesting?'

'Well, unfortunately, you can't search based on breast size,' I say, having known Tom long enough to be familiar with what his idea of 'interesting' is. 'I do have a list of matches, but there's no one on it who really takes my fancy.'

As Tom picks up the laptop and sits down on the sofa, I grab myself a bottle of beer from the fridge and join him. 'What about her?' he says, scrolling through my match list, and pointing to a picture of a blonde girl who's dressed in a rather tight-fitting school uniform, which I'm hoping is a photograph taken at a St Trinian's fancy-dress party rather than her normal weekday wear. 'She seems nice.'

I reach across, click on the photo, and skim through her profile. 'Gemma. Aged nineteen. Oh well.'

Tom looks at me as if I'm crazy. 'Why the hell not?'

'She's nineteen, Tom.'

'So?' he says, running the mouse pointer over her breasts, as if to emphasize her finer points. 'What's wrong with that?'

'Tom – I might have said that I love kids. But that doesn't mean I want to go out with one.'

Tom grins, and turns his attention back to the screen. 'When was the last time you slept with someone in their teens?'

'That would be when I was in my teens too.'

He stares wistfully at Gemma's photo. 'Remember how it was? All firm, and—'

'Tom, I'm going to be thirty-one very soon. And I need someone who's in the same boat as me, age wise. Someone younger isn't going to want to commit to a life of child-rearing. Not just yet, anyway.'

Tom shrugs. 'Seems a shame. Okay,' he says, scrolling through my list of 'recently viewed', before stopping suddenly at Sandra's photo. 'What about this one? She's got nice—'

'Tom, please,' I say, snatching the laptop back and shutting the lid, nearly trapping his fingers in the process. 'I can do without your input at this stage, thanks very much.'

'Suit yourself,' says Tom, getting up from the sofa and heading towards the spare room. 'Game of pool instead?'

'No!' I say, jumping up and rushing to block the doorway.

Tom eyes me suspiciously. 'What's going on? You haven't got someone in there?'

'Chance would be a fine thing. No, it's just . . .'

'Come on,' says Tom, using his considerable weight advantage to barge past me. 'Let's see.' He pushes open the door, and stops in his tracks, as if he's not sure he's gone into the right room. 'What have you done to the pool room?'

'It's now the, er, baby's room.'

Tom stares at me in disbelief. 'First the car, then the child locks, and now this? You've lost it. Big time.'

I shrug. 'It's like I said. I want everything to be right. The fewer changes I have to make at the time, the better. But I still think it's missing something.'

Tom scratches his head. 'What? Apart from the pool table.'

'And a baby, obviously. But it's just got no child-friendly touches. Or a cot. Which is why you're coming with me to Mothercare.'

'Mothercare? On a Saturday?' Tom swallows hard. 'What's in it for me?'

'Beer?'

Tom takes another swig from his bottle. 'Already got one, thanks.'

'Lunch?'

'You'll have to do better than that.'

'Not telling Barbara what you really got up to on your stag night?'

Five minutes later, we're in the TVR, heading off towards Kew retail park which, strangely, has been built next door to the council tip, a planning decision that doesn't always make for the most pleasant of shopping experiences. Fortunately, the wind's blowing in the opposite direction this afternoon, as I steer the TVR carefully through the car park, which seems to be full of almost identical four-by-fours, and pull into a space in front of Mothercare marked 'mother and baby'.

'It never says "father and baby" does it?'

Tom gets out of the car with what looks like fear in his eyes. 'You'll see why.'

As I peer through the window, the place appears to be crammed with crying children and harassed-looking parents, and when Tom and I make our way inside, a wave of noise hits us. For a moment, the screaming and sobbing threatens to get the better of us, and that seems to be just the parents. There's a café down at the far end, which seems a little more tranquil, and I have to grab onto Tom's jacket to prevent him making a run for it.

We push through the various aisles, full of expensive-looking baby bits and toddler technology. There's a bicycle with no pedals which, the box informs me, is actually easier for a child to learn to ride than a bike with pedals, which at twice the price of a normal one, I suppose it should be. And while it occurs to me that you could just buy a normal bicycle and take the pedals off for half the money, it seems out of place to mention it. Confused, I pick up a strange-shaped device, and hold it out to Tom.

'What's this?'

Tom smirks. 'A breast pump.'

'What on earth is it for?'

Tom rolls his eyes and takes it from me. 'For when a woman needs to express herself,' he says matter-of-factly.

I frown. 'They never seem to have a problem with that, in my experience. I mean, Barbara didn't shut up when she was pregnant.'

Tom stares at me for a second or two. 'You have so much to learn, my young apprentice.'

I stand there blankly, not knowing where to turn, before picking up a huge pink bunny rabbit, which I'm shocked to see costs almost sixty pounds and, of course, also comes in blue. As Tom grabs the blue one and pretends to mount mine with it, an assistant materializes from behind the soft-toy display and taps him on the shoulder. She's about sixty, and wearing a name badge that says 'Ethel', and looks like she'd be more at home in Grandmothercare.

'Can I help you?'

Tom quickly hides the rabbit behind his back. 'Er . . . yes. My good friend here is looking for some baby furniture.'

Ethel frowns. 'Baby furniture? You mean . . .'

'You know,' says Tom, 'things to kit out a baby's room. So it feels at home.'

I nod. 'I'm afraid I've never done this before.'

Ethel smiles sympathetically. 'Your first, is it?'

'And last,' interrupts Tom.

Ethel looks at the two of us for a minute, and then grabs me by the hand. 'Well, I know some people don't agree with the principle, but I just think it's wonderful.'

'What is?'

'The fact that nowadays it's okay for you to have a child of your own.'

'Thanks,' I say, wondering whether it's her first day here. On the planet, I mean.

Ethel smiles warmly at Tom. 'And who's the father, if I can ask?'

'He is,' says Tom, pointing towards me with the blue rabbit. 'Well, he will be, I mean.'

Ethel looks like she's intrigued. 'And if I can ask,

how did you decide? Which one of you it was going to be, I mean.'

I'm starting to get a little confused. 'Well, Tom's already got two . . .'

Ethel pats the back of my hand. 'And the two of you wanted one of your own. That's lovely.'

Tom and I exchange confused glances, before the penny drops. 'Not again,' he says. 'You and I are obviously spending far too much time together.'

'No – I'm the one who's having the baby,' I say, blushing furiously. 'Well, not having it myself, you understand. With a woman. This is my friend, Tom, who's married. To a woman. And I've asked him along to give me some of his advice. About baby . . . stuff.'

Ethel looks as though she'd like to hide behind the display. 'Oh sorry. I thought . . . I mean . . .'

'Never mind,' I say, grabbing Tom's hand. 'Easy mistake to make.'

'No it *isn't*,' says Tom indignantly, shaking me off and stalking away to look at what appear to be some pretty impressive four-wheel-drive buggies.

'So,' says Ethel, trying desperately to regain her composure. 'Do you know what you're having yet? A boy or a girl, I mean?'

'No – it's going to be a surprise.'

'You're telling me,' interrupts Tom, test-pushing a two-seater in front of us that's the width of the aisle.

'So, when's it due?'

'Er . . . I'm not sure.'

'Well,' says Ethel patiently, 'when was the baby conceived?'

'Um . . . It hasn't been yet.'

Ethel starts to look even more confused than before. 'But your wife does know that you're having a baby?'

'I, er, don't have a wife.'

'Girlfriend?'

'Nope.'

By now, Ethel is looking around anxiously, as if she's about to call security, while I'm starting to wonder whether you need some sort of proof-of-parenthood passport to buy things here, like when you have to prove you're a shopkeeper to shop in a cash and carry. Fortunately, we're interrupted by a couple looking to get Ethel's advice on which kind of nappy-changing mat is the best, and although they all look the same to me, I'm grateful for the chance to escape. Though not as grateful, I suspect, as Ethel.

As Tom and I get back into the car to drive home, I grip the wheel and shake my head. 'Why do people always assume I'm mad when I tell them what I'm up to?'

'I think you've answered your own question there, mate.'

'Is it so strange, what I'm trying to do?'

Tom thinks about this for a minute. 'Not what you're trying to do. How you're trying to do it, perhaps?'

'But what's my alternative? I've tried the traditional route, and it just hasn't happened.' I stop abruptly at a zebra crossing and wave a mother with a pushchair across, causing the car behind to beep me furiously. 'And besides, this is what I tell my clients every day. If you want something in life, focus on the goal, and work backwards from there. The more you put things in place to achieve that goal, the more likely you are to achieve it. And that's all I'm doing. Getting everything in place.'

Tom shakes his head. 'But surely there are some things that don't quite work like that.'

'You're wrong, Tom. Everything works like that. I mean, it's fair to say that on balance women usually have a stronger drive to have kids than men do, right?'

'I suppose.'

'And so whenever a woman looks at a man, she's sizing him up as a potential father to her children?'

'Well, when you put it like that . . .'

'So all I'm doing is taking the same approach. Making sure I've got everything ready, everything in place, and then just flipping it around. Women decide they want to have a baby and either go out and find a man to start a family with, or they mould, force, coerce, convince, whatever word you want to use, the bloke they're with to have one. I should be the easy choice. The no-brainer. Women should look at me and think: great – here's a ready-made dad. Off the shelf. Off the peg.'

'Off his head, you mean.'

'Why?'

'Will, however you look at it, while it might seem logical to you, what you're doing doesn't follow the natural order. The historical way of doing things. I'm not saying it's the best way, I'm not even saying it's the right way, but whatever, it's the way. And maybe you need to think about that.'

'If that was true, then nothing new would ever get done. If someone had said to Columbus, "Sorry, mate, but you can't discover America because the world's flat and you'll just sail off the end of it," then he wouldn't have gone. People need to do new things. In new ways.'

'Will, you having a baby and Columbus sailing across the Atlantic are different things. Although they seem to be taking about the same time, though.'

And as we park outside my flat, it suddenly occurs to me that this is exactly what I'm doing. A voyage of discovery. And it's one that I've been on for years. And I've wasted half of my reproductive life stopping at every island I see, in the hope that maybe this time it might just turn out to be the place I've been searching for. I need to actually find America to see whether it's the promised land or not, and stop this constant island-hopping that's been so draining.

'It's just ... I've got a nice flat, a decent car, a good job,' I say, letting us in through my front door, 'and I don't have anyone to share it with.'

'You could share it with me and Barbara, if you like?'

'I'm being serious, Tom. It's no fun, not having anyone to enjoy it all with. And more importantly, someone to leave it to. At this rate, Battersea Dogs Home is going to do very well out of me when I'm gone.'

'Oh yes,' says Tom, picking up his copy of the *Guardian* from the coffee table and handing it to me. 'I almost forgot. Before you go any further, take a look at this.'

I stare at the headline on the front page. '"Spice Girls To Re-form". What's that got to do with me? Unless one of them wants a baby instead?'

Tom snatches the paper back, and points to an article at the bottom of the page. 'Not that. Below it.'

He hands it back to me, and I read the opening sentence. '"The average cost of raising a child nowadays is £180,000, say experts . . ." So? That's not all at once, surely?'

'No, thank goodness,' says Tom. 'Up until they're eighteen, apparently. That's nursery costs, school fees, food, clothing . . . I tell you, mate, the list is endless. I had to hide this from Barbara in case she panicked and sent me out to get a proper job.'

I shrug, and throw the paper down onto the coffee table. 'So? That's only ten grand a year, and I spend that on the TVR. And anyway, how can you put a price on something as miraculous as having a child? Surely whatever it costs it's worth it? You just have to prioritize.'

'Sure you do,' says Tom. 'But sometimes those priorities might mean you missing out on something else important to you. And don't forget, with your little scheme, you've not got only two mouths to feed. There's the mother to take care of too, seeing as she's not earning anything.'

I sit down, and help myself to a chunk of Tom's chocolate. 'Not for that long, surely? I mean, once the kid's out of nappies, she can go out and get herself a job, can't she?'

Tom starts to laugh, and sits down next to me. 'You have so much to learn, my child. Looking after children, whatever their ages, *is* a full-time job, even when they finally go off to nursery or school. You've got to take them there, clean up after them, pick them up, feed them, entertain them, and even in the few hours you don't have them getting under your feet, you've still got to make sure that the house is a safe place for them to be when they come home, and that there's food on the table. Fortunately, Barbara went back to work because she wanted to, and even then, it's only three days a week. But most women? The first five years are so knackering that you can see why they need the next thirteen or so to recover.'

I pick up the paper again, and skim through the article. 'Tom, it's just as expensive being single as it is having kids, you know. Possibly more so.'

'How do you work that out?' asks Tom disbelievingly. 'What on earth do you spend your money on?'

'Trying not to be single, for one thing. Everything about me has to suggest attractiveness. I can't just drive any old car, or wear any old thing like you do.'

'Thanks very much.'

'No offence, mate, but you hardly dress to impress, do you?'

'That's because I don't have to,' says Tom, a hurt expression on his face.

'And that's precisely my point. I may not have to buy kids' clothes and toys, but I've got to buy *my own* clothes and toys, just so I can attract a woman who I might be able to have kids with.'

'But that hardly adds up to ten grand a year?'

'Aha. But then there's the dating side itself. When was the last time you and Barbara went out to eat?'

Tom folds his arms smugly. 'Last Saturday, I think you'll find.'

'Taking Barbara and the kids to Burger King doesn't count, Tom. I mean just you and Barbara. Somewhere nice.'

Tom thinks for a moment. 'Ah. That would be . . . her birthday.'

'Which was this time last year?'

He widens his eyes. 'Er, might have been. Yes. And thanks for the reminder.'

'Well, think of it from my point of view. Every time I take a girl out for dinner, it costs me, what, a hundred pounds? And I might have to do that four or five times before I know whether we get on enough to become boyfriend and girlfriend, right?'

Tom gets up and helps himself to another beer from the fridge. 'I suppose.'

'So, that costs me at least five hundred quid. And say I do that once every couple of months. That's about three grand a year. And that doesn't include any little spontaneous presents, weekends away, and so on.'

'That's still not quite what it says in the paper, is it?'

'I've hardly started, Tom. When you and Barbara do go out to dinner, what do you wear? Your one good suit. Which you bought when?'

'Er, for my wedding.'

'Precisely. I've got to look good every time, which means I have to dress well, which isn't cheap. And then there're the miscellaneous things like the insurance for my car, which probably costs more a year than you spent on actually buying yours. And the aftershave. And the gym membership. It all adds up to a little more than the odd trip to Hamleys, I can tell you.' I get up to grab a Diet Coke from the fridge, then collapse back down next to Tom. 'Dating's bloody expensive. I'll be glad when I finally get this baby sorted. It'll be a chance to save a bit of cash, as far as I can see.'

Tom shrugs, grabs the remote control, and switches the television on. 'Speaking of which,' he says, taking a mouthful of beer. 'Aren't you supposed to be some-where this afternoon?'

'Shit,' I say, looking at my watch and jumping up from the sofa.

Ten minutes later, I'm hurrying breathlessly towards Starbucks, just about in time for my blind date with Julie. I've already had to phone Tom twice on the way down – once to remind myself what her name was, and then again to get a better description of her, although his 'about Barbara's height but with bigger tits, apparently' isn't perhaps the detailed depiction I was hoping for. She's seen my photo, apparently, so should be able to recognize me, and I'm hoping I'll be able to spot her in the crowd, but when I get there, and anxiously scan the occupants of the café, I can't seem to find her.

I check my watch, and I'm only a few minutes late, so it's doubtful she'll have left already. I find a corner table with a good view of the door, and sit down. Every time the door opens, I try not to look up expectantly, but I can't help myself, and as I wait, I wonder why I've never met this colleague of hers before. Is it because Barbara's always thought I'd be a bit unsuitable for her, and has kept us apart? Or maybe she's only just got over being dumped – sorry, splitting up with her boyfriend – and therefore it's never been appropriate?

A few minutes later, when there's still no sign of her, I walk over to the rack next to the door and help myself to a newspaper, using this as the perfect cover to take another look around just in case I've missed her come in. There is one single woman, who's sitting reading a book a few yards away from me, and who was here when I came in, but it can't be her. She must be at least forty, and while she's quite attractive and matches most of Barbara's description, she looks a little taller, although it's hard to tell because she's sitting down. Plus she's more attractive than I was expecting, even based on Barbara's glowing portrayal, which I think was probably exaggerated a little anyway to get me to turn up, and as I watch her surreptitiously over the top of my paper, I wonder whether it is Julie. She's not drinking anything, which could suggest she's waiting for someone.

After a further couple of minutes, and with still no sign of anyone else, I think perhaps that it might be her. After all, Barbara's a little older than Tom, and it's not totally beyond the question that she might have older workmates. I look at the woman again, and while I wouldn't say she was prime child-bearing age, she's certainly not unattractive. She looks as if she works out, there's a not-unimpressive cleavage on display, and although there are a few lines round her eyes, she's still young enough to be described as pretty.

By now, she's aware of my occasional gaze. And the next time I glance over, she looks up from her novel and smiles back at me. It's not the friendliest of smiles, but it doesn't exactly say 'piss off' either. I take it as a signal, put my newspaper down, and walk over to her table.

'Hi,' I say. 'I'm Will.'

The woman lowers her book and looks up at me. 'Hello.'

I stand there awkwardly, leaning on the back of the vacant chair next to her. Should I sit down? Or wait until I'm asked? 'I'm sorry. I've never done this before.'

'What? Said "hi" to a woman in Starbucks?'

'Its just, well, I don't quite know the etiquette.'

She leans back in her chair and folds her arms. 'Well, you could start by buying me a coffee.'

'Oh. Sure. Yes. Of course,' I say, and start to move off towards the counter, but when I look at the board behind the till, I notice that there are rather a lot of different types of coffee. I head back over to the table sheepishly.

'Er . . . What kind would you like?'

She smiles at my obvious embarrassment, which I'm hoping is endearing. 'Surprise me.'

I walk over to the till, and gaze up at the options board, wondering what 'surprise me' actually means. Is this some kind of test? Will the choice of coffee I bring back to the table say volumes about me? Or will it tell her what I think about her? The obvious surprise would be to order her a cup of tea, I suppose.

I glance back towards where she's watching me from the table. Can you tell what kind of coffee someone likes by how they look? Is she a cappuccino girl, or more of a latté type? And if I order her a skinny latté, is she going to worry that I think she's fat, and could do with losing some weight? Or what about one of these new flavoured coffees? Aargh.

As the woman behind the counter turns round to take my order, I jump slightly. It's Emma – the girl I met in the toilets yesterday. She finishes tying her apron, evidently just starting her shift again, and smiles at me.

'On your own today?' she asks, looking around exaggeratedly for any abandoned children.

'Yes. I mean, no, but no kids. I had to give them back.'

Emma nods. 'Probably just as well.'

'Quite. Listen, I just wanted to say thanks again for yesterday.'

Emma shrugs briefly. 'Don't mention it. And sorry to hurry you, but' – she nods towards the growing line of people behind me – 'what can I get you?'

I look back at the table, where Julie has started reading her book again, panic, and order the first thing that comes into my head – a cappuccino – but then when Emma says, 'Tall, grande or venti?' I face my second dilemma. If I buy her a small one, she'll think that I'm a cheapskate. Medium, and she might think that I can't make my mind up, or am not very generous. Large, and she might think I'm trying to be flash. Why does everything have to be so difficult?

I throw caution to the wind and order a venti, and wait there nervously as Emma makes up a small bucketful of coffee, which I'm going to need two hands to carry back across to the table. But as I'm sprinkling chocolate over the top, it occurs to me that this might be a huge mistake. What if she turns out to be the blind date from hell? I've then got to sit and listen to her droning on for the next two hours while she struggles to finish the gallon of coffee I've stupidly just got her.

I get back to the table, wondering whether I should have got an espresso instead, and as Julie puts her book to one side, she surveys the huge mug of coffee I've just put down in front of her.

'What's this?'

'Well, you said to surprise you, so I got them to make up a special blend of coffee, topped with frothed milk, and a sprinkling of chocolate powder . . .'

'A cappuccino, you mean?'

'Er . . . yes.'

'And is this for the both of us to share?'

'Ah.' In my rush, I've forgotten to get myself one. 'Back in a sec.'

I join the end of the queue, cursing silently to myself. But just as Emma's about to take my order for the second time, I feel a tap on my shoulder.

'Will?'

When I turn round, there's a girl standing there with a quizzical expression on her face. She's about five foot two, with short dark hair, and very pretty. And pretty much as Barbara described, as well.

'Hi,' I say, an awful realisation suddenly dawning. 'You must be . . .?' I don't want to take any chances.

'Julie,' says Julie. 'Of course.'

'Of course.'

Bollocks. I glance anxiously across to my table, where the woman I've assumed up until now is Julie is watching me. Watching me talking to the real Julie, that is.

'Can I, er, get you a coffee?'

She smiles. 'That's very kind of you. Shall I go and find us a table?'

Shit. 'Why not. What would you like?'

She looks up at the board behind the counter. 'Surprise me,' she says.

As the real Julie peers around the café, trying to locate an empty table, I turn back towards the counter, worried that I am going to surprise her, but not in the way she's expecting. What on earth do I do now? For a split second, I wonder whether I can pull it off. If she manages to find somewhere to sit out of the view of the other woman, then maybe I can extract myself from that in time to ... Oh, who am I trying to kid? I'm screwed. Particularly when I feel a hand on my arm.

'Will?' says woman-from-the-table, stepping in between Julie and myself.

'Oh, hi.' I turn back to Julie, who's looking a little confused. 'Julie, this is ...'

'Susan,' says Susan, a little coldly. 'Have you got yourself a coffee yet, Will?'

'No, not quite. I was just ...'

I stop talking abruptly, hoping the ground will swallow me up. I don't know why I've introduced them. It seemed like the thing to do, but we're hardly all going to sit down at the same table and have a pleasant chat. And now Julie's going to be wondering why on earth I'm apparently here with another woman while I'm supposed to be waiting for her, while Susan is going to think ... Well, I can't imagine exactly what Susan's going to think.

'Will,' says Julie, breaking the stand-off, and pointing towards an empty table. The table that Susan's been sitting at. 'I'll be waiting for you over there.'

'That's my table,' says Susan. 'Find your own, love.'

By the look on her face, I've got a feeling she's not just talking about the table.

'But he's supposed to be meeting me,' says Julie.

'Well, he met me first,' says Susan, taking me by the arm and pulling me back towards where she's been sitting. After a second's hesitation, Julie grabs my other hand and, for a moment, I'm the rope in a tug of war between the two of them.

'But we're on a blind date,' protests Julie.

Susan looks her up and down. 'He'd have to be blind to want to go on a date with you.'

As the two women regard each other confrontation-ally, I'm wondering whether there's going to be a fight, which under any other circumstances I'd be happy to watch. And while the prospect of two women fighting over me has always seemed like a story that I'd want to tell to my grandchildren – which, at this rate, I'm never going to have – at the moment, it doesn't seem like quite such an attractive option, particularly as, given the raised voices, everyone else in the café seems to be watching. But just as my arms are about to pop out of their sockets, and the two girls are squaring up to each other, Emma comes out from behind the counter and steps in between them.

'Is there a problem here?'

For some reason, although the girls are the ones behaving menacingly, it's me she's addressing this remark to.

'No,' says Julie, letting go of my arm abruptly, causing Susan and me to nearly fall on top of each other. 'No problem at all. In fact, I was just leaving.' She gives me a dirty look, turns on her heel, and storms off.

I stand there, open-mouthed. 'But . . .'

'Me too,' says Susan, picking up her book from the table and stomping out of the door.

I'm too stunned to try and stop either of them, and although I want to leave as well, I don't want to run the risk of bumping into either of them on the street outside. Instead, I sit down at the table and pick up Susan's untouched cappuccino, trying to pretend nothing's happened. But when I've taken a long sip, which doesn't seem to have any noticeable effect in terms of reducing the amount of coffee in the oversized mug, I notice that Emma is looming over me like a schoolmistress.

'Well?' she says, standing there with her hands on her hips.

I look up at her, trying rapidly to come up with an excuse, but decide that on this occasion, perhaps honesty is the best policy. When I explain about my misunderstanding, Emma's face breaks into a grin.

'You seem to be making a habit of getting into trouble in here,' she says, sitting down across from me.

'I'm sorry,' I say, sounding like a scolded child. 'I won't do it again, miss.'

'So,' she says. 'Blind date, eh?'

I take another sip of my coffee, and look at her over the chocolate-frothed rim. She's actually very attractive, and even makes the Starbucks uniform seem sexy.

I nod. 'Which is well-named, because now I'll never see her again.'

Emma smiles. 'That looked like it might have turned nasty.'

I nod again. 'Thanks for rescuing me. Perhaps you might let me buy you a cof—' I stop myself, realizing I've just made quite possibly the most unoriginal suggestion to someone who, in fact, works in a coffee shop. But maybe she'll take it as ironic. 'I mean, a drink, sometime?'

Instead, Emma suddenly becomes all defensive. 'Oh, no, that's okay, Will. Thanks, but . . . I can't. I mean . . . I don't really like coffee.'

I don't know what's more embarrassing – having two women argue over me in public, or being turned down by Emma. But from where I'm sitting, it's absolutely the latter. 'Oh,' I say, trying to keep from blushing. 'Right. Not a problem. Just thought I'd, you know, ask.'

'And it was sweet of you to,' says Emma, sensing my discomfort. She looks over towards the till, where a small queue is starting to form again. 'Listen,' she says, standing up. 'I'd better get back and . . .'

'Sure,' I say. 'I'll just finish this and –' I look at the gallon or so of coffee in front of me, pick the mug up, take a deep breath, and drain it all in one – 'be on my way.'

And as Emma walks back towards the counter, I get up and, trying hard not to burp cappuccino as I go, head miserably out through the door.

Chapter 7

When I arrive at Tom and Barbara's for lunch the next day, Barbara doesn't say a word, but just glowers at me.

'I made a mistake . . .'

Barbara shakes her head. 'That's the last time I try and set you up with any of my friends. What am I supposed to tell her now?'

'That it wasn't my fault?' I say, as I chase Jack and Ellie around the sofa.

'And how wasn't it your fault, exactly?'

'Well, she was late, for one thing. That's hardly the most encouraging start, is it?'

Barbara sighs. 'Will, she's a woman. Of course she was late.'

'True,' says Tom. 'It's genetic. Just like they can't read maps, they can't tell the time either.'

Barbara digs him in the ribs. 'Why do you men always think it's a bad thing?'

'How do you mean?' I say, as Tom rubs his side gingerly.

Barbara shoos the kids into the conservatory. 'The

reason we're never on time is because we're getting ourselves ready for the likes of you. Take it as a compliment next time. We're probably just choosing what to wear, so we can look good for you.'

'Is that why it's called "fashionably late"?' I ask, making sure I'm out of elbow range. 'And why don't you just start getting ready earlier? Or is that too difficult a concept for you to grasp?'

Tom smiles. 'You're assuming there's a finite time that women take to get ready, mate. Not so. It's not like us − shower, shave, squirt of deodorant on the old nether regions, and we're ready. Girls are always changing their outfits, or making last-minute tweaks and adjustments.'

'Which normally go unnoticed by you gorillas, as all you want to do is stare at our tits, once you've stopped being all moody because we've kept you waiting, that is.'

'Not true,' I say. 'You can be hours late, and we don't dare leave, and then when you eventually turn up looking gorgeous, we forgive you anything. Whereas if we're not punctual, you give us five minutes and then you're off. What we don't understand is what on earth takes you so long.'

Barbara shrugs. 'We've got to shave our legs, for example. It only takes you five minutes to shave your chin.'

'Even if you've got two of them, like Tom,' I suggest.

Barbara sighs. 'Look at the Mona Lisa. You don't hear people saying, "Bloody hell, Leonardo, why'd it take you so long to paint it?" People look at the end result and they're happy. And that's how you men should view us.'

'Which we do. Assuming it's worth the wait,' adds Tom, adeptly dodging another poke in the ribs. 'Which it always is for you, my love.'

'So,' I say, 'did Julie say anything else? About me, that is. Anything . . . positive?'

Barbara puts an arm around my shoulders. 'I'd like to be able to say yes, Will, really I would, but . . .'

'But what?'

'Well, she said you seemed really nervous. Although, on reflection, I can probably see why.'

'I *was* nervous,' I say. 'It's tough, meeting someone for the first time like that. Particularly when, well, you're asking them to do what I am. I'm just not good at it.'

'Well, you're the life coach,' says Tom. 'What would you advise someone to do in that situation?'

I think about this for a second. 'Well, role play is normally a good idea. It gets the person used to the situation they're going to find themselves in.'

'Excellent idea,' says Barbara, sitting down and patting the seat next to her. 'Come on, then, Will. Try and chat me up.'

I look at her blankly. 'What?'

She nudges me. 'Come on. Imagine we're on a blind

date. And remember, first impressions, and all that.'

'Okay. Er. Hi . . .'

Barbara shakes her head. 'Properly, Will. Pretend you're meeting me for the first time.'

I sigh loudly, then get up, walk out of the door, and come back in again.

'Hi. I'm Will,' I say, extending my hand.

Barbara takes it and shakes it, rather formally. 'Pleased to meet you, Will. I'm Dolores.'

From behind me, I hear Tom snigger.

'Dolores?' I say. 'Where on earth . . .?'

'Be quiet, Will. This is role play, don't forget. I can be who I like.'

'Fine. Dolores. Nice to meet you too. Can I get you a drink?'

Barbara – sorry, Dolores – smiles. 'Yes, please. A cup of tea, please. Two sugars,' she adds, looking over at Tom.

Tom sits there obliviously, before realizing that he's evidently in the role play too. 'Fine,' he says, standing up and heading towards the kitchen. 'Will?'

'If you're making one.'

'Apparently, I am,' says Tom, disappearing through the doorway.

As we listen to Tom banging about in the kitchen, Barbara turns back to me.

'Well?'

'Er, well, so, I want to be a father, and . . .'

Barbara shakes her head. 'No, no, no, Will. Don't

just go straight for it. This isn't a business transaction we're talking about here. Start again.'

'Oh. Right. Sorry. Anyway, Barbara, I mean, *Dolores*. That's a pretty name. Where's it from?'

Barbara stares at me in disbelief. 'Will, is that really the best you can do? *That's a pretty name.* This is a crucial meeting to discover whether I'm going to be the mother of your child. And your opener is straight out of the pages of the paedophile's handbook.'

'Sorry,' I say, blushing. 'It's just that, well, it's difficult, isn't it?'

'Will, you've got to come across like you're sorted. Like this is the most natural thing in the world for you. Not like some hormonal teenager who's only after a quickie behind the bike sheds.'

'Sorry. Let's start again.'

'Fine. Hello, Will.'

'So, you found the place okay?'

Barbara puts her head in her hands. 'Will – this is why women despair of you men. If I'm quite plainly sitting here in front of you, then of course I found the place okay. What do you think – that I had to fight my way here through crowds of warring Red Indians? That I've been kidnapped by someone from a rival coffee shop chain? Or that, because I'm a woman, I'm unable to locate a branch of Starbucks just off the high street?'

I wince slightly at Barbara's onslaught. 'I'm just making small talk.'

'Well, what you see as small talk, we see as inane.

Pay me a compliment, perhaps, or ask me something interesting, but for God's sake don't patronize me with the first words that come out of your mouth.'

Tom plonks the mugs of tea down on the coffee table, careful to use coasters this time, and catches my eye, although I'm not sure whether his expression is one of sympathy or pity.

'How's it going?' he asks. 'Will managed to talk you into bed yet?'

'Well, he's in danger of sending me to sleep,' says Barbara. 'Which isn't quite the same thing.'

I clear my throat. 'Can we get on with this, please?'

'So,' says Barbara. 'What makes you think you'd make a good father?'

'Well, for a start, I love kids.'

She stares at me. 'And?'

'Er . . . I used to be one. So I can relate to them, you know?'

Barbara sighs. 'Will, that's like applying for a job working in a bank because you like spending money. Give me something more concrete.'

I think for a moment about something more concrete, but it doesn't seem to be setting. 'Er . . .'

'Well, what about how you've always wanted kids? What about the fact that you're godfather to Jack and Ellie? How about the fact that you work for yourself so you're always going to be available to help out around the house, and you'll never miss a school play or sports day? How about the fact that your dad left when you were young, so you're determined that when you have a child you're going to make sure they don't lack for anything?'

'You couldn't speak to these women for me, could you? Or do me a reference?'

'Will, remember, you've got to sell yourself. You don't have the luxury of time like Tom and I did. When you've known someone for a while, you get an understanding of how good they are with children, because you see first and foremost how they are with you, and other people and, more importantly, other people's kids.'

'Okay.' I clear my throat. 'Let's go again.'

'So what are you offering me?'

'Well, I've got a good career, and I have a nice flat, so . . .'

'You live in a flat? What floor?'

'What's that got to do with it?'

'Because I'm going to be the one who's going to have to struggle with the baby, pushchair, and the shopping, up several flights of stairs, not you.'

'But there's a lift.'

'And anyway, what makes you think we'll be moving into your place? I might have a lovely house. With a garden.'

'So?'

'So you can sell your flat and come and live with me in the arse-end of Hounslow, if you like.'

'Er . . .'

'Do you see my point, Will? You've got a lot of stuff to cover in terms of practicalities before you actually bother to work out if you like each other. But having said that, for a woman, if she really likes a guy, she'll forgive him an awful lot. We think that we can meet someone and, assuming they show potential, we'll be able to subtly mould them into an approximation of a human being. Just like I did with Tom, for example.'

From the sofa, Tom snorts. 'Don't mind me.'

'I'm serious. You remember what he used to be like. No home skills, couldn't cook, didn't know what that funny noise was when you pressed that button on the side of the vacuum cleaner. Now? Well, he's not perfect, but at least I know I can leave him on his own for a few days and he won't starve, kill himself, or neglect the twins.'

'So how does that affect what I'm trying to do?'

'Because what you're doing is asking someone to ignore that forgiving stage. You expect them to make a decision based on the presentation you're making to them of you as an adequately sorted male. Which, trust me, there are very few of in this world.'

'So you're saying that no matter what I do, I'm always going to come up short?'

Barbara smiles. 'It's not just that. We want a bit of a project. And if we see you're already sorted, well, we may not be quite so interested.'

'Mind you,' says Tom, 'that's assuming you ever actually get the chance to go on another date, of course.

And speaking of which, how are you getting on with that internet dating lark?'

'Oh yes,' says Barbara. 'Tom's told me all about that.'

I give Tom a contemptuous look. 'Thanks, mate. And actually, I do have a date. Well, maybe . . .'

'Who with?' asks Tom incredulously.

'That one whose photo you saw yesterday.'

'The teenager?' says Tom. 'Good on you.'

I can't stop myself from blushing. 'No. Not her. The dark-haired one.'

'You've got a date? With her?'

'Might have,' I say. 'Well, she's asked if I want to meet up. Only problem is . . .'

'Is what?' says Barbara.

'Where on earth do I take her? I don't want to risk any of my usual haunts, given that I'm trying to project this new, er, father figure. If you see what I mean.'

Tom thinks for a moment while he sips his tea. 'You've never actually met her before, right?'

I shake my head. 'Well, not physically. I mean, we've spoken. Over the internet, that is.' I decide not to add the word 'once'.

'And where does she live?'

'London. I think.'

'You think?'

'Well, that's what it says on her profile. But we're not allowed to give out addresses. In case one of us turns out to be a stalker.'

'What if both of you turn out to be stalkers?' observes Barbara. 'Surely that'd be a match made in heaven?'

'I have had one idea,' I say, ignoring her.

'Which is?'

'Well, I was thinking about the London Eye.'

Tom shakes his head. 'Bad idea.'

'Why?'

'Because you can't get off. Imagine if she's awful. Or she smells.'

'Or I could meet her at the Eye and take her to the pictures?' I suggest.

'True,' says Barbara. 'There's that IMAX cinema near there.'

'Even worse,' says Tom. 'You may want her to get a crick in her neck at some point on the date, but not from staring up at the screen.'

Barbara nudges him. 'What about the Tate Modern?'

'Great idea,' says Tom.

'The Tate Modern. The art gallery?'

Tom nods. 'That's right.'

'For a date?'

'It's perfect,' says Barbara. 'In fact, that's where Tom took me the first time we went out.'

'But . . .' I frown. 'I don't know anything about art.'

'Which is precisely why you're not going anywhere near the galleries.'

'Nope,' agrees Tom. 'Head straight up to the café on the seventh floor. Grab a table by the window. You

can see the whole of the city across the Thames.
Beautiful view.'

'Which is important,' says Barbara, 'if your date turns
out not to be.'

'And,' adds Tom, 'the lifts are right next to the
toilets, which means you've got a guaranteed escape
route.'

'Which had better not be the reason you took me
there,' says Barbara accusingly.

'Seriously,' says Tom, 'it's ideal. The view's really
impressive, you can have a coffee and a chat, and then,
if you want to extend the date, just take her for a
stroll along the South Bank. And it's free.'

'You big spender, you,' I say. Although I have to
hand it to Tom, it's not a bad idea. What better than
a coffee in an impressive environment, followed by a
romantic stroll along the river? And if it's still going
well, there are loads of restaurants on the South Bank
for an even more romantic lunch. Next time I speak to
Sandra, I'll suggest it.

'Just remember to add "modern art" to your profile,'
advises Tom. 'In case it's raining, and you have to take
her round the gallery.'

'But I don't know my Dalis from my –' I struggle to
think of another modern artist, and fail – 'daleks.'

'Doesn't matter,' says Barbara. 'Nor did Tom. And
his pathetic attempts to pretend that he did, when
I could see that he was reading off the little cards next
to each painting, were somehow endearing.'

'Why?'

'Because I thought he was obviously trying to impress me. And that meant he thought I was worth impressing. Which was the biggest compliment he could have paid me.'

'So no flashy restaurants?'

'Will, do you really want the kind of woman who's going to be impressed by that kind of thing? You're asking her to be rather un-flashy for the next few years, don't forget.'

'And remember, be attentive, not overly keen,' suggests Barbara. 'And do more listening than talking.'

Tom laughs. 'Which isn't normally a problem where women are concerned.'

Chapter 8

But chance would be a fine thing, as there's no sign of Sandra that evening, or even the following morning, when I try surreptitiously to log on at home without Magda seeing what I'm up to. And what's more, there don't seem to be many other women beating a path to my inbox. Even though I'm not in the best of moods, I still have to head into work; but as I walk into reception, I realize that I'm not the only one having a bad day, as I get to the front desk just in time to see Jen slam the phone down angrily.

'That customer service training course was money well spent, then.'

Jen glowers up at me, but then her face softens. 'Sorry, Will. It's just . . . men.'

'All men, or one in particular?'

Jen smiles. 'All of them, in my experience.'

I don't know quite what my next line should be. Jen, I know, has a boyfriend. Josh, he's called. I've met him on a couple of occasions, when he's picked Jen up from work. And from what I've seen, he's a bit of a git.

I think the technical term would be 'rugger bugger', all striped shirts and turned-up collars. He's evidently the product of some stuck-up school, and has an arrogance to match. And from how I've noticed he treats Jen, he clearly thinks women are somewhere below amoebas on the evolutionary scale.

'Do you, you know, want to talk about it?'

'You're just trying to get me on that couch of yours. Anyway, I can't.' She pats her desk. 'Phones to answer, people to receive.'

'Tell you what, I'll nip out and get us both a coffee. Then we can have a chat here. If you like, that is.'

Jen considers this for a minute, and then reaches for her purse. 'Why not. Thanks, Will.'

I wave her money away. 'On me.'

'Watch what you say, or it might be,' says Jen, forcing a smile.

I head back out and across the road, dodging the charity muggers again, and nip into Starbucks. When I get to the counter, Emma regards me suspiciously.

'Dare I ask?' she says, looking warily over my shoulder.

'Just a cappuccino and a latté. To go, please.'

Emma raises one eyebrow. 'To go? You are still allowed to drink in here, you know.'

To be honest, I'm still a little embarrassed after our last encounter, and I'm quite pleased to have a reason not to linger. 'I would stay. But bit of a crisis in the office.'

'What's that?' asks Emma, as she presses coffee into the filters, then sticks a jug of milk under the steamer. 'Children running amok? A couple of women slugging it out in reception?'

'Colleague with boyfriend problems, actually.'

Emma stops mid-froth, and turns to look at me. 'And she's asking *you* for advice?'

By the time I get back, Jen seems to have calmed down a little; that is, until she starts talking. Fortunately, it's a quiet morning, because for the next half an hour the floodgates well and truly open, as Jen tells me all about her and Josh.

And as she talks, it makes me realize that she's typical of a lot of my clients – and of a lot of people in general – hanging around in unsuitable relationships, letting their partners treat them badly, and putting up with it, all because they're more scared of being single and out there, even when they're as attractive as Jen is. And it's a philosophy that I certainly don't subscribe to.

'So,' says Jen eventually. 'What do you think?'

I scratch my head, more to give myself a bit of time to come up with an answer than because I've got an itch. 'It's a tricky one.'

'And?'

Ah. Obviously she wants more than that. 'Well . . .'

'Aren't you going to ask me if I love him?'

'Sometimes, Jen, that's the least important thing.'

'How so?'

'Because love can make us do all sorts of strange

things. Act in completely illogical ways. And love means we're always more likely to get hurt. If you'd told me all that, but said that you didn't love him any more, I'd obviously say you should leave him. So why should it be any different if you do love him? It doesn't alter the facts of the case. Would you treat someone you loved like Josh treats you?'

'No. Of course not.'

'So, turning that around, would you expect someone who loved you to treat you like that?'

'I guess not.'

'Do you think someone who loves you could treat you like that?'

'No . . .'

'So, what does that tell you?'

Jen doesn't answer at first, but just stares at her half-drunk coffee. There's a tiny blob of foam on the end of her nose, and I have to stop myself from reaching over and wiping it off.

'That he doesn't, I mean, he might not . . . love me.'

'Jen, in any relationship, if only one person is in love, that's not a recipe for success. Especially if the other person is taking advantage of that. Which I have to say, Josh sounds like he is.'

'But I thought he might be the one, Will.'

'Jen, you're still young. Too young, even. So is Josh. Look at it from his point of view. And he's a man, don't forget.'

'What's that got to do with it?'

'Because a guy of that age, well, he might tell a girl that he's looking for the one but, in reality, he's just looking to give her one.'

Jen half smiles at this. 'But I can't split up with him, Will. It'd break his heart.'

If he's got one, I think. 'Yes you can, Jen. As long as you're sure it won't break yours.'

The phone rings, and Jen stares at it for a second or two before picking it up and asking the caller to hold, before turning back to me. 'You're too good at this, you know,' she says. 'Only one thing puzzles me.'

'Which is?'

'Why, if you're such an expert, are you still single?'

The conversation with Jen puts me into a reflective mood, so I spend longer than normal with my clients today, pausing every couple of hours to check NewFlames, but there's still no sign of Sandra. I'm starting to think that she's 'met' someone else, or maybe I'm not her type – in both senses of the word.

I'm home by six, and it's not raining. There's nothing on television, and it's too early for dinner, so I'm faced with no alternative: I go for a run.

I refuse to call it 'jogging'. That's what unfit people do – and besides, jogging's just more of a fast walk, really. And how can you tell the difference? Well, according to the textbooks, if you have difficulty holding a conversation while you're doing it, it's running.

But I'm not running with anyone, and I'd look stupid trying to talk to myself.

But running or jogging, it's still a sad, single man's activity. If I was half of a couple, I wouldn't waste my time pounding the streets every evening. I can never understand those sad couples who go out jogging together. What's the point? Is the guy so pathetic that he can genuinely only run as fast as a girl? And besides, can't they think of another, more fun way to get some exercise together? I know I could.

If I was part of a couple, I wouldn't be wasting my time going out for a run every evening, like some sad Billy-no-mates. We'd be in the kitchen, opening a bottle of wine, and chatting about our working days as we cooked something delicious, which we'd eat on the sofa in front of *EastEnders*. Pasta, maybe, or something with couscous. I long to have the kind of relationship where we eat couscous together. And I'm not even sure what couscous is.

Because running in the dark is the saddest thing of all. It says, 'I've got nothing better to do with my evenings, so I'm going to go for a run in the hope that my slim physique will make me more attractive to the opposite sex.' And it's a vain hope, in more ways than one. If women were really attracted to runners, you'd see them hanging around at athletics tracks, or mobbing the winners of the London Marathon.

I entered a 'fun run' last year. 'Fun' and 'run' – two words that have absolutely no business being in the same sentence. It was round Richmond Park, so at least the scenery was pleasant, and I enjoyed it at first, particularly because people seemed to be applauding me whenever I passed. In fact, I soon got caught up in the spirit of the thing, and started to wave back at them, acknowledging their support, and it was only after the third mile that I realized that they were actually cheering the blind guy running with his guide dog a few yards behind me. The last mile was the worst. It was supposed to be a fun run but this other guy kept trying to overtake me. I'd speed up a little and so would he. As if he was waiting for his moment. His opportunity to sprint past me on the final stretch. Which he did. Quite convincingly. And I wouldn't have minded, if he hadn't been wearing a gorilla suit.

I first got into running at school. It was something I could beat the bullies at. A way to stop them teasing me about my dad. Because it's hard to take the piss out of someone if you're fighting for breath yourself. Unlike the rest of the kids, I'd look forward to cross-country days. The loneliness of the long-distance runner? Not if you prefer your own company. And now here I am, some fifteen years later, pulling on a pair of reflective trainers, choosing an appropriate playlist on my iPod, and ready to go out and pound the streets until my chest hurts and my knees ache, all in the name of 'fitness'.

I head out of my flat and break into a light jog down towards the river front, then speed up and bound along towards the railway bridge. I dodge the drinkers outside the Slug & Lettuce, who seem to be happy to stand outside clutching their pints even on the foulest of days, then past the slipway, down by the White Cross pub, and along the towpath. There are a few joggers coming the other way, but being a proper runner I ignore them, and concentrate on getting into a rhythm.

And why do I do this? Put myself through this torture every evening? This reminder of my sad single status? Running is my thinking time, you see. If ever I've got a problem, I just have to stick on my running shoes and hit the pavement, and soon a solution will come to me. I don't know why it is, but the moment I start breathing hard, my mind begins to process whatever it is that's bothering me, and this evening, it's Jen's parting comment. Why *am* I still single? And although I do a long loop, all the way to Twickenham and back in fact, by the time I've finished, the only answer I can come up with is maybe it's because I spend my evenings running, rather than trying to meet someone new.

As I walk back in through my front door, breathing heavily and sweating profusely, I catch sight of my lap-top on the kitchen table, and realize that I've left myself logged on. But just as I'm about to sign out, I hear a ping – I've got mail. It's not the Instant Messenger that Sandra used last time but hoping that it's her, I click on the envelope icon, and open up the message.

'Hi,' it says. 'I'm Cat Lover.'

Uh-oh. *Cat lover.* I click on the link, and open

Cat Lover's profile. She's pretty enough, but cats and babies don't exactly mix, I seem to remember from some news item I watched a while ago. Given her feline friendship, I'm just about to hit 'delete', before I notice on her 'About Me' section that she doesn't actually like cats. 'My name's Catherine,' she explains, 'but my friends call me Cat.'

Hmm. Suddenly, Cat Lover sounds exciting, rather than sad. I'm sitting trying to compose my answer, while wondering whether I should jump in the shower first, when there's another ping. Congratulating myself on my popularity, I click on the link, and see it's from Cat Lover again.

'I can see you're still online. Did you get my message?'

She's keen, I think. 'Yes, thanks,' I type. 'How are you?'

And as I sit there, we have a conversation of sorts, exchanging emails for the next hour or so. And while it's not quite the instant connection that Sandra and I seemed to have – in both senses of the word – we get on well, although I find myself struggling to match her speed on the keyboard. Either she's the world's quickest typist, or she's already written these out and is just cut-and-pasting them into her replies, as it seems like I've hardly pressed 'send' before her reply appears in my inbox.

I'm interrupted at around eight o'clock by the phone ringing. It's my mother, calling to see how I am, and after a cursory five-minute conversation assuring her that I'm fine, and that no, she's not a grandmother yet, I hang up, and hurry back to my laptop. When I refresh my inbox, I'm a little surprised to see a further eleven messages. However, instead of excitement, I feel a little lurch of dread. They're all from Cat Lover. Anxiously, I click them open in turn.

'Are you still there?'

'You haven't replied to my last mail.'

'Where are you?'

'HELLO?'

And so on, each with an increasing number of capital letters and exclamation marks.

I look at my watch to check whether I have, in fact, been gone for only a few minutes, rather than having hit my head and been passed out for longer, but it's still only five past eight. And eleven messages over the course of five minutes works out to one every thirty seconds or so, which occurs to me is rather on the needy side of keen. As I'm wondering how on earth to reply, a final ping makes me jump. It's Cat Lover again. With mounting apprehension, I click 'open'.

'This'll never work out,' it says. 'Don't contact me again.'

Brilliant. From picked up to dumped within five minutes. A new record, even for me. Out of safety's sake, I put a block on Cat Lover's profile, then log off and head for the shower, pausing only to double-lock the front door on the way.

Chapter 9

A strange thing happens at lunchtime today. I'm walking round Richmond, trying to kill some time instead of heading straight back to the office, and, as usual, decide to go in and read the magazines in WH Smiths. I always feel a little guilty about this, even though I know I'm not the only one who does it, as every time I go in there are about twenty blokes stood there reading *What Hi-Fi* or *Nuts*, along with a similar number of women on the other side of the aisle desperate to get an update as to whether Pete/Kate are on/off.

Anyway, I'm stood there looking through a copy of *GQ*, having been attracted by the particularly nice photo of Cameron Diaz on the front, and flicking past the collection of adverts for clothes I'll never fit into and watches I'll never be able to afford, when out of the corner of my eye I spot a woman pushing a baby in a buggy stop by the end of the aisle and pick up a copy of *For The Bride* magazine. I smile to myself, as the words 'shutting the stable door' and 'after the horse has bolted' join together in my mind, but just as they're forming a sentence I see that it's Anita. *My* Anita.

I refer to her as 'my' Anita, because she is. Well, was. Anita is my significant ex. The one that got away. Maybe even the love of my life, if you want to put it in more sentimental terms. Only at the time, I didn't know it. And I certainly wouldn't admit it to Tom and Barbara.

Anita and I met six years ago, and went out for the next three, on and off. We talked about moving in together, and at times I even dared to think we might have a future together, but it wasn't to be. Nerves or some sort of strange male pride stopped me from taking that next step. I couldn't even tell her that I loved her. Not until after she dumped me, that is. And by then it was, of course, too late. And when we split up for the final time, on a bench on Richmond Green, I sat there and cried.

I tried all sorts of romantic gestures to win her back after that. Declarations of love, promises of commitment, but to no avail. And it taught me a valuable lesson: You snooze, you lose.

Up until a year or so ago, Anita and I would still meet up on a regular basis, even occasionally ending up in bed together, and then regretting it the next morning, although her more than me, I always felt. And when she finally met someone else – Mike, I think his name is – as she was bound to, our meetings and, of course, the sex, stopped. It wouldn't be fair on him, she told me, when what she probably meant was that it wouldn't be fair on me to let me think there was still some hope, a tiny chink in their relationship that might let me back in. When there wasn't.

As my eyes flick between her and the buggy, for a moment it doesn't compute. Anita and I last saw each other, what, a year ago by my calculations? And if I remember it correctly, we ended up having sex. And she's now pushing a baby around . . . I mean, I know she's only known Mike for six months or so, which means either she's a fast worker, or . . . No. It can't be.

I stuff my copy of GQ hurriedly back into the slot on the shelf, but for some reason, can't get it in. I seem to have lost all co-ordination, and end up just jamming it in half way, crumpling the picture on the cover in the process, and giving Cameron a set of wrinkles that, unless she's been Photoshopped to within an inch of her life, I'm pretty sure she doesn't have in reality.

I can't remember if I've seen Anita in the last six months or so, or if I have, whether she was looking unusually fat. Surely she'd have told me. And anyway, we were always extremely careful. Besides, *she* dumped *me*, as I seem to remember. And surely she wouldn't have if she was . . .

Anita heads towards the greeting-card section, so I make my way along the magazine aisle, peering over a copy of *Practical Parenting* while deciding what my next move should be. As the security guard watches me suspiciously, I try and get close enough to sneak a peak at the baby, before wondering what on earth that's going to tell me. They all look the same at that age, after all, so it's hardly like I'm going to be able to tell if I'm the father from the fact it's got my nose.

I follow her surreptitiously around the store for a few minutes, watching as she finally selects a birthday card, then wheels the buggy towards the checkouts. As she pays for her purchase, adding a Terry's Chocolate Orange on impulse at the till, and makes her way towards the exit, I follow her out of the store and tail her along Richmond High Street, still unable to get a proper look at the contents of her pram.

By the time we've been down as far as the station and back, I decide there's nothing for it but to confront her. I'm just catching her up, rounding the slow-moving pensioners who always seem to walk along the pavement in pairs, and have to dodge into the road to get past one particularly obstructive couple, causing a bus to beep me. But just as I'm about to stop her, she ducks into Ann Summers.

I stop in the doorway. Ann Summers? With a baby in tow? I hope she's covering its eyes. And what on earth is she doing going in there? From what I remember, we never needed any assistance between the sheets. But perhaps this is what Tom was telling me about, and maybe she's after something to spice up her love life post-production.

Now, I don't know what to do. I can't go into Ann Summers after her – after all, I don't want her to think that I'm the kind of person who frequents this type of establishment, and besides, what am I going to find her looking at? More importantly, what might I see? Even though I walk past the place every day, I've never been inside, and I'm secretly worried that it's full of battery-operated *things* that might make me feel more than a little inadequate. But, equally, I can't hang around on the pavement outside and try and keep tabs on her movements by peering through the window, because one of my clients might walk past and think I'm a pervert.

I look up and down the pavement in desperation, and then have an idea. There's a group of chuggers milling around outside Boots – and if one of them were to stop me for a chat, I'd have a legitimate reason to hang around here and wait for her to come out of the shop, with the added benefit that when Anita sees me, she'll think I'm a great bloke for being so charitable. And this would be a fantastic plan, if it weren't for the fact that unlike their usual modus operandi, which is to virtually rugby-tackle everyone who walks past, right now the chuggers look like they're taking a break.

I hop around near them for a moment or two, even clearing my throat and getting my wallet out expectantly, but can't seem to get any interest – they're too busy chatting to each other, or rolling their own cigarettes with some suspicious-looking tobacco. Eventually, I decide that I'll just have to go over and interrupt them. I pick the nearest one, a dreadlocked girl with piercings in both ears, both eyebrows, and, by the look of her, several other places that would stop her going through airport security untroubled, and tap her on the shoulder. Her name badge, I notice with a sense of irony, says 'Charity'.

'Excuse me.'

The dreadlocked girl jumps and spins around, hiding her roll-up guiltily. 'But I'm on a break.'

Well, now you know what it feels like to be interrupted in the street, don't you, I want to say. 'Oh. Sorry. But I was wondering, I mean, I'd, er, like to make a donation.'

She looks anxiously at her colleagues, who seem as astounded as she is.

'Oh. Right.'

'What are you collecting for, anyway?'

She's so stunned, she seems to have momentarily forgotten, and stares blankly at her clipboard. 'Er, it's for . . .'

I take it from her unresisting grasp and speed-read through the form. It's Help the bloody Aged again. At this rate, the aged will soon be able to help the rest of us. 'Fantastic,' I say. 'I love the aged. In fact, I'm going to be one soon. Where do I sign?'

'Er . . . here.'

Charity reaches across and flicks straight over to the direct debit form, then hands me a pen. But as I start to fill my details in, I glance over her shoulder and realize there's a slight flaw in my plan. We're standing about ten yards away from Ann Summers, and if Anita comes out while I'm concentrating on this, I might miss her and, more importantly, she might not see me.

In desperation, I start quizzing Charity about how the money will be spent, while imperceptibly edging closer to her, invading her personal space as much as possible in an attempt to move her along the pavement. And it seems to do the trick – not surprisingly, Charity starts backing away from me and, ever so slowly, I manage to edge her towards the entrance.

After five minutes, and with Charity glancing anxiously back over at her colleagues like a wildebeest separated from the herd, I'm starting to run out of questions about the aged, and there's still no sign of Anita. What can she be doing in there? Surely they don't let you test the products out? I've never heard any suspicious noises coming out of the back of the store, so I don't think that can be the case. By now, I'm looking over Charity's shoulder so regularly, I'm sure she thinks I've got some sort of facial tic. But, thankfully, and after I've probably signed up to pay for at least a couple of old folks' homes, Anita finally comes out of the store, although I'm somewhat dismayed when she doesn't see me, and heads off in completely the opposite direction.

I break away from a very pleased and not a little relieved-looking Charity to resume my tailing, but after a few yards Anita stops suddenly and, as if she's just remembered something important, turns and spins the buggy around, heading straight back towards me. So straight, in fact, that she bangs it painfully into my ankle.

'Why can't you watch where you're— Will?' Her angry expression changes to one of pleasant recognition.

'Anita?' I put as much surprise into my voice as I can muster, trying hard to come across as someone who's just casually bumped into her on the street, rather than someone who's been stalking her around town for the last fifteen minutes.

'Long time no see,' she says, leaning across and kissing me on the cheek. 'How have you been? Busy?'

Not as busy as you, evidently, I want to say. 'Yup. Good, thanks. And you?'

'Oh, fine.'

'Good.'

'Great.'

We stand there for a few moments, Anita seemingly oblivious to the thing on the pavement between us. I steal a few furtive glances down, trying to work out if it's a he or a she, but even though it seems to be dressed in some sort of pink outfit, I really can't tell. It doesn't look like me, but it doesn't not look like me, if you see what I mean, so I'm none the wiser. I decide to give her an opening to confess.

'So, what's your news?'

Anita smiles. 'Oh, not much.'

Come on, for Christ's sake, I'm thinking. There's an

elephant in the room here, or rather in the buggy. 'No? Not been up to anything exciting?'

She puts a hand on my arm. 'Well, actually, I'm glad I bumped into you, Will. I was going to call you. There is something I wanted to tell you. Have you got time for a coffee?'

My legs suddenly feel all wobbly. *Finally*, I think, although Anita seems to be sounding a bit vague. Maybe she wants me to be sitting down when she tells me? And given the way my heart is thumping, it's probably not a bad idea. 'Sure. Of course. Why not?'

'Starbucks?' suggests Anita, nodding towards the branch near my office. 'There's that new one just around the corner.'

'Let's try somewhere else,' I say, having seen Emma in there earlier, and worried about getting myself banned if I end up causing another scene in front of her.

We stroll down the high street towards Carluccio's, and even though Anita's not confirmed anything yet, I can't stop glancing proudly at the contents of the buggy. I can't believe that I might be a father already. I'll be able to call off the search when it's hardly begun. Which, given the success I'm having so far, will be no bad thing.

I direct Anita towards one of the tables in the window, sit opposite her, and order two cappuccinos from the waitress. But as we make small talk, she seems a little nervous, like she's skirting the issue. And if she's a little nervous, then I'm on the edge of my seat. In an attempt to distract myself, I pick up the menu and scan through it, looking at the array of Italian food on offer, and wondering idly whether if pasta ever meets antipasti there's some kind of black hole effect. But it doesn't work, and once the waitress has delivered the coffees, I can't stop myself from asking.

'Is that mine?' I say, my voice shaking slightly.

'What?'

I put my coffee down on the table. 'Is that mine?'

'Is what yours, Will?' She looks at her cup. 'The coffee? No – they're both cappuccinos.'

'No,' I say, nodding towards the buggy. 'That.'

Anita follows my gaze, before a look of surprise crosses her face. 'What? This?' She nods down towards the pink-clad blob, then throws her head back and lets out a short laugh. 'Not unless you've been sleeping with my sister.'

'What?' I don't understand. I've only met her sister the once, and although it was a long time ago, I'm pretty sure I haven't.

'It's not even mine,' laughs Anita.

I'm both relieved and disappointed at the same time. 'What do you mean, not even yours. Have you stolen it?'

Anita puts her cup down, reaches into the push-chair, unbuckles about a million safety straps, and hoists the baby up and onto her lap. 'Will, meet Elizabeth. Elizabeth is my sister's baby.'

I hold out my hand as if to shake Elizabeth's, before I realize what I'm doing and stop myself. 'Ah. Oh. Right.'

'You thought . . .' Anita shakes her head in disbelief. 'My, that is funny.'

I feel myself starting to blush, and try to explain. 'It's just that, well, it's been a year since I've seen you, and we, you know, one last time, and, well, I thought you'd, you know, and hadn't told me.'

'Will, if I didn't want to have a baby with you, I'm hardly going to want to have our baby without you, am I?'

I stare at my coffee glumly. 'I suppose not.'

'Exactly.'

Anita jiggles Elizabeth on her knee for a while, until the baby proceeds to drool down the front of her romper suit, then straps her back into the buggy. And as I watch her with a child in her care, a strange feeling washes over me, particularly when I replay what she's just said.

'Tell me, Anita. Why didn't you want a baby with me? Didn't you think I'd be a good father?'

Anita regards me for a moment, before reaching down to wipe Elizabeth's chin with her serviette. 'Well, for one thing, you never asked me.'

I pick up my coffee and take a sip, more for something to do than because I'm actually thirsty. 'Do you ever think about you and me?'

Anita lays a hand on mine, and I have to stop myself from pulling away, as it's the hand still holding the drool-soaked napkin. 'Of course I do, Will. We had some great times. You'll always be special to me.' She picks up her cappuccino. 'You know that.'

'No, I mean, you and me, now. Or rather, in the future. What might have been.'

Anita puts her coffee back down again. She's got a slight chocolate moustache from the foam, and it's quite possibly the sexiest thing I've ever seen, particularly when she sticks her tongue out and licks it off.

'Will, there never was a might have been.'

'Why not?'

'Because you never gave me the slightest indication that you wanted any more than the here and now. Until I dumped you, that is.'

'Well, I might not have said as much, but . . .'

'Rubbish,' snorts Anita. 'You were quite happy for things to carry on as they were, despite my hints to the contrary.'

'What hints?'

Anita shakes her head. 'That's the trouble with you blokes. You've really got no idea.'

'Hang on. I'm confused. So if you wanted so much more out of it, why did you dump me?'

'Will, it's not as simple as that. We women are a lot more practical than you men give us credit for. Which means we reach a point that, well, let's just say that there's no going back from. So by the time you've finally been shocked into action, from our point of view it's usually too late.'

'And what about whatshisname? Mark.' I know it's childish, but I always get his name wrong on purpose.

'Mike,' she says, with a little annoyance. 'What about him?'

'Are you going to have to shock him into action?'

'Quite the opposite,' she says, a dreamy look coming over her face. 'In fact, that's what I wanted to talk to you about.'

Anita holds her hand out, palm down, on the table. Her left hand. And for the first time I notice the ring with a rock the size of Gibraltar on her third finger.

I feel like I've been punched in the stomach. And the head. I need to get outside and get some air, but my legs won't move. And all the time, my mind racing, my heart thumping, Anita is still talking, and I have to force myself to concentrate on what she's saying.

'. . . to be honest, his proposal came as something of a surprise. It was Christmas Eve. We were in Paris, at the top of the Eiffel Tower.'

'With the hundred other couples there doing exactly the same thing?' I say, finding a focus for my anger.

Anita ignores me and carries on. 'And, I mean, we hadn't been going out for that long, really, but when he went down on one knee . . .'

'He managed to get up again all right, did he? I mean, I know he's a little bit older than me.'

She snatches her hand back and looks at me disdainfully. 'I won't let you spoil it for me, Will. It was really romantic, actually.'

'Sorry. I'm just ... surprised,' I say, not wanting to say the word 'jealous'. 'And you're sure you're doing the right thing?'

Anita picks up from her saucer the little sweet that's not sure whether it's a coffee bean or a chocolate, unwraps it, and pops it into her mouth. 'Not really, no. But I'll never know unless I give it a go, will I?'

I can feel the coffee rising in the back of my throat, and have to swallow hard. If she was one of my clients, I'd be helping her work that sentence through to its logical conclusion. 'And what about kids? Have you thought about that?'

'Well, Mike's already got a couple of his own, and he says he probably doesn't want any more.'

'But I thought *you* wanted a family?'

'I do. Did. But as I said, he's already got a couple, and while they live with his ex—'

'You're marrying a divorcee? With all the baggage that goes with that?'

Anita folds her arms defensively. 'Mike's baggage is all neatly packed away, thank you. He's even let me have a rummage through his cases.'

I can't believe what I'm hearing, and I'm still feeling a little shaky. Maybe it's the fact that this is my third coffee of the day, or maybe it's what I'm about to say. I grab her hand – the hand without the ring on it – and

I'm relieved when she doesn't try and snatch it away. At first, anyway.

'Marry me instead.'

At this, Anita tries to pull her arm back with such force that she nearly knocks her coffee over, but I've got a firm grip.

'What?'

'Marry me instead. Not Mark.'

'Mike!'

'Mike. Sorry. I mean, we get on great. And I'm desperate to have kids.'

'Will, that's not fair.'

Life's not fair, I want to tell her. Nothing is. It's not fair that it took her finally dumping me for me to realize what I'd lost, and it's not fair that it's taken someone else proposing to her to make me realize how much I want her back. Plus, it's not fair that us blokes are so useless at telling people how we feel about them that we end up losing them. And it's not fair that Mark/Mike's already had one chance at this, and he's mucked it up, and abandoned his family into the bargain, just like my dad did. And just like I won't.

'I'm serious, Anita. I haven't stopped thinking about you since the day we split up.'

Anita tries to pull her hand away again. 'Will, we didn't split up,' she says. 'I chucked you. Because I was fed up with the fact that we weren't going anywhere. And besides, I'd fallen out of love with you.'

This is a slap in the face which, on top of the earlier

punch in the stomach and the head, has me reeling. And it takes a lot of quick thinking to try and turn it around. 'Aha!'

Anita looks confused. 'What do you mean, aha?'

'Just that, well, to have fallen out of love with me, you must have been in love with me. Once.'

'So?'

'So that means you can be again. If you give it a chance. Give us a chance.'

Anita finally succeeds in removing her hand from mine, but probably only because my palms are sweating so much that I can't hang on to her any more, and rubs her fingers where I've been squeezing so hard.

'Will, it doesn't work like that. Love isn't one of those things that you just switch on and off. It builds. Over time.'

'Aha!'

'Will you stop aha-ing. What now?'

'You said it builds over time. How much time?'

Anita shrugs. 'I don't know. I don't think there's a set rule.'

'A month? A week? Six months?'

Anita looks at me like I'm a candidate for care in the community. 'All right then. Ten months, four days, six hours.'

'And you've known whatshisname for how long?'

'Very clever, Will. You're not going to catch me out like that.' She stands up, and puts one hand on the buggy. 'Listen. I've got to get this little one home. So let's forget this conversation ever happened, shall we?'

'Which part?' I say, hoping she means the 'getting married to Mike' bit.

'You know which part!' Anita leans in and kisses me on the top of the head. 'And I hope you'll come to the wedding. It'll mean a lot to me and Mark.'

'Don't you mean Mike?' I say, as I watch her wheel Elizabeth away from the table and out through the door.

I wait five minutes, then pay the bill, and walk out of the restaurant. On my way back to the office, I feel more miserable than ever, and when one of Charity's colleagues tries to accost me outside Tesco's, it's all I can do not to punch him in the face. And later that evening, when I'm back in my flat, I slump down on the sofa and stare at the wall. I've never felt more alone. More stupid. And like I've lost my one and only chance at real happiness. Why wasn't I more decisive when Anita and I were together? I'm reminded of that song that says something about not knowing what you've got until you've lost it. Well, today, I lost it. Big time.

I need to talk to someone, and it's unfair of me to keep burdening Tom with my concerns so, instead, I get changed into my running gear and hit the streets again, mulling the problem over in my head. What would I do if I came to me for advice? What would I say? I'd say get over it. I'd say that what in retrospect looks like a mistake quite clearly wasn't a mistake at the time, so it wasn't a mistake to make that particular decision there and then. I'd also say that we learn from our mistakes, and the most important thing that can come from it is that I'd recognize if I was ever in a similar situation again, and then I hopefully wouldn't do the same thing. I'd also say that the only thing I can do is to try and put that mistake right, which I've done, and if that doesn't work, which it didn't, then I just have to move on. It's called reframing. Looking at things in a positive light, rather than a negative one. And moving on from there. And the best way to achieve that would be to take someone else to that wedding. But, as things stand, that might prove rather difficult.

Chapter 10

I get back home from my run earlier than usual, shower, and fix myself a sandwich, before sitting down at my laptop. And the second I log on to NewFlames, the winking eye appears again. I check cautiously that it's not Cat Lover, but when I click through, it's an instant message from Sandra.

'Will, I am sorry I have not been here.'

'That's okay,' I type.

'I feel bad.'

Uh-oh. 'Why?'

'I feel bad because I have not told you everything.'

Here we go, I think. She's married. Or she's met someone else.

'Are you angry with me?' she asks, before I get a chance to reply.

I look at her photo again. It's not anger I feel, but lust. 'How can I be angry with you? I don't even know you.'

'I hope you will soon know me,' comes the reply. 'But . . .'

I wait for her to complete the sentence, but after a couple of minutes, it's clear that she's not going to. I check my internet connection, just in case, but it's still working fine.

'But?' I type.

'BUT I LIED TO YOU ON MY PROFILE. I AM NOT IN THE CITY OF LONDON.'

I suddenly notice that her English isn't sounding as good as it might, and more worryingly, she's got her Caps Lock on. I do the same.

'NOT TO WORRY. WHERE ARE YOU?'

There's a pause, and then 'LAGOS.'

I pause myself. Lagos? It sounds Welsh to me. I look at her photo again and quickly decide that I don't mind the odd trip down the M4.

'THAT'S NOT A PROBLEM. I HAVE A CAR.'

'IT MIGHT TAKE SOME TIME,' types Sandra.

Rubbish. I've driven to Wales before. It's not that far. And I've got a TVR now.

I quickly type 'Lagos' into the AA route planner, to see how far it actually is, but, surprisingly, the AA doesn't recognize it as a destination. Confused, I type it into Google instead, which comes up with twenty-one million answers. And by the looks of things, the majority of them seem to say that Lagos is in Nigeria.

Nigeria.

Ri–ight.

'ARE YOU THERE ON HOLIDAY?' I type tentatively.

'I AM STUCK HERE,' replies Sandra.

'WHAT DO YOU MEAN, STUCK?' I type, picturing her, a poor model, stuck in Nigeria after some photo shoot. Bikini modelling, probably. Hopefully.

'I HAVE LOST MY PASSPORT. THERE IS ONLY ONE WAY TO GET IT BACK.'

'WHICH IS?'

'I NEED MONEY.'

Despite thinking that I might regret typing this next question, I can't help myself. 'HOW MUCH?'

'FIVE THOUSAND DOLLARS.'

Five thousand dollars? I do a quick exchange-rate calculation in my head. 'THAT'S A LOT OF MONEY. WHAT ABOUT YOUR PARENTS?'

'I CANNOT ASK MY FAMILY.'

'WHY NOT?'

'THEY ARE DEAD.'

Ah. I don't quite know how to reply to that. And five thousand dollars! I'm pretty sure I only paid about sixty quid to renew my passport the last time. But then, she is really good-looking, and if she really is in trouble . . .

I'm still thinking about how to respond, when Sandra writes again. 'DEAR WILL, I HAVE TO GO. THE MEN ARE BACK. IF YOU CARE ABOUT ME, MEET ME ON HERE THIS TIME TOMORROW AND I WILL GIVE YOU MY BANK DETAILS FOR TRANSFER. I WILL BE SO GRATEFUL WHEN I MEET YOU IN LONDON CITY AND WE ARE MARRIED.'

I allow myself a few moments to daydream about exactly what her being grateful might involve, before I reread the last sentence, and spot the word 'married'. And it's only then that the first alarm bell starts to ring. We've only chatted twice, and already it seems like Sandra sees me as a potential fiancé. Trouble is, I'm worried that she's spelling it 'f-i-n-a-n-c-e'. I'm just typing 'WHAT MEN?' when I see that she's logged off, and despite my pressing 'refresh' continuously for the next five minutes, Sandra doesn't reappear.

I'm somewhat confused about what's just happened, and log out of NewFlames a little nervously, and I'm just checking my emails before I shut the computer down when a message pops into my inbox. It's from a D. Smith, with 'Long Time No See' in the subject line, and I'm just about to delete it as Spam when I remember that the D might stand for 'Debbie'. She must have got my message via Friends Reunited. Fan-bloody-tastic!

Suddenly forgetting all about Sandra, I open the email excitedly and, sure enough, it is Debbie. There's a bunch of stuff about how great it is to hear from me, what it is she's doing now, and how pleased she is that I managed to decipher her 'message'. I'm not sure exactly what she means by that, but when she asks if I want to meet up with her for a drink tomorrow evening, I'm only too happy to agree. She still lives in Shepherd's Bush, and when she suggests meeting at a pub that we used to drink at all those years ago, I'm all too happy to agree. Maybe it'll be a trip down memory lane in all senses.

'So,' says Tom, when I meet him for lunch the following day to update him on my progress. 'Debbie Smith.'

I nod. 'Yup.'

Tom takes a bite of his bacon sandwich and chews thoughtfully. 'I seem to remember she was a bit of a goer. Wonder if she's calmed down any?'

'I sincerely hope not.'

'Where are you meeting her?'

'The Anglesea Arms.'

Tom puts his sandwich down. 'Not *the* Anglesea Arms? The place we used to drink after school. It's a bit spit–and–sawdust, isn't it?'

I shake my head. 'Not any more,' I say, through a mouthful of cream cheese bagel. 'It's a gastro–pub now, apparently.'

Tom makes a face. 'It used to be more gastro-enteritis. Well, give her my best.'

I grin back at him. 'I intend to give her better than that. It's been a while, after all.'

'Really?' says Tom. 'Well, you'd better make the most of it, then. Especially if she turns out to be the one.'

'What do you mean?'

'Well, it's different, isn't it?'

'What is?'

'The sex. When you're trying for a baby.'

I frown. 'How do you mean?'

'Well, you're more worried about the long-term outcome, aren't you?'

'I suppose. But how does that make it different? And different better? Or different worse?'

'Just ... different,' says Tom. 'It's a bit like every time you have sex you're buying a scratch card, and you wait a few weeks to see if you've won. You try not to think of it like that but it drives you mad. I mean, if I'd thought every time Barbara and I were doing it that it was for the express purpose of having a baby, I don't think I'd have been able to do it half of the time, if you see what I mean.'

'Er ... not really.'

'You don't just think "bombs away" and then wait a couple of weeks to see if you've got lucky.' Tom gestures towards me with his sandwich. 'You can't. Otherwise you'd just get in there and do your job as quickly as possible.'

'Which you did, right?'

'Well, some of the time, admittedly. But it wasn't like we said "Okay – sex is now for the express purpose of fertilization." We kept doing it – more often than usual, of course, but we just stopped using any sort of protection. That way we thought we could make it more natural. Less – clinical.'

'Which is ironic, seeing as you ended up having to go to a clinic to get pregnant in the end.'

'Whatever,' says Tom. 'But the fact of the matter is, that's what sex is all about. Procreation. And yet when most of us do it, for the majority of the time we take steps to ensure that we don't actually procreate. So when you start actually doing it for real ... I tell you, Will, it's best almost not to think about it.'

I'm not following this at all. 'What do you mean?'

'Well, the first time we did it bareback, so to speak, it was weird, as if the outcome really mattered, like those films you see of spacecraft trying to dock precisely with space stations, and if they don't deliver their precious cargo it's all over. Beforehand, we were quite, er, wasteful, if you get my drift, but all of a sudden it becomes this precious substance that you're afraid to splash around. Who knows if one of your little fellows is going to get through and score? And so you want to ensure you're giving them all the best chance.'

I push my bagel away from me, not hungry any more. 'Please tell me you've finished?'

'Which was just what Barbara would say, funnily enough,' laughs Tom.

'What?'

'Well, you know how you always try to be considerate on the timing front? Making sure that it's good for her, if you see what I mean? Suddenly, that all goes out of the window. There were times when Barbara would just lie there and say, "Don't worry about me — you just go ahead and do what you have to."'

'But that's good, isn't it?'

He shakes his head. 'You'd think so, wouldn't you? But, actually, it kind of had the opposite effect. Took the fun out of it, as it were. Made it quite mechanical. And even though we ended up going down the IVF route, in a funny way, I'd have hated a baby to have been conceived from one of those less involved sessions.'

'Why?'

Tom shrugs. 'I don't know. It just wouldn't have felt right. Rather like winning the lottery with a lucky dip, I imagine. The result's the same, but you'd rather have chosen your own numbers than just let fate decide.'

And while I don't necessarily believe in fate, as I think about my date this evening with Debbie, I do wonder whether I'm going to get lucky. In both senses of the word.

Chapter 11

When I walk into the Anglesea Arms, although I can't say the same about the pub, I recognize Debbie instantly. For some reason, I've been picturing her in her school uniform – a not altogether unpleasant reminiscence – and while I'm a little disappointed to see her dressed normally, she looks just as good in a pair of jeans and a black, tight-fitting jumper.

She's still as flirtatious as ever, greeting me with a kiss on the lips even though we haven't seen each other for over twelve years, and telling me that I look good. I return the compliment, and as we get a bottle of wine and sit down at one of the stripped-wood tables in the corner, I realize that it's good to be back visiting one of my old haunts. Well, two of them.

I tell her about my job, and she seems interested, and when I ask her what she does, she tells me she works as a copywriter in advertising.

'"I'm Lovin' It,"' she says. '"Just Do It!"'

I sit back in my chair and raise my eyebrows appreciatively. 'You wrote those?'

Debbie shakes her head. 'No, I just like them.'

She still smokes, which is the only black mark I can give her, and I find it funny that something we all used to think was so sophisticated and exotic back then should be the complete opposite now. But despite the Marlboro fumes that I have to fight not to constantly wave away from my face, we have a nice evening. So much so that the time flies by, as we spend most of the time talking about who we remember from school, what they're up to now, and who we used to fancy, which of course included each other. And when Debbie admits that she still fancies me now, I start to think that my Friends Reunited subscription was the best seven pounds fifty I've ever spent.

The evening goes so well, in fact, that when Debbie invites me back for coffee, I don't even have to think about it. We even kiss a little at her front gate, and although I can taste the cigarettes on her breath, her tongue is still as agile as it ever was. Eventually, she breaks away, and fumbles in her handbag for her house keys, and I follow her up the path, kissing the back of her neck as she attempts to put the key in the lock.

'I can't get it in,' she giggles.

I nibble her ear suggestively. 'Let's hope that won't be a problem later.'

As we make our way into the hallway, I'm mindful that we haven't actually discussed the real reason why I'm here, and my conscience suddenly gets the better of me.

'Debbie, your "three is better than two" comment . . .'

'Shhh!' She places a finger on my lips, and then replaces it with her mouth, and after a moment's hesitation, I pick her up and carry her into the lounge, trying to ignore the sudden twinge in my back. Still kissing, we collapse onto the sofa, but when I try and raise the subject once more, she shushes me again.

'Why do we have to be quiet?' I whisper, watching Debbie pull her jumper off over her head.

'So we don't wake him,' she says, reaching round to unfasten her bra. 'Let's have a bit of time on our own first.'

'Wake him? Wake who? Your lodger?'

Debbie shakes her head, before jumping up off my lap and unzipping her jeans. 'No, silly. My husband.'

It's as if a bucket of cold water has been poured over my groin. 'Your . . . *husband*?'

Debbie nods. 'He's asleep upstairs, so let's try and keep the noise down. We don't want to get him down here just yet.'

Just yet? I'm still in a state of confusion, but one thing is clear to me – I don't want to get him down here at all. 'You didn't tell me you had a husband.'

She nods towards a framed photograph on the bookshelf, where a tattooed bruiser has his arm round Debbie on a beach somewhere. He's grinning at the camera, and judging by the way that he towers over Debbie, I'm in serious trouble.

Bollocks. He's going to come downstairs any second and find me about to shag his wife, and when he does, I'm going to get seriously beaten up. I haven't been in a fight since my school days, and I lost that one. And while, admittedly, nowadays I work out on a regular basis, it's my running ability that might come in handier, because from the looks of him, Debbie's husband can more than take care of himself.

'He's a . . . big bloke, isn't he?'

Debbie smiles mischievously. 'I've never had cause to complain. But don't worry. I'm sure you'll measure up.'

The bucket of cold water on my groin has now turned into ice, and as Debbie sits down next to me and wriggles out of her Levis, I stand up awkwardly.

'But . . .'

Debbie pats the sofa next to her. 'It's okay. We've got an arrangement.'

'What kind of arrangement?'

'You know – if either of us wants to bring someone home, we can. Like I said on my profile?' She shrugs, her not-inconsiderable breasts jiggling up and down as she does so. 'I don't think human beings are meant to be monogamous. Do you?'

I do, actually. In fact, I think fidelity is one of the most important things in the world. There's no justification for any kind of arrangement I can imagine, and certainly not the kind of arrangement that Debbie has in mind. And as I look down on my nearly naked ex-classmate, it all suddenly becomes horribly clear to me. It's not broody that she's feeling, but horny. Three might be better than two for Debbie and her husband, but it's not exactly the kind of 'plus one' I was hoping for.

It's time for me to extricate myself – only trouble is, I'm not sure how. What is the etiquette here, exactly? Does one turn down the prospect of sex with another man's wife with a simple 'no thank you', or will that appear a little rude? While Debbie may be particularly attractive, and I haven't had sex for a while, I can't let myself get distracted from the matter in hand. Plus, even if I did decide to go through with it – and I can't believe that I'm describing the act of sex with someone as gorgeous, horny, and quite obviously available as Debbie as 'going through with it' – what if Debbie's husband comes downstairs and decides he wants to watch or, even worse, join in? There's only one man that I want to see me having sex, and that's, well, *me*.

I consider my options, which include either bolting for the door, or, well, bolting for the door, really. 'Debbie, I'm flattered. Really I am, but . . .'

I hear a noise behind me and suddenly stop talking, and by the way a huge shadow has just fallen over the sofa, I don't need to turn around to know that it's Debbie's husband, standing in the doorway. As he walks into the room, he extends a hand towards me which I shake, rather formally, and rather carefully, given the fact that he's completely naked, and his hand isn't all that's extended in my direction.

'Hi,' says Debbie's husband, returning my handshake firmly before walking past me and sitting down next to his wife, who proceeds to kneel on the floor in front of him. 'Come and have a go,' he says, beckoning me over. 'If you think you're hard enough.'

'I've told him all about you, Will,' says Debbie, looking over her shoulder at me, before sticking her head in his lap. 'He's excited to meet you.'

And while that is plainly obvious, what's also clear is that now would be a good time to go. I surreptitiously pat the front of my jeans, though the only swelling I'm interested in locating is my car keys in my front pocket, and as Debbie's husband seems a little distracted, probably due to what Debbie's doing with her mouth, I seize my chance.

'May I, er, use your bathroom first, please?' I ask, although I'm probably overdoing it on the politeness front, given what else they're obviously happy for me to use.

'Help yourself,' he grunts. 'Left down the hall, door at the end.'

'Thanks,' I say, and walk briskly out of the lounge. But when I get into the hallway, I turn right instead, run out through the front door, and don't look back.

Chapter 12

It takes a good ten minutes for Tom and Barbara to stop laughing when I tell them the story the following day, possibly because I decide to confess all about my NewFlames experiences as well.

'I meant to tell you to watch out for those scams,' says Tom.

'What scams?'

'It was on *Watchdog* the other night. Big burly blokes from Africa join these dating websites pretending to be beautiful model types, then tell you they're in some kind of trouble, and need some money to get out of it.'

'Thanks for the heads-up,' I say sarcastically, trying to ignore Tom's continuing sniggering. 'So, anyway, I've decided to give up on internet dating.'

'How about speed dating?' suggests Barbara, putting a mug of tea down on the table in front of me.

I shake my head. 'I'd already thought of that. But I hardly think that three minutes is going to be long enough to vet the potential mother of my child.'

'Even though that's twice the time it'll take you to have sex with her,' jokes Tom.

'I could always try and set you up on another blind date, assuming you don't two-time this one the second you meet her,' offers Barbara, heading back into the kitchen to fetch the biscuit tin.

'Thanks, but no thanks. I think I need to do this under my own steam.'

'So what's next?' asks Tom. 'Any other plans as to how you're going to get yourself a family?'

'Well, actually, I've realized that the easiest way is to have you two bumped off. That way I get Jack and Ellie, being their godfather, and all that.'

'Not before my sister,' shouts Barbara from the kitchen.

'You couldn't have her bumped off instead, could you?' whispers Tom. He and Barbara's sister, Jackie, have never seen eye to eye.

'Speaking of sisters, what about yours, Tom?' says Barbara, heading back into the lounge and putting the tin down on the coffee table. 'She's always had a soft spot for Will.'

'Between her ears, sadly,' says Tom.

I stick my tongue out at him. 'No offence, Tom, but . . .'

'But what?' says Tom, helping himself to a couple of chocolate fingers while trying to ignore Barbara's disapproving gaze.

'But . . . Well, she looks a bit like you. A bit too

much. Not that you're not a good-looking chap, of course. But every time I kissed her, it'd be like kissing a female version of you . . .' I shudder.

'Kissing a male one's bad enough,' adds Barbara.

Tom shrugs. 'Fair enough.'

We sit in silence for a while, sipping our tea, until it's Barbara, bless her, who comes up with the idea.

'What about advertising?'

I frown across the top of my mug at her. 'What about it?'

'Have you thought of doing some? To find this woman, I mean.'

'What – some big picture of me up on a billboard next to the M4? I don't think so.'

Tom dunks a chocolate finger into his tea. 'It's not a bad idea, you know.'

'No – it's not a bad idea,' I agree. 'It's a terrible one. Whoever heard of anyone advertising to find someone to start a family with?'

Barbara pulls a copy of *Woman* magazine out from the magazine rack. 'Well here, for a start.' She flicks through and points out a particular article to me.

'"Who Wants to See A Millionaire". What's this all about?'

Barbara takes the magazine back from me. 'It's this guy who can't find anyone to go out with, despite being filthy rich.'

Tom nudges me. 'He must be incredibly ugly, then.'

'So he put an advert in his local paper,' continues

Barbara. 'And the following week, he got around four hundred responses.'

I look at the article again. There's a photo underneath the title. And he is, in fact, incredibly ugly. 'And I suppose he lived happily ever after? Found the woman of his dreams?'

'Or just died happy,' suggests Tom. 'And they couldn't get the coffin lid down.'

'I'm serious, Will. If you're finding this person so hard to track down, why don't you advertise?'

'Where, exactly?' I snort. 'Take out a full-page ad in the papers?'

'No,' says Barbara, slapping Tom's hand away from the biscuit tin. 'Why not start small. Put an ad in the personals section.'

'Personals? What makes you think this is something for the personals? Surely it's more along the lines of "help wanted"?'

Barbara sighs. 'Will, you're looking for someone to have a baby with.'

'Exactly,' adds Tom. 'Can I shag you and get you up the duff? It doesn't get much more personal than that.'

'I suppose so . . .' I say, absent-mindedly scraping at what turns out to be a crack on the lip of my mug.

Tom nips into the kitchen, and returns with a pad and paper. 'Right,' he says. 'What do we think?'

I pick up the newspaper and scan through the ads. 'How much does it cost?' I ask tentatively.

Barbara takes the paper from me and looks at the

bottom of the page. 'Five pounds per column inch.'

'That'll be about a tenner, then, for Will,' says Tom. 'Oh sorry. You mean . . .'

I make a rude gesture at him with a chocolate finger. 'Thanks, mate.'

'They've all given themselves titles at the front,' says Barbara, ignoring our rather puerile banter. 'Look – Lonely Larry, Horny Harry . . .'

Tom smiles. 'It has to alliterate, does it? Now, what word starts with a W, and describes Will?'

I look at him menacingly. 'Don't you dare.'

'Okay,' says Barbara. 'How about Desperate Dad?'

I shake my head. 'No. That makes me sound . . .'

'Desperate?' suggests Tom.

'No – more like I'm already a father, and I'm desperate for something else.'

Barbara sucks thoughtfully on the end of her pen. 'Okay – what about a different approach? Something like "Let Me Be The Father Of Your Children"?'

'Nope,' says Tom. 'Sounds like he wants to be a stepdad.'

'True,' says Barbara. 'What about just "Let Me Father Your Children"?'

'What about "Have My Baby"?'

As Tom and Barbara toss suggestions back and forth, I sit and drink my tea in silence. Eventually, I have to interrupt.

'What if I'm just . . . me?'

Barbara frowns at me. 'How do you mean?'

'What if I just list everything that I've got ready?'

She puts her pen down. 'Don't you think that they might find that a little . . . scary?'

'Why on earth would they think that?'

Tom smiles. 'Barbara's right. Picture it this way. You go out with a girl a couple of times, then drive her back to your place in your child-friendly four-by-four, then once inside, she excuses herself to go to the toilet, only to stumble into the spare room by mistake, which she suddenly discovers is all newly decorated and full of baby furniture. Only trouble is – there's no baby. And then there's you, all chomping at the bit to get her impregnated.'

'What are you saying?'

'Just that a woman might find that a little in-timidating,' says Barbara. 'Like she's just up for a production-line role.'

'Just a womb on legs,' adds Tom. 'The walking womb-ed. A womb with a view . . .'

Once she's sure her husband's finished, Barbara smiles at me. 'Because she'll have no doubt that you're only after one thing. And that's to get her pregnant as quickly as possible.'

'But, surely, if she wants that too then there's no problem?'

'Ah,' says Barbara. 'That's where you're wrong. Because even though she might want it as much as you, or even more, this is a woman you're dealing with. She still needs a little romance. A little wooing. She'll want to feel that this baby is conceived out of love. Not just out of your desire to get yourself in and it out as quickly as possible.'

'So you don't think I should tell her what I'm up to?'

Barbara shakes her head. 'No – that's not what I'm saying at all. I just mean that you need to be a little more sensitive. Not quite so coldly mechanical about the whole process. Like it's some service she's providing for you.'

'How do you mean?'

'This baby's going to be as much hers as yours, don't forget. Maybe even more so. She'll always be its mother. And she'll be doing most of the primary caring. So don't think that thirty seconds of huffing and puffing followed by eighteen years of paying the bills suddenly makes you in charge, just because it's you who's funding the whole venture.'

'Barbara, you make it sound very impersonal.'

'And so do you, Will. That's the problem. And maybe that's why you haven't had much luck so far.'

And as I drive home later, I can't help thinking that maybe she's right.

Chapter 13

I'm out on my usual early evening run when I have
the idea, and although it hits me the moment I leave
my flat and run past the auction house on the corner,
it takes me a good forty minutes – until I'm running
back up my street again, in fact – before I've managed
to convince myself that it's actually a good plan. I rush
through the shower, grab a bottle of beer from the
fridge to steady my nerves and, switching on my laptop,
find my favourites list and click on eBay. Because, let's
face it, who needs to advertise when there's a place
where millions of people are browsing every day?

Almost before the page has loaded in front of me,
I take a deep breath, and click on 'sell'. But as soon as
I've decided that an online auction might be a better
option than a fixed-price sale, I hit my first hurdle:
'Select A Category'. How on earth do I classify myself?
I scroll through the categories on offer, stopping briefly
at the 'baby' section, but it doesn't have a sub-heading
of 'father', so instead I settle on 'everything else'. As my
sub-heading I put 'services', but refrain from putting

'baby' – after all, I want people to find me, and don't want to be buried in between all the other weirdos selling, shall we say, less reputable items.

Choosing my item title is easy – 'Me' – and after an hour or so of careful editing, I'm pretty pleased with my description. For 'Delivery Options', I've replaced 'Royal Mail First Class' with 'natural or caesarean', not knowing if there's a third. Once I've uploaded a photo – the same one I've been using, albeit without much success, on NewFlames – and set my starting price, which I've kept at a pound so as not to exclude anyone, I'm ready to hit 'list'.

It's not that I'm actually planning to take the auction through to conclusion. I'm just looking at it as another area where I can reach the widest possible audience in the quickest possible time. And given the response I've had even when I've sold complete junk on eBay – like the collection of Beanie Babies that a former girlfriend insisted on buying me – I'm pretty confident that the prospect of a *real* baby should get me more than a few enquiries.

I take one last look at my listing: 'Male, thirty, good-looking or not – you decide. Solvent, successful, own business, lives west London. Fertile. Would make ideal father. If you're looking to start a family now or in the near future, and you think we might be compatible, happy bidding. More details available on request.'

Satisfied, I click on 'list your item', and log off. But when I pop round to tell Tom the following afternoon, he evidently doesn't seem to think it's quite as good an idea as I do.

'eBay?'

I nod. 'eBay.'

Tom gives me a look that seems to question my sanity. 'What were you thinking?'

'Why ever not?'

'Well, it's just . . . *eBay?*'

I shrug. 'They seem to sell everything else.'

'Yes, but not –' Tom shakes his head incredulously – 'eBabies. Tell me you haven't done it already?'

I nod. 'Afraid so. Auction ends next Friday night. At midnight, to be precise.'

'Just when all the drunks get back from the pub,' laughs Tom. 'Brilliant timing, Will.' He walks over to the PC on the desk in the corner and switches it on. 'Show me, then.'

I take a seat in front of the screen and log on, click onto my listing, and then swivel the screen round so Tom can see it.

'You idiot,' he says, staring in disbelief as my picture slowly loads. 'What on earth made you think this was a good idea?'

'Well, er, you did, actually.'

'Me? How on earth do you work that out?'

'Ages ago. When you were banging on about those old clothes you sold because you'd grown out of them.'

'They'd shrunk. I hadn't grown out of them,' says Tom crossly.

'Whatever. "People will buy anything on eBay," you told me. Well, I've decided to put that to the test.'

'Put what to the test?' asks Barbara, following the twins in through the front door. They run over and grab onto my legs, nearly pulling my jeans down as they try and climb up me.

'Will's put himself on eBay,' says Tom.

Barbara does a double take. 'What do you mean, put himself on eBay?'

'He's selling his, er, seed,' Tom keeps his voice low to prevent the twins from overhearing.

'There's not a photo, is there?' says Barbara, aghast.

'Well, actually . . .' I lean down and tickle Jack and Ellie, which has the desired effect of getting them to let go of my trousers, then they run off, giggling, into the conservatory.

Barbara walks over to where we're standing and elbows Tom out of the way. 'Do I really want to see this?'

'It's a photo of me. Not my . . . you know.'

'Thank goodness,' says Barbara, reading through the listing on the screen. 'But do you really think people are going to be on here looking for that kind of thing?'

'I don't care. Apparently, a lot of things that people purchase on here are impulse buys.'

She looks up from the screen. 'So you're hoping that some poor girl is going to be looking on here for a pair of Jimmy Choo's, but instead she sees your photo, and suddenly thinks to herself, "I know. I'll put a bid in. He seems like the kind of guy I want to tie myself to for the rest of my life on a whim."'

'Well, when you put it that way . . .'

'What other way is there to put it?' asks Barbara.

'But I don't really want any money. I just want to see what the interest is, and then I'm going to withdraw before the finish, as it were.'

Barbara shakes her head. 'There's something missing from your listing.'

'Which is?'

'The fact that you're insane!'

'I prefer the term "enigmatic".'

'Have you got any bids yet?' asks Tom.

I hit 'refresh'. 'No. It hasn't even had that many hits. I mean, it's only been on the site for—'

'Yes you have,' interrupts Tom, pointing at the screen. Sure enough, there's a 'one' in the bids column.

'Click on it,' says Barbara, excitedly. 'See who she is!'

'No, I don't want to . . .'

'Just do it,' says Tom, grabbing the mouse and clicking through onto the 'bid history' section to reveal the bidder's name. 'Here. Opening bid – one pound. Bidder – David69.'

As Tom starts to snigger, I wonder whether I've read it correctly. 'David69? That doesn't sound like a—'

'It's a bloke!' says Tom. 'You haven't put "women only" on your listing.'

'I didn't think I'd need to.'

Barbara puts her arm round my shoulders. 'Well, don't you think you'd better? It's legally binding, this auction, you know, particularly once they've paid for your, er, services. And besides, you don't want anyone leaving you bad feedback.'

'Particularly when you won't sleep with him on the first date,' laughs Tom.

Chapter 14

Today gets off to the worst possible start. I'm sorting through my post at home, and even though it's not Valentine's Day yet, I'm excited to find what appears to be a card amid the usual collection of bills and junk mail. But when I rip open the envelope and peer inside, instead of the lovey-dovey message I'd been expecting, it's Anita's wedding invitation.

For a minute, it occurs me to rip it into tiny pieces and throw it out of the window, but that would be childish – not to mention littering – so instead, I just hold it up to the light and examine it suspiciously. Why on earth has she invited me to see her get married to someone else? Surely I wasn't so bad to her when we were going out that this is how she wants to get her revenge, by proving to me that she is, in fact, marriage material, and I'm the one at fault for not seeing that when we were together.

'Your Anita?' says Tom, when I call him for advice.

'Of course my Anita. How many other bloody

Anitas do you know? Why on earth would she want to invite me to her wedding?'

'Same reason she's invited Barbara and me,' says Tom. 'Because she wants to have her friends there.'

I can't quite understand why Tom doesn't see this as an issue. 'But ... we went out. As a couple. Together.'

'Well, maybe she thinks you're over her now, and getting on with your life?' suggests Tom.

'I am.'

'Yeah, right. That's obvious, given the way you're reacting.'

I put the phone down, and stare at the silver-embossed invitation jealously, still unable to believe that Anita's actually going through with it – with someone else, that is. I know deep down it's just an ego thing: men never want to think that their exes are having a better time – and especially better sex – with their latest boyfriend. As far as we're concerned, ever since we split up, their life has been one long episode of longing and regret, unfavourably comparing every man they've had the misfortune to sleep with since to how great it used to be with us. So the realization that, actually, they might like this new boyfriend more than they did us, and in fact, like them enough to marry them, is pretty hard to take.

Even though I don't know what I'm trying to achieve, I pick the phone up again, and dial Anita's mobile number. When she answers, I feel a twinge of guilt, but I can't help myself.

'Hi,' I say. 'It's me.'

There's silence for a moment, and then Anita's voice comes back on the line.

'Will?'

'Who did you think?'

'Sorry, Will. It's just, well, you're not "me" any more. If you see what I mean. I've got another "me" now. As you well know.'

'Oh. Of course. Mark.'

'*Mike*!' says Anita, the irritation plain in her voice.

'Mike. Sorry.'

There's a pause, and then, 'So?'

'So I was phoning to ... Well, I got my post this morning, and I was, well ...'

'Oh, you got the invitation?' says Anita. 'They're nice, aren't they?'

I look again at the silver-embossed card, noting the weight of it in my hand. In truth, I hadn't even noticed the design.

'Yes. It's lovely. Very professional.'

'Mike had them done at work,' says Anita proudly.

'What is he – a printer or something?'

'No,' says Anita. 'He's a merchant banker.'

'A merchant banker?' Or something like that, I think. 'That's ... impressive.'

'Isn't it just?' says Anita. 'So I hope you're not

phoning up to say you can't make it. Like I said, it'd mean a lot to me, well, Mike and me, if you could come. I'm inviting Tom and Barbara, so at least you won't be there on your own.'

There on my own? Bloody cheek. What makes you think I'll be there on my own? And what exactly would it mean to you, I wonder, if your ex-boyfriend appears at your wedding? Are there going to be any of your other exes there, or is it just me who qualifies for the humiliation due to my length of service? And what about Mike's ex-wife? Will she be there? Is it going to be some kind of sick parade of the runners-up in your emotional sweepstakes? The ones who fell at the final hurdles? And what the hell would it mean to Mike? Who, unless I'm very much mistaken, I've never met?

And at that instant, I feel something change inside me. Something bristles. If her game is to rub my nose in it, then I'm damn well going to play her at it.

'No – I just wanted to ask if I could, er, bring someone?'

'Bring someone?' says Anita. 'I didn't realize you were seeing anybody.'

I try and see if I can detect any malice in that, but there isn't any. And immediately I feel guilty. Of course there isn't. Why would there be? Anita's not a malicious person. At least, she wasn't when we were dating, so unless going out with a merchant banker suddenly turns you . . .

'It's just that you haven't put "plus one" on the

invite, and I didn't want to turn up with someone without . . .'

'No,' says Anita. 'That's fine. Do I know her?'

'I don't think so,' I say enigmatically. And I'm not lying, of course, because I don't know her either.

'What about Kate?' says Jen, when I explain my dilemma to her later.

'Kate? Along-the-corridor Kate?'

She nods. 'Why don't you ask her?'

I look at Jen across the reception desk. 'And why, exactly, would I want to ask Kate?'

'Because you fancy her?'

I feel myself start to blush. 'And why on earth would you think that?'

Jen shrugs. 'No reason. Apart from the fact that I've seen your occasional attempts to accidentally bump into her by the water cooler. Or how you sometimes coincidentally time when you go home so you can ride down in the lift with her. Or the fact that you're always wanting to use the photocopier when she does.'

'Okay, okay. I get your point.'

'And what do you ever need to photocopy anyway?'

'Lots of things.'

'Such as?'

'Er . . . confidential stuff. Client stuff, actually.'

'So, does she have a boyfriend?'

'No. I mean, I don't know. I've not asked her.'

'Want me to?'

'Don't you dare.'

'But you admit you're interested.'

'Well, she seems very . . . pleasant.'

Jen shakes her head. 'Pleasant. Which is why you practically drool whenever she walks past.'

'Anyway, what's your point?'

'My point, Romeo, is that it's Valentine's Day tomorrow. So if ever there was a time for a grand romantic gesture, it's now.'

'So what do I do? Just go up to her and say, "Are you doing anything on Valentine's Day?"'

Jen rolls her eyes. 'Nope. Just use your imagination.'

'My imagination. Right.'

And as I sit in my office, wondering what on earth to do, I begin to question whether I've actually got any.

I get into work early the next morning, determined to put my plan into action. I've stolen the idea from one of my clients – Stephen, the trader, in fact – who I remembered told me it was how he finally got his future wife to go out with him. So a couple of hours later, I just happen to be hanging around reception and talking to Jen when a delivery arrives for Kate. Jen buzzes through to her, and as she walks up the corridor, she breaks into a huge smile.

'Roses. How lovely.'

'You lucky thing,' says Jen, handing them over a little reluctantly. 'All I got was a card. Are they from your boyfriend?'

'I, er, don't have a boyfriend,' says Kate.

'Who are they from, then?' I ask, trying not to sound too interested.

'I don't have a clue,' she says, inhaling the flowers' scent, which is wafting around the reception area.

'Perhaps you've got a secret admirer?' suggests Jen.

'Perhaps,' says Kate, turning to walk back towards her office.

'There's a note,' I say suddenly, and a little too loudly, causing Kate to look at me strangely. 'I mean, is there a note?'

Kate examines the bouquet closely, and finds the tiny envelope, which must have slipped in between the stems. She slits it open and reads the message to herself.

'Come on. What does it say?' asks Jen.

Kate hands the note to Jen. '"From your secret admirer,"' she reads. '"And if you want to find out who the flowers are from, meet me in Paradise at eight o'clock."' She turns the card over in her hands, as if checking for any clues, then hands it back to Kate. 'How exciting.'

'"Meet me in Paradise"?' says Kate. 'That sounds romantic. I wonder what it means?'

'It's a restaurant. On Paradise Street,' I say quickly. 'I believe. Isn't it, Jen?'

'That's right,' says Jen. 'I keep asking Josh to take me there, but he doesn't seem to think it's my kind of place.'

'That's probably because it's quite expensive,' I say.

'Not that you're not worth . . . I mean, he probably doesn't want to spend . . .'

As Jen crumples the envelope into a ball and throws it at me, Kate makes to carry the flowers off towards her office, before turning round and walking back towards reception. She fixes me with a quizzical expression.

'Will, can I ask you something?'

I swallow hard, and try to keep my voice even. 'Sure. Fire away.'

'These flowers. And the note.'

'What about them?'

'You don't think they're a little . . . creepy?'

'No way,' I say, after leaving what I hope is a long enough pause to suggest that I've given her question the proper consideration.

'I mean, it could be some weirdo. He knows my name, where I work . . .' Kate shudders, and regards the flowers with suspicion.

Ah. In my experience, there's a fine line between being romantic and stalking, and I'm starting to worry that I may have crossed it. 'No way. I'd look at it as more of a grand romantic gesture. I mean, that's not a cheap bunch of flowers. So even if he is a weirdo, he's a rich weirdo. I mean, not that I think he's a weirdo. Or that if he was, it'd be okay if he was rich . . .'

I look across to Jen for help, conscious that I'm digging myself into a very deep hole. Fortunately, she pulls me out of it.

'No. Romantic is what it is,' agrees Jen. 'Absolutely.'

Kate takes another look at the bouquet, which is quite impressive, even if I say so myself. But then, at fifty pounds, it'd better be. 'So I should go?'

'Definitely,' says Jen. 'If you want to find out who your secret admirer is, of course.'

'I'm not so sure,' says Kate, chewing nervously on her lower lip.

'Oh go on,' says Jen. 'If someone liked me enough to go to all this trouble, I'd be there like a shot.'

Kate thinks about this for a moment or two. 'Maybe you're right. It is quite exciting, I suppose.'

With that, she turns and heads back towards her office, smelling the bouquet as she goes. And as Jen winks at me from behind reception, and I mouth 'Thank you' back at her, I start to feel a little excited myself.

I'm at the restaurant by seven forty-five, and I've chosen a table with a view of the window, just so Kate's arrival doesn't take me by surprise. The place is pretty full, and as I sip my fizzy water apprehensively, I realize I'm the only single guy in a restaurant full of couples. But as I look at all the loved-up diners around me, none of whom look like they're on a first date, I start to have serious doubts that Kate'll turn up. Going on a blind date is bad enough, but a blind date on Valentine's Day? How desperate do you have to be? And even though – thanks to Jen – I know that Kate doesn't have a boyfriend at the moment, she doesn't look like she's the desperate type.

By eight-fifteen, I'm on my third bottle of San Pellegrino, and trying to look as relaxed as possible, even though it's quite obvious to everyone else in the restaurant that I'm in serious danger of being stood up. I try and tell myself that Kate's just being 'fashionably' late, and remember Barbara's comments that she's probably making herself look beautiful, and that I mustn't resent it when she arrives. Trouble is, my bladder's starting to resent the amount of water I've drunk while I've been sat here, and yet I can't risk getting up to go to the toilet in case Kate turns up, sees the empty table, and leaves without me even knowing she's been here.

Finally, when I'm just about to give up hope, I see her peering through the window, and fix her with my best smile, although when I catch sight of my reflection, and probably due to the litre-or-so of water I've consumed, it looks a little pained. I'm not that hard to spot – after all, every other table has twice the number of people sitting at it – but as Kate catches sight of me, instead of returning my smile, she appears to duck down out of sight. I sit there, puzzled, for a few seconds, then stand up, before sitting back down again, wondering whether perhaps she might just be fixing her make-up outside before coming in to join me. And if she is just fixing her make-up, then it'll look pretty bad if I go out to see where she is. I don't want to appear impatient, after all.

After a further quarter of an hour, it occurs to me that maybe she hasn't ducked down to fix her make-up. No one takes this long to fix their make-up – not even clowns. But if she's not fixing her make-up, where on earth is she? I'm pretty sure she recognized me through the window and, judging by the look on her face, she seemed pretty surprised. Maybe it wasn't surprise, I tell myself, but excitement, and in her enthusiasm she's rushed towards the restaurant door and has tripped over the kerb, and now might be sitting on the pavement outside, nursing a broken ankle. And maybe it's because I've overdosed on fizzy water, and the carbon dioxide has affected my brain, but, suddenly, this seems like the most rational explanation of all.

I think about going outside to see if she's okay, but just as I'm about to leave the table and walk towards the door, a couple come in. After a brief conversation with the waiter, they're shown to an empty table. And I remember that they're not the first couple to have come through the door in the last fifteen minutes. Surely, if Kate had been sat outside in pain, someone would have seen her as they came in, and said something to the waiter? Or helped her inside, even, and called an ambulance. And I'd have seen if an ambulance had come to pick her up.

Ten minutes later, and with still no sign of her – or an ambulance – I take a deep breath and stand up, as it's obvious that that's what she's done to me. Besides, by now, I'm the desperate one – desperate for the toilet, that is, as I've got through the best part of two litres of water. I sprint-walk to the Gents, then pay the bill, and beat the path of shame to the door, past all the sniggering couples, and out into the chilly February evening.

I fob Jen's 'So?' off with a 'Too busy to talk' when I come in the next morning, and manage to avoid both her and Kate for the next few hours by shutting myself in my office and refusing to answer the phone, and it's not until I'm heading out to meet Tom for lunch that I bump into either of them. In the worst possible way. Because Jen spots me trying to sneak down the stairs, and comes out from behind her desk to try and intercept me, at the exact moment that Kate walks past.

'Don't think you're getting away with it so easily,' says Jen.

'Getting away with what?' says Kate, a little alarmed.

Jen glances mischievously in my direction. 'Last night, of course.'

'Oh. I er . . .' Kate stammers, and I can tell she's wondering whether Jen knows what happened and is accusing her of standing me up. I can also tell that Jen thinks that it must have gone well, because I've been avoiding talking about it this morning, and so Jen is trying to put me on the spot.

'So, who was it?' Jen winks at me, making sure Kate can't see, and obviously assuming she's doing me a favour. 'Tell all . . .'

Kate seems a little relieved that Jen doesn't actually seem to know. Which is not how I'm feeling. 'Oh. No,' she says, pointedly avoiding my gaze. 'I, er, didn't go, in the end.'

'No?' Jen suddenly looks a little embarrassed. 'Why ever not?'

'Kate's said she didn't go, Jen. No need for the third degree. Just drop it.'

There's an awkward silence as Kate hits the lift button and stares fixedly at the LCD panel, waiting for it to arrive. When Jen mouths 'You didn't tell me' accusingly in my direction as she moves back behind the reception desk, I just shrug, then walk slowly down the stairs, leaving a suitable amount of time for Kate to have left the building before heading out into the street.

Tom's already waiting for me in All Bar One and, like the mature father-of-two he is, he makes a face at me through the window when I walk past. When I break my usual don't-drink-at-lunchtime rule by ordering a pint of lager, his expression changes to one of concern.

'What's up with you? No eBabes locked in a bidding war over you yet?'

I sigh, and swallow a huge mouthful of beer. 'This is all one big joke to you, isn't it?'

'Sorry, mate. It's not a joke. Although parts of it are funny, you have to admit.'

'Tom, you've obviously forgotten what it's like to be single.'

'More's the pity,' he says, gazing towards a nearby table, where a couple of good-looking twenty-something women are giggling to each other.

'I'm serious,' I say, clicking my fingers in front of his face in an attempt to get his attention. 'It's all right for you – you've got company whenever you want it. Me? I'm sick and tired of going through the same old find/fancy/meet/go-out-with process, only to find that it all comes to an end because I ultimately work out that we're incompatible. And what is incompatibility? It's not like, say, going out with a vegetarian when you like steak. It's finding out you don't like the same things, i.e. each other. Finding you prefer your own company. And look how it affects us single people. You might meet someone, start going out with her, enjoy spending time together, but then you have to make a decision. Is this a female friend who I sleep with, or actually my girlfriend?'

'You have female friends you sleep with?'

'You know what I mean.'

Tom frowns. 'I'm not sure I do, actually. And when do they become a girlfriend, exactly?'

'Ah, well, I've thought about this. It's when you see them every Saturday night. Because Saturday nights are traditionally male nights out. So when you decide to forgo the company of your male friends for your new female one on a regular basis – *voilà*. She's your girlfriend.'

'But you don't have any single male friends. Not any more.'

'Which is why I'm trying to make some new female ones. And without putting myself – and them – through the same old cycle, which ultimately leads to one of us being dumped.' I drain half of my pint in one go, and Tom picks up his and does the same. 'Because there's only one thing worse than being dumped, and that's doing the dumping yourself.'

'I thought it was always better to give than to receive,' says Tom, stifling a burp. 'Apart from where oral sex is concerned, of course.'

'Nope. I'd always much rather be the one who gets dumped. Because, first, it's a really unpleasant thing to have to do to anyone, particularly if you don't want to hurt them; secondly, you've got to come up with a good and plausible reason to be breaking up with them, which can be harder than it sounds; and thirdly, you've got to decide if the agony of the break-up is actually something you want to put the two of you through, given your emotional state, the time of year, and so on.'

'What's the time of year got to do with it?' asks Tom, glancing hungrily at the menu.

'You have been married a long time, haven't you? There are five key dates,' I say, counting them off on my fingers, 'Christmas, Valentine's Day, your birthday, her birthday, and the summer.'

Tom looks mystified. 'How do you mean?'

'Christmas. No one wants to be alone at Christmas. It's no wonder more suicides happen then than at any other time of year. If you break up with someone at Christmas, there are good points and bad points. The good points? Well, there's only one, really. You save yourself money on their present. The bad points? You don't get a present from them. Plus, they'll always remember you as the person who dumped them before Christmas, which makes you heartless, tight-fisted, or both. Ditto on birthdays. Dump her just after yours, and you'll feel duty bound to give her present back, even though it might be something you like. Dump her just before hers, and again you look like you're callous and tight, plus she'll always remember her birthday as the time you dumped her, giving her an extra reason to tell her friends how heartless you are.'

'And Valentine's Day?'

'Pretty obvious, really. It doesn't matter whether you're being dumped or doing the dumping. That feeling when the postman doesn't pop a card through your letter box is the worst one in the world. And every single single person is desperate to have a date on Valentine's Day. Because if you don't, you'll find yourself stuck at home in front of the telly, where there's always some crappy film on to remind you how great it is to be in a relationship. As you stick your dinner for one in the gas oven, you wonder if you should stick your head in there too.'

Tom takes another mouthful of lager. 'So what's the deal with the summer? I'd have thought someone like you would love the browsing possibilities. Girls, short skirts, walking in high heels, the way every footstep sends a ripple through their—'

'Please, Tom. Summer's the absolute worst, and I'll tell you why in two words: summer holidays. While you, Barbara and the kids are preparing for your two-week jaunt to Florida, anyone who has just been dumped is stuck with either staying at home, or considering booking one of those God-awful singles holidays, which are really just shag-fests for people with terminal acne. At least when you have a girlfriend, you've got someone to go on holiday with.'

Tom looks like he's wilting, although whether it's from my verbal onslaught or through lack of food, it's hard to tell. 'Well, when you put it like that . . .'

'You see, it's not just about the basic physical need to be with someone. Ours is a society that's all about couples. Go to a restaurant and ask for a table for one, and they'll either tell you they're full or seat you next to the toilets. Take a trip to the cinema on your own and people think you're a pervert. Go to the swimming pool without kids in tow, and you're branded a Speedo Paedo. Even your car insurance is more expensive if you don't have a partner. I tell you, there're huge pressures on us to pair up just so we conform with society.'

'But I thought you liked being single? The freedom? The, er, freedom . . .'

'Single's fine some of the time. But the problem with some of the time is that it's not most of the time. And most of the time is when I want to be happy. I like kids, and therefore having a baby will make me happy too. And it also means that I get the mother – and therefore I'm not single any more – into the bargain.'

Tom wags his finger at me. 'But what if you turn out to have nothing in common with the person you have the baby with?'

'Aha – that's where you're wrong. We will have something in common, and it's the best thing there is to have in common. A child.'

'But what about all those things you've talked about in the past? The love of culture. The different interests.'

'Tom, with all due respect, look at you and Barbara. Where did you last go on holiday?'

'Well, er, Center Parcs.'

'And was that because you and Barbara particularly wanted to stay in a log cabin and go swimming every day?'

'No – of course not. The kids love it there.'

'So you didn't think about taking them to Florence instead? Going to visit the Uffizi, for example?'

'Yeah, right,' says Tom. 'I can just see Jack and Ellie loving a load of old paintings and sculptures.'

'And what do the two of you talk about whenever Barbara gets home? Politics? The arts?'

'Sometimes,' says Tom, a little defensively.

'Well, what did you discuss over breakfast this morning?'

Tom thinks for a second. 'Well, it was about Ellie's painting that she'd done at school, and how Jack's in the ninetieth percentile for his vocabulary. Not that you'd know it, though.'

'Precisely. So this life you talk about – it doesn't really exist outside of the kids, does it? Everything you do, everything you talk about, wherever you go as a couple – it's all with the kids in mind. You put your own interests on the back burner because the thing that's most important to you both is those two little angels. And it's going to be like that up until they're eighteen and off to university, I'll bet. Which means that as long as the two of you keep going like this, you're not going to have time to get on each other's nerves, because that's just not an option.'

Tom looks at me, dumbfounded for a moment. 'Ah. But you're forgetting one thing.'

'Which is?'

'We had a lot in common before we had Jack and Ellie. We had a life before them.' Tom scratches his head. 'I think.'

'But that's my point. And that's why what I'm doing

will work. Because even if you did, it's all completely gone by now. It's like these couples who describe their other half as "my best friend". What is all that bollocks? The only reason they say that is because they've become so bloody insular during the whole time they've been together and they've let their real friends, their true friends, fall by the wayside.'

Tom folds his arms. 'That's bollocks, Will. Look at you and me, for example. We still see a lot of each other.'

'Tom, that's because I don't have a family. And you don't have a proper job. And because I make the effort to try and drag you out of the house at least once a week. What would you have done last night, for example, if it hadn't been Valentine's Day?'

'It was Valentine's Day yesterday?' says Tom, his eyes widening in horror.

'You didn't forget?'

'You'd be visiting me in hospital and feeding me through a straw if that had been the case,' says Tom, picking up the menu. 'But, actually, Barbara was too tired to do anything, so we just fed the kids, put them to bed, and collapsed in front of the TV. Like any other night, really.'

'That's exactly my point. A lot of people, when they get married and settle down, lose the will to live. And I don't mean live as in their heart stops beating, but *live*, as in have a life. The family becomes the focus, and the kids fill the gap between the partners. Not that I'm suggesting you and Barbara don't have any interests outside of the twins, you understand.'

'Yes you are.'

'Well, not completely. But you have to admit, it's a lot easier to just keep your head down and deal with your family responsibilities. Why do you think a lot of couples get divorced when the kids leave home?'

Tom almost drops his menu in shock. 'They don't, do they?'

I shrug. 'Probably. And if they do, it's because they realize, when it's finally just the two of them again, that they've got nothing left to talk about. Which is why my approach is the only logical one.'

As Tom stares miserably at the 'specials' board, I feel a little guilty for bringing him down. But I'm right. I know I am. Which is why have to keep on going. However long it takes.

Chapter 15

It's been a week, and my total of new eBay bids so far is a big fat zero. Nothing. Nada. Zilch. In fact, apart from David69, only two people have actually looked at my listing, and one of those, as far as I'm aware, is Tom, so in desperation I've re-listed myself. What's more, NewFlames is proving to be a bit of a waste of money as well, although maybe I'm just a little too wary after my experiences with Sandra and Cat Lover. And with less than two weeks to go until my birthday, I'm starting to feel under a little bit of pressure.

And to tell the truth, I can't understand it. I'm not a bad-looking guy. I don't smell. I'm pretty successful. I've got the sexiest car in the world. And I'm prepared to do the one thing that most women want, apparently. Settle down. Commit. Well, perhaps that's two things. And stay faithful. Three. Anyway, you get my point.

I've even done my research and, apparently, in London, fifty-two per cent of the population my age are women. That's an extra four per cent when compared to us blokes – allowing for, er, uncertainties on both sides, I suppose. So unless an awful lot of men are dating two women at the same time, or there's a much higher proportion of lesbians than gay men, I can't work out for the life of me where on earth all these single women are. Apart from doing other things with their time instead of looking on eBay, obviously.

'You'd think they'd be becoming less choosy the older they get,' says Tom, when I share my concerns with him and Barbara over lunch on Sunday. 'Which is lucky for you.'

'Thanks very much.'

'Why should they be less choosy?' asks Barbara, easily pulling the cork that neither Tom nor I could shift out of a bottle of wine.

He shrugs. 'Once they hit their thirties, women start to worry they'll never meet Mr Right. It's a fact. Time is running out for them, so you'd think they'd leap at the kind of opportunity Will's offering them.'

Barbara fingers the sharp end of the corkscrew, obviously considering where to stab Tom with it. 'Is that a fact?'

'Yup,' says Tom, unaware of the potential impending violence. 'But for a guy, it's completely different. Why tie yourself down now when you can spend the rest of your life dipping in and out of an increasingly desperate female population?'

'Which is why I can't understand why I'm not having more luck,' I say. 'Particularly when I've got a trump card.'

Barbara looks at me strangely. 'Which is?'

'Well, what's the one thing that you women always complain about in us guys?'

She scratches her head. 'One thing? I'm not sure there's just *one* thing . . .'

'All right, then. The main thing. Before you met Tom, what was the thing you and your girlfriends would always moan about in relation to us blokes?'

'Er . . .'

I'm starting to get exasperated. 'Come on, Barbara. It was our lack of . . .'

'Will, there are so many things. I can't pick one.'

I roll my eyes. 'Begins with C?'

'Cash?' says Barbara, nodding towards Tom.

'Commitment. Our lack of commitment,' I almost shout. 'From the dawn of time, women have moaned about man's lack of commitment. You – you're genetically programmed to be monogamous and faithful, whereas we – well, let's just say we're rather well equipped to sow our seed as widely as we can.'

'Some better equipped than others,' interrupts Tom, making a face by sticking his tongue into his cheek.

'I suppose so . . .' says Barbara, somewhat reluctantly.

'And so that's why I'm going to succeed at this. Because I'm committed.'

'Or need to be,' says Tom, looking up from where he's laying the table.

Barbara sighs. 'It's a fine line, remember, Will. It's lovely that you're not scared of commitment, really it is. But whatever you do, don't go rushing in brandishing a ring from day one, or you'll only scare us off. That'd be like having sex and going straight for the orgasm. What about the foreplay?'

'I don't have time for foreplay, Barbara. That's my problem.'

'You and most men,' she says, flicking her eyes across at her husband. 'I'm serious, though. Don't offer it to us on a plate. We need to feel that we're competing for your affections at least a little bit. Otherwise, we just won't be interested.' She shrugs. 'Ridiculous, I know.'

I shake my head. 'So I can pitch up offering to be everything that you women normally moan about, and it will actually have the opposite effect?'

Barbara nods. 'Possibly. Look at when you buy a house. If you know that it's been on the market for a while, you begin to wonder what's wrong with it. If no one's made any offers, you're not going to be rushing to make one yourself. But if the agent tells you that there's a lot of interest in one particular property, that's only going to make you more interested yourself. It's the psychology. You're asking someone to make a long-term commitment to you, Will. And to do that, she's got to know that she's chasing after a desirable property.'

'But surely it's more about the partnership? What you both bring to the party?'

'And love, don't forget.'

'Barbara, you're wrong. Look around you. Successful relationships are just that – a partnership. Forget love – all you need is affection. All the starry-eyed and passionate stuff just dies out sooner or later, and if you're lucky it's replaced by a working arrangement where the couple is more than the sum of two individuals. And surely that's more likely to be the basis of a successful family unit, rather than all this romantic rubbish?'

'Who on earth gave you that idea?' snorts Barbara. I glance across at Tom, but he's giving me a 'don't you dare' look.

'It's obvious, isn't it?' I say, rearranging the spoons that Tom always puts down the wrong way round. 'Sometimes, decisions you make because of "love" are the most illogical, emotional ones, and therefore by definition not necessarily the right, or most sensible, ones. Whereas decisions you make out of practical necessity are so much better, because they keep the emotion out of it.'

'Well, maybe, but . . .'

'So that's all I'm doing. Starting the partnership part early. Bypassing all the emotional stuff – which, let's face it, is a bit of a waste of time anyway – and making sure the arrangement is rock solid in the first place.'

'That's ridiculous!' says Barbara, heading back into the kitchen.

But I know it's not ridiculous. I spend half my time discussing it with my clients, and they all tell me the same thing.

'And in actual fact, one of the big problems a lot of couples have is because the men struggle to deal with the change in status. I won't, because there won't be any change.'

Tom finishes laying the table and pours himself a glass of wine. 'What change in status? What are you talking about?'

'Well, think about it. For years, it's just been you and her, right? And so, hopefully, you've been the biggest priority in her life up until then. Then along comes this little bundle of noise, and suddenly your place in the pecking order is bumped down by one. Or two, in your case.'

'You're joking?'

'Nope. Watch this. Barbara?'

She pops her head around the kitchen door. 'Yes, Will?'

'If it was a choice of saving Tom's life, or saving Ellie and Jack's, what would you do?'

Barbara looks weirdly at Tom, then back at me. 'What on earth are you asking me that for?'

'Just humour me.'

'Well, Ellie and Jack's, of course.' Barbara shakes her head then disappears back into the kitchen, muttering to herself.

'See?'

Tom stares blankly at me. 'See what?'

'Well, let me turn that round. What would your answer be?'

Tom shifts uncomfortably. 'What? My life or the kids'? The kids', of course.'

'Nope. The twins', or Barbara's?'

'Er . . .'

Tom hesitates, and I see that he's starting to get it. 'And let me put it to you another way. That parachute jump I got you for your thirtieth.'

'What about it?'

'We asked Barbara if she wanted to come too, remember?'

'And she chickened out. So what?'

'She didn't chicken out, Tom. She made a decision. She'd done one before, right?'

He nods. 'Before she had Jack and Ellie . . . Oh.'

'You see? A man will risk his life for fun. A woman will only risk hers if absolutely necessary. And that's the difference between most mothers and fathers. But me? Once I have this baby, that'll be my last jump for a long, long time.'

Tom grins. 'You may be right there,' he says. 'But just remember, as much as we love having the kids, it's not all "proud parents at sports day", you know.'

'I'm aware of that.'

'In fact,' he lowers his voice, 'there are times when it can be quite draining.'

'And how would you know?' interrupts Barbara. 'You only get them for a few hours a day.'

Tom ignores her and carries on. 'For example, every morning you have the battle to get them up, washed, dressed, and then you've got to try and get their breakfast down them, rather than down the front of your shirt, and all before you can even think of getting yourself anything more than a rushed cup of coffee. And you can forget your fancy clothes and designer suits. It's more important that whatever you wear is wipe-clean.'

I nudge him with my elbow. 'And there's me thinking that the reason your only suit is so shiny is just because it's old.'

'Well, it's hardly because he wears it to the office every day,' says Barbara.

Tom ignores us. 'And then at night, you come home knackered, and they still want to play some inane game with you, or show you an unintelligible squiggle that they've drawn at school, when all you want to do is collapse in front of the TV with a large glass of wine.'

'Maybe so . . .' I say, as Barbara rolls her eyes at me.

'And every weekend, when you're desperate to have a lie-in, or just read the paper in peace, you get woken up at some ungodly hour to play hide-and-seek, or read them a story that you've read them a million times before. And then it's a forty-eight-hour marathon of trying to keep them entertained, especially if you're stuck indoors if it's raining, or you end up going to some child-infested café where you can't move for buggies, or even hear yourself think above the screaming that's coming from the ball-pit.' By now, he's getting quite animated. 'And holidays? Forget two weeks of luxury in the Maldives. You have to go ahead and book some child-friendly hotel, which generally means adult *un*friendly, and where you don't dare swim in the hotel pool because the water's a strange yellow colour, and you're pretty sure what's causing it. Plus, when they get to school age, you have to go away at the same time as all the other parents and their kids, which not only costs you an arm and a leg but means being stuck on a plane for three hours with a hundred or so *other people's children*, which is so unpleasant that there are times when you'd actually consider it a relief if you crashed, and even when you get there you can't relax – a trip to the beach turns into some nightmare scene from *Lord of the Flies*. And then, for the next ten years, you're tied into a succession of theme-park holidays where you have to pretend that chugging round in a large plastic teacup at five miles per hour in the Florida heat, accompanied by some would-be child molester in a mouse costume, is the most fantastic thing you've ever done. By the time you realize that it's cost you the price of a good meal for two at a London restaurant just to buy burger and chips for the four of you, it's too late; you're sucked into a Disneyesque nightmare from which the only escape is when they become surly teenagers . . .'

Eventually, Tom runs out of steam, and takes a huge gulp of wine, much to my and Barbara's relief.

'I, er, didn't know you felt so strongly,' I say.

'Nor did I,' adds Barbara, looking at her husband strangely, before walking back into the kitchen.

'But don't get me wrong,' says Tom, topping his glass up. 'Having said all that, I wouldn't change them for the world. I just want you to know the reality of the situation.'

I shrug. 'All that doesn't matter. This is something I definitely want to do. Whatever the cost.'

Chapter 16

Today is Barbara's birthday, and tonight, as is customary on this annual occasion, Tom is taking her out to
dinner. Their babysitter has cried off sick, and rather
than Tom and Barbara cancel their one night out of
the year, I've offered to come round and look after
the twins. To my surprise, Barbara has agreed, and I'm
sitting in my office trying to work out what I'm going
to do with them later, when Jen rings through.

'Will, I've got Lisa on the phone for you. She says
it's an emergency. Again.'

Lisa was one of my first clients, and I tend to see her
regularly every few weeks now. She's about ten years
older than me, not unattractive, and desperate to settle
down, but with a bad habit of always going for the
wrong men. To use a technical term, she's a 'humpty
dumpty' – the men she meets just want to hump her
and dump her – but she'll typically fall head over heels
within the first week, meaning that they can't get rid of
her that easily, and so resort to treating her badly in an
attempt to try and get her to leave them. Ironically, in

many ways, her dilemma and mine are the same, except I come from the 'dumping' side – which is probably what gives me such a good insight into what she's going through.

I look at my watch, conscious that it's lunchtime, and I'm hungry. Lisa's calls usually take the best part of an hour. 'No worries, Jen. Put her through.' There's a click, and then I hear a sniff at the other end of the line.

'Will Jackson.'

There's another sniff. 'Will, it's Lisa. I need you.'

If only those words were uttered by someone else. 'What's the problem?' I say, struggling to keep the words 'this time' from the end of the sentence.

'I just ... It's ...' is all that I hear, before Lisa starts crying down the phone.

'What time can you get here?'

'I'm just outside now,' she says, in between sobs. 'Two minutes?'

I sigh, trying to ignore my rumbling stomach. 'Fine. Tell Jen to send you straight in when you get here.'

Almost as soon as I've put the phone down, there's a knock on the door, and a red-faced Lisa comes in and makes her way automatically towards the couch. Even if I hadn't just spoken to her, it'd be obvious that she's been crying.

I walk over and shut the door behind her, and I'm just about to tell her to take a seat when I see she's already assumed the position. I reach into my desk drawer for the box of tissues, hand it to her, and sit down in my chair.

'So,' I say, 'do you want to start at the beg—'

'Richard and I might be breaking up.'

Oh well. Start at the end, then. 'What makes you think that?'

'A couple of things he's said recently.'

'Such as?'

'That he needs some space. Some time on his own. And how he loves me, but he's not "in love" with me.' She dabs at her eyes with a tissue. 'What does that mean?'

Ah. Lisa and Richard have been together for nearly six months, and, despite her regular appearances here during that time, six months is a record for Lisa ever since I've known her. And there was me thinking that maybe this one had some legs.

I shake my head. 'Lisa, you need to think carefully about what he's said. You love him, yes?'

She nods enthusiastically. 'Yes. Of course.'

'So, technically, given that fact, and the fact that he's said he loves you, then the two of you are actually "in love", wouldn't you say?'

Lisa frowns. 'But he says that he isn't.'

'And so what does that mean?'

'That . . . he's lying? About loving me?'

I nod, still marvelling at the fact that the easiest approach to this life-coaching lark is just to turn the question back onto the person who's just asked it. 'And do you really want to be with someone who can lie about something so important?'

Lisa helps herself to another tissue from the box and blows her nose. 'Do you think he's going to break up with me?'

'It looks like it.'

'How do you know?'

Because I've used those lines myself in the past, I want to say. Or had them used on me. And this is why I'm qualified to talk about this kind of stuff. I've not learned it from a book, or at any college. This is classic University of Life, Bachelor's Degree in Modern Relationships.

'Lisa, how many times has Richard had you here in tears?'

Lisa shrugs. 'I don't know. Two? Three?'

I open her file and flick through. 'Nine. In the past six months. And that can't be good, can it? Especially for your bank balance.'

'I suppose not.'

'And how many Richards have there been?' I ask, tempted to use the shortened form of his name.

Lisa shrugs. 'But I really thought he was the one.'

'Did you? Or were you just desperate for the next one to be the one?'

'No!' says Lisa defiantly.

I adopt a more conciliatory tone. 'You know what the really frustrating thing is? We sit here and talk and talk about your problems, and just when I think we're making some progress, you go and fall into the same trap again. And do you know what's more frustrating than me giving you the same advice time and time again?'

'No . . .' she says, a little more meekly this time.

'You not taking it. Why on earth do you sit here and agree with everything that I say, and then walk through that door and forget it all?'

Lisa gazes up at me and, for a moment, I think she's in danger of bursting into tears again. She knows the answer as well as I do. Because the real problem is that Lisa is desperate to meet the right guy. But the kind of right guy she's desperate to meet must also be a forty-year-old millionaire, so she can get married and live happily ever after in the style to which she'd like to become accustomed. And the problem with that is that, by definition, forty-year-old single millionaires tend to have rather a lot of choice on the woman front – no matter what they look like. And usually, that choice doesn't tend to favour forty-year-old single women who are blatantly trying to marry a millionaire of their own.

'Maybe . . . maybe I'm just a hopeless romantic?'

'You're telling me.'

'But I just want to be happy.'

'Lisa, you say that. But you've got this weird idea of happiness.'

'How do you mean?'

'Because you're . . . objectifying it. Happiness isn't

something that you can buy, or get off the shelf. Happiness is a state you achieve through a set of circumstances. Not through a cheque book.'

Lisa stares at a spot on the floor. 'But I know I could never be happy with someone who's . . .'

'Poor? Why ever not?'

'Because they couldn't ever give me what I want.'

'Which is?'

'Like I said. To be happy.'

'And what will that person give you, to make you happy?'

'A big house. Two cars. Nice holidays.'

'Lisa, those are all very material things. And trust me, while you think they might be the key to your happiness, there'll come a time when you realize that those things are just . . . things. And not what life's about.'

'But they'll help to numb the pain . . .'

'Of what? A bad relationship?'

'I suppose so.'

'Well, why not do something radical and go for a good relationship instead? That way, there'll be no pain to numb.'

Lisa blows her nose loudly. 'There's always pain, Will. You just need to know how to control it.'

And as Lisa talks, I start to feel strange. Empty, even. And I don't mean in a haven't-had-lunch-yet kind of way, but it's more of a hollow feeling deep inside me. For a while, I can't quite put my finger on why that is, and then, suddenly, I realize that it's because as I'm sitting here, trying to advise her, I'm starting to have doubts myself. Not about my advice, but about how I'm trying to achieve what I'm trying to achieve. Because Lisa just wants to be happy. And she's fixated on the one thing that she thinks will make her happy. But in order to achieve that, she's prepared to sacrifice an awful lot else – maybe too much, in fact. And maybe, like Lisa, I'm in danger of falling into the same trap. And also, again like Lisa, I might not be going about it in quite the right way.

An hour later, Lisa leaves, feeling a little better, I think. I, on the other hand, am thoroughly depressed, not to mention starving, and I've got another appointment at two, so I quickly rush out and grab myself a coffee and muffin from Starbucks. As I'm heading out of the door, clutching my purchases, I spot Emma coming the other way.

'I'm beginning to think you're avoiding me,' she says, looking at the coffee-to-go in my hand.

'Sorry,' I say. 'Not at all. I've just been busy. And no, not with lots of women, before you ask. Well, apart from professionally . . .' I stop talking, conscious that I'm in danger of getting myself into trouble again.

'And how about those two delightful kids? I'm assuming you've not been trusted with them again?'

'Well, actually, I'm babysitting them this evening.'

Emma raises one eyebrow. 'Babysitting?'

'Don't look so surprised.'

She looks at me strangely, as if she's considering something. We're still stood in the doorway, and I have to move out of the way to let a couple of teenagers in. As they mumble what could be either thanks or a threat, I roll my eyes at Emma, and then move to walk out of the door, conscious of the time.

'Will . . .' she says.

I stop and turn around. 'Yup?'

'I was just wondering.' She takes a deep breath. 'Does that offer of a coffee still stand?'

'I thought you didn't like the stuff?'

She blushes a little. 'You know what I mean.'

'Sorry.' I'm a little taken aback. 'Yeah. Sure.'

'Don't sound so enthusiastic.'

'No. I'm sorry. I mean, yes. I'd love to. Buy you a coffee, that is. Or any other drink of your choice. Soft or, er, hard. When's good for you?'

Emma smiles. 'Tomorrow night? Meet me here? Say seven o'clock?'

'"Seven o'clock,"' I say, as instructed.

Chapter 17

I'm sitting on Tom's sofa with Jack to my left, Ellie on my right, some Disney film playing on the TV in front of me, and about two hundred assorted toys and games laid out on the floor in readiness for the end of the DVD. Barbara is upstairs getting changed, while Tom waits by the dining table, sipping a beer and agitatedly looking at his watch approximately every thirty seconds. He's wearing his best suit, or rather his only suit, and it, like him, has seen better days.

After a while he stands up and starts pacing the room, probably as much due to the waistband of his trousers cutting into his stomach as Barbara's apparent disregard for their reservation time, before making for the bottom of the stairs.

'Come on, love,' he shouts. 'We don't want to lose our table.'

'What time is it booked for?' I ask him.

'Eight. But I've told Barbara seven-thirty. An old trick to ensure we get there in time.'

'Does it work?'

He sighs, and looks at his watch again. 'Apparently not any more.'

'Are you sure you don't want me to drive you?'

Tom shakes his head. 'No thanks, mate. We'll get the tube. And besides, you've got the kids to look after, remember?'

'That's okay. I thought I'd just leave them here on their own, maybe with a box of matches and a packet of razor blades to play with.'

Tom smiles mirthlessly. 'Very funny. Now, you know where everything is?'

'Seeing as he virtually lives here, I'd be surprised if he doesn't,' interrupts Barbara, who's come silently down the stairs. She looks fantastic, wearing a tight-fitting evening dress, black shoes, and a simple silver necklace that I helped Tom pick out from Tiffany's the other afternoon.

As we stare at her, open-mouthed, and even the twins do a double take, she blushes slightly. 'What?'

'Nothing,' Tom and I say in unison.

'It's just . . .'

'You look . . .'

'Fabulous?' suggests Barbara. 'I'm still a woman under all those mother clothes, you know.'

'Change of plan,' I say to Tom. 'You stay here. I'm taking her out.'

'No fear,' he says, picking up his keys and escorting his wife towards the door. 'Now, you've got Barbara's mobile number, just in case?'

'Just in case of what? No – on second thoughts, don't answer that.'

'And don't forget the naughty step,' adds Tom, gesturing towards the bottom of the stairs. 'If you need it.'

'How could I? You've made me sit on it often enough.'

'You're sure you'll be all right?' says Barbara, although I fear this is a question directed towards the twins rather than me.

'Of course. You kids enjoy yourselves.'

Tom's already half out of the front door when Barbara turns back to face us.

'Bye, Jack. Bye, Ellie. Mummy'll see you later,' she says, adding the word 'hopefully' and fixing me with a stern look.

As Jack and Ellie don't even glance up from the television screen, I smile confidently at Barbara, before turning my attention back to the twins. Fortunately, they're already in their pyjamas, so that's one trauma I won't have to face. In fact, all I have to do is occupy them for the next hour and, if possible, get them tired enough so they'll go to sleep without any trouble.

As the door slams behind Barbara, I pick up the remote control and hit 'mute'. Jack and Ellie continue to gaze at the screen for a few seconds before turning round and staring at me.

'So come on, kids. What do you want to do?'

The twins look at each other, and then back at the TV. 'Watch television.'

'I'm serious. Don't you want to play a game or something?'

'We want to watch television,' demands Ellie. 'Now.'

'What about I-Spy?'

Jack looks suddenly interested. 'What's I-Spy?'

As I educate the twins in the finer points of the game, before running through a couple of examples, it doesn't take me long to realize that there's a fundamental flaw in trying to play I-Spy with a couple of five-year-olds who have the spelling ability of, well, five-year-olds, particularly when they don't get the concept of 'something beginning with'. As their attention drifts back towards the TV screen, I rack my brains for other games to play.

'What about hide and seek?'

Ellie sighs, as if I'm the child and she's humouring me. 'All right, then.'

'It'll be fun,' I say, although the twins don't look convinced. 'Tell you what – I'll hide, and you count to twenty and come and find me.'

Jack and Ellie look at me and nod, rather reluctantly, it has to be said.

'You can count to twenty?' I take the twins' silence as confirmation, and stand up. 'Okay,' I say. 'Go!'

I leave the two of them looking blankly at each other, and then hurry excitedly out of the front room and up the stairs. After a moment's deliberation, I decide on the perfect hiding place – under Tom and Barbara's bed – and, congratulating myself smugly on my brainwave, cram myself in under the bed frame, trying hard not to sneeze at the dust I disturb. Despite a muttered 'fuck' when I bang the top of my head on one of the handles of Tom's rowing machine, which seems to be where most of the dust is coming from, I make sure I'm completely concealed, and lie in wait.

After a minute or two, and with no sign of either Jack or Ellie, I wonder if I should perhaps leave a foot sticking out, or some other clue as to my whereabouts. After five minutes, I'm thinking that it's taking them an awfully long time to count to twenty. And after ten minutes, I'm doubting whether five-year-olds can actually count that high. And then, above the asthmatic wheezing sound that I'm shocked to discover is actually my own breathing, I realise that I can just about make out the sound of the television.

'Kids?'

There's no answer, and so I squeeze myself out from under the bed, managing to bang my head in exactly the same spot in the process, and make my way back downstairs, brushing the dust off my trousers as I go. When I walk into the front room, I find Jack and Ellie sat in front of the television again, transfixed by what I've heard in the background enough times to know is *The Lion King*.

I squat down between the two of them. 'Couldn't you find me?'

'No,' says Ellie, without even taking her eyes from the screen.

'How hard did you look, exactly?'

Jack and Ellie exchange the briefest of glances. 'We looked everywhere,' insists Jack.

'Well, why don't you two go and hide now, and I'll—'

'We don't want to play any more games' interrupts Ellie.

'Well, what do you want to do?'

'Watch TV,' they chorus.

I look at the two of them in disbelief. On the screen, a hyena who sounds suspiciously like Whoopi Goldberg has just burst into song.

'What's happening?'

'Shh!' says Ellie.

I give up, help myself to one of Tom's beers from the fridge, and flop down on the sofa behind them. But it's not until I've read the paper from cover to cover, and even got halfway through the crossword, that the magical words 'The End' appear on the screen.

'Right,' I say to the two of them, checking the time, and noticing with a start that it's gone nine. 'Bed.'

'But it's not time for night-night yet,' says Ellie, her forehead creasing into a frown. Beside her, Jack is nodding furiously, before realizing he perhaps should be shaking his head, which results in some strange head-circling movement.

'Well, what time do you normally go to bed?'

'Bedtime,' says Jack.

'Very funny,' I say, although the irony is lost on Jack. 'Ellie?'

'We go to bed at ten o'clock,' says Ellie triumphantly, as if she's been saving this particular trump card.

'Oh really?' I know for a fact that Barbara and Tom always put them to bed at eight. I lean forward from my position on the sofa. 'Well, look at my watch. Do you know what time it says?'

The twins both stare blankly at the Breitling on my wrist.

'It's not bedtime yet,' insists Ellie.

'Can you actually tell the time?' I ask her. She shakes her head, and turns her attention back to my watch, twisting the dial and enjoying the clicking sound that it makes. 'How about you?' I say to Jack.

'No,' he admits, biting his bottom lip.

'Well, I'll teach you. You see the big hand is pointing to the number two?'

Jack nods. 'Two.'

'And the little hand is pointing to which number?'

Ellie concentrates hard on my watch. 'Nine?'

'Well done, Ellie. So that means it's what time?'

Jack and Ellie look as if they're about to burst. 'We don't know.'

'Ten o'clock,' I say. 'Which I think you said was bedtime, Ellie.'

She grabs me by the hand. 'Please, Uncle Will. Can we stay up a little more?'

'Please,' says Jack, grabbing hold of my leg.

I look down at them fondly, cute little buggers, and although I'm now worried that I'll be sent to the naughty step for real when Tom and Barbara get home, I cave in.

'All right. Five more minutes. I don't want your mummy telling me off because you're too tired in the morning.'

But by ten-fifteen, neither Jack nor Ellie is showing any signs of being tired whatsoever, and in fact it's me who's starting to flag. We've watched another DVD, played hide and seek with the lounge curtains, and even built what's surely the world's tallest Lego construction in the front room, narrowly avoiding breaking Barbara's favourite fruit bowl when Jack decides to play demolition.

In a vain attempt to relax them a bit so I can get them ready for bed, I switch the TV on again, and sit the kids up next to me on the sofa. I can't face another Disney film, and so rifle through Tom's DVD collection, but decide that the *Die Hard* movies aren't exactly suitable viewing, and as tempting as Tom's compilation disc of his own acting parts is, I'm sure the twins have seen the five commercials and his walk-on in *Doctors* more often than all their copies of *The Lion King*, *Finding Nemo* and *Narnia* put together.

Instead, we settle for some twenty-four-hour cartoon channel that I find somewhere on Sky, and the kids snuggle up against me and settle down to watch. And as

I sit there, my attention focused more on the two of them than on the action on the screen in front of us, I realize absolutely that this is what I want.

The next thing I know, it's eleven-fifteen, and I'm startled awake by the front door closing, and I'm still trying to get my bearings when Tom and Barbara walk into the lounge. Jack and Ellie are asleep either side of me, although Jack seems to have wriggled himself upside down, and Ellie is hanging precariously off the end of the sofa, so Barbara places a finger on her lips and shushes me before she and Tom pick the twins up and carry their still-sleeping bodies upstairs to bed. A couple of minutes later, Tom comes back down and walks into the lounge, where I'm trying to put half a ton of Lego back into the toy box, and wondering why, when I saw it all come out of there, I can't seem to get it all back in.

I look up at him from my position on the floor. 'Good evening?'

'Good evening to you too,' he says, slurring his words slightly.

'No – good evening, as in did you have one?'

Tom nods. 'Yes thanks. For once Barbara didn't call home every half an hour to check on the kids. Which is a first, to be honest.'

'I'll take that as a compliment.'

'Don't. It's only because she couldn't get a signal on her mobile in the restaurant.'

'Ah.'

As Barbara comes back down the stairs, I survey the mess. 'I'll give you a hand to clear up, if you like?'

Tom and Barbara exchange slightly squiffy glances, before Tom puts an arm around my shoulder and escorts me to the door.

'Thanks, Will, but no need.'

'No, I don't mind.'

'We'll do it in the morning,' says Barbara. 'Honestly.'

As I look at him uncomprehendingly, Tom smiles. 'Will, for once, the kids are fast asleep, and there's only one thing we want to do. Which is why we appreciate your kind offer, but we'd really just like you to leave, so we can have . . .'

I stand there, confused, before realization dawns. They're going to have sex. The moment I leave, they're going to pounce on each other like . . . like . . . I don't want to think about it. Tom and Barbara are the closest I've got to having a brother and sister, and the thought of them . . .

'Please, Tom,' I say, holding my hands up. 'Spare me the details.'

'. . . a decent night's sleep,' he continues.

'What did you think we meant?' asks Barbara.

'Well, you know, sex,' I say.

Tom starts to chuckle. 'Will, haven't you been listening? Nowadays, for us, sex is like the Isle of Wight. We remember it being a nice place, but we don't go back there very often.'

'More's the pity,' says Barbara, giving me a hug. 'Thanks again, Will.'

I return the squeeze. 'You are most welcome.'

'So, same time next year, then?' says Tom.

I look at him, expecting him to be joking. 'You're kidding, right?'

Barbara shakes her head. 'Will, you have so much to learn.'

'Why? What's wrong with going out once in a while?'

'This *is* once in a while,' says Barbara. 'It's like we said. And it's not that we don't want to. We're just too tired the rest of the time. Or we know we won't enjoy ourselves, because we're too worried about how the kids are. And to tell you the truth, most of the time, we'd rather be with them, and stay at home knowing they're safely tucked in upstairs.'

Tom nods. 'That's parenthood, Will.'

'Well, it won't be the way I do it.'

And five minutes later, as I'm letting myself in through my front door, I can still hear them laughing at me.

Chapter 18

I spend most of the morning in a state of nervous excitement, and I'm sitting in my office wondering where to take Emma this evening when the phone rings. It's Jen.

'Will, there's a journalist waiting to see you. Something about you putting yourself on eBay?'

A journalist? 'Tell him . . .' Bollocks. Tell him what? 'Er . . . tell him I'm busy.'

'It's a her.'

'Well, tell her I'm busy, then,' I say, a little exasperatedly.

I hear a muffled exchange and then Jen's voice comes back on the line. 'She says she'll wait.'

'Fine. Well, she'll have a long one, then.'

I sit down at my desk, and hurriedly log on to eBay, and when I click on my listing I'm shocked to see it's been viewed approximately twenty times. What's more, there are a series of messages, and when I open them I find they're all from the same woman. Probably the same woman who's waiting outside for me now. 'We're very interested in what you're selling,' is the gist of them, 'and we'd like to do a piece on you.'

I chew the end of my pen anxiously, not quite sure what to do. This has all suddenly got out of hand. I consider asking Jen to sneak me out of the back door with a blanket over my head, but then I realize that I'm overreacting and, actually, this could even work in my favour. Speak to the press now, get it over and done with, and what's the worst that could happen? On the plus side, I might get a bit more exposure, and if it's not quite as flattering as I'd like, then today's news will be tomorrow's chip wrapper, as Tom always says – unless it's one of his acting reviews, which I know he always cuts out, laminates, and keeps in a special box in the attic that only he has the key to.

I pick up the phone to buzz Jen back, and tell her to let the reporter in. A couple of seconds later, there's a knock on my door, and a young, bleached-blonde woman comes in. She's wearing a pin-striped business suit, and carrying a large bag over her shoulder.

'You don't look like a journalist,' is all I can think to say.

She smiles, and hands over her business card, which identifies her as Victoria Baker, freelance. 'What were you expecting?'

I blush immediately. 'I'm not sure, actually. I mean, I just thought that all hacks would be, you know, grizzled, lecherous, chain-smoking old—'

'That's me at the weekend,' she laughs, taking a

pair of glasses out from her inside pocket and putting them on. 'But during the week I like to dress up for the job.'

I ask Victoria to take a seat, but, unfortunately, my office only has the one chair, and the couch for consultations, so I don't know quite where to put her. 'Do you want to lie down?'

'Is that what you say to all the women you get in here?' she asks.

'Well, yes, actually. I find it helps them to . . .' I stop, because I see she's getting her tape recorder out from her bag, and suddenly realize that that could be misconstrued. 'So, who did you say you write for? And how did you get my details?'

Victoria smiles. 'Oh I'm freelance, so anyone who'll pay me, really. And I just happened to see your entry on eBay, and thought there might be a piece in it.'

'So, are you going to interview me, or what?'

Victoria looks at me over the top of her glasses. 'I thought I'd just do a little gentle probing first. If that's okay. Get behind the story. If there is a story, of course . . .'

'Fine,' I say, sitting down. 'Fire away.'

Half an hour later, my head is buzzing, as Victoria's gentle probing proves to be like the Spanish Inquisition. All the while, I'm careful not to say anything that can be misinterpreted or might make me look like I'm a pervert, or worse − if there is anything worse, that is. Eventually, Victoria stops writing and looks up at me.

'So, you do genuinely just want to be a dad? Simple as that?'

I nod. 'Simple as that. But finding the right person is proving somewhat difficult.'

'Join the club.' Victoria sucks the end of her pen for a moment. 'How about . . . No, forget it.'

'What?'

'No, it's probably a silly idea.'

'What?' By now, I'm actually interested to hear what she's got in mind. She is, after all, rather attractive, and maybe she's going to suggest that the two of us go out on a date, and wants me to do some gentle probing of my own. Which I wouldn't, of course, because I'm seeing Emma this evening. But it's a nice thought.

'Well, I was thinking, what if I pitched it as a feature? You know – do a big piece on you. Some papers do a "hunk of the month", and you— Well, "hunk" might be stretching it' – she smiles as she says this – 'but I'm sure I could drum up some interest, if you like. And it'd probably get you lots of dates. Think about it.'

Ah. 'I don't need to think about it,' I say. 'No way. I'm not in this just to meet women. I'm looking to start a family. And I don't quite see how that kind of thing is going to help me.'

'Suit yourself,' says Victoria. 'But it's a numbers game, don't forget. And from what I know about your relationship history—' She stops talking abruptly and stares at her notepad, possibly because she's just seen the look on my face.

'My relationship history? How exactly did you get my details again?'

Victoria shifts uneasily on the couch. 'eBay. Like I said.'

'But my contact details aren't on there. And my relationship history certainly isn't. Who told you?'

Victoria smiles nervously. 'I couldn't possibly reveal my sources . . .'

An hour later, and Tom is buying me lunch by way of an apology.

'How could you have given my details to a journalist? Of all the stupid—'

'I just thought you could do with a bit more coverage. Given your lack of success, and all that.'

For a moment, I consider telling him about my date with Emma this evening, but decide not to. After all, it's only a drink at the moment, and although I'm not at all superstitious, I don't want to jinx it. Besides, I can just see Tom marching into Starbucks and trying to do me another 'favour'.

'And who does she write for, exactly?'

As Tom rattles off a list of mainly tabloid news-papers, I shake my head. 'Thanks, mate. I'd love one of the readers of the *Sunday Sport* to be the mother of my child. I can just picture it now, going down to meet her. And her five other kids and their five different dads.'

'Ah,' says Tom. 'Good point. But I wouldn't worry about it, if I were you. Nobody takes much notice of these things. But leave it to me, anyway. I'll sort it.'

I meet Emma outside Starbucks at seven, as arranged. It's the first time I've seen her out of her uniform, but immediately find myself hoping it's not the last. She's dressed in jeans and a simple white top, and what looks like a snorkel parka, but somehow she manages to make even that seem sexy.

I decide against taking her to Paradise after my experience there the other evening, and instead we stroll over to the White Cross, a pub down next to the Thames. It's a chilly evening, and not many drinkers have braved the night, so we're able to grab the table nearest to the fire.

As per Barbara's advice, I've decided not to mention my baby quest – I don't want to scare her off, after all – so, instead, I tell her about my job, and my life, and my friends. In return, Emma talks to me about how she never thought she'd find herself working in a coffee shop, but she used to be a professional musician, playing the piano on tour for some groups that I've actually heard of, and has decided to go back to college to study to be a music teacher, and so she's working in Starbucks now to pay her way through the course.

'Isn't that a funny choice of job for someone who hates coffee? Surely you've got to at least like the thing you're working with?'

Emma sips her white wine. 'Will – don't take this

the wrong way, but if you had to serve the same thing a hundred times every day, you'd probably end up hating it.'

'I suppose,' I say, deciding not to contradict her, although I seem to remember that Hugh Hefner doesn't seem to have the same problem in the Playboy mansion.

'Do you like hearing about all the problems people come to you with?'

I shrug. 'Not especially. But I like helping them to deal with them.'

'Is that why you went into it? To help people?'

'That's right,' I say, before admitting guiltily, 'Well, that, and the hundred pounds an hour they pay me. But it is very rewarding.'

'You're telling me,' laughs Emma.

And we have a nice evening. I don't get into trouble, or embarrass myself, and Emma seems to genuinely find my jokes funny, even when she tells me she's only five foot one, and I tell her she's the smallest pianist I've ever seen.

Finally, Emma looks at her watch. 'Ohmigod,' she says, standing up quickly.

It's an automatic reaction, but I stand up with her. 'What?'

'The time. It's gone eleven,' she says, noticing for the first time the bored bar staff putting stools on top of tables around us.

'You're not about to turn into a pumpkin, are you?'

Emma smiles. 'No. Nothing like that. It's just ... Well, I ought to be getting home, is all.'

I try to hide my sudden feeling of disappointment. 'I suppose it is a school night, and all that.'

Emma looks at me strangely. 'You could say that,' she says, fumbling in her handbag and retrieving her mobile phone from amongst the lipstick, tissues and various other unidentifiable items that women seem to be unable to leave the house without.

'What are you doing?'

She looks up from the keypad. 'Just calling a taxi.'

'Don't be ridiculous. My car's just around the corner. I'll give you a lift.'

Emma stops dialling, and looks up at me. There's a suspicious expression on her face, as if she's trying to work out whether there's some hidden meaning in my suggestion.

'I don't want you to go out of your way.'

'It's no problem at all. Unless you live in Birmingham, or something.'

'Will, that's very kind of you. But I'm afraid I won't be able to invite you in for coffee.'

I'm slightly taken aback by this. I mean, it's not as if I'd expect to be asked in, and it's certainly not the reason I've offered to drive her home, but to have it flagged up even before we've got into the car seems a little, well, harsh.

'That's okay,' I say, forcing a smile. 'I don't really like coffee either.'

Eventually, and as if she's not sure she's made the right decision, Emma puts her mobile back in her bag, and we head out of the pub and walk round the corner to where I've left the TVR. When I blip the doors open, Emma whistles in admiration.

'A TVR,' she says. 'Nice.'

'You're rather up on your cars,' I say, opening the door for her, and offering my hand as she climbs awkwardly down into the passenger seat. I try not to watch, but I can't avoid seeing a flash of her cleavage as she swings her legs into the footwell. 'Most women, I mean, *people* think it's an E-type.'

Emma shrugs. 'You soon learn the difference between a TVR and a Jaguar when you've got a, er, interest in these things.'

It's a five-minute drive to her house, and we don't talk much on the way, although that's mostly due to the ridiculous noise the TVR's engine makes.

'It's very . . . loud, isn't it?'

'Pardon?'

'I said it's very . . .' Emma reaches over and flicks me on the ear when she sees that I'm just pretending not to have heard her. But as I indicate to pull into her street, and before I've even stopped, she unclips her seat belt. 'You can drop me at the end of the road, if you like.'

'No, that's fine. It's late. I should see you to your door,' I say, hoping I don't sound too much like a stalker.

'I'm more worried you'll wake up the neighbours.'

I pull up outside Emma's house, but leave the engine running, to show that I'm not intending – or expecting – to stay. Unfortunately, this also makes our parting conversation difficult.

'Well,' she yells, 'thanks for a lovely evening.'

'You too,' I reply, at a similar volume.

And it's now that I'm reminded of a further disadvantage of driving a car that Tom refers to as a 'babe magnet' – the deep, figure-hugging bucket seats that hold you in place when you're negotiating a sharp bend at somewhere north of the speed limit are no good when you want to lean over and give your passenger a goodbye kiss on the cheek, particularly when you're further handicapped by a somewhat high centre console that houses both the gear stick and the rather sharp-ended handbrake. As attractive as Emma is, I decide that a visit to the osteopath or even the A&E department isn't worth the effort. Indeed, it's all I can do to turn my body slightly sideways, and I don't want to get out of the car and risk that she'll feel intimidated.

'So . . .' shouts Emma.

'So . . . I'll call you?'

Emma nods. 'That would be nice. But not from the car. Or, alternatively, just come in for a coffee. At work, I mean. Tomorrow?'

'Oh. Of course. Sure.'

'Well, goodnight, then.'

Emma's just trying to locate the door handle, and has

so far only succeeded in opening the window, when a light comes on from inside her hallway.

'Who's that?' I ask, slightly suspicious after my recent evening escapade. 'Don't tell me it's your husband?'

I watch as her front door opens, keeping one foot on the clutch in case I have to make a quick getaway, but after a second or two, a twenty-something girl emerges from the house and walks down the path towards us. She stares at the car appreciatively, and then sticks her head in through the open window.

'Hi,' she says. 'Nice motor.'

'Hi,' I say. 'And thanks. I'm Will.'

'Will, this is Amanda,' says Emma awkwardly. 'She's my, er, baby—'

'Baby sister,' says Amanda, with a grin. 'Nice to meet you, Will.'

Ah. So that explains why Emma won't, or rather, as I'm quick to assume, *can't*, invite me in.

'Everything all right, Amanda?' asks Emma.

'Fine,' says Amanda, the grin not leaving her face. 'Just wanted to say hello. I'll leave you two to say your goodbyes.'

As Amanda skips back up the path, Emma smiles at me one last time, then finally locates the door handle and climbs awkwardly out, and even though I try hard not to look again, I'm treated to a view of her pert denim-clad behind.

I wait outside until she closes the front door safely behind her, then put the TVR in gear and execute a three – well, seven, given the narrowness of the street and the lack of visibility over the bonnet – point turn, possibly waking up any of Emma's neighbours who might still be asleep, and head back home. And as I drive, I do the customary post-mortem of the evening. On balance, it seemed to go well – all apart from the reluctance to invite me in for coffee, or even accept a lift home in the first place, that is. But maybe she's just a little more independent than I'm used to. Or playing hard to get. Or even just being cautious. But whatever it is, I'm intrigued to find out.

Chapter 19

The rest of the week passes fairly uneventfully. Emma's busy at the weekend, and because I don't feel I can quite pry into what she's doing, I settle for a couple of nice conversations with her when I'm in buying my coffee, which I admit has become a little more frequent since the other night. I've still not mentioned our date to Tom and Barbara, and although I feel a little disloyal about this, I want to wait until I've actually got some real news to tell them – assuming I ever do, of course. And besides, they're still giving me more than enough stick on the eBay and NewFlames fronts for me to want to give them any additional ammunition.

The following Monday evening finds me sat round at Tom and Barbara's with the twins perched on my lap. Two months ago, Tom filmed a supermarket commercial, and I'm round here because tonight is, to use his word, the 'premiere'. I'm trying to sip champagne from the glass that Tom's just handed me, which is proving somewhat difficult given the fact that Jack and Ellie are trying to tickle each other, while on the TV in front of us *The Bill* is just about to end. Tom's got the sound on mute, while looking anxiously at the time every five seconds, and suddenly, as the credits begin to appear on the screen, Tom shushes us all loudly.

'Attention please, ladies and gentlemen, boys and girls,' he says, causing the twins to start giggling.

Tom aims the remote control at the DVD player, presses 'record', then un-mutes the sound. With a blast of the familiar theme tune, the final credits roll, and suddenly we're all on the edge of our seats.

As the well-known music starts, followed by various shots of people picking groceries off the shelves with the same amount of pleasure as if they've won the lottery with each can of beans, Barbara nudges me. 'Doesn't look like any supermarket I've ever been in,' she mutters, looking at the spotless aisles, well-dressed, smiling clientele, and the fully stocked shelves.

'Shh!' says Tom, leaning in so close to the TV that he's in danger of falling onto the carpet.

We stare silently at the screen for a further thirty seconds, with Tom becoming increasingly anxious. The commercial's ending soon, and I'm about to ask Tom whether his part's been cut, when he shushes us again, even though no one's actually talking, and announces that this is his bit. Sure enough, we see the briefest sight of Tom pushing a heavily laden trolley through the checkout, screen wife and children in tow. There's a half-second close-up of his smiling face, as if the supermarket's his absolute favourite place to be in the world, followed by an even briefer shot of him patting himself on his back pocket.

The advert finishes, and Tom hits 'stop', and leans back in his chair with a smug expression on his face. Barbara puts her champagne glass down and starts to clap, ironically, I'm sure, and then nudges me to join in.

Tom grins. 'What did you think?'

I make eye contact with Barbara, and then look back at Tom, who's already re-winding the recording so he can watch it again.

'I, er, you were, er . . .' says Barbara.

'. . . very good, I thought,' I say. 'Don't you think so, kids?'

Jack and Ellie don't say a word, but, instead, and showing a wisdom beyond their years, run off to play in the conservatory.

'Oh well,' I continue. 'Never mind. Kids can be the harshest critics.'

'That's first-class acting,' says Tom, nodding at the screen. 'Even though I say so myself.'

'I'll give you that,' says Barbara. 'You hate going to the supermarket.'

I nod appreciatively. 'Show us the action again, mate.'

Tom puts his glass down on the carpet, stands up, takes a deep breath, does a couple of stretching exercises, clears his throat, and then finally pats his backside, which invokes a further round of applause from Barbara and me, although I'm trying to keep a straight face.

'Don't take the piss,' says Tom. 'The auditions were particularly tough.'

'Had to beat off lots of other blokes, did you?' I say, as Barbara struggles to stop herself from laughing.

'Don't be disgusting,' says Tom.

'So, basically, they got a load of guys in a room together, and got them to pat their collective arses?'

'Yup,' he says proudly.

I nod back towards the screen, where Tom has freeze-framed it on his face.

'And what did they pay you for that?'

He grins. 'About five grand.'

I whistle as he tops up our glasses again. 'Beats working for a living.'

'Look who's talking,' says Barbara archly.

But as we settle down to watch the advert again, I can't help feeling a little depressed. We're the same age, Tom and I. We're probably quite similar in the attractiveness stakes, albeit there is more of him than me, although, of course, that's not necessarily an advantage. And yet here he is, with his perfect nuclear family – and even another one on screen – whereas I'll be going home after dinner to my empty flat, and waking up alone in my bed tomorrow morning. Where's the supermarket ad that shows what real life is for a lot of us, featuring the single guy in the 'nine items or less' queue, buying his microwave-ready meal and his box of tissues, or maybe slipping a packet of condoms into his basket at the last minute, just in case he gets lucky on the way home?

I cheer up a little when I kiss the twins goodnight, and as Barbara puts them to bed, I give Tom a hand setting the table, but for some reason, by the time we've finished, there's a fourth place laid out. And when Barbara comes back downstairs, even though I have a strange feeling that I'm going to regret asking, I can't help myself.

'Is, er, someone else joining us?'

Tom and Barbara look at each other conspiratorially. 'Oh. Did I not mention?' says Barbara. 'There's a friend of mine coming.'

'And this would be a female friend, I suppose?'

'Might be,' says Tom.

'Oh great,' I say, with as little enthusiasm as I can muster. 'Another blind date.' My mind suddenly flashes back to my coffee-shop tug-of-war, and it occurs to me to go and get my coat, but Barbara's cooking lasagne this evening, which happens to be my ultimate favourite. Now I come to think of it, that's probably why it's on the menu – to make sure that I stay.

Barbara looks at me guiltily. 'Now don't be like that, Will. Her name's Sarah, she's divorced, and—'

'And what's wrong with her? Apart from the fact that, being divorced, she's probably going to be extremely bitter, and hate all men on sight?'

Tom hands me a glass of wine. 'Why do you have to assume there's something wrong with her?'

'Because you've invited her here. This evening. On an obvious set-up. What is it? She's only got one leg – and even that has a fat ankle? And please don't tell me she's got a nice personality.'

Barbara holds up a hand to silence me, walks across to the bookshelf, takes down a photo album, and hands me a photo from the loose ones inside the front cover. In it, there's a college-days Barbara with her arm round a girl who I have to say is a level or two above the normal type Tom and Barbara have tried to set me up with in the past. And from what I can tell, all her limbs are present and correct.

'How old is this photo?'

Barbara shrugs. 'About ten years? But she hasn't changed much.'

'Oh yes? When did you last see her?'

'Today, actually.'

'And why have you never mentioned her before?' I say, still a little suspicious.

'Because today was the first time I've seen her for ages. I bumped into her in town. And it turns out she's just got divorced, so . . .'

I hold my hand up. 'Hold on. "Just" as in how recently, exactly?'

'I don't know. I think it's just about to become final. Anyway . . .'

'Oh great. The ink isn't even dry on her divorce papers, which means she's so on the rebound that she'll probably come bouncing in through the front door.'

Tom sighs. 'Will, we're hardly, I mean, *Barbara*'s hardly going to set you up—'

'Introduce,' corrects Barbara.

'Sorry, *introduce* you to someone if they're damaged goods. Sarah's pretty sorted, apparently.'

'And what have you told her about me, exactly?'

'Not much,' says Barbara. 'Just that you're a friend of Tom's, and that you're single, and that you happen to be coming round here for dinner this evening.'

I check my watch and wonder whether it's too late to just head home with a takeaway, particularly since I had such a good time with Emma the other evening. But just as I'm about to make my decision, which is made harder by the cooking smell that's wafting in from the kitchen, the doorbell rings.

And as it transpires, Sarah's not only pretty sorted, but she's also extremely pretty. About five foot four, with short blonde hair, a nice figure, and an even nicer smile, she even blushes when she's introduced to me.

Tom hands her a glass of wine, and I'm a little shocked to see the speed at which she nervously gulps it down, and when we sit down at the table some half an hour later, she's already on her third. As we tuck into our lasagne, the conversation flows, but not as well as the Chardonnay down Sarah's throat, and by the time we get onto dessert, it's not only the pears that are stewed.

'So, Will,' she says, gesturing towards me with her

spoon. 'Barbara tells me you're desperate to be a father?'

I shoot an accusing glance across the table, where Barbara seems to have found something especially interesting in her wine glass.

'It's, er, something I'm considering,' I say.

'Did you and James want kids?' asks Barbara, handing Sarah the jug of custard, which she puts unsteadily down on the table.

At the mention of her ex-husband's name, Sarah's face darkens. 'Well, James did,' she snorts. 'Literally. Which is why he's shacked up with one at the moment, I imagine.'

Tom and I exchange confused glances. 'Oh really?' he says, through a mouthful of pudding.

'Yes,' says Sarah, taking another huge gulp of wine, before sliding her empty glass across to Tom for him to fill up. 'The work experience girl at his office. She can't be more than seventeen. Pervert.'

As Sarah gives us a step-by-step, or rather, shag-by-shag account of the breakdown of her marriage, I don't know if I'm imagining it, but she seems to be giving me the eye across the table — at least, I'm fairly sure she is, given that her eyes are each looking in opposite directions. But by the time we're on to coffee, I'm in no doubt at all, given that Sarah's leg is rubbing against mine, which is quite a feat given that Tom's sitting awkwardly in between us.

Despite the caffeine, and as on most weekday nights, Tom and Barbara's eyes are beginning to shut, and it's not even eleven o'clock. Sensing an escape route, I look at my watch exaggeratedly, and yawn.

'Well, thanks, Tom, thanks, Barbara, for a lovely evening,' I say, standing up from the table. 'And Sarah, it was, er, pleasant to meet you.'

Tom starts awake. 'Oh. Right. You off, then, Will?'

I nod. 'And not a moment too soon. You two look like you're ready for bed.'

'They're not the only ones,' slurs Sarah, in what I guess is meant to be a suggestive manner. As she struggles to her feet, knocking over her thankfully empty wine glass, she catches her handbag on the arm of her chair, spilling half of its contents onto the floor as she does so. 'Could you possibly call me a cab?' she says, gathering the assorted items together and stuffing them back in. 'Unless . . .'

The word hangs in the air, until I ask, fearing I already know what the answer is going to be.

'Unless what?'

Sarah flutters her large, brown, and somewhat out-of-focus eyes in my direction. 'Unless Will can drop me off?'

We all follow her gaze to where she's staring at the car keys I've been jingling unconsciously in my haste to make my escape. Off of what? I'm tempted to ask.

'Er . . .' Now I'm stuck with a dilemma. I've quite plainly got the car, so the polite thing to do is offer to give Sarah a lift home. Only problem is, I'm worried she'll throw up all over my pristine leather upholstery, plus, I'm not sure how I'm going to get her out of the car at the other end, let alone escape from her potentially drunkenly amorous clutches. My alternative is to tell her that I've drunk too much and will have to leave the car here and get a cab myself, but then, of course, she'll offer to share hers, and that puts me in pretty much the same position. Plus, I'll have to shell out for the cab fare, along with an extra tenner for the cabbie when Sarah throws up all over his seats instead of mine, and then get another cab to come and rescue my car in the morning before the wardens impound it. I'm standing there hopelessly when, suddenly, I hit on a solution. 'I would offer you a lift home, Sarah, but I've drunk a little too much, and I probably shouldn't be driving myself, let alone risk having anyone else in the car.'

Brilliant, I think, congratulating myself on my inventiveness. I can see the admiration in Tom's eyes, and he's even imperceptibly nodding at the genius of my escape. Sarah, on the other hand, looks like she might burst into tears.

'But . . . Oh.'

And I don't know why Barbara does this – perhaps because she's feeling sorry for Sarah, or maybe because she's desperate to see me give it more of a go with this friend of hers, but she walks over to me, grabs my arm firmly, and escorts me to the door. 'You've not drunk that much, Will, have you? And I'm sure Sarah would really appreciate a ride.'

As Tom tries his hardest not to burst out laughing, and Sarah follows us through the hallway, I glare at Barbara. Because now, of course, I do feel incredibly guilty. Do I really want to trust this poor, upset and, it has to be said, incredibly pissed and potentially randy woman to some lecherous minicab driver, when I know I'm absolutely fine to drive her home?

Five minutes later, we're heading down the A316 towards Whitton, which we've managed to work out between the three of us, the phone book, and Tom's A to Z is where she lives, Sarah herself being a little bit hazy on this particular detail. I'd been worried about making small talk on the way home, but, fortunately, and in between burps, Sarah does more than enough talking for the both of us, and while I'd normally be trying to put my foot down, I steer the TVR carefully round the corners, more than a little worried about Sarah regurgitating Barbara's lasagne all over my carpets.

When I eventually pull up outside her house, I prepare myself for her drunken attempt at a goodnight kiss, wondering what's the best way to play it. Am I better off getting out first, thus ensuring Sarah gets out too, and therefore giving me the option of getting straight back in the car, or do I stay in my seat, assuming that she'll just attempt to lean over, then let her get it over with, at which I'll grit my teeth and take it like a man, and hope her tongue – or the lasagne – doesn't come my way too? I decide on the latter of the two options, but Sarah makes no attempt to do either, despite my parking in the middle of the road.

I think about reaching across to open her door from the inside, but don't want it to be misinterpreted, as indeed any move in her direction might. After a couple of awkward minutes, having made sure she is, in fact, still awake, there's nothing for it, and I revert to plan A.

'Well, lovely to meet you, again,' I say, climbing out of the car and walking round to the passenger side to open her door. I hold out my hand to help her out of the low-slung seat, but it takes her three or four unsuccessful attempts to get up before she realizes she's still got her seat belt fastened, which prompts another two minutes of uncontrollable giggles.

'Oh, look at me,' she says, unclipping the belt at the fifth go, while dabbing at the corners of her eyes with a tissue. 'Is my mascara running?'

For its life, I'm thinking, wishing I could do the same. I reach down and heave her out of the seat and into a more or less upright position on the pavement, but just as I do, the car engine, which I've left running in an attempt to reinforce the fact that I'm not intending to hang around, stalls.

'Maybe it's trying to tell you something,' says Sarah, licking her lips in what I imagine she hopes is a suggestive manner, but looks more like she's just come back from a rather painful visit to the dentist.

It's pretty clear to me that sex is on the cards. In fact, it'd be pretty clear to even someone who'd never met a woman before that sex is on the cards. Sarah's certainly not unattractive, and even by my standards it's been a while. But she is very, very drunk, and there's no way I'd ever want to take advantage of that.

Sarah gropes in her handbag, and after what seems like an eternity, produces a set of keys. Cursing Tom and Barbara, I realize that unless I physically help her into her house, there's a danger that she won't actually be able to negotiate the five or so yards to her front door and, even if she did, the chances of her managing to get the key in the lock are somewhat remote.

'I'll walk you to your door,' I say, grabbing her elbow, and then half escort, half carry her up the garden path. But after fumbling with the keys, Sarah can't seem to get the door open.

'What's the matter?' I say.

She stares at the key in her hand as if she's never seen one before. 'S'not working.'

'Here,' I say, taking it from her. 'Let me try.'

Normally, I'd find this amusing. But tonight, all I want to do is get the door open, shove Sarah inside, and close it after her. Although, try as I might, I can't seem to get the key to fit.

'You're sure this is the right one?' I ask, as Sarah slumps heavily against the wall. Then, as if by magic, a light comes on, and the door swings open by itself. Or rather, thanks to the dressing-gown-clad woman who's just unlocked it from inside.

Sarah stares at the woman through glazed eyes,

before a look of recognition crosses her face. 'Rebecca,' she says, enunciating the word extremely carefully. 'What are you doing in my house?'

Rebecca folds her arms. 'This is my house, Sarah. You live next door. Remember?'

As Rebecca gives me a look as if to imply that this isn't the first time, I mouth 'Sorry', pick Sarah up, put her over my shoulder and, as she squeals with delight, carry her back down Rebecca's path and up what I'm hoping is hers. Perhaps not unsurprisingly, the key fits first time in her own front door, and so I walk her through to her lounge and deposit her on the sofa. I leave her keys on the coffee table, find a duvet from the bed upstairs and drape it over her now-sleeping form, then retrieve a bucket from the kitchen, which I leave next to the sofa, just in case.

And later, as I'm driving back home, I find myself thinking about Emma, and wondering whether I'd have been quite as much of a gentleman with her.

Chapter 20

I'm sitting by the window in the seventh-floor café in the Tate Modern, marvelling at the view of St Paul's Cathedral across the Thames. But I'm not just here to enjoy the scenery – I'm waiting for Emma to arrive. She's got the day off college, and isn't working until tomorrow, and to my surprise, since I only mentioned it in passing yesterday, she's agreed to meet me for lunch.

There're a few families in here too – foreign tourists, I'm guessing, judging by the fact the kids aren't at school, plus the way the adults aren't fussing over them like most of Tom and Barbara's friends seem to when-ever they take their children out in public – and it's lovely to see the kids playing happily around the tables, or fascinated by the bird's-eye view of the river.

It's five minutes to midday, and I'm nursing a cappuccino while taking bets with myself as to just how late she's going to be, when there's a tap on my shoulder. I'm assuming it's going to be someone else asking whether the empty stool I've had to guard for the last twenty minutes is free, but instead, and to my astonishment, it's Emma.

I don't quite know how to greet her. I mean, we didn't kiss goodnight the other evening, therefore it hardly seems appropriate to kiss her hello, so I just sort of half stand up, prompting a couple of what appear to be scruffy art students leaning on the counter next to me to point at my stool and ask whether I'm leaving. When I shake my head, they look most put out.

'You look surprised to see me,' says Emma, taking off her coat and jumping up onto the seat next to mine.

'No, not at all. I'm ... Well, yes. Actually. Because you're early, I mean. Not because I thought you wouldn't come.'

Emma shrugs. 'I hate people who are late. I think it shows a lack of respect. Like they're saying that their time is more valuable than yours. Don't you?'

'I haven't really thought about it that much. But now you put it that way ... Can I get you a drink?'

She looks at my coffee, and then at her watch. 'Glass of white wine, please. Seeing as it's not a school day.'

When I get back from the bar, Emma is scowling at the students, who have grabbed a nearby table.

'What's wrong? Did they say something to you?'

Emma shakes her head. 'No. But they're rolling a bunch of cigarettes. And from what I can tell, it's not just tobacco they're filling them with.'

I look across to where they're sitting, one of them laying out a series of Rizlas, and the other blatantly crumbling what even to my untrained eye appears to be cannabis resin into the pile of tobacco. 'Well, I'm sure they're not going to smoke them in here.'

'That's not the point, Will. There're lots of children about. And if they drop some of that ... stuff on the floor, who knows what could happen?'

I look at the two students. They're both taller than me. And certainly taller than Emma, even when they're sitting down. 'Do you want me to go over and say something?'

'No need,' says Emma, jumping down from her stool before I can stop her, and walking across to where they're hunched over the table. She clears her throat, and they both look up from their assembly line.

'What?' says the scruffier of the two, although it's a close-run thing.

Emma folds her arms. 'Should you really be doing that in here?'

'What's it to you?' says his mate.

'Well, it's illegal, for one thing.'

'So? They should legalize this stuff, anyway. People are going to do it whatever.'

'That's a ridiculous argument. That's like saying they should reduce the age of consent because paedophiles are going to sleep with children. And it doesn't change the fact that, as of today, it's against the law.'

It's a good line, and I can tell that the two of them are struggling to come up with a rebuttal. 'So?' says the scruffier one eventually, leaning back in his chair defiantly. 'What are you going to do? Arrest us?'

As I brace myself to dive in at the first sign of trouble, Emma nods over in my direction. 'Well, my friend over there is an off-duty policeman. Perhaps you'd like to discuss the legal intricacies with him down at the station?'

They both swivel their unkempt heads towards me, and I nod in agreement. Ten seconds later, they're heading for the lifts, obviously assuming that by 'station', Emma didn't mean Waterloo.

'Impressive,' I say, wondering whether I should be pleased or not that they thought I looked like a constable. 'You'll do well as a teacher.'

Emma shrugs, and takes a sip of her wine as she sits back down next to me. 'Most men are big kids, really. You just need to know how to talk to them.'

'And how do you know that, exactly?'

'It's a secret.' She taps the side of her nose. 'Fabulous view, by the way.'

'Isn't it just,' I say, not strictly referring to the London skyline.

'So,' she says. 'Tell me a secret about you. Something that you've never told anyone else.'

'Like what?'

She smiles. 'I don't know. Anything you like. But it's got to be a secret.'

'Ah,' I say. 'But if I told you, then it wouldn't be a secret, would it?'

'It would be *our* secret.'

Why do women ask these kinds of things? What am I supposed to say now? Something mysterious about my past that makes me look interesting, or something that I'm ashamed of doing, that shows I'm capable of opening up to her. Where's Barbara and her role play when I need her?

'Er ... I don't like mushrooms,' is the best I can come up with.

Emma peers at me over the top of her wine glass. 'That's not much of a secret, is it?'

I shrug. 'It's still a secret. What else did you have in mind?'

'I don't know. Something like ... having a third nipple.'

'Is that *your* secret?'

Emma blushes, then turns and looks out of the window. 'No.'

'Well, what, then?'

She tears her eyes away from the view and looks at me earnestly. 'You're the first person I've been on a date with for over a year.'

'Wow. I'm flattered.'

'Don't be. It's only because no one else has asked me out.'

As my ego deflates with an almost audible whistle, Emma breaks into a grin. 'I'm teasing you, Will. Are you always this easy to get?'

'I'm beginning to worry that I might be.'

'Listen,' she says. 'I hope you don't think I'm being

too forward, but what are you doing on Saturday?'

'Saturday?' Whatever it is, I think to myself, I'll cancel. 'I'm not sure. Why?'

'I wondered whether you might like to come over. For lunch. I'll cook something.'

'Really? You wouldn't prefer to go out?'

'No. Come to the house. Besides, I like to cook.'

'You see! I knew we were compatible.'

'How do you mean?'

'Well, you like cooking. I like eating . . .'

'And how about you, Will. Can you cook?'

'Oh yes. My cooking is legendary.'

'Really?' says Emma. 'I'm impressed.'

'No, legendary as in you hear stories about it, but never actually see any evidence of it. I mean, the kitchen, it's just not our natural habitat.'

'And it is ours, is it?'

I know better than to answer this with a yes. I haven't known Barbara for years for nothing. And I've got the scars to prove it. So I take the only sensible option, and change the subject.

'Listen, speaking of food, are you hungry?'

Emma looks at me for a second. 'I could certainly eat something,' she says, and although I'm not sure if she's flirting with me, there's a distinct possibility that she might be.

And it's only now that I'm sat here with Emma that the absurdity of what I'm doing is starting to hit home. Because here I am, with someone I like, and who I think likes me, and I can't think of how on earth I'm going to bring up what it is I'm trying to achieve without sounding like a nutter, or scaring her off, or both.

We ride down in the lift, then stroll along the South Bank towards Tower Bridge, and we're just heading past the Globe Theatre when Emma spots a restaurant down one of the side streets.

'Ooh,' she says. 'Mediterranean food. Is that okay for you?'

I don't know, actually. The last time I was anywhere near the Mediterranean was on a holiday to the Costa del Sol when I was eighteen. I can only remember eating either burger and chips or pizza then, and I'm pretty sure that's not what Emma's getting so excited about. 'Love it,' I say, hoping it's not an entire cuisine based around mushrooms.

'Great,' she says. 'I hope they do couscous. I love couscous.'

We walk into the restaurant, where we're met at the door by the manager. 'Table for two?' he asks, and when I nod, he leads us to an alcove in the corner.

'That always makes me laugh,' whispers Emma. 'We're obviously a couple, so what do they think we're going to say? Two tables for one?'

I smile back at her, but don't answer. Because I've heard her say 'we're obviously a couple', and that's made my day.

Chapter 21

On the Wednesday I have to go into town to get a replacement wireless card for my laptop – my original one having evidently packed up through overuse these past few weeks, and I'm leaning against the door on the tube when I first notice a woman sitting just along the carriage staring at me over the top of her copy of *Metro*, the free morning newspaper. At first, I think she's just accidentally caught my eye whilst gazing off into space, any actual interaction frowned upon under normal tube etiquette, so I smile briefly back at her, but she just looks away, embarrassed, and doesn't make eye contact again. At Kew Gardens, she stands up and peers at me intently, before hopping off the train.

I shrug, and make a 'what can you do' face at the woman standing in front of me who's witnessed the whole thing, but she too gives me a strange look, and turns back to her paper. When this happens a third time, I begin to get paranoid, and surreptitiously check that my trousers are done up, before examining my reflection in the window in case I've got a Frostie stuck on my chin. There's nothing obvious so, instead, when another seat becomes free, I pick up the discarded copy of *Metro* that's been left on it, sit down, and attempt to hide behind the pages. But this proves to be a mistake, because there seems to be a picture of me on the page I'm trying to hide behind.

I stare at the newspaper in disbelief. 'Is this the father of your baby?' screams the headline, followed by a rather unflattering picture of me sitting on the bonnet of my car, which looks very similar to a picture Tom and Barbara have in their photo album at home. And as worrying as the headline is, the picture couldn't be worse, particularly given that the presence of the TVR means it has 'penis substitute' written all over it.

I glance around the carriage in shock. As usual, everyone is reading *Metro*, which they've probably picked up at Richmond station, which was three stops ago. And my photo's on page fourteen, so, by my calculations, most of them should be turning to it round about now. I read on hurriedly.

'Thirty-one-year-old Will Jackson is so desperate to be a father that he's put himself on eBay. The Richmond-based life coach and self-confessed woman-izer has signed up with internet dating agencies, been out on blind dates, and even taken to asking out random women in the street in his attempt to meet someone to have a baby with. But now, he's even listed himself on the online auction site, so come on, girls, help Will out in his "bid" to be a dad . . .'

Oh. My. God. So much for Tom's promise to get Victoria to keep it under wraps. I can't bring myself to read any further, and suddenly feel the need to be anywhere but on the tube, so jump off at Hammersmith and make my way quickly along the platform. As I dive into the anonymity of Tesco's, my mobile rings. It's Tom.

'Hello, mate,' he says. 'I just wanted to call and tell you that I might not have remembered to phone Victoria the other day. . .'

'Oh really,' I say, trying to get as much sarcasm into my voice as possible. 'This wouldn't be something to do with you having read a copy of this morning's *Metro*, would it?'

There's silence on the other end of the line for a second or two, before Tom comes back on. 'You've, er, seen it, then?'

'Tom, not only have I seen it, but so have approximately half a million Londoners on the tube this morning. And where the hell did they get the photo from?'

'Ah,' says Tom sheepishly. 'There may be a small chance that I might have had something to do with that.'

'How small a chance, exactly?'

'Well, a pretty big one, actually. Still, look on the bright side.'

'Bright side?' I'm virtually shouting into the phone by now, causing a couple of pensioners in Tesco's to give me a wide berth. 'How can this possibly have a bright side?'

'Well,' says Tom, 'it means you're sure to get some responses now.'

I give Tom the only appropriate response, and head nervously back down to the station, careful to avoid anyone's gaze, taking the first Richmond train that comes along. When I get back to my office, I anxiously log on to eBay, and scroll down to my 'hits' counter, which is slightly up from yesterday's total of seven. Three thousand, four hundred and five up, in fact. There's also a list of one hundred and nine questions, and, somewhat worryingly, there have even been fifty-seven bids. In fact, my current eBay worth seems to be in excess of two thousand one hundred pounds.

I frantically scroll through some of the questions, clicking on several at random. Hidden among the expected rude responses and offers of cheap Viagra, which, quite frankly, I'm going to need if this level of interest keeps up, seem to be a few genuine enquiries, although it's hard to tell, given what's happened, whether they're just journalists after a story.

Without a moment's thought I remove my listing and, for good measure, cancel my NewFlames subscription too. Damage limitation. That's what it's all about now. And I'm just wondering what else I need to do to stop this spreading any further, when I suddenly remember that Emma's doing a day shift today. Which means she'll have taken the tube into work.

I run out of my office, along the corridor, past a bemused Jen on reception, take the stairs three at a time, and sprint round the corner to Starbucks. There's no sign of Emma, but there are certainly a few copies of *Metro* around the place.

I hurry over to the counter, and attract the barista's attention.

'What can I get you?'

'I don't suppose Emma's in?'

He shakes his head. 'She was earlier. I saw her reading the paper before starting her shift, then suddenly she said she had to go.'

Great. I jog back up to the office, and find Emma's number. When her mobile rings a couple of times, and then kicks into voicemail, I think about leaving a message, but stop myself. What exactly would I say? I leave it a minute, and then call back, and this time the phone's answered, although with a pretty unfriendly tone.

'What do you want, Will?'

Ah. No chance she hasn't seen the paper, then. 'Well, er, I'm calling to see if you fancied a drink this evening?'

She lets out an exasperated sigh. 'What do you think?'

'Emma, I can explain. It's not like—'

'I don't want to be just a number, Will,' she interrupts. 'I can't afford just to be a notch on someone's bedpost.'

'It's not like that at all. They've exaggerated ...'
I start to say.

'What is it like, then, Will? You didn't tell me about
any of this, so why should I believe anything else you
say?'

'Because ...' She's got me there. 'Er ...'

'Will, I've got to go,' she says, cutting me off
abruptly.

'Wait,' I say. 'What about this evening?'

'I don't think so.'

'Well, how about Saturday, then? Are we still on for
lunch?'

'I can't, Will. I'm ... busy.'

As I'm pleading with her down the phone, I hear a
noise in the background, and the sound of Emma
putting her hand over the mouthpiece. And although
it's hard to make out, I think I hear her say the words
'it's nothing' and 'go back to bed'.

I get a sudden lump in my throat. 'What's going on?
Is there someone else?'

There's a pause, and then, 'Yes, Will. Yes there is.'

I start to protest, but then realize I'm talking to a
dead tone.

Chapter 22

I hit 'do not disturb' on my phone, switch off my mobile, and for the next half an hour, sit at my desk with my head in my hands, wondering just how more surreal the day can possibly get. As it turns out, quite a bit, because when I eventually emerge from the sanctuary of my office and walk past reception to get a drink from the water cooler, Jen stops me.

'There's an Ellen Waters on the phone for you, Will. She's called five times already this morning.'

I look at my watch. It's still only eleven-fifteen. 'Did she say what she wanted?'

Jen shakes her head. 'Nope. But she did say she was from the BBC.'

I do a double take. 'The BBC? As in . . . the BBC?'

Jen nods. 'One and the same.'

And in my addled state, I forget to put two and two together. Perhaps this is it – the silver lining that every cloud has, or so I tell my clients. Maybe the Beeb are looking to do another one of these makeover or life-changing programmes, and having seen my picture in the paper, they want me to be the resident life-coaching expert. I feel my heart start to race a little. This could be my big break.

'Well, you'd better put her through, then.'

I sprint back down the corridor, through my office door and run over towards my desk, where the phone is already ringing. 'The BBC for you,' says Jen, in a rather clipped tone. I hear a click, and then announce myself.

'Will Jackson.'

'Will,' says an over-friendly voice on the other end of the line. 'Ellen Waters here. From the BBC.'

'Er . . . Yes?'

'You are the same Will Jackson I've been reading about in all the papers?'

All the papers? I thought it was just *Metro*. I stand up and pace around the room, peering nervously through the window in case there are any paparazzi lurking outside.

'Well, I . . . yes, I suppose so.'

'Splendid, splendid,' says Ellen. 'Well, let me get straight to the point. We were wondering if you'd like to come on *Today's the Day*.'

'*Today's the Day*?'

'It's our morning programme. Surely you've seen it?'

I don't like to tell her that I haven't, because I have a life. 'Of course. But . . . what for?'

'What do you think?' Ellen chuckles down the

phone. 'We love the idea that you've gone to such desperate measures to have a baby. Quite frankly, we think our viewers would love to hear more about you. And how you're getting on.'

Ah. Scratch my plan to become TV's Mr Life Coach. 'You can't be serious?'

'Deadly, Will. As long as you are about this baby nonsense, that is.'

Baby nonsense? By now, one or two alarm bells are ringing, and I'm beginning to wonder whether it's a wind-up. 'Did Tom put you up to this?'

'It's no wind-up, Will. I can give you a number to call me back on, if you don't believe me.'

'Fine.'

I jot down the number she reels off, then ring her back. 'Hello, BBC,' says a bored voice at the end of the phone.

'Ah. This is the BBC? The television people?'

There's a sigh at the other end of the line. 'That's correct, sir.'

'Er, and does someone called Ellen Waters work there, please?'

I hear the noise of someone typing on a keyboard. 'Yes,' says the voice.

When they don't elaborate, I have to speak again. 'Well, could you put me through to her, please?'

There's another sigh, a click, a few seconds of 'Greensleeves', and then Ellen comes back on the phone.

'You see, Will – I can call you Will, can't I? – we're legit. So how about it?'

'And why, exactly, should I come on *Today's the Day*?'

'So you can put your side of the story, of course. I've read the papers – some of them haven't been that complimentary, have they?'

I swallow hard. 'Haven't they?'

'Well, the *Daily Mail* has got you on page five. But the *Express* has got your photo on the front page. With the caption "Have you slept with this man?"'

I feel my mouth go all dry, and I suddenly need to sit down. 'You're kidding?'

'I bet you wish I was, don't you?'

'But I just want this to go away. And surely coming on national television will only keep it alive for longer.'

'Not at all, Will. It gives you the chance to put the matter to bed. Once and for all. Tell people you're not a crank. Or a pervert.'

While Ellen tries her best to convince me, I start to realize that she's got a point. And as much as the prospect of appearing on a live television chat show scares me, I'm more worried that the newspaper coverage has left me with a reputation that I'm going to have trouble shaking.

'Well, what would be involved?'

Ellen's voice perks up, like an angler who's just got a bite. 'Oh, not much to worry about. You come in, sit on the sofa for ten minutes, and just have a chat with Martin and Trudy. Nothing to it.'

Martin and Trudy! Television's A-list couple. 'I presume I'll get to see the questions I'll be asked beforehand?'

'Oh, it's normally not a scripted show,' says Ellen dismissively. 'But you'll be fine. They won't ask you anything you'll be uncomfortable with. We'll turn it into a feature, if you like. Kind of a "what men are looking for in a woman nowadays" piece. Topical stuff. Always goes down well with the audience.'

'Let me think about it, will you?' I say hesitantly. 'When were you thinking of having me on?'

But Ellen doesn't hesitate at all. 'How about tomorrow?'

'Tomorrow. As in ... the day after today? You're joking?'

'Not at all. It needs to be current. Topical. Today's news is yesterday's news tomorrow, if you see what I mean. Except for where your reputation is concerned, of course. So strike while the iron's hot.'

'So, what you're saying is that if I don't go on national TV before my story dies a natural death, it'll die a natural death anyway?'

'Aha,' says Ellen. 'But you want it to die the right natural death, surely?'

'Ri–ight.'

'Excellent. So we'll see you tomorrow? We'll send a car? Nine o'clock?'

'Don't you need my address?'

'Already got it, dear boy.'

Before I can ask any more questions, the phone clicks off. I stare at the receiver for a moment, wondering what on earth I've got myself into, then rush out to reception and, in front of a bewildered Jen, switch the large Plasma TV on the wall over from its usual news channel to BBC One. On the screen in front of me, Martin and Trudy seem to be locked in a vigorous debate about which supermarket has the most eco-friendly carrier bags, and it certainly looks innocuous enough – the only time voices get raised are when Martin shushes Trudy too often for her liking.

As I watch, I start to feel a little more confident. After all, how tough can it be on a peach-coloured sofa, anyway? Perhaps I'll be able to give the business a plug too. And if I can get Emma to tune in, maybe it'll be a good chance for her to hear my side of the story. Back in my office, I call Tom to tell him the good news, but his reaction isn't quite the one I was expecting.

'You bastard!' he says, loudly enough for me to have to hold the receiver an inch or two away from my ear.

'What do you mean?'

'I've been an actor for nearly ten years, and it's still just as tough for me to get any kind of exposure. You put yourself on eBay and, five minutes later, you're all over the bloody media.'

'Thanks to you and your reporter friend, don't forget.'

'Ah. Right. Sorry. So are you nervous?'

'Not really. How hard can it be?'

'Have you ever seen *Today's the Day*?'

'Yes. Of course. I saw a bit of it this morning, in fact.'

'And you're sure you want to go on?'

'Why wouldn't I?'

I hear a commotion behind him, and wait as he gives Barbara a quick update. As Barbara starts to snigger, Tom comes back on the line. 'It's just that . . . I mean, it's hardly . . . Never mind. I'm sure you're doing the right thing, Will.'

I'm just about to ask Tom what he means, when I hear a struggle at the other end of the line, followed by Tom grunting in pain.

'What time are you going on?' says Barbara, who's obviously just wrestled the phone out of Tom's grasp.

'Why?'

'Just so I can set the DVD recorder. After all, it's not often you see someone you know skinned alive on national television, is it?'

'I'm hardly going to be skinned alive. It's just a cosy little chat on the sofa, after all.' I swallow uneasily. 'Isn't it?'

Barbara struggles to contain her laughter. 'Sure, Will. Whatever you say. A cosy little chat. Anyway, I'd better let you go – I'm sure you've got a lot of things to sort out for tomorrow.'

'Such as?'

'Well, what you're going to wear, for one thing.

You're on national TV, don't forget. Play it smart and this'll be a great advert for you. And at least you want to look the part. Just in case there are any eligible women watching . . .'

'Barbara, the kind of women I'm hoping to meet are hardly going to be watching *Today's the Day*.'

'You never know, Will. I watch it sometimes.'

'Exactly,' I say, and put the phone down in victory.

I get Jen to reschedule my afternoon appointments, and hurry back to my flat, because Barbara's right – what *do* I wear? I'm used to dressing to impress in an out-on-a-date kind of way – I've got a whole wardrobe full of trendy shirts and designer jeans, which, it seems to me, the more they cost the scruffier they look. But they're all my pulling clothes – outfits that lend me an air of style without looking like I've tried too hard, although I'm beginning to suspect that most women can see straight through that, particularly the trendily ripped pair I bought on a whim and then wore the once. I tried to take them to a charity shop recently, but they rejected them on the basis that they looked too far gone.

I've never been on television before, unless you count the video that Anita and I made once when we were drunk, and we certainly weren't bothered about what we were wearing on that occasion. But, as Barbara mentioned, there might be eligible women watching, so what do I wear that says 'dad-to-be'?

Looking at the way Tom dresses, a trip back to the charity shop would be in order, but, realistically, that's not an option. I need to convey smart without being flash; well dressed and stylish, but not someone who minds spilling baby food on his shirt.

But then it occurs to me that maybe I'm approaching this the wrong way? Just because Tom and, let's face it, most of the other fathers I know lose the will to dress well the moment the kids arrive, that doesn't mean that I have to follow suit, so to speak. In fact, I'm going to be one of those trendy dads. One of those fathers who still looks good in a suit, rather than making it look like it's been made to measure for someone smaller. I'll be the kind of dad who the other mothers look at appreciatively. And who their husbands see and think: Why did I let that gym membership lapse? Why can't I look like that Will Jackson over there? My, he's good-looking for an older man.

Because you don't have to let it all go once the kids arrive. And, surely, if I still look good, then the mother of my baby will feel she has to do the same, which in turn should help us stay together? And I want her to want to stay with me too – and not just for the child's sake. Because there's no way I'm going to be one of these part-time fathers, playing at being the attentive parent in McDonald's or Starbucks when they've got the kid for their forty-eight hours every other weekend, before taking them back home for one of those border hostage handovers like you see in Cold

War spy films. That'd never happen to me. Never be something I'd do. We'd stay together because of the kids, and never let them know even if we were having problems. No – I'll definitely put on a united front. Unlike my bloody dad.

I pull my black Hugo Boss suit out of the wardrobe, slip it on, and check my reflection in the mirror, but it's not quite right – there's a fine line between the cool one from *Reservoir Dogs* and looking like you're on your way to a funeral. And even if I did decide to wear it, I'd still have the tie dilemma. It's not an interview – well, not really – and I never wear a tie in everyday life (or a suit, for that matter), so would I really want to be sat there under the studio lights with this constricting thing round my neck? And besides, it's all open necks nowadays, isn't it? With shirts tucked in. Again. I think. Plus, would I ever wear a suit and tie on a date? Doubtful. And surely not if I want her to think that I'm a fun kind of guy, and not one of those stiffs I see on the tube all the time poring over their BlackBerries like they're waiting for the lottery results, or having a panic attack whenever they temporarily lose reception on their mobiles.

I put the suit back on its hanger, and look for something a little less formal. I could wear jeans, I suppose, but then there's the risk of appearing too scruffy. Or there's always Chinos, but then I don't want to look too 'preppy'. This is turning out to be trickier than I thought, and after another fruitless search through my wardrobe, I come to the only possible conclusion. I need to go shopping. And fast.

Ten minutes later, I'm heading back into Richmond, and after an hour trawling up and down between the likes of Marks & Spencer's and Moss Bros, realize that I really must add this to my list of things that are crap when you're single. When you're a couple, clothes shopping is a doddle – fun, even – and there're not many shopping-related activities that you can say that about. When you're shopping for clothes with your girlfriend, you know you can't go wrong – there's no way she's going to let you be seen dead in anything embarrassing, you've always got a willing helper there to pick things out for you, bring you different sizes while you hide in the changing room, and then cast her expert eye over your new ensemble. With a woman's help, the changing room becomes a refuge from the normal hustle and bustle of the high street. A chrysalis from which you'll eventually emerge, resplendent in your new, carefully selected outfit. And, occasionally, a venue for a quickie.

On your own, however, it's a different story. In desperation, you take a random armful of clothes to the changing room, only to be told off by the bored teenager guarding the entrance who, by the way he casts a scornful eye over what you've selected, obviously thinks he's got a degree in fashion, whereas the only real piece of paper he owns with his name on has the letters ASBO printed firmly underneath.

I'm on my third circuit of the town centre, walking so quickly that even the chuggers don't dare to try and stop me for fear of whiplash, and beginning to despair that I'm never going to strike the balance I'm desperate to achieve, when it hits me. Gap. I never normally shop in Gap, not particularly liking their selection of faded T-shirts and baggy combat pants, but as I peer through the window, it strikes me that this is what dads actually wear, particularly the young, trendier ones I see pushing their four-by-four buggies around Richmond Park. Perfect. Dress myself in their version of smart-casual and I can't go wrong.

I push through the large swing doors and follow the signs towards the menswear department at the back of the shop, and I'm staring at the various dummies, all identically decked out in a variety of loose-fitting striped polo shirts, cargo pants – whatever they are – and what I understand from GQ to be a 'man-bag', when one of the dummies moves.

'Can I help you?'

'No, it's okay. I'm just looking,' I say.

The assistant, whose name badge identifies him as 'Kevin', looks at me resentfully, as if letting him help me might lend a sense of purpose to his otherwise dull afternoon, before walking off to re-fold a pile of T-shirts that don't look as if they've been disturbed in the first place.

After five minutes or so, I've managed to locate the constituent items that I think might make up the 'casual dad about town' look that I'm trying to recreate, and head over towards the changing rooms. Kevin, who's obviously been watching me surreptitiously as I've moved around the shop, fairly sprints across to meet me at the entrance.

'Can I try these on?' I ask, conscious of the need to say something even though I'm carrying an armful of clothing and standing by the entrance to the changing rooms.

Kevin does a quick inspection of what I'm carrying, and looks up at me in a so-you-want-my-help-now kind of way. 'It's five items max,' he says.

'I've got ten,' I say.

'It's five items. Max,' repeats Kevin, as if I haven't understood him the first time.

'Yes. But I need to try on ten at once,' I reply, stopping myself from adding 'because I don't have a girlfriend to go and get alternative colours and sizes while I'm in there'.

Kevin reaches under the small table by the entrance to the changing rooms, and retrieves a plastic tag with the number five stamped on it. 'But it only goes up to five.'

I stare at him for a moment, wondering how to get around this impasse. 'Well, how about you give me two of those little tags. Then we'll both be happy.'

Kevin tries to process this piece of information, peering towards the tills, as if he's considering whether he needs to check this most radical of requests with the manager. 'Okay,' he says, as if he's just agreed to donate one of his kidneys to me. 'But just this once.'

I thank him profusely, even though just this once will be fine as I'll probably never come into Gap again, and carry my prospective-dad outfit into the changing rooms, where I draw back the musty curtain of the first cubicle I see, and walk inside. The floor is covered in ripped-off labels and security tags from when, I'm guessing, previous occupants have nicked the clothes they've been trying on, and the hook on the back of the door is missing, so I have to pile all the clothes, including mine, on the shelf-like wooden seat. What's worse, it's one of those dual-sex changing rooms, and when I try and shut the curtain behind me, and manage to close the gap at one end, I end up revealing an inch or two at the other, through which I spot a gaggle of skiving teenage schoolgirls disappearing into the cubicles opposite.

After ten minutes of mixing and matching, I think I've managed to assemble a decent-enough outfit, although it's hard to tell, given the cramped confines of the cubicle and the size and orientation of the mirror. I don't want to emerge into the middle aisle to use the larger mirror there and run the risk of being laughed at by the teenage girls who, judging by the noise emanating from behind their curtains, seem to be having some kind of party, so, instead, I try and adjust the angle of the two mirrors on the adjacent walls in my cubicle to get a view of how I look from the back,

but only succeed in cricking my neck. The main
mirror's only four foot high, and I can't seem to get far
enough away from it to get a full view of myself without leaving the safety of the cubicle, so, in desperation,
I try and take a picture of myself on my camera phone
by standing with my back to the mirror and taking
the shot over my shoulder, but even then, it's too dark
to get a proper photo.

Eventually, I decide that the only way I can get a
decent look at the trousers is by standing on the seat,
thus bringing them level with the bottom of the mirror,
so I move the rest of the clothes into a pile on the floor
and climb up onto the bench. My phone is still in
the hand I'm hanging on to the top of the cubicle
wall with, and I'm trying to tuck my shirt into the front
of my trousers with the other, and as I crane my neck
around to try and get a proper view, I hear a shout
from one of the teenage girls opposite. As I look automatically across, I suddenly realize that because I'm
standing on the seat, my head and shoulders are poking
over the top of my cubicle, giving me a clear view
across the aisle and into where the girls are changing.

As I duck out of sight and jump down off the bench,
the curtain is suddenly swept aside to reveal Kevin,
surrounded by the girls from across the aisle. I catch
sight of my reflection in the mirror, one hand down the
front of my trousers, the other clutching my camera
phone, and realize that this might not perhaps look
too good.

'That's him,' spits one of the teenagers. 'Pervert.'

'Get a good view, did you?' shouts her friend.

Kevin stands there mutely, not knowing quite how to react.

'Actually, no,' I say. 'I mean, it's just that these mirrors are too small. And I was trying to look at—'

'Us changing,' interrupts the first girl.

'No, I wasn't. I . . .'

And this is why I need a girlfriend. And fast. Because if I had a girlfriend, I wouldn't have been manhandled to a room at the back of the shop by the security guards. And if I had a girlfriend, I wouldn't have had to explain to the police what I'd been doing standing on the bench in the changing rooms with my camera phone. And I wouldn't have had to prove my case by showing a policeman some grainy photographs of my own backside. And if I had a girlfriend, I wouldn't have been in bloody Gap in the first place trying to buy something to wear so I could go on television to discuss my single status, which, quite frankly, is looking more and more like a permanent state.

Chapter 23

Today's the day, as it were. The car comes at nine exactly – a large, silver Mercedes that's possibly not the best use of licence-payers' money, but looks extremely comfortable, a fact I am happy to confirm as I jump into the back seat for the short drive to Shepherd's Bush. I'm wearing my Hugo Boss suit jacket – the shops having been shut by the time I eventually got out of the police station the previous evening – with a white shirt open at the neck, and my best pair of jeans, which I'm hoping will give me the right mix of respectability and come-and-get-me sexuality that every prospective father appearing on national television wants to achieve.

I've texted Emma to tell her to tune in if she gets the chance, but she's not replied to my message, or indeed to any of the other ten or so voicemails I've left her, so I'm assuming that she's given up on me. And as depressing as that is, I've got no choice but to try and put it to the back of my mind and get on with the task at hand.

By nine-thirty we're pulling into the BBC car park, and I'm led into reception, where I sit down nervously on the squeaky leather sofa and scan the assorted faces, trying to spot anyone famous. But just when I think I might have recognized someone who used to be a weathergirl before some incriminating photographs of her caused a bit of a storm of their own, a short, fat, blonde woman comes out from one of the security doors and bustles over in my direction.

'Will?' she says, a couple of seconds before her perfume cloud almost asphyxiates me. 'Ellen Waters.'

I shake her hand, wondering whether I should be giving her one of those media-type double kisses, but Ellen doesn't hang about long enough for me to get the chance. Instead, she ushers me through the security with a wave of her badge on the scanner, barking instructions as we go.

'Slight change of plan,' she says, leading me through into make-up. 'We thought we'd do a bit of a phone-in.'

'What kind of phone-in?'

Ellen pushes me into a chair, resting a hand on my shoulder as the make-up girl stuffs tissue paper into the neck of my shirt. 'Nothing to worry about. One where we ask people to call in to the show if they like the look of you. If you get on, then we thought they could perhaps win a date or something.'

Win a date? With me? 'So, sort of a phone-in competition?'

'That's right,' smiles Ellen, patting my arm in a patronizing I-don't-expect-you-to-understand-the-intricacies-of-live-television kind of way. 'A competition. So how about it?' she asks, in an as-if-you've-got-a-choice voice.

I'm smiling as I consider the idea, but when I catch sight of myself in the mirror, it's more of a grimace. What could possibly be worse? I've come on here to try and rescue my reputation after being made a laughing stock, and now I'm going to be offered up as some kind of prize.

'Well . . .'

'Splendid,' says Ellen. 'I'll go and tell them you're thrilled with the idea.'

Thrilled? Scared stiff, more like.

After my make-up's been done, which seems to consist of just dabbing on some brown powder to stop my forehead reflecting the studio lights, I'm led through to the green room, which I realize is so called because I'm feeling sick with nerves. There's coffee and doughnuts on a table in the middle, but I don't dare have anything in case it gets stuck in my teeth or even worse, makes an unscheduled reappearance when the cameras start rolling.

After a couple of minutes, a young girl with a clipboard comes and fetches me, and a few moments later – during a break for the news, apparently – I'm sitting on the famous peach couch being introduced to Martin and Trudy. Trudy smiles warmly at me, and although she's old enough to be my mum, she's still attractive enough for me to blush when she tells me she likes my jacket and fingers one of the lapels appreciatively. Martin, on the other hand, gives me the weakest, clammiest handshake I've ever felt. He's got the orangest face I've seen, and after checking himself on one of the monitors, he summons one of the assistants over to adjust his hair, tutting loudly when she accidentally tugs his microphone wire. As Trudy rolls her eyes at me, the assistant looks like she wants to strangle him with it.

As I stare at the bank of cameras in front of me, I'm starting to sweat, though more from the combination of the hot studio lights and the jacket I'm wearing. I wonder if it's too late to take it off, but the microphone that's just been clipped to the lapel might make that a bit difficult.

'Tell me something, Trudy,' I say. 'What would you think is the demographic of your viewers?'

Trudy smiles. 'Oh, it varies, really. Students, stay-at-home mums, pensioners . . .'

'And which of those do you think will be appropriate for what I'm looking for, exactly?'

Trudy looks like she's about to answer when a hush falls around the studio, and from behind one of the cameras, Ellen counts down, 'Five, four, three . . .' and then makes the 'two' and 'one' signs with her fingers. I'm feeling like making some finger gestures towards her of my own, but suddenly there's a camera in my face with a blinking red light on the top, and my throat goes very, very dry.

'Welcome back,' says Trudy. 'Well, for all you ladies watching this morning, we're joined on the sofa by Will Jackson, who wants to make an honest woman of you ... or perhaps a dishonest one? Let's find out. Welcome, Will.'

The red light seems to glow even brighter on the camera in front of me. 'Hi,' I say, in my best manly voice, but what actually comes out is little more than a squeak.

'So, Will,' says Martin. 'Tell us about your little plan.'

Condescending git. 'Well, it isn't a plan, really, Martin. It's just that, well, I love kids, and I didn't seem to be having much luck in my relationships, so I thought I'd, you know, try and find someone. A woman, that is. To start a family with ...'

As Martin and Trudy nod encouragement at me, I'm conscious that I'm gabbling on, but for some reason, I can't stop myself. I start talking about my disastrous internet dating, and the nightmare blind dates, and I'm even just about to tell them about the time that Debbie invited me back for a threesome when, thankfully, Martin interrupts me.

'Well, that's all really interesting, but we've got a surprise for you, Will. Someone who knows you very well, in fact. On the line, we've got Claire. Are you there, Claire?'

Claire? I rack my brains quickly for any Claires that I know, but I can only come up with the one. Claire who I dated for around six months two years ago, and who I split up with because she ... Well, because she was a bit thick, really. Very attractive, but not the brightest of girls. And once you've got past the physical side – which, admittedly, took the best part of five of those six months – you've got to have something to talk about.

It takes me a second or two to remember how I finally dumped her, and when I do, underneath my make-up, my face goes as red as the light blinking away in front of me. We'd been out for dinner, and she'd said she wanted kids, and I'd said I didn't. Which was a lie. Because even back then I did want kids. Just not with Claire. Oh *no*. Please don't let it be her.

'Hello, Will.'

As a disembodied female voice booms into the studio, taking me a little by surprise, it doesn't take me long to recognize that it is Claire. The tightness in my throat increases, and I reach forward for the glass of water on the coffee table in front of me, wishing it was something stronger.

And as Claire lays into me, encouraged by Martin and Trudy, I feel I should start defending myself. But what do I say? The truth about how we split up? Or will that make me come across as callous? After all, I don't want to insult her live on air, do I?

But five minutes later, I do want to insult her live on

air, as that's all she's done to me so far. I look frantically across at Ellen, willing her to go to another caller, but she just gives me a thumbs-up and mouths what I think is supposed to be 'good television'. Eventually, thankfully, when Claire runs out of steam, Martin turns back to me.

'So, Will. Perhaps not the best advert there?'

'Yes, but then she's one of my exes. What did you expect? A glowing reference?'

Trudy smiles sympathetically at me, then turns to the camera.

'Remember, we're here with Will Jackson,' she says. 'Will wants to be a dad. So much so that he was prepared to auction himself on eBay. All he needs is that special lady. Could it be you? Email in your details, telling us in twenty words or less why you'd like to have Will's baby, and . . . anything else, Will?'

I feel like a rabbit caught in the headlights, conscious of the camera in my face, and realize that even though Emma might be watching, I've got no choice but to go along with this. And although I want to try and represent that I'm not a typical, fickle male of the species, I want to blurt out 'a photo'. Really want to. So I do.

'A photo. Please. Not that that's the most important thing. But it's essential that we're . . . compatible?'

'A photo, then,' laughs Martin. 'And clothed, please, ladies,' he adds, leering into the camera.

After Trudy announces that we'll be back in two

minutes, we cut to the weather. I'm considering getting up and walking out, but my microphone seems to be caught on the sofa, and I just collapse back onto the cushions instead.

'That was great,' says Ellen, rushing forward as the red light blinks off on the camera in front of me.

'Great?' I say, a little shell-shocked. 'What's next? Asking another of my exes to rate my sexual technique?'

As Ellen tries to work out whether I'm being ironic or if I've in fact made a brilliant suggestion, the studio hushes once more, and I'm shepherded off the set and back to the green room. After a feature on cooking with tofu presented by some bloke who used to be on *Big Brother*, which I watch on the large flat-screen television in the corner, and a further news break, I have my make-up retouched, and I'm installed back on the sofa just in time for the last fifteen-minute segment.

'And welcome back,' says Trudy. 'Now, thousands of you have been calling and emailing in your pictures for Will Jackson, our desperate dad. What do you think of that, Will?'

'Thousands? Really?' Surely she's exaggerating for effect.

'Exactly,' says Martin. 'And of the pictures we can show, you naughty ladies you, we've selected five for Will to choose from. Remember, the lucky winner will go out with Will on an all-expenses date to a top London restaurant. Our cameras will be there to record how it goes and, who knows, in nine months, we could be hearing the patter of tiny feet – live on air. So come on, Will, pick one.' He beams across the sofa at me, as if he's actually done me the biggest favour in the world.

'Yes, Will,' chimes in Trudy. 'Don't be shy. Pick one.'

On the huge screen at the back of the set, five photographs of women are arranged side by side. I look at the photos, conscious of the dead air as I don't speak. They're all reasonably attractive, and although a couple of them have a slight scariness about them, from what I can see none of them appear to have fat ankles. But being here, and being made to select one of them in some daytime-television nightmare is hardly the situation I wanted to find myself in when I started this quest. Perhaps I don't have to agree to go out with any of them? Maybe I can hang it out until the credits roll without choosing one? Or maybe I'll go out with all five? Like some sort of *X Factor* elimination contest?

'Well, it's difficult, based on just their photos, you know . . .'

'Come on, Will,' says Martin, his voice full of encouragement, although his expression is a little creepy. 'Pick one.'

'I couldn't possibly.'

'Yes – pick one,' insists Trudy.

'Pick one,' mouths Ellen, from next to the camera.

And as I sit helplessly on the sofa, the ridiculousness of my situation finally gets to me. How deranged or desperate do you have to be to send your details in to national television offering your services as a mother? Possibly as deranged as you'd have to be to come on the programme looking for one in the first place, I'm beginning to think.

'No!' I say, standing up abruptly.

'No?' says Martin incredulously. 'What do you mean, no?'

'No, as in "no I'm not going to pick one,"' I say. 'This is ridiculous. It's not a game. All I want to do is meet someone special, who needs me. Not' – I nod towards the pictures on the screen – 'someone with special needs.'

And with that, I rip off my microphone and walk out of the studio, leaving a stunned Martin and Trudy on the sofa, and side-stepping Ellen's attempt at a rugby tackle as I go.

The silver Mercedes seems to be missing when I walk out of Television Centre, and I'm forced to make my own way to Shepherd's Bush tube station. As I'm waiting on the platform, my mobile rings. It's Tom.

'Well, that went well,' he says.

'You think?'

'Absolutely. Great television. You should have seen the look on Martin's face.'

'Yes, but now I'm going to be known forever as the guy who stormed off *Today's the Day*.'

'Nah,' says Tom. 'It'll all be forgotten by tomorrow.

Unless it makes it to one of those "bloopers" programmes, of course.'

I'm hoping that's a joke, albeit a feeble one, because
at the moment I'm in dire need of cheering up. 'Tom,
tell me something.'

'Sure. What's on your mind?'

'It's just, well, this kids thing.'

I can almost hear Tom rolling his eyes. 'Here we go
again. What now?'

'Well, I was just wondering. I've been questioning
my motivation lately. Particularly after everything that's
happened. And I was just curious as to how much it
was your decision, and how much Barbara's.'

'Like everything we do, it was pretty much
Barbara's,' he admits. 'I was pretty easy either way. I
certainly didn't have this insane drive that you seem to
have, but then—'

'But then your dad didn't leave when you were
young, did he?'

'Point taken. Sorry, mate. But no, I'd kind of always
thought one day I might have a family but, like most
men, hadn't given it much thought, to tell you the
truth. And when I met Barbara, and we'd been
together for a while, I kind of ran out of excuses. I'd
always thought I'd be happy either way, and kind of left
it up to Barbara to decide when the right time was.'

'But isn't that a little, you know' – I struggle to find
the right word – 'unthinking? Starting a family – bringing a new life into this world just because your other

half suddenly decides her hormones are firing on all cylinders?'

'Well, it's not quite as simple as that, is it? Besides, isn't that what we're all here for, in the grand scheme of things? To reproduce? Maintain the old human race, and so on? And that's not such a bad reason.'

'Huh?'

'Will, most men will tell you the same thing. There're only a few of us who do it for any other reason than to keep the woman in their lives happy. Sure, you occasionally hear about guys who are determined to keep going until they produce a boy, a son and heir, someone who they leave everything to. Although in our case, at the rate Barbara spends money on the twins, it looks like there won't be much to leave.'

My train is pulling into the station, so I jump on and grab a seat as far away from anyone else as possible. 'But don't you feel kind of uninvolved from the whole process? I mean, you do your bit at the start, obviously, but from then on you're really only playing a supporting role.'

'In more ways than one,' laughs Tom. 'And you'd think so, wouldn't you, particularly if you're not that bothered about it in the first place. But then look at my career – I'm only ever going to get supporting roles there too, realistically. But if it comes down to a choice between that, and not being in it at all, then it's still no contest. I tell you, Will, having kids is a gift. A miracle.'

For a moment, I swear I can hear Tom's voice crack a little. 'I've never heard you talk about it before in this way, mate.'

'Yes, well,' sniffs Tom. 'I know this sounds like a cliché, but having kids is the most amazing thing in the world. Ever. Nothing can prepare you for the way you feel when you first lay eyes on that screaming little thing. You suddenly have this incredible about-face when you realize that whatever you've done before, no matter what you've experienced, this makes it look like nothing on earth. You've created a life. Another human being. And what's more, you've done it with the woman you love, and this little baby . . .'

'Or babies, in your case.'

'Sorry – these little babies are part of you. Made from you. And they're still a work in progress. Every day, you see a change. Something different. They learn a new skill, or a new word. And what's incredible is that these little miracles of human engineering are here because of you. And it's the most wonderful thing you can imagine.'

'But surely that's why what I'm doing is so good? Because if I really, really want them, then I'm going to appreciate it even more. It's not going to take me by surprise. I've got all this time to prepare for it.'

'Ah, but that can have a negative side too.'

'How do you mean?'

'Well, you're building this up like it's the most important thing ever. So when it actually happens, there's a risk that you're going to end up disappointed.'

'Why?'

'Well, look at your car. You'd wanted one of those TVRs for ages, right?'

'So?'

'So when you actually got it, was it all worthwhile?'

'Well, yes. Apart from the fact that it keeps breaking down. And I can't drive it anywhere fast because London's so congested. And it can't get over speed bumps.'

'But that's what having a baby's like, Will. Lots of speed bumps. It's hard work. There's lots of stress. Lots of disappointment. You can't just lock it in the garage and take a taxi when you feel like it. It's constant twenty-four-seven attention, even when you're asleep. What happens if you build this up into the life-changing event you want it to be, and find it's not actually changed your life for the better?'

And as the train disappears into a tunnel, and I lose the reception on my phone, for the first time I'm starting to wonder whether he may be right.

Chapter 24

I wake up before the alarm, as usual, and groan loudly as I remember the date. Today is my thirty-first birthday, and I'm officially past it. I lie there for a few moments, wondering whether I can just stay in bed all day, when the phone goes. It's my mother.

'Do you like your card?' she asks, which means 'Do you like the fact that there's some money in it?' Even though I earn more in a year than she's earned in her entire lifetime, my mother still thinks it's a good thing to slip a fiver into the envelope every year. At least she doesn't insist on knitting me a jumper instead. Any more.

'Mum, the postman hasn't arrived yet. It's only' – I groan again as I catch sight of my alarm clock – 'twenty to eight.'

My mother sighs, and goes into some tirade about how postmen are much lazier than they used to be in her day. 'So I'll see you for dinner?' she asks.

'Of course,' I say. I've had dinner with my mother on every single one of my birthdays I can remember, and while I think it's a tradition we've kept going more for her benefit than mine, to be honest, I don't really mind.

I put the phone down and try and go back to sleep but, twenty minutes later, a loud ringing on the doorbell wakes me up. I jump out of bed and stagger, bleary-eyed, to the door.

'Someone's birthday, is it?' says the postman.

'How ever could you tell?' I say, as I stare at the pile of brightly coloured envelopes on the mat by my feet.

'I need your autograph as well,' he says.

Oh no. It's started already. Yesterday's disastrous appearance on *Today's the Day* is going to haunt me. 'Listen, just because I've done one television show, I hardly think it's appropriate,' I say, secretly chuffed. 'Who do you want it made out to?'

The postman looks at me strangely. 'Just your name will do,' he says, holding out a parcel and the delivery slip for me to sign.

'Ah. Right. Of course.'

I take the package from him and close the door, then pick the cards up from the floor and sort through them unenthusiastically. How birthdays have changed. When did I lose all the excitement of opening my cards and presents? Perhaps if I don't open any of them, I can pretend that the day's never happened? That I'm still just thirty, rather than *in my thirties*.

There's the usual one from my mother, with some

sickly poem and 'for the best son in the world' written across the front, above a montage of racing cars and sporting equipment. The next card looks like it's been made by a pair of five-year-olds, and when I finally decipher the squiggly handwriting, I realize it has. In the same envelope – well done for saving on postage, Tom – is a more grown-up card from him and Barbara, with a picture of a screaming baby on the front, which raises the barest of smiles from me.

Still half asleep, I shuffle through into the kitchen, but nearly jump out of my skin when I find Magda lurking next to the refrigerator.

'Morning, Magda,' I say. 'What are you doing here? It's not Monday. Is it?'

'I change day,' says Magda.

'Oh,' I say. 'Right.'

As I wonder why she didn't say anything on Monday, Magda points towards the kitchen table. 'I make coffee,' she says. 'And toast.'

Sure enough, there's a steaming mug of rather anaemic coffee next to a plate which appears to hold a couple of charcoal sheets.

'That's fine,' I say. 'Help yourself.'

Magda blushes slightly. 'No. I make for you.'

'Oh.' In two years, she's not made me a single thing to eat or drink. And just as well, by the looks of things. 'Er, thanks.'

'Come,' she says, pulling out a chair and wiping the seat. 'Sit.'

I do as I'm told, although a little nervously. 'What's all this in aid of? My birthday?'

Magda blushes even more. 'It is your birthday?'

As she bends down to butter my toast for me, I notice she's wearing a glittery, rather low-cut top – rather low cut for cleaning, that is. And a skirt, which, for Magda, is a first. And if I'm not mistaken, what looks like make-up.

'Are you off somewhere nice today, Magda? Or perhaps you've just been out on a late one?'

Magda stands up and smoothes down her skirt self-consciously. 'No. This my normal clothes.'

'For work?'

'You not like?'

'No, you look very nice, Magda. And thank you for my breakfast. It's very . . . thoughtful of you.'

Magda smiles. 'You are welcome.'

I take a sip of coffee, and have to work hard to swallow it, so think better of picking up the toast. I decide to open the package which, instead of a present, turns out to be a book on children's names that I forgotten I'd ordered from Amazon. When I look up, Magda seems to be cleaning the same part of the fridge door over and over again.

'Is everything okay, Magda?'

She puts her cloth down and pulls a copy of Wednesday's *Metro* out of her bag. It's open at the article on me.

'I read. About you wanting baby.'

It's my turn to be embarrassed. 'Yes, well, you shouldn't believe everything you read. That's the English papers, Magda. They like to exaggerate . . .'

Magda looks crestfallen. 'So it not true?'

'Well, yes, it's true, but . . .'

'I can help,' she beams.

'How, exactly? Don't tell me you know some poor desperate Polish girl who's prepared to marry me and have my child?'

Magda nods enthusiastically. 'I am she.'

I almost spit out my coffee for a second time, but now it's from surprise.

'You?'

She pulls out the chair next to me and sits down. 'Why not? I clean. I cook too,' she adds, pointing to the untouched pile of carcinogenic bread with its centimetre-thick coating of butter on my plate. 'And I good at the jiggy jiggy.'

She stands up again and makes a movement with her hips that's probably the height of seduction in Poland, but actually just makes her look like she's giving birth to a large Mr Whippy ice cream.

'Ah. Oh. Well, that's very kind of you, Magda, but . . .'

'It not kind. You need baby, I want to live in nice house in Richmond. It is simple. We trade. What do you think?' Magda looks at me expectantly, as if she's just asked for something as straightforward as a pound-an-hour pay rise.

Ah. What do I say, without hurting her feelings? The truth. 'I don't think so, Magda.'

Magda frowns. 'I thought you just wanted baby?'

'So did I.' I pat the chair next to me, and Magda reluctantly sits back down. 'Magda, it's extremely ... nice of you to offer your services, as it were, but I'm not looking at this as some kind of business arrangement. I've realized that I want a relationship out of it as well. I need someone who wants to do this for the right reasons too. Because they want a family as well. With me.'

Magda looks at me for a moment or two, and then simply shrugs. 'Okay.'

'Okay?'

Magda nods. 'But, how you say, your loss,' she says, before sashaying out of the kitchen.

While I'm considering whether that needs a response my mobile goes, and when I answer it, I'm greeted by the sound of someone strangling a cat. Or that's what I assume it is, until I eventually realize that it's Jack and Ellie, with their own unique version of 'Happy Birthday'.

'Morning, birthday boy,' says Tom, once the 'singing' has finished.

'Morning,' I grunt down the line.

'What are you so miserable about?'

'What do you think?'

'Look on the bright side,' says Tom. 'At least your car insurance will be cheaper now.'

Car insurance. Great. That only serves to remind
me that I'm due to swap the TVR for the Toyota
tomorrow, which will be the final nail in the coffin
as old age finally catches up with me. I thank Tom
and the twins for their birthday wishes and tell them
I'll see them tomorrow, then jump into the shower,
being careful to lock the bathroom door in case Magda
decides to demonstrate exactly what it is I'm losing,
and, in the absence of anything better to do, head
into work. I'm too depressed and embarrassed to even
think about calling into Starbucks to see if Emma is
there, particularly given my disastrous experience on
Today's the Day yesterday, and apart from Jen appearing
at eleven o'clock with a coffee and a chocolate muffin
with a candle stuck into the top, which apparently
we can't light inside the office due to health and safety
reasons, my birthday passes pretty normally.

I'm just packing up to leave for the evening when
Jen buzzes through from reception.

'There's a David Smith here to see you, Will. He
doesn't have an appointment, but he's wondering
whether you can fit him in.'

Bollocks. David Smith. It's not Debbie's husband,
is it? I crack open my door and peer down towards
reception, but, from what I can make out, the man
sitting there has got his clothes on, and doesn't appear
to have an erection. He also looks about sixty, so I'm
pretty sure I'm safe. I look at my watch; it's only five-
thirty, and I'm not meeting my mother until eight.

'You've explained the rates to him?'

'Yes. He says he'll pay cash, if that's okay?'

'No problem, then. Just give me a moment.'

I unpack my briefcase and stroll out to reception, where a smartly dressed, grey-haired man is sitting on the sofa with his arms folded. As I walk towards him, he rises stiffly from his seat.

'William?' he asks, tentatively.

'It's Will, actually. Pleased to meet you.'

The old man takes my hand and shakes it for a long time. 'And you, son.'

'Son?' I laugh. 'I'm older than you think!'

I lead him back along the corridor and into my office, indicating the couch by the window. After staring at it for a second or two, he sits down without unbuttoning his coat.

'So,' I say, picking up my notepad from the desk and taking a seat opposite him. 'How can I help?'

He peers around the office, his eyes eventually settling on the certificate on the wall, before looking back at me.

'Nice office. Business good?'

'I get by,' I say. Sometimes this is the pattern with new clients. They'd rather talk about anything – even the weather – than go straight into admitting what's brought them here. And to tell the truth, I don't mind. Especially not when they're paying me by the hour. 'How about you? What do you do?'

The old man smiles at me. 'Oh not much nowadays.

I used to work, but then I retired last year. And since then, well . . .' His voice tails off, and he stares out of the window.

'Mr Smith . . .'

'Please, call me . . . David.'

'David. Sure. I was just going to ask you whether you missed work?'

He smiles again. 'It's not work I miss.'

'It must be good to have more time to spend with your family, though? You do have a family?'

He looks up sharply. 'Well, that's kind of why I'm here.'

When he doesn't elaborate, I stop making notes and smile back at him. 'How do you mean?'

'I don't have a family. Not any more. I used to, but . . .'

So far, this isn't following the normal pattern. David looks like he's keen to admit something. Confess, even. But it seems that he can't quite get the words out.

'Did your wife die?'

He swallows hard. 'I did something terrible.'

'What do you mean by that? What did you do? And did she leave you afterwards?'

I start to worry he's murdered her. After all, you read about this in the papers. Pensioners going mad after they've retired, not able to deal with the futility of their post-work existence, and beating their partners to death with their Zimmer frames. I furtively look around the room to check there are no sharp implements within easy reach, while hoping Jen hasn't left yet, just in case it gets nasty.

'No. Quite the opposite.'

I lean forward and place a reassuring hand on his arm. 'David, I see a lot of people who have been affected by divorce. It's more common than you'd think. And sometimes, the biggest feeling is guilt. Let's come back to that later. Now I want to focus on you. What are you doing here?'

David thinks for a moment. 'I'm not sure, really. Well, I know why I came, but I'm not sure it was such a good idea.'

'What's important is why you're here. Not whether it's the correct thing to do or not. We need to clarify what your goal is in seeing me.'

'I know what my goal is. I just don't know if it's . . . fair.'

'Well, why don't you let me be the judge of that?'

I place my notepad down on the desk and sit back in my chair, and David looks at me for the longest time, before taking a deep breath.

'A few years ago – quite a few years ago – I was married. She was a lovely woman. Really lovely. And I loved her. But for some reason we weren't – well, I wasn't – happy. We thought starting a family might fix it, but . . .'

'But?'

He looks at me earnestly. 'But it didn't. And we talked about it. And tried to work it through, but we couldn't. So I did something that I've always regretted. Every single day.'

'Which was?'

'I left them. When my son was only a baby. Can you imagine what that feels like?' he asks, his voice trembling with emotion.

Yes I can, actually. I suddenly feel my face go pale, and an icy hand squeezes my chest.

'I'm not here to judge you, David. I can't give you forgiveness.'

'Yes you can, in fact.'

'How do you mean?'

He sits up on the couch and looks deep into my eyes. 'Happy birthday, son.'

And as the tears start to roll silently down his cheeks, I suddenly feel like I've been slapped round the face. Because the way he's just pronounced that last word makes me comprehend something very, very important. He's not just any old man. He's my old man.

'Wh-what?'

I want to stand up and run out of the room, but I can't get my legs to work. It's all I can do not to cry. And as I sit there, not knowing what to say, David reaches over and takes my hand.

'William, I'm your father.'

For some reason I find this insanely funny, and I can't help thinking of the scene in *The Empire Strikes Back* when Darth Vader utters something similar. I laugh, but there's no mirth in the sound.

'But ... you can't be.' And yet, as soon as I say that, I know, of course, that he can. And is. I get up unsteadily, pushing my chair backwards with such force that it bangs against the desk and knocks the lamp over. 'What are you doing here?'

David — my father — stands up and holds out his hands towards me. 'I ... I wanted to see you. I have done for years, in fact. And when I read about you in the paper, and how you were desperate to be a father yourself, I couldn't help myself. So I found out where you worked, and—'

'And tricked your way into my office. Does Mum know you're here?'

'I haven't spoken to your mother in nearly thirty years, William.'

'Stop calling me that. It's Will. No one calls me William, except for her. And she's the only one who's allowed to.'

My mind is racing. I don't know how to react. My father, who I've missed, hated, despised, and wondered about for most of my life, is standing in front of me, and I don't know whether to punch him or hug him.

'I know this must be a bit of a shock ...'

'That's the understatement of the year. Don't you think you might have warned me? Called, perhaps?'

'And risk that you might not want to see me? I couldn't take that chance. I needed to see you face to face. Talk to you. Explain.'

I'm angry, now. Angry, and upset. 'Explain what?

Why you walked out on Mum and me? What possible explanation could there be for that?'

My father opens his mouth to speak, but instead, just sits back down on the couch. 'There's no excuse,' he says eventually. 'You're right. But there was a reason.'

'Which was?'

My father shakes his head slowly, and utters the same words that I've heard Tom use with the twins a thousand times, although it's usually when they're asking him for something like another biscuit or an ice cream, rather than why a family was torn apart.

'You'll have to ask your mother.'

I'm still on my feet, and he beckons for me to sit down too, but I shake my head. 'I'll stand, thanks.'

My father sighs. 'Son, I understand you're angry with me, but I need to tell you something. This search you're on. Are you sure it's for the right reasons?'

'What do you mean, the right reasons? And what business is it of yours what I'm doing?'

'William, all I'm trying to say is this. Having a child is the most wonderful, precious thing. But having one for all the wrong reasons is the worst thing you can possibly do. Just be careful you don't get yourself into a situation you'll regret.'

'Like you did?' I spit.

'Like I did,' he says softly.

As I collapse back into my chair and put my head in my hands, my father stands up wearily and walks towards me, as if he wants to comfort me, but I wave him away, trying to ignore the look of hurt on his face.

I look up at him angrily. 'Even if I am making a mistake, one thing I know. I'd never run out on my wife and child.' I don't add the words 'like you', but we both know I don't have to.

'Son, I . . .'

I ignore him, and swivel my chair round to face the window. 'I'd like you to leave, please.'

I can feel my father staring intently at me, perhaps conscious that this might be the last time we see each other, and for a moment, just a moment, I feel sorry for him. When I catch sight of his reflection in the glass, he seems to have visibly aged from when he first came in.

'William . . . Will.'

'Now!'

He walks past me and rests a hand on my shoulder, pausing as if to say something, but then just carries on going through the door, down the corridor, out through reception, and back out of my life, almost as quickly as he came in.

I jump out of my chair and slam the door shut behind him, switching the light off for some reason I can't quite fathom, then slump down on the couch, my mind racing. My first thought is for my mother, and whether I should warn her that – and the word doesn't seem quite right as I visualize it in my head – *Dad's* back in town. I don't know what to do, and so just sit there in the darkness.

After what seems like five minutes, but could be an

hour, I hear the door open, and Jen walks in. She hasn't seen me lying there in the gloom, and as I clear my throat, she almost jumps out of her skin.

'Jesus!'

'No, it's me, Jen,' I say.

'You scared the life out of me. What on earth are you doing sitting here in the dark?'

For a moment, I want to tell her. But where would I start? 'Oh, not much. Just thinking about a couple of things.'

She flicks the light on, making me squint in the sudden glare. 'Did you manage to help Mr Smith? He seemed like a nice old man.'

'Yes. Well. Appearances can be deceptive.'

Jen gives me a puzzled look. 'Are you okay, Will?'

I gaze up at her from the couch, not quite knowing what to say. So instead, and completely to my surprise, I burst into tears.

Jen comes and sits down next to me, puts her arm around my shoulders, and just holds me until I've finished sobbing. And when I've regained what's left of my dignity, I tell her the story from the beginning up until what's just happened, and she listens sympathetically, and then I cry some more.

'How are you feeling?' she says, when I've finished.

I help myself to a tissue from the box in my desk drawer and blow my nose. 'I'm not sure, Jen. This is just . . . huge. And I can't really take any of it in at the moment. I mean, I've wondered about my dad all my life. What he was like. Whether I looked like him. If we walked the same. Stupid stuff, really. And now, when I've finally met him . . .' I stop talking and shake my head slowly.

'It's probably quite a big deal for him as well,' says Jen. 'If you look at it from his point of view. Which is what you always tell other people to do.'

'I suppose. But, presumably, he's had a while to prepare for it. I didn't exactly get much warning.'

'Are you going to get in touch with him again?'

'I don't know. I mean, even if I wanted to, I've only gone and thrown him out, haven't I? He's hardly going to want to see me again after that, is he?'

And as the reality of what's happened hits home, I understand that I've probably blown my one chance to find out who he really is. And that I've therefore lost an opportunity to find out a little bit more about who I really am too.

'Don't be ridiculous,' says Jen. 'Of course he will.'

'Well, that's fairly academic, isn't it? Because I've got no way of getting back in touch with him.'

'Er, that's not strictly true,' says Jen.

'How do you mean?'

'Well, I've got his address and telephone number out at reception. Just in case you decide you ever need them.'

'What? How come?'

'In my appointments book. Just like I take details down for everyone else who comes to see you.'

As Jen and I walk out through reception a few minutes later, I turn to face her. 'Thanks,' I say. 'For listening.'

'Don't mention it,' says Jen. 'I owed you one from the other day.'

'Oh yes. And how are things with Josh?'

'Well, he's treating me a lot better since I realized who was actually in control in our relationship.'

There's a pause, and then, 'Which is you, right?'

'Of course.'

'I'm pleased,' I say. 'How come?'

'Something I learned after our last conversation. Women can use sex to get what they want. Men can't, as sex *is* what they want. Works a treat.'

'You got that from me?'

'Nope. I read it in *Cosmo*.' Jen grins. 'Are you going to tell your mother?'

I look at her for a moment. 'Well, I don't think she'd really be interested. I mean, *Cosmo*'s not really her kind of magazine, and besides, she's a bit old to have a boyf—'

'No, Will,' says Jen. 'I meant about your dad.'

And as we ride down in the lift, I realize that that's a very good question.

Chapter 25

Still a little shell-shocked, I head out of the office, apprehensively checking the street in both directions in case my father is hanging around, then hurry along to the restaurant, knowing my mother will be waiting for me outside in the cold. Despite my repeated reassurances, she never likes to sit in a restaurant on her own, worried that she'll look like a lonely old woman – which I do my best to ensure she isn't. As I turn the corner and spot her standing by the window, she breaks into a huge smile, which I return gratefully, pleased to have some semblance of normality back in my life. She's dressed in her new winter coat, purchased from M&S with the vouchers I gave her at Christmas, and straightens it self-consciously as I approach.

'Happy birthday, William,' she says, giving me a kiss as we walk in through the door together.

'Mum, not so loud,' I say, wiping her lipstick off my cheek.

'What's wrong? Are you worried they're going to think you're my toy boy?' -

For some reason, I can't think of a right answer to that question. Instead, I just follow her to the table and we sit down, ordering a couple of gin and tonics from the waiter.

'Now, have anything you want,' says my mother, giving my hand a squeeze. 'After all, it is your . . .'

'. . . special day. Yes, I know.' She says that every year, although this year it's probably more special for her. Particularly since I'd rather just forget it.

I pick up the menu and, having missed out on my run this evening, flick through the choice of starters trying to find something that isn't deep fried. Even the salad comes with bacon and crispy croutons, and although the food here is always pretty good, this afternoon's events have dulled my appetite somewhat. As we sip our drinks, my mother tells me how she's planning to have her garden paved over, because she's heard about how dangerous these nuclear plants are that the government keeps mentioning, and she's worried that there might be some growing in there without her knowledge.

And while normally I'd find this funny, and wonder whether there's any point trying to correct her, not surprisingly I've got other things on my mind. Although I'd planned to wait until the end of the meal to tell her, I can't help myself, and as soon as the waiter has read out the specials, I blurt it out.

'I had a strange thing happen at work today.'

'Hmm?' says my mother, still engrossed in the menu.

'Dad came to see me.'

My mother suddenly stops reading, and her mouth tightens. She doesn't say anything for a moment or two, then puts her menu down carefully and takes a large gulp of her gin and tonic. 'Oh. What did he say?'

We're interrupted by the waiter, and I can tell it's a relief for my mother to have a few moments to collect her thoughts. I order for both of us and, over the first course, outline this afternoon's conversation. Although my mother hardly touches her food, the same can't be said for her drink, and when I finish, she takes a deep breath.

'William, there's something I haven't been quite honest about.'

'What? Now you're going to tell me I'm adopted?' I'm joking, but when she doesn't reply immediately, the room starts to spin.

'No. Nothing like that,' she says, a little too slowly for my liking. 'It's just, your father, well, he didn't decide to leave, exactly.'

'How do you mean?'

My mother grabs my hand tightly, as if she's afraid I'll try to get up and go.

'I asked him to.'

I drop my fork in shock, causing the waiter to rush over. He picks it up and hands it back to me, before realizing that's probably not the most hygienic thing to do, and fetches me another from a nearby table.

'What? Why?'

'Because . . .' She takes a deep breath. 'He'd been having an affair. When I was carrying you. Well, for a long time before that, actually. And although he was prepared to come back to me because of you, for me, the prospect of being stuck in the house with someone who didn't love me was worse than bringing you up on my own.'

'But . . . He said he did love you.'

My mother, who I've never seen cry in thirty years, dabs her eyes with her napkin, and it nearly breaks my heart.

'Maybe,' she sniffs. 'But he loved someone else more. And I wasn't prepared to live with him knowing that. So I asked him to leave. And he did. And even though me asking him was the hardest thing I'd ever done, I know that, for him, leaving you was even harder.'

'It doesn't seem like that to me. I mean, thirty years, and he didn't even try and get in touch once.'

'He did. Several times. And I did mean to tell you, William. When the time was right. It just never seemed to be. And the longer I put it off, the harder it became.' She squeezes my hand. 'Can you forgive me?'

I sit there in stunned silence as the waiter clears our plates, and I still haven't spoken by the time the main courses arrive. I've got so many questions, but don't have a clue which one to start with. As my mother beckons to the waiter for another gin and tonic, I find my voice again.

'But . . . Why?'

'Because I was trying to protect you. And I didn't want you to be let down, like he'd let me down. I knew what he was like – he'd left me before, you see. And as painful as it was, I knew that it was better for you that he walked out when you were six months old. Before you'd had a chance to get to know him. He'd cheated on me, which meant he'd cheated on us. And I wasn't prepared for him to hurt you in the future in the way he'd hurt me in the past. But we did okay, didn't we? You and me?'

By all rights I should be angry with her. You see this kind of scene played out in films all the time, when the aggrieved son suddenly finds out that his life's been a tissue of lies, and everything that he's ever been told is untrue. Maybe I should be storming out, not giving her a chance to explain any further, leaving my shame-faced mother here on her own, the waiters wondering what on earth could have been said that would make me abandon an old lady in a restaurant on a cold February night.

And while I am angry, it's with my dad. Fair enough, my mother might have been the one who sent him packing. But he didn't have to go. He could have decided what was really important, and tried to make it work.

And yet, strangely, the only thing I feel is pity. And love, I realize. And an awful lot of respect. Here's a woman who was prepared to do a difficult thing all by herself, rather than compromise her principles and live a lie. Nowadays, divorce is more common than successful marriages but, back then, it certainly wasn't something you took lightly. And as I look at her, I understand something else too. My mother didn't just sacrifice her marriage for me. She sacrificed her life as well. Gave up all hope of meeting someone else, of finding happiness with someone else, just so she could concentrate on giving me the best start possible. And didn't she just? What's more, she did what she thought was right at the time, and after four years of telling my clients they should never blame themselves for doing exactly that, I'd be a hypocrite if I resented her for it.

So I do something that I haven't done for ages – reach over and give her a huge hug – and, for the first time, I notice how small and frail she's become. And although she brushes me off in the embarrassed way that she normally does, I can tell by the squeeze she gives me back that it's the best possible response. Even though, from where I'm sitting, it's the only possible response.

'Mum, we did more than okay.'

My mother seems to find her appetite again, and although we've both got a lot to think about, we chat pleasantly through the rest of the meal. She quizzes me about where I'm up to on what she calls my 'baby quest'. I even give her an abridged version of my recent few dates, and when she laughs it's good to hear the

sound. Eventually, the waiter comes over and clears our
plates away, placing the dessert menu in front of us as
he does so.

'Let me tell you about the special,' he says. 'Rasp-
berry Surprise.'

'No thanks,' I say, making eye contact with my
mother across the table. 'I've had enough surprises for
the day.'

I pay the bill and walk her back home, taking her
arm as we stroll up Richmond Hill, and she seems
happy to let me take the strain. When we reach the
house, she beckons me inside.

'Hold on, William,' she says. 'I've got something
for you.'

'Mum, I thought we agreed. No presents.'

'Sit down for a moment,' she tells me. 'You might
want this one. In fact, I should have given it to you a
long time ago.'

I pace around the lounge as she disappears upstairs,
but when she reappears a few minutes later clutching
a shoebox, my heart sinks.

'You've bought me shoes?'

'Inside the box, William.'

I lift the lid, and survey the contents. It's full of
envelopes – and what look suspiciously like the kind
of envelopes that have cards inside. They're all
addressed to me, but in a handwriting I don't recognize. And what's more, there seem to be nearly thirty
of them.

'What's this?'

'Birthday cards. From Dav— From your father. I was going to send them back to him, but I thought you might like to have them one day. And it seems like today's the day.'

I wince a little, both at what these cards represent, but more at the memory of the stupid television programme.

'He sent me birthday cards?'

My mother nods. 'Every year. Without fail. Plus quite a bit of money that he put in each one.' Her voice falters a little. 'Don't you want to see them?'

I think about this for a moment. 'I don't know. I'll have the money, though.'

She manages a smile. 'Shall I put the kettle on?'

'But I thought he didn't ... I mean, that he ...' I slump down onto the sofa. This is all becoming a little bit much to take.

'William, I know this all must have come as a shock to you. But your father loved you. Really he did.' And as I stare at the pile of envelopes, my mother comes and sits down next to me, and puts her arm around my shoulders. 'Do you want to see him again? I wouldn't mind, you know.'

I shrug. 'I'm not sure, Mum. Maybe. I don't know the first thing about him.'

'Well, perhaps it's time you found out. And reading those might be a good place to start.'

So this is how I spend the evening of my thirty-first

birthday – reading through the cards sent to me for my previous thirty. And in a strange way, I think it might be the best birthday I've ever had.

Chapter 26

I wake up feeling surprisingly okay about being thirty-one and a day. But what's perhaps more surprising is that I'm also kind of fine about what happened yesterday. And while there's a part of me that feels duty bound to my mum not to contact my dad again, there's a bigger part of me that feels I owe it to myself to get in touch. Admittedly, I haven't quite achieved my goal of finding a woman that I can start my own family with, but for some reason that seems to be a little more in perspective too. And although Emma hasn't responded to any of my messages or texts, which also means I'll probably have to stop getting my coffee from Starbucks, in the overall scheme of things I'll just have to accept this, move on, and get on with my search.

With that in mind, I take a last, lingering look at the TVR before jumping in, and for once find myself wishing it won't start, but take it as an omen when it does, first time. I check that I've got all the documents I need, along with the service history – which by now is quite a weighty document – and head down through

Richmond and across the bridge, trying to ignore the appreciative looks from a couple of small boys on the pavement as I roar past.

It's a short drive down the A316 to Toyotas R Us, and although it occurs to me to keep on going round the roundabout and back home, I pull onto the forecourt and switch off the engine with one last throaty blip of the throttle.

Alan, the salesman, comes out to greet me, with a cheery, 'Heard you coming. Five minutes ago,' and I climb out of the car. But instead of the engine note, it's Tom's advice – 'Only sell this when you have to' – that's ringing in my ears.

Alan runs a hand along the TVR's nearside wing. 'She's a looker, eh?'

I stare at the TVR as if seeing it for the first time. 'Yup.'

'Bet the women love her?'

I nod. 'Yup. But not as much as the blokes. If you, er, know what I mean.'

'You sure you want to do this?' he jokes, nodding towards the new silver RAV 4 parked outside the showroom that he's ordered for me.

I look at the large, squat vehicle. Even though it's quite stylish for a four-by-four, it still looks like my car's fat ugly brother. Is it me? I keep asking myself. I mean, I know it's a car, and not me, but is it *me*?

'Er, no, actually.'

Alan laughs nervously. 'Let's not get cold feet now.

I've got all the paperwork ready inside, if you'd just like to follow me . . .'

He puts a hand on my shoulder, and tries to steer me into his office, but I just stand there, rooted to the spot, gazing at the two cars side by side.

'Hold on a moment.'

'What's the matter?'

'I . . .'

It's at that moment I realize I just can't do it. At least, not yet, anyway. And it's not a case of wanting the TVR more than a baby – of course it isn't. It's just . . . I love the TVR. It's been with me through thick and thin – although mostly thin, when I think about it. But it's a part of me. And Tom's right. Why get rid of it until I have to? Particularly – as Alan's just helpfully pointed out – it might even help me in my quest to meet the mother of my baby. And although it occurs to me that while I might be able to pull her in the TVR, I could actually have sex with her in the Toyota, I realize that this isn't quite a good enough justification.

As Alan pleads with me to change my mind – although deep down, on some level, I'm sure he understands – I just shrug and jump back into the car. My car. The TVR. With a grin on my face I push the start button and the engine roars into life, startling an old couple coming out of the showroom with the keys to a new Yaris, then screech out onto the A316 and back towards Richmond. And even before I accelerate through the traffic, nearly forgetting to brake hard for the speed camera on the bridge, I know I've made the right decision.

Five minutes later, I'm pulling up outside Tom's house, where he and the twins are washing the Volvo. Or rather, Tom's trying to wash the Volvo, but Jack and Ellie are more interested in throwing handfuls of soap suds at each other.

'Aha!' he says. 'I knew you couldn't do it.'

'I will,' I tell him, picking up a squealing Jack under one arm and a giggling Ellie under the other, and pretending to dunk them in the bucket. 'When the time is right.'

Barbara appears at the front door. 'Not you again,' she says, kissing me on the cheek. 'Happy birthday for yesterday. Get anything nice?'

I shrug, which is a little difficult with a five-year-old under each arm. 'Just the usual stuff. And a bunch of cards. From my dad.'

I put the twins down on the ground, and they immediately run back towards the bucket, where Ellie proceeds to give Jack a soap-suds hair-and-beard combination. On top of his red tracksuit, he looks like a dwarf Santa.

Tom puts down his sponge and looks up at me in surprise. 'From your dad?'

'I'll put the kettle on,' says Barbara.

We leave the kids outside with strict instructions not to touch the hose and head into the lounge, where

I recount the previous afternoon's events over a cup of tea.

'Blimey,' says Tom, when I've finished. 'Well, that kind of puts a different slant on things, doesn't it?'

'How do you mean?'

'Duh.' He stands and pulls Barbara up from the sofa. 'Okay. Have it your way.'

'What are you doing?'

'Come on,' says Tom. 'I'm serious. On the couch.'

As he stands there with his arms folded, I stare at him for a second or two, then walk silently over and lie down. Tom clears his throat, pulls up a chair, and sits next to me.

'So,' he says, in a strange accent that I recognize as a poor copy of my own. 'When did this all start?'

'Tom, do you mind not doing the voice, please.'

'Sorry.'

'And when did what all start?'

'All this. Your inability to commit?'

'I'm not scared of commitment.'

'Bollocks, Will. Up until now, the second any of your girlfriends have mentioned the C word, you've broken the sound barrier on your way out of the door.'

'That's not true. I . . .'

As Barbara rolls her eyes, Tom frowns at me. 'So tell me, then, how many women have you committed to, exactly?'

'Define committed.'

Tom sighs. 'All right. Gone out with for longer than

a year, then. Continuously,' he adds, obviously referring to my on–off relationship with Anita.

I hold my hand up. 'Okay. I get your point,' I say, mentally running back through my relationship history.

'And the answer would be?' asks Tom, when I don't say anything further.

'Fine. None. Happy now?'

'It's not my happiness we're trying to work on, is it?'

'Stop being a smart arse.'

Tom stands up, and starts to pace around the room. 'Okay. Let's try a different tack. Tell me about your childhood.'

'You know all about my childhood. My dad left when I was six months old—'

'Aha!' interrupts Tom. 'Now we're getting somewhere. And how did that make you feel?'

I sigh, and try to stand up. 'Tom, I was a baby. I didn't feel anything, apart from a constant need to shit, eat, and cry.'

'Well, how do you feel about it now?' says Tom, pushing me back down again.

I shrug. 'Okay, I guess.'

Tom glares at me. 'How do you really feel about it?'

'I told you. Fine. It was a long time ago.'

'Will,' says Tom, in what I imagine he thinks is his best soothing voice, 'it's okay to be angry.'

'I'm angry at you for wasting my time with this ridiculous—'

I start to sit up, but Tom leans over and grabs me by

the shoulders. 'For Christ's sake, Will. I'm trying to help you here. Now will you just think about the question for a minute? Or would you rather just spend the rest of your life sad and alone and walking out on every girl that shows the slightest bit of interest because you haven't got over the fact that your dad walked out on you?'

And suddenly, although I want to get up and walk out on Tom at this moment in time, this stops me in my tracks. Because Tom's right. It's classic. And if I had someone sat on the couch in my office saying exactly the same things to me, it's precisely the conclusion that I'd come to.

'So . . . You're saying that the simple reason that I've never been able to commit to women is because I'm scared that they'll eventually leave me just like my dad did? And therefore the moment it looks like I might be getting in deep enough to be hurt if this is actually the case, I walk out on them instead?'

Tom shrugs. 'Could be.'

'And . . . And so the reason that I'm desperate to have a child with someone now is because I know I'd never walk out on a baby the way my father did, and therefore it gives me an excuse to commit to someone without *actually* committing to her, because in fact it's the child I'm making the commitment to?'

Tom nods. 'Sounds like a theory.'

'Plus, I'm desperate to be a great father, because my own father never was?'

'Precisely,' says Tom. 'Whereas, if you think about it, it's all bollocks, because all your commitment issues are actually based on your own misconception.'

'How do you mean?'

'Because your dad didn't leave you, as it turns out. Your mum asked him to go. So you don't have to be worried about anyone else leaving you.' Tom smiles. 'Piece of piss, this psychoanalysis bollocks. How much do you charge again?'

As I look at Tom in disbelief, I realize that he's pretty much nailed it. And although I'm slightly concerned that I couldn't see it myself, sometimes it takes a third party to make sense of this kind of stuff. A bit of distance. After all, that's what my clients all pay me for.

I swing round on the couch, put my feet on the floor, and put my head in my hands. 'So assuming that is, in fact, the case, what on earth do I do about it?'

Tom puffs air out of his cheeks. 'I dunno. You're the life coach. You work it out.'

Barbara comes and sits next to me, puts her arm around my shoulders, and gives me a squeeze. 'I'm sorry you didn't make it, Will.'

'Make what?'

'Paternity. Wasn't it supposed to be by yesterday?'

I stare out of the window, where Ellie is chasing Jack round the front garden with the sponge. 'Yes. Well. You can't rush these things, can you?'

Tom sits down on the other side of me. 'So, just to recap, you didn't actually meet anyone suitable?

Despite being splashed all over the internet, eBay, the newspapers, and even daytime TV?'

'And not forgetting our best attempts to set you up,' says Barbara.

'Well, there was one person,' I say quietly.

'You sly old dog, you,' says Tom. 'You didn't mention anything.'

'Who?' says Barbara, suddenly intrigued.

'Her name's Emma,' I explain. 'She works in that new Starbucks next to my office. But don't get too excited. I seem to have scared her off with all this baby stuff.'

Barbara does a double take. 'Emma? So you've met Archie, then?'

I look up sharply. 'Archie? Don't tell me she's married? That would explain it.'

'No – Archie, her *son*.'

'Her . . . son?'

Barbara nods. 'He's in Jack and Ellie's class. Nice little lad. Ellie's quite sweet on him, actually.'

I stare at her in disbelief for a moment or two, trying to process this piece of information, and suddenly it all becomes clear. The fact that she only works the day shifts. Her lack of evening and weekend availability when I asked her out. And, of course, her not inviting me back to her place for coffee that night.

Tom grins. 'Didn't she tell you?'

'Judging by the look on his face, obviously not,' laughs Barbara.

'Yes, well, I wasn't exactly honest about my motives either,' I say. 'But she won't seem to give me a chance to apologize.'

Barbara smiles. 'Well, from where I'm sitting, I'd say she owes you an apology too.'

When I ring Emma's doorbell, there's no-one in, and for a moment I stare up at the front windows, wondering whether maybe she's heard the car coming and has decided not to answer her door. I curse silently to myself, thinking that I should have parked the TVR out of earshot, but then I'd have had a very long walk, and I'm just about to give up and go home when I hear a voice from the next-door garden.

'They're at the park.'

I peer over the hedge to see an old lady, barely as tall as the rake she's leaning on for support.

'Who are?'

'Emma and Archie. She always takes him to the park on Saturday mornings.'

'Oh. Of course.'

'You should catch them there if you hurry,' says the old lady.

'Right. Thanks.' I turn and walk back to the car, but then stop and run back towards her garden. 'And which park would that be, exactly?'

The old lady gives me directions, and I thank her and sprint back towards the car. A few minutes later, I find the park. There's a football game going on, where a bunch of overweight thirty-somethings, some of whom look like they're more likely to have a heart attack than touch the ball, are all trying to prove they've still got 'it', while a bunch of dutiful girlfriends and bored children stand and watch on the touchline. There's no sign of Emma, and I'm worried I've missed them when over in the corner I spot the kids' play area. There's a small figure running towards the roundabout, and a woman sitting on one of the benches nearby. From what I can just about make out, she's wearing a snorkel parka.

It's a cold day, and cursing the fact that I'm not wearing a coat myself, I hurry across the grass, being careful to avoid the various mounds of dog poo, walk up behind the bench, and clear my throat.

'Will?' Emma gets up from where she's been sitting and turns around. 'What are you doing here?'

'I thought it was about time you told me the truth.'

Emma looks guiltily over her shoulder to where the small boy is hanging upside-down on the monkey bars. Even to a thirty-one-year-old, it looks like fun.

'You can talk. Why didn't you tell me you were so desperate to have a child?'

'Why didn't you tell me you already had one?'

Emma starts to say something, but stops herself, as we both know I win this particular argument. Instead, she just sticks her hands in her pockets and shakes her head slowly. 'Will, you've got no idea what it's like, have you?'

'What what's like?'

'Being a single mum.'

Perhaps more than you think, I want to say, given my upbringing. But I realize that now's the time to let Emma talk, rather than try and assert my credentials.

'I know what it's like to be single.'

'That's not the same thing at all.'

'Well, why on earth didn't you tell me? About Archie?'

'When?'

'Well, when we first met might have been a good time. Or on our first date. Or even the second one. It's quite a major thing, you know.'

'I'm sorry. I was planning to. When I invited you round for lunch.'

'And your "baby sister"? Any other family members I don't know about?'

Emma blushes. 'Babysitter, actually. But that was her idea not mine. I just . . . went along with it.'

'Why?'

Emma sits back down on the bench, careful to avoid the bird droppings, and as I sit down next to her, I can see her eyes start to mist up. 'Mention the fact you've got a child to most blokes and they run a mile. Amanda knew that too. And I liked you. And didn't want you to run a mile.' Emma shakes her head slowly. 'Then I read that stuff in the paper about you, and I got scared. I've already been left once when someone decided that being a father didn't actually fit in with his great life plan. And I certainly didn't want that to happen again.'

'But didn't you see me? On *Today's the Day*? I wanted to explain.'

'Will, I have a life. And a job. And college. And a five-year-old son who's been off school for the past couple of days. That doesn't exactly leave much time for daytime TV. Or anything, come to think of it.'

I nod towards Archie, who's trying to get himself started on the roundabout. And as I watch him playing on his own, I realize how lucky the twins are to have each other. And Tom. 'Where's his dad?'

Emma shrugs. 'That's a very good question. I guess he didn't want to face the responsibility.'

'But you do know . . .'

'Who he is?' Emma punches me on the shoulder. 'Of course I do, Will. Who do you take me for? But I don't know where he is. And I don't care, actually. He didn't even have the decency to hang around until Archie was born.'

'I'm sorry, I . . .' I swallow hard. This is all painfully familiar.

We sit there in silence, watching Archie as he climbs onto the swings, before Emma forces a smile. 'Do you remember those days, Will? When you didn't have a care in the world? When you could just please yourself? Maybe you're still there. But I haven't had that 'for five years now. Because everything I do is for him now. Every decision I make, I have to think what it will mean for Archie. And as for letting someone else into

my life, well, I thought that maybe I could. But . . .'
Her voice tails off.

'I do, actually. Which is why I thought maybe you
might want to go out to lunch.'

'Will, haven't you been listening to anything I've
been saying? I've got Archie . . .'

'I meant the two of you. And me, obviously.'

Emma looks across at the swings, where Archie is
swinging himself higher and higher with a huge grin on
his face. 'I'm not sure, Will. I've had boyfriends before,
and ultimately . . . I don't want him to be let down.
Again.'

As Emma stares stonily ahead, I realize that now's the
time to play my trump card. So I tell her all about my
childhood, and how I know what a struggle it was for
both me *and* my mum. I fill her in about what I've
been going through recently, and just why it is that I
was so set on having a family of my own. And then
I tell her why I'd never let her down. Because I know
just how bad it feels when it happens.

And then something unexpected happens: Emma
starts crying. And it's not just small drops-of-
water-from-the-corner-of-the-eyes crying, but huge,
shoulder-heaving sobs. I sit there like an idiot for a
second, trying to ignore the accusing glances from
some teenagers on a nearby bench, before putting an
arm round her shoulders in an attempt to comfort her.

Archie jumps down from the swings and comes running over, looking at me suspiciously before grabbing

Emma protectively round the leg. Already he's half as tall as she is, looking very much the boy in his striped rugby shirt and turned-up jeans. Emma regains her composure, then reaches down to re-fix the Velcro straps on his trainers, before picking him up and resting him on her lap.

'Archie, this is Will,' she says, drying her eyes on her sleeve and taking a deep breath. 'Will, this is Archie. My son.'

I'm not really sure what to do, as I've never been introduced to a five-year-old before. I've known both Jack and Ellie since they were born, so I'm not sure what the correct etiquette is. I'm also conscious that Emma might be reading a lot into what I'm like with kids from this. But then again, she's seen me with Jack and Ellie.

'Hi, Archie,' I say, ruffling his hair, having decided not to shake his hand.

Archie just stares at me for a moment or two, smoothes his hair down again, then wriggles off Emma's lap and heads back towards the slide.

'Well, that went well,' sniffs Emma, but with a smile on her face for the first time today.

'Yes. I'm a natural,' I say. 'As you well know.'

She slips her hand into mine, and we sit and watch as Archie climbs back up the slide. He's an independent kid, obviously used to playing on his own, and although he looks slightly nervous when he gets to the top, he looks across to where we're sitting and waves.

'Be careful,' shouts Emma, but before she can move, Archie launches himself down the slide head-first. We watch in horror as he reaches the bottom and crashes onto the ground.

Like a sprinter out of the blocks, Emma leaps up from the bench and runs towards where Archie's lying. Although her speed has surprised me, I'm not far behind, but by the time I reach them she's already crouched down next to him, cradling his limp body in her arms. He's obviously caught the side of his head on the metal end of the slide, and there's a worrying amount of blood seeping out of the gash.

Emma looks up at me, an expression of panic on her face. 'Help me,' she says, fumbling in her bag for her phone. I take one look at Archie and make a decision. He's still breathing, but there's no way we can afford to waste any time.

I hurriedly pull my sweatshirt off over my head, and hand it to her. 'Here. Press this against the cut. It'll help to stop the bleeding.'

'Should we call an ambulance?'

'No time for that,' I say. 'I'll drive us to the hospital.'

I pick Archie up and run towards where I've parked the car, Emma doing her best to keep up behind me. She jumps into the passenger seat, and I lower Archie in and onto her lap. As she holds my sweatshirt over the gash on Archie's head, I try not to notice the blood dripping down onto the cream-leather seat.

'Sorry,' says Emma, as I fire up the engine and slam it

into gear, spraying gravel as I wheelspin out of the car park.

'Don't worry,' I say, and then utter the words I never thought I'd hear myself say about the TVR. 'It's only a car.'

I put my foot flat to the floor, and the TVR rockets forward and onto the A316. We accelerate over the bridge, and are doing seventy by the time I have to jam the brakes on for the speed camera on the other side of the hill. As I weave in and out of the traffic, I'm suddenly grateful for the fact I haven't traded the car in for the Toyota, and there's actually a part of me enjoying having a reason for driving like a lunatic.

I screech round the roundabout, occasionally veering onto the other side of the road to overtake other motorists, and ignoring the fingers they flick at me as I pass. Fortunately, Emma's too absorbed in Archie to notice my driving.

'How's he doing?' I say, glancing across. Archie's face is incredibly pale, and Emma's isn't far off the same colour.

'I don't know, Will. Hurry, will you?'

Under other circumstances this would be funny, given the speed I'm going at and the way I've been driving, but instead I just turn my attention to the road in front of me and aim for the hospital. After what seems like forever, but in reality is little more than three minutes, we pull into the ambulance bay, and I've

hardly screeched to a stop when Emma leaps out of the
car and sprints for the entrance.

'You take him in and I'll just go and . . .' I say, to her
rapidly disappearing figure, 'park the car.'

I drive round the corner to where the parking
signs are, and squeeze the TVR into the first space I
see, which turns out to be a good four hundred yards
from the hospital entrance. As I leap out of the car and
sprint back towards the A&E department, I suddenly
remember I've got no shirt on, and there's blood on
my chest, which is probably why the security guards
are looking at me rather strangely as I burst in through
the door, breathing heavily and sweating profusely.

'Can I help you, sir?' says one, or rather that's what
I assume he's saying as he rugby-tackles me to the
ground.

'I'm here with . . . Archie . . . My, er, girlfriend just
brought him in . . .' I pant, enjoying the feeling that the
words 'my girlfriend' conjure up, even though I'm in
a rather painful headlock.

Fortunately, I'm rescued by one of the reception staff,
who saw Emma come in with Archie a few minutes
previously. I'm lent a hospital gown, and directed
through to the X-ray department. And when I finally
find Emma, she's waiting anxiously by the coffee
machine.

'How is he? Any news?'

Emma takes one look at my ridiculous attire, but
doesn't seem to register what I'm wearing. 'They're

doing X-rays now. The bleeding's stopped, but ...'

And as her eyes fill with tears again, for the first time in my life, I understand what it means to really, truly, love someone. Sure, I've seen Tom and Barbara concerned when one of the twins has fallen over and hurt themselves, but it's never been anything like this. Emma is genuinely scared. Terrified, even. And it's all I can do not to take her in my arms and hold her tightly. So I do.

Eventually, the doctor appears. As Emma stares mutely at him, I clear my throat.

'How is he?'

The doctor smiles. 'He's fine. He's got a nasty cut, and lost a bit of blood, and he'll have a bit of a headache for a few days, but there's no lasting damage. We'll keep him in overnight, just to make sure.'

Emma bursts into tears again, but they're tears of relief, and as she wipes her nose on the sleeve of my gown, I'm struck by the realization of just how hard it must be for her to go through this kind of thing on her own. And maybe she is too, because when she looks up at me, there's a genuine vulnerability in her expression.

'Can I see him?' she sobs.

'Sure.' The doctor nods, and indicates that she should follow him.

I stand there, not quite knowing my place, before Emma walks back towards me, grabs me by the hand, and leads me in behind her. And although I think that might be more for her benefit than for mine, I don't mind at all.

Later, when I'm driving her home to collect a change of clothes, she smiles for what seems like the first time in a long while.

'Thanks, Will.'

I shrug manfully, which is a difficult thing to carry off in a pink hospital gown.

'Don't mention it.'

'And I'm sorry about your sweatshirt. And your upholstery.'

'S'all right.'

We drive in silence until we reach her house, but when I drop her off, Emma leans back in through the open window.

'He likes pizza, you know.'

I turn the engine off so I can hear her properly. 'Pardon?'

'Archie. He likes pizza. Just so you know, when you take us out to lunch.'

'Great,' I say. 'Me too.'

Emma's expression hardens – although with a hint of a smile – and she reaches across and grabs me by the shoulders.

'Will, if you ever break my heart – our hearts – I'll break both your legs.'

And for some reason, that sounds like the most romantic thing anyone's ever said to me.

Chapter 27

I'm stood in the church, my neck chafing slightly from the tie that it's taken my shaking hands three attempts to knot around my neck. There's a nervous hush, as if we're all waiting to see if, rather than when, the bride will turn up, and it's a real effort to stop myself from turning round to check whether she's coming.

'Maybe she's got lost?' whispers Tom.

'Difficult to do,' I reply. 'The church. On Church Road. How hard can that be to find. Even for a woman?'

Tom's stood to my right, and as I catch his eye he gives me a supportive smile. 'Are you sure you're doing the right thing?' he asks me.

I nod. 'As I'll ever be.'

Tom's got his hand on Jack's shoulder, and next to him, Ellie is holding tightly onto Archie's hand. I can hear the two of them chatting animatedly to each other, and Jack starting to giggle, before Barbara shushes them.

After what seems like an eternity, the strains of 'Here

Comes the Bride' start up, and the whole congregation turns round in unison. I'm feeling surprisingly calm. Relaxed, even. And surely this is how a wedding should be? Not a stressful event, but something to enjoy. A celebration of a couple's love. And a declaration of it in front of the people who matter.

As the music stops, I take a deep breath and turn to my left. Emma looks beautiful, and she meets my gaze and squeezes my fingers.

'No second thoughts?' she whispers.

I smile back at her. 'None whatsoever.'

'Well, thanks for asking me.'

'Thank you for saying yes.'

As the kids whisper excitedly to each other, I look down at them, winking at Archie as he catches my eye. My mother had offered to take him for the day, but I'm pleased he's here with us. Besides, she's got more important things to think about. Like lunch with my father, which I've arranged for the four of us tomorrow.

And fifteen minutes later, when the vicar is asking if there's anyone present who knows of any just cause why Anita and Michael shouldn't get married, I'm too busy thinking about the feel of Emma's hand in mine to even consider shouting something.

At the reception, I'm only recognized twice from my *Today's the Day* appearance, and apart from one slightly awkward moment when Anita asks where we met and Emma says, 'In a Ladies toilet,' we have a good time.

Great, even. But not as great as later that evening, when I carry a fast-asleep Archie from the taxi and into Emma's house, then turn round to find out that she's sent the driver away.

'Oh,' I say. 'There goes my ride.'

'Not necessarily,' says Emma mischievously. 'I thought you might want to come in.'

I smile. 'For coffee?'

'No,' she says, kissing me long and hard on the lips. 'For sex. I don't like coffee, remember?'

'Er . . .' I say.

'Don't sound so enthusiastic,' she says, putting on a hurt face.

'No, I didn't mean it like that. It's just . . . Are you sure?'

Emma presses her body against mine. 'Well, it certainly feels to me like you are.'

And after she's put Archie to bed, she comes back downstairs wearing just an old sweatshirt and a pair of boxer shorts, and it's possibly the sexiest outfit I've ever seen. I kiss her on the forehead, and she kisses me back, and then I can't help myself and I kiss her again, but on the mouth, and suddenly we're moving through the hallway locked together by the lips, and crashing down on her couch. Eventually, she breaks away from me.

'What's the matter?'

'I, er, haven't done this for a while,' she says.

'Don't worry. It's just like riding a bike.'

'Really?' says Emma. 'Not the way I used to do it.'

I kiss her again. 'Well, perhaps you haven't been doing it properly.'

'Shall we go upstairs?' she says, a little breathlessly.

Without a word, I get to my feet, picking Emma up from the sofa in the same movement. As she wraps her arms around my neck I carry her up the stairs and, after accidentally carrying her into the bathroom and out again, find the bedroom and lower her onto the bed. All of a sudden, I stand up abruptly.

'Bollocks.'

Emma sits up. 'What's the matter? You haven't put your back out?'

'No I ... And this is going to sound silly, but I haven't got any condoms.'

'Ah. And I suppose we'd better ...'

I sigh, and collapse onto the bed next to her. 'Yup.'

'Do you want to go out and get some?'

'Kind of kills the mood, doesn't it? Plus, it's a bit embarrassing to walk into a chemist's and ask for some at this time of night.'

'Especially with a hard-on,' says Emma playfully. 'We could always do ... something else.'

'What do you mean? Play Scrabble?'

'No, you idiot.' She pulls her sweatshirt off over her head. 'Come here and I'll show you.'

Some months later . . .

I'm sitting by the window in my new office, looking out across Richmond Green, and looking forward to meeting Emma for lunch, like I do most Fridays when she doesn't have a lecture to go to. And no offence to Tom, but whilst I still enjoy meeting up with him for our regular blokes' beer and burger at All Bar One, I much prefer these Couple Lunchtimes with Emma. And the Family Saturdays that invariably follow them.

It's Kate's old office – she moved out a few weeks after Valentine's Day, although nothing to do with our disastrous non-date, Jen assures me – and it's a little smaller and slightly more expensive than my old room but, let's face it, I'd rather pay that bit extra than stare at Ann Summers' rear for one day longer, if you know what I mean. Besides, a view of the Green means that on the long summer evenings, I can open the window and call out to Emma and Archie as they play on the grass below, waiting for me to finish work and walk them home, maybe stopping for a coffee on the way.

It's gone one o'clock, and there's still no sign of her, so I pick up my phone and dial Emma's number. Her mobile rings twice before she picks up, sounding a little out of breath.

'Hello?'

'It's me.'

'I can tell,' says Emma. 'You have a distinctive ring.'

A few months ago I'd have found that amusing, but I'm more mature now. Responsible even. Which I have to be, because I've got responsibilities.

'Just wondering where you are?'

'I'm late.'

I shrug, then realize it's a pointless gesture, as we're still talking on the phone. 'Not to worry. I haven't booked anywhere. I thought maybe we'd just get a sandwich and sit by the river.'

'No, Will. I'm *late*.'

It takes me a good five seconds to understand what she's talking about.

'Ah. Oh. Right. As in—'

'I'll be with you in two minutes,' she says, hanging up.

I stand there with the phone in my hand. Two minutes doesn't give me a lot of time to digest this particular piece of news. I mean, we've discussed how great it would be for Archie to have a brother or sister, and while we haven't necessarily been *trying*, we haven't been trying not to, if you see what I mean.

I still haven't quite managed to hang up the receiver

when Emma walks in, kisses me hello, and sits down on the couch.

'So . . .' I say. 'Late. As in . . . late?'

'Yup.'

'And have you . . . you know?'

'Not yet.' She reaches into her handbag, and produces a pregnancy testing kit. 'But I bought one of these from Boots on the way here. I thought you might want to find out at the same time.'

And I do want to find out. As soon as possible. And I'm sure I know what I want the result to be. I know that Emma knows what I'm hoping for too – after all, we've promised not to have any secrets any more. But either way, it doesn't matter as much now as I used to think it did. After all, we've already got Archie.

'Well, wish me luck, then,' says Emma, as she heads down the corridor towards the toilet.

It's a long wait – perhaps the longest wait of my life, and my fingers are starting to go numb from having them crossed so tightly, but eventually she comes back into the room, and although I'm trying hard to read her expression, she's not giving anything away.

'Well?' I ask, my voice an octave or two higher than normal.

Emma sits back down on the couch and doesn't say anything. But, judging by the smile on her face, she doesn't need to.

Acknowledgements

Thanks, as ever, to Patrick Walsh, and the team at Conville & Walsh. To Kate Lyall Grant and everyone at Simon & Schuster, and Digby Halsby, publicist extraordinaire. To my parents, for their love and support. To Tina – ditto. To Tony Heywood, Lawrence Davison, Chris Raby and Stewart Holness, because I couldn't make it all up myself. To Mike Gayle, for being such a great bloke. To Kate Harrison, for the coffee and sanity. And lastly, to the Board – without you, my days at the office would be much lonelier affairs.